The Lions and the Wolf

The Brood at Trasimene

Garrett Pearson

Published by Morepork Publishing

Cover Design: More Visual Ltd

ISBN: 13-978-0-473-52591-0
ISBN: 13-978-0-473-52594-1

*For Paul and Debbie, Colin and Melissa
May you live forever in peace, free from the Gods of
war.*

Glossary

Ancient Country & Place names

Arretium – Arezzo, Italy

Ariminum – Rimini, Italy

Carthage - Founded by the Phoenician's, now within modern day Tunisia

Cartagena Nova – Cartagena, southern Spain

Drepanum – Trapani, western Sicily

Gades – Cadiz, Spain

Gaul - France, Belgium, Switzerland, Holland and Northern Italy

Icosium - Algiers

Iberia - Northern Spain

Igilgili – Jijel, Algeria

Lilybaeum – Marsala, western Sicily

Massilia – Marseilles, France

Nubia - Northern Sudan

Numidia - Algeria

Perusia – Perugia, Italy

Placentia – Piacenza, Italy

Rusucurru - Delles or Dellys, Algeria

Saguntum – Sagunto, Spain

Salamantica – Salamanca, Spain

Saldae – Bejaia, Algeria

Spoletium – Spoleto, Italy

Tarraco – Tarragona, Spain

Tarascon – Provencal, France

Victumulae - Outpost or township somewhere in the Po valley. (The exact location is unknown)

The 'She Wolf' Howls!

The She Wolf retreats to her den
And throws back her head to howl
Her yellow eyes look ever northward
The Lion's brood has come to prowl.

The rising mistress of the middle sea
She thought she'd rule the nations all
Now with her tail and den afire
She rues the Lions call.

Bloodied this thrice in battles sore
She wonders how and when
She will howl in triumph
And drive the Lions from her den.

She has given freely of her litter
So many, so young and brave
Only to see them torn apart by Lions paws
The open field and woodland now their grave.

The Lions roam at will and without fear
Across mountain, plain and wood
Driving the She Wolf's cubs before them
Washing their spears in Roman blood.

The She Wolf throws back her head again
Once more to mournfully call
Another bloody reckoning there must be
The city of Rome shall not fall.

Prologue

Italy, late spring of 217 BC

After their great victory over the Roman legions at the Trebbia River in December 218 BC, the Carthaginians made winter camp on the plains of the river Padus in northern Italy. Hannibal made use of the time to recondition and further train his men and to seek recruits among the Gauls and the Italian tribes disaffected from Rome. Late spring of 217 BC saw them begin their march southwards.

The Romans, recovering from their two defeats the previous winter and in readiness for the coming campaigning season had raised four new legions, reinforcing and for the most part replacing those of Consuls Longus and Scipio, decimated at the battle of the River Trebbia.

The two new Consuls elect, Gnaeus Servilius Geminus and Gaius Flaminius Nepos marched their new legions, two each, plus auxiliary troops, to the northeast and northwest of the Apennine mountain ranges, thus covering and opposing any logical march southwards down either coastline by the Carthaginians.

Hannibal, anything but predictable took neither route, choosing instead to march directly south through the centre of the country and over the Apennine mountains, then crossing the river and marsh of the Arno onto the Etruria plain. However, despite this fast and secretive march, which placed his army ahead of and south of Flaminius and effectively between the two Consular armies, no further contact between the combatants had come.

Flaminius, though initially pushing north and west hoping to pin Hannibal between himself and the western seaboard, suddenly found the Carthaginians had bypassed him and were now south of his position. Forced to halt and about-turn, he encamped within the city of Arretium while considering how and where to fight Hannibal. This halting and about-turn movement enforced upon Flaminius and a full Consular army by Hannibal, is the first ever such tactic done on this scale in recorded military history and would not be repeated successfully until the early 19th Century.

Consul Geminus seemed content to shadow the Carthaginian march southwards while staying well to the east and at this time making no determined push to confront Hannibal.

Hannibal had also halted and made camp expecting Flaminius, being the closest to him, to come out and meet him in battle. Flaminius however, wary of the open plain and the Carthaginian reputation for trickery and fast movement sat impotent and undecided, thus Hannibal devastated the surrounding countryside slaughtering or enslaving the people in an attempt to bring him to battle.

Despite the despoliation and wanton killing, the Carthaginians remained unmolested, seemingly free to roam at will, the Romans failing to retaliate or even place cavalry units into the field as screens or pickets.

Thus the 'she wolf's' tail is afire with the 'lion's cubs' loose in her den.

It is amongst this slaughter and despoliation that we find Baldor. He, newly promoted to Captain of a cavalry unit after his successful storming and capture of the fortified township of Victumulae earlier in the spring. He struggles with the unwanted burden of command and his orders in what he sees as merciless harassment and murder of the local populace with no relation to the Roman military machine.

Cornelius has also advanced to the rank of Centurion. After his escape from the debacle at the Trebbia and subsequent recuperation in Rome, he is set to join Flaminius and his legions on the march northward to confront Hannibal again.

Part 1

A man may ask; whom is the harder master, the God Bacchus or Hannibal?

Anon

Chapter One

The Etruria plain, south of Arretium, Italy. Late spring of 217 BC.

Baldor sat his mount watching sullenly almost disinterestedly as the white washed farmhouse went up in flames. The deliberate blaze had grown quickly on the freshening spring breeze and now roared and crackled in the dry thatch sending billowing gouts of grey-green smoke skyward adding to the already dark stained sky. Patting his horse's withers and talking softly to settle its nervous stamping, he wiped at the smoke and swirling ash that clouded his vison, stung his eyes and burned his throat raw.

The courtyard was full of his men, most already dismounted and engaged in ransacking the buildings. Chaos ensued with men shouting, running and herding the fire-fearful cattle and horses clear of the burning byre and stables, while giving the half dozen, still tethered Mastiff guard dogs a wide berth. The frustrated dogs howling, snarling and barking in alarm while straining savagely at their leashes to be loose amongst the raiders.

"Kill the damned dogs!" Armaco bawled then had to point when his words were drowned by the whickers of horses and terrified mooing of the cattle. Some of the still mounted warriors wheeled their horses about hurling javelins at the dogs, most found their mark amidst sharp yelps and pitiful cries and much of the barking cacophony died away. Before they could reach for a second javelin to finish off the last pair of dogs, the frightened, milling cattle stampeded forward seeking refuge or an exit from the growing flames and making for the open gates. Men and horses leapt to one side as the cattle thundered past, their heads dropped low, hooves loud on the paved yard and horns flailing in a careering, heaving crush of bovine weight and muscle. Funnelling through the gateway they tore the already damaged gates and frame clear of the wall demolishing some of the masonry. As the herd cleared the courtyard, some riders turned their mounts and trotted after them ready to round them up once they'd run themselves out of their fear.

Baldor, his Standard-bearer and two officers formed a small group in the middle of the courtyard while the remainder of his men stood their horses back a little way from their angry and baleful looking commander. Baldor looked about at the chaos and madness and felt sick to the stomach, pondering grimly that he'd lost count of the homesteads they'd burned and the number of folk they'd slain since emerging like Hades sent Harpies from the marshlands of the river Arno. They'd grown ruthlessly proficient at their work and countless columns of smoke and the bodies of those who'd violently resisted bore testament to their efficiency, and there had been many during the first days before word of the advancing Carthaginians had spread like smoke on the wind.

On his orders, his men drove out any folk that had not already fled before ransacking the farms and small settlements for anything edible or of use before burning and destroying what remained. Grain storage pits had been emptied, larders stripped, wine stores pillaged and livestock herded while the un-ripened crops in the fields were trampled and spoiled. Carts, tools, clothing and any coin that could be found, anything that may be of use to the invading army had been taken and passed back to the quartermasters in the vast column which spread like a colony of soldier ants over the plain. Bodies of dead folk and animals were thrown into wells and streams to pollute and poison the water to help complete this scorched earth offensive in a bid to bring Rome and her legions to battle.

Thus, Baldor's mood was black and his temper foul for this harrowing of civilians and wanton destruction of property with no direct relation to the military was not to his taste. It found him drawing uncomfortable parallels to earlier in the year and another village high in the hills of Cisalpine Gaul and more destruction and murder and where he'd slain an unarmed Roman Officer in cold blood for similar acts. Thus, he snapped and barked orders at his men seeking to imbue tight control as they went about the business with what he could see was a will and clear delight. Forbidding rape and murder of those that could not defend themselves, he'd enforced it by hanging two of his men earlier that morning when they were caught in breach of his orders. Again, he railed at himself judging he was a hypocrite for had he not also slain unarmed warriors in a fit of temper at the fall of Victumulae. Now his men were wary of their brooding young Captain and struggled to understand a man whose humours were known to swing from gently compassionate to blind, deadly fury in the blink of an eye.

His sombre thoughts were interrupted by shouts followed by a howl of agony and the clash of weapons from around the gable of the farmhouse. Reaching behind his shoulders he drew the two falcatas he wore crossed on his back and kicked his mount forward guiding it expertly with his knees. He whistled to a handful of warriors busily applying fire to the thatch of the outbuildings and the tiny roof over the courtyard well. Catching their attention, he nodded his head in the direction of the cries.

As he turned the corner, one of his men staggered past backwards clutching at the handle of a long-shafted scythe that was buried in his guts, the bloodied point protruding from his back. As he sank groaning to his knees, his hands and ruptured mail shirt a welter of blood, his comrades appeared alongside, their weapons outstretched defensively and facing front. Most had left their shields on their mount's tack and now gave ground as a tall man advanced swinging a double-headed felling axe in huge figure of eight strokes. The man was fast and the axe hummed like the winter wind in a gable's eaves as it cut the air. Behind him came two others, one with a pitchfork and the other picking up the sword dropped by the warrior with the scythe in his guts.

As the three men drove the raiders back past the end of the house, they exposed their flank allowing Baldor and the approaching warriors to attack them from the side. Heavily outnumbered by professional warriors and having to fight to their front and flank simultaneously the outcome was inevitable. The first farmer died when his sword was battered to one side as another chopped heavily into his shoulder smashing his collarbone and cleaving his chest almost to his heart. The man with the pitchfork swore savagely and wailed a name as he saw his comrade fall, before he too was forced on the defensive, having to twist body and weapon from side to side quickly as he warded off the encircling raiders. As the warriors closed in, they feinted and sidestepped to evade the thrusting, probing tines until a sword point flicked out like a striking serpent catching him in the shoulder. As he recoiled in pain, a warrior drove his sword through his ribcage into his lungs and the farmer gasped, dropping the pitchfork and clutching at the blade. The swordsman twisted the weapon brutally when it lodged between the man's ribs then had it pulled from his grip when another warrior, swinging at the farmer's neck almost decapitated him with the blow killing him instantly, his body falling backwards, blood arcing fountain like from the torso. The axeman was still holding the encroaching warriors at bay though he was tiring from the exertion. He made strange, almost pitiful, mewing sounds as he swirled his axe; the warriors cautiously content to shadow him while standing off just out of reach of the humming death. He'd already left two of them rolling on the cobbles in agony, their shields splintered into matchwood and them, though un-bloodied suffering broken ribs and the other a smashed pelvis. Baldor stared hard at the man then rode forward into the fight.

"Hold! … Hold! Back, away!" Pointing with his swords, he motioned his men away while his mount stamped nervously in front of them, the smell of the fresh blood unsettling it further.

"Enough! Throw down! … Throw down and live!" He called to the axeman as the horse continued to wheel, whicker and toss its head.

The man slowed the whirring axe, pulling it into his body holding it prone but defensively in front of him. He glanced warily at the warriors still edging closer on either side of him, his chest rising and falling like hard worked bellows as he gasped for breath.

"Back away I said!" Baldor bellowed.

His men stopped and looked up, their faces snarling and bitter, like lions chased and cheated from their prey. Everything went un-naturally still and all eyes fell on Baldor.

"Throw down!" He called again to the axeman.

As the man looked up at him, Baldor saw his head was abnormally large and strangely misshapen with a jutting brow that twisted his face leaving one eye higher than the other. His eyes were bulbous and wild looking from a mixture of anger, adrenalin and fear. Seeing no immediate threat from Baldor, his slack lips changed from a twisted snarl to a lopsided, moronic grin as he tilted his head like a curious dog. He slavered from the corner of his mouth and his tongue, which seemed abnormally large, flicked out and in repeatedly. Up close,

Baldor confirmed his suspicions; the big and strong seeming man was actually very young, a boy just, perhaps fifteen or sixteen years old at most and plainly not right in the head.

"Enough now." Baldor said quietly. "If you understand me, throw down the axe and go!" He gestured with one of his swords towards the broken courtyard gates behind him.

The simpleton smiled again showing big gums full of misshapen and misaligned teeth then mouthed some unintelligible sounds while slavering and spraying spittle. He lowered the axe a little more and Baldor stepped his horse backwards offering an exit.

"Down … down!" Baldor repeated slowly while pointing to the axe then the ground.

The simpleton grinned widely then looked around at the warriors; his tongue flicked out again licking his lips and he gave a short manic laugh before gently offering the axe to one of the men. The warrior took it then quickly moved back a pace as the simpleton suddenly stepped in too fast too close. Seeing the warrior's wary move, he laughed again, hooting loudly and making a childish face. Having surrendered the axe, he mumbled more unintelligible words and grunts amidst sprays of spittle and a flopping tongue then turned and took half-a-dozen paces away. Suddenly, he spun around, jumping back towards the watching men raising and waving his arms wildly, and shouting. "Waaah!"

Instinctively, a sword stabbed forward catching him in the lower belly, the force of the jump driving it hilt deep. Groaning like a butchered bull then falling to his knees, he looked askance at the blade and his lifeblood spilling onto the cobbles. He panted with the pain then howled like a wounded animal. His eyes filled and he wept pitifully like a child, the sobs punctuated by more slurred mumblings that made no sense. Seeing neither an enemy nor a man in front of him but a dying, retarded boy horrified Baldor and he urged his men to help him, though he'd seen enough wounds to know the boy was beyond aid. The men knew it too. One stepped behind the boy discreetly drawing his dagger and speaking quietly, trying to calm him.

"I said help him!" Baldor shouted.

"But sir, he's …"

"Baal Almighty!" He cursed.

The warrior sheathed his dagger and crouched down to the boy who was now bent double with the pain, his jutting brow resting on the ground, hands holding the sword hilt as if they could ease his hurt. When the warrior tried to help him up, he howled like a trapped wolf as the movement brought fresh pain. Baldor recoiled as if in pain himself and bellowed:

"Finish it! For the love of Baal, have done!"

The warrior redrew the dagger; putting his arm around the boy's shoulders as if comforting him, then deftly drew the blade quickly across his throat. The boy's whimpers turned to obscene gurgles then a cough. As more blood sprayed then coloured the cobbles, he shivered then went mercifully quiet. The warrior lowered the still twitching body slowly to the ground.

"Tanith in heaven!" Baldor shouted. "He was just a boy! And a simpleton at that!"

"Aye, but old enough and deadly enough with that axe!" Armaco retorted from his mount behind Baldor.

Baldor turned to face Armaco, his brow knotted and eyes narrowed as he glared at his officer. Making a visible effort to restrain himself from further outbursts he retorted hotly.

"I think that's enough murder for one day."

Armaco held the stare and when he didn't reply, Baldor snapped again while looking from Armaco to the watching warriors.

"Do I make myself clear? ... Do I?" He snarled.

The warriors mumbled their ascent and Armaco nodded curtly then turned his mount away.

Thus, when the flames drove an elderly couple from the farmhouse some moments later and the woman set about the warriors with her stick they looked to Baldor for direction. As she rained her feeble blows, Baldor trotted forward catching the stick in mid-strike wrenching it from her grip.

"Enough, old mother! ... Away I say! Take yourselves hence and go! Go, while you can!"

The woman stood back to look up at him, her hand coming up with a crooked, aged finger pointing accusingly.

"Destroyer! Barbarian! ..." She hissed then paused, forced to catch her breath. Her hand came up suddenly to cover her mouth and stifle a scream as she saw the bloodied corpses of the three men laid in the courtyard amidst the dead and injured warriors, the pitchfork, scythe and felling axe. "Murderers! ... Murderers, all of you!" She wailed and stepped close to beat at his leg with her fist, while her husband wrestled with her trying to pull her away, less she join the bodies on the ground.

Shrieking hysterically, she forcibly shrugged the old man off then began weeping pitifully amidst further curses.

"I hope you all die spitting blood! You killers of innocents … murderers! I pray you rot in Hades for what you've done … my sons … my sons … they weren't warriors, they could do you …"

"They wouldn't throw down! We warned them!" Baldor shouted above her tear-filled tones and the whinnying of his horse as it stamped then reared in fright as a collapsing roof beam sent a shower of bright red sparks and black debris spiralling skyward. The horse knocked the old woman over as it stepped and staggered sideways trying to regain its balance.

She fell heavily, cracking her head on the cobbles, her wailing cries abruptly cut off. The old man knelt beside her, trying to raise her up while looking aghast at the reddening gash in her greyed scalp. The horses continued to bridle and whinny as more of the house roof collapsed, crashing loudly and sending flames roaring in all directions. A flailing hoof caught the woman in the face sending her and the old man reeling backwards, Baldor cursed savagely and started to dismount. With his back to the old man, he was half off the horse when there was a gasping noise akin to bursting bellows. The old man staggered into him knocking him off balance and pushing the horse in turn. As Baldor regained his balance and snatched for the hilt of his sword, he saw the old man had fallen to his hands and knees in front of him with a javelin lodged between his shoulder blades. The man coughed and gagged blood then gasped for breath as his punctured lungs collapsed. Baldor glowered at Armaco who was kicking his horse forward and pointing at the ground with his sword. About to verbally lash his second in command for the killing, Baldor's words stuck in his throat as he followed the pointing blade to a short, broad bladed dagger that had fallen from the man's hand and he held his peace.

"For the love of Tanith, Baldor! Have a care! The old bastard would have stuck you." The one-eyed warrior snarled. "Enough of this chafing and worrying over farmers and the like, they're a treacherous bunch! Slay them all and have done with it I say, ere they slay us!"

Embarrassed at his failing, Baldor stared at the one-eyed warrior and curtly nodded his thanks, he checked for signs of life in the old woman and finding none remounted.

"Are we done here?" He growled to the mounted men closest to him.

"Aye sir!" Mumbled quickly back.

Without another word, he sawed on the reins pulling his mount sharply about, trotting it out through the ruptured courtyard gates towards the road. Behind him, Armaco had a trumpeter sound the recall and the men quickly left their mischief to mount and form a column and follow their commander.

With eyes streaming from the acrid smoke that followed their passage south and the sweet, sickly stench of burning bodies that stuck in their noses, they rode in silence. Baldor turned to Armaco and announced they would stop to eat and rest the horses at midday. Armaco nodded and turned his horse, trotting back along the length of the column advising of the coming break.

The cavalrymen were a cosmopolitan mix of Spaniards, Carthaginians and Gauls, their weapons and equipment as different as the men themselves. All however, had the same lean, hungry look of warriors who'd campaigned too long and hard with too little to eat and not enough rest. Which for most was in fact true; for this unusual polyglot unit, from an even stranger multi-cultural, mercenary army. Who'd fought its way across the length of Spain before traversing the Pyrenees, crossing the wide Rhone then the Alps in the dead of winter amidst snow, ice and hunger! They'd endured and fought off determined attacks from the local Gallic tribes before finally spilling onto the plains of the Padus and defeating the Romans at the rivers Ticinus and Trebbia. Their road had been long and hard but it was their most recent obstacles; the crossing of the Apennines, where they were almost swept off the crags by a lightning storm whose ferocity had seemed to herald the end of the world. Then, wading and blundering through the mud and stagnant water of the marshes of the river Arno that had probably taxed them the most and pushed them closest to breaking point. Forced to sleep on the carcasses of the dead pack animals to keep dry, they'd endured flies, mud and the rotten water which brought the flux of the bowels to many, sickness and agues to others. Many had fallen to disease, puking and shitting their life force into the marsh, some never to recover.

Thus, Armaco reasoned it wasn't surprising that the men behaved like mad dogs loosed from the leash when they entered the rich, soft country of this Etruria plain, with orders to burn and destroy the land of the whole world's enemy, Rome. Now it seemed he had an additional battle on his hands, that of preventing the men and Baldor from savaging one another instead of the enemy. He cursed beneath his breath for the position he found himself in, for acting peacemaker was neither his nature nor his trait. Pushing his horse alongside Baldor's, he sought the right words with which to speak to his friend and latterly, his Captain. Baldor glanced at him as he reined alongside but said nothing. His brow knitted; his face set in an angry scowl as black as the cascading plumes that fell from the dome of his helmet. When the tactful, calming words wouldn't come, Armaco adjusted his eye patch, took a deep breath and blurted out his concerns in his usual blunt style.

"You're scaring the men to death, Baldor!"

"What?"

Armaco set his jaw, his one eye glaring brightly at Baldor as he motioned him to one side while waving the column onward.

"I said; you're scaring the men to death!" Baldor went to interrupt but Armaco pressed on quickly. "They don't know what to do for the best, they're under the General's orders to loot, burn and destroy everything in our path and ..."

Baldor grimaced and tried again to interrupt. Armaco however continued, his voice rising in volume to assert command of the conversation and rid himself of the words and pent-up anger.

"And with that comes killing, for most folk will not give up their homes without a fight, whether they're farmers, warriors, simpletons or women. How do you expect our men to follow their orders when they're under threat of a hanging if they get it wrong?"

"So, you're condoning murder and rape now?" Baldor interjected tetchily.

"No, damn you! I'm not." Armaco replied sharply, his patience already thin and his nerves raw. "I'm saying you can't do one thing without expecting to do some of the other."

"I will have order! We're not savages!"

"No, we're not! We're flesh and blood! Flesh and blood, that's been to Hades and back these last months and more than likely going there again. These aren't ploughboys you can bully into doing what you want, nor are they eunuchs who won't look twice at a comely wench! They're men! Warriors! But they're also fathers, brothers and sons of folk who've died or suffered Roman rule and savagery ere this …"

"So that makes it right, does it?"

"No! … Damn you Baldor, listen to …"

"Captain! You'll address me as Captain!"

Armaco's face twisted into a bitter snarl as he leant towards Baldor and though lowering his voice the menace in it amplified.

"No, damn you … Captain!" He added with vicious sarcasm. "It doesn't make it right but woe is the vanquished and the dead, and dead is where you may find yourself if you don't ease up."

"What …"

"Baldor … Captain, you've hung a Gaul and a Carthaginian warrior for slaying the enemy."

"Rape! I hung them for rape and murder of peasant folk! They knew my orders! All were told!"

"Rape? Murder? It shouldn't matter, they're Roman …"

"It does matter! Damn it! … Damn you, Armaco! I gave strict orders; I will have discipline! I won't tolerate …"

"Hark the noble, virtuous Baldor! You weren't so damned prickly at Victumulae."

"They slaughtered my men and my friend while under the white spear of truce and they … they crippled you!" Baldor's face clouded as he snapped his justification.

"Aye! And your vengeance was going unappeased?"

"They had their chance to surrender and …"

Baldor coloured with the memory of the slaughter and realising he was losing this war of words changed tack.

"Must I remind you sirrah that I command here? Rightly or wrongly, I command! And that's a fact!"

"I need no reminding! Though the fact is … Captain, that warriors are dead and at your hand, and for what the Gauls will see as no good reason. Slaying them in battle is bad enough but hanging them …? Oh, for Baal's sake man! They're a vengeful people and you of all of us should know and understand that, for you were raised by one!"

Baldor looked as though he'd been struck and his hot reply dissolved into a jumbled stutter. Seeing the hesitation and sensing an advantage Armaco pressed on, though attempting to swallow his temper and changing to a more conciliatory tone, he pointed to the passing warriors.

"These men follow you because of your reputation. For the way you led them to victory over the Cenomani at Victumulae and for slaying Lugobelinos, their warlord in single combat and for your courage! Damn it Baldor! Don't squander that hard won credence for the sake of some Roman peasants."

Baldor found his voice again though some of the anger and surety had gone from his tone.

"We're a military unit Armaco, not some rabble of rampaging tribesmen on a hot trod for blood."

"We may see it like that Baldor but they see it differently." He flicked his head towards the Gallic horsemen trotting past. "They've been provoked, attacked and slaughtered by the Romans for years. What you see here's exactly what they've already suffered and worse, this is the nearest they've come to payback."

"But! We …"

"I know, we're a military unit and as high principled as you'd like to be or us to be, we have our orders. Anyway, see it from their point of view. Remember how you felt and reacted at Victumulae when you saw what the Cenomani had done to me?"

Baldor nodded resignedly, remembering all too well his murderous rage at the sight of the starved, beaten and crippled husk of a man, Armaco had been when he'd found him and replied quietly.

"Aye, I remember. My wrath knew no bounds … we slew them all." He looked at the passing column and the grim faces and saw the eyes turn quickly away less they catch his malevolent gaze. "But I slew men, warriors who'd fought … I … "

"Baldor, I'm not asking you to justify your …"

"We kill … I kill when I must but I cannot abide this of cruelty and rape, I won't tolerate it."

Seeing he was making little progress, Armaco sighed resignedly. "Fair enough Baldor and as you say, you're the Captain."

"I didn't mean that to sound the …"

Armaco raised his hand. "With respect Captain, I hold both you and your rank in great esteem but I'm blunt and will have my say, especially when I feel I must protect you from yourself. I trust we're friends enough to allow me the privilege? Captain or not?"

"You have the right Armaco, never the less the privilege … you're my closest friend."

Armaco heard and saw the sincerity and wondered at his strange companion, his friend. One moment he was angrier and more dangerous than a bear roused early from its winter sleep, the next he was childlike, worrying and chafing over little.

"Humour me then Baldor and humour the men. No rape as you command but let them take those that won't run or look to resist, a man needs a woman to see to his meals and his gear and Baal knows we all lack a little feminine company of an evening." Armaco smiled with mock coyness in an attempt to lighten the conversation. "And not all are unwilling given time ... surely you must have found that so?"

Baldor however, was still tetchy and fraught with the burden of command and trials of the day and his temper flared again as suddenly as it had previously calmed.

"No! I haven't found it so! Lasairiona ... the Gallic woman." He corrected himself. "If that is to whom you refer? She need fear nothing from me."

Armaco continued to smile despite Baldor's irritation and seeing his friend hiding his embarrassment behind anger, he ventured further while risking a snigger.

"So, you haven't bedded the bitch yet then?"

"She's, my servant."

"Hah! The big titted, old fishwife, Sulis is your servant. But the fiery, red headed bitch ..." He bowed his head mockingly. "Your pardon ... this Lasairiona, she's your slave by right of conquest and thus yours to do with as you please!"

"And I'm pleased to treat her as a servant."

"As you say Captain." Armaco grinned good-naturedly.

Baldor coloured and brought the subject back to the men.

"Very well Armaco! Let the men keep what women they will but I'll see no savagery in my presence or out of it! And I stand by my decision to have hanged the last perpetrators."

When Armaco's jibing was replaced by another look of concern Baldor snapped at him.

"Baal in heaven man! They were but children they snatched up and forced themselves upon."

"What?"

Armaco saw Baldor's brow knit and his face cloud as the terrible anger built in him again at the thought of what he'd witnessed.

"Aye, did you not see?" He asked bitterly. "Did the complainers not tell you that the pair I hung were caught having raped two girls, children just! Before butchering them to keep them from speaking out to condemn!"

It was Armaco's turn to look embarrassed for his lack of support for his friend and Captain and for not securing the full story before bringing the complaint. He stared at Baldor who now just looked weary and physically sick.

"No sir! I didn't see, I was told and …."

"Told and presumed no doubt, that I was being too noble towards the enemy?"

"Yes sir, I did." He answered honestly. "Though I know you to be an able warrior I've warned against such niceties ere now. I'm sorry, for in this I've misjudged you."

Baldor waved the sentiment away but Armaco continued as his own countenance turned grim.

"I should've known there was more to it when Andulas raised no complaint; he's instilling order on his people on your behalf before some lunatic Gaul tries to kill you because of blood feud."

Baldor sneered, shaking his head slightly he answered bitterly.

"Blood feuds, vengeance trails, pay back, honour! Tell me something new. I'm weary of it all! No! Sick to the stomach of it!"

"It's the way of the world Baldor, the face of war!"

"Spare me the justification Armaco." He said with finality. "We stop at midday; just leave me in peace till then, eh?" He kicked his mount on leaving Armaco mumbling at his back.

Chapter Two

The Villa of Lucius Aemilius Paullus. Rome, late spring 217 BC

Cornelius announced himself to the guards outside the gates of the Aemilian villa. Beckoned into the shade of the magnificent, marble-pillared portico, the first guard disappeared through the small door set in the main gate seeking the Steward to tell of the visitor. The second guard, a grizzled veteran from previous wars going by the old scars on his weathered face and forearms remained stoically at his position, eyes facing front, leaving Cornelius idling until he was admitted or otherwise. As young as he was, Cornelius was not intimidated by the elder, dressed in the full panoply of war himself and a veteran now of three battles, two of which he'd fought in this new war against Carthage, he felt he had some credence and right to respect. As he waited, he mused a marching song and tapped cadence to it with his vine cane against his greave. It was the Steward himself who appeared alongside the first guard, he all smiles and apologising profusely for the delay.

"Centurion Scipio, sir! My Lady Aemilia bids you most welcome. Please, if you'll follow me through to the house she awaits you in the reception room along with her parents."

Cornelius slipped the magnificent trans-crested helmet from his head, the sun reflecting from it in a blinding white flash as he passed it to the Steward while he untied and removed the felt under cap. Beneath it, his cropped, blonde hair was sweat damp from the morning sun, which was already becoming hot. His chest was covered in a short sleeved, mail shirt that hung to mid-thigh with a second layer of mail laid over his shoulders like a stole and covering his white linen tunic beneath. A harness over his shoulders and chest denoted his phalerae, the badges of his rank. His gladius and dagger hung from his left and right hip respectively. The late spring's heat had seen him remove his heavy war cloak; it being transported along with his effects on the legion's northbound supply wagons. Reaching for his helmet, he paused to reposition a simply made child's bracelet of brass and copper twists that sat snugly about his wrist; comfortable at last, he tucked the helmet beneath his arm and followed in the lee of the Steward.

Once through the cedarwood gate they followed a paved pathway through ornate gardens of manicured bushes and colourful late spring blooms. Their scent was both strong and sweet and as the breeze wafted the fragrance, it caused Cornelius's nose to wrinkle and him to sneeze. The lazy drone of working bees competed with the clicking of grasshoppers creating a peaceful almost lethargic aura. Statues of an austere Jupiter and Juno wrought in greened bronze and set upon plinths of creamy marble held prominence with effigies of the lesser Olympians and Gods of the garden set up in the more private areas. Fishponds filled with yellow and pink waterlilies completed the vista, the soft trickle of water adding to the feeling of peace and tranquillity. Leaving the garden, they entered an open pillared corridor leading to the house itself. Exiting the corridor, a grand but gently rising flight of steps led up to the main house.

He hesitated, then taking a deep breath stepped forward boldly.

Entering the reception room, he saw his prospective father-in-law, Lucius Aemilius Paullus standing by the window whilst his betrothed, Aemilia and her mother sat somewhat tensely on a settle.

"Sir, my Ladies; may I present, Centurion Cornelius Publius Scipio."

The Steward bowed deeply and backed from the room; he paused at the double doors to bow again then closed them gently behind him. Cornelius cleared his throat to speak but was pre-empted by the older man.

"Centurion!" His voice boomed and resonated in the room. "I bid you welcome to my house." The greeting was formal and without warmth.

"Father, please! This is your Good Son to be! Cornelius!"

"Aye, but a Centurion never the less and he shall have his rank. A drink, Centurion?"

"Thank you, sir, but no. My visit must be brief as my Century is already on the road north and I must make up the time and catch them ere I depart here."

The elder huffed, shrugged and poured himself a drink.

Aemilia made to rise but catching a warning glance from her mother sat back down. A moment later and somewhat determinedly she rose, walking across to Cornelius and kissed him gently on the cheek while slipping her arm through his. Her father remained looking out of the window while her mother shifted uncomfortably on the settle. Aemilia squeezed Cornelius's arm as he began to speak.

"Sir, I come to ask …"

"I know what you would ask and the answer is the same as which I gave you before …"

"But sir! I beg you, hear me …"

"No Centurion! No, I will not! I've no objection to your betrothal to my daughter, in fact I rejoice in it for you are of good character and family. However, I warned you of conditions to that and hence marriage long ere you set your foot on the path you've chosen."

"Sir, I cannot stand back when my city calls! I …"

Lucius finally turned towards Cornelius. "Yes! Yes, you can! Could have!" He pointed accusingly. "You've served bravely in the Gallic uprising and fought this twice against these Carthaginian savages! Your honour is proved you need do no more!"

"But sir …"

"No, Centurion! No, no and again no! Betrothed you are and maybe but as long as you march under the eagle, I'll not sanction a wedding to my daughter."

"Father!"

"Silence Aemilia, I'm firm upon this as is your mother." He glanced towards his wife who nervously nodded her assent. "We've not raised you to see you wed then your heart broken when your husband doesn't return from the wars. I'll not sanction a wedding only to see you widowed before we even have grandchildren!"

"Father!" Aemilia exclaimed as she blushed.

Lucius Aemilius Paullus waved away his daughter's embarrassment. "I'm firm upon this daughter, firstly as your father and secondly because as a soldier and a General I know of what I speak. The Centurion here …"

"Cornelius, father!" She corrected petulantly.

"The Centurion here." He repeated and pointed again, "If he's as honest as I think him to be, will tell you of the risk."

"No father!" She snapped defiantly, her face twisting into a scowl. "I see no difference! All soldiers run the same risks when they take the field; be they legionary, Optio, Centurion or ..."

"No daughter, it's not the same! Is it Centurion? ... Tell her! Tell her frankly and honestly how it will be!"

All eyes turned to Cornelius. He cast his eyes downward to hide his disappointment and to gather his words.

"Well?" Lucius prompted impatiently.

Cornelius shifted slightly then began in a reluctant, quiet tone.

"My Lady." He dipped his head respectfully to the elder woman. "Aemilia, the General ... your father, is correct. The risk of mortality is greater for me as my rank demands that I lead my men into battle personally." Aemilia shrugged and went to interrupt but Cornelius continued. "And lead them from the front, where the fighting's the thickest and fiercest, and these ..." He pointed to his helmet crest and two silver phalerae decorating his chest. "These mark me as a target for the enemy; it would be an honour for them to kill me." Aemilia clearly not understanding and downcast at his capitulation tried to interrupt again, smiling ruefully, he held his hand up to quell her words. "What I'm saying is; you don't find many old Centurions."

Aemilia's countenance clouded and her eyes grew large and misted, Lucius raised his hands as if to say 'I told you so' then with a lowered but triumphant voice said.

"There! Now do you understand daughter? Perhaps you'll believe it now that you hear it for yourself?"

Aemilia's eyes were full and as she tried to hide her upset, the first tear spilled and rolled quickly down her cheek. She cuffed it away while sniffing hard, trying to regain her composure while looking angrily at Cornelius.

"You, you didn't tell me this ... of the greater risk!"

Cornelius shifted awkwardly, unsure as to whether he should comfort her; else stand his ground and just answer. Aemilia's mother came to his rescue.

"Cornelius is a thoughtful young man, Aemilia." She said tentatively while glancing at her husband, when he didn't interrupt she carried on. "Which is why we welcomed your choice of him in the first place, I'm sure he'd not wish to worry you with details of war."

"But there is ... was to be, no secrets between us?" She said firmly while looking hurtfully at Cornelius.

"Sometimes ... sometimes a secret can save much pain and anguish?" He ventured.

She wiped again at the tears that now fell copiously. "I can't bear it!" She said with a voice already unsteady with emotion. "I don't want you to go, especially ... especially after you tell ..."

"I'm sorry! I had no choice, I ..."

"Damn you! You did have a choice!" She shouted as her anger vented.

"Aemilia! Please!" Her mother scolded.

"That's enough daughter!" Lucius intervened levelly.

"No, it's not! I'll not be treated as a child, someone to be lied to and placated!"

"I said that's enough!" Lucius growled.

"Enough, all of you, I beg you!" Her mother interrupted sharply. When she had quiet, she continued in a more conciliatory and calming tone. "Are we to send this young man off to war with harsh words and arguments ringing in his ears?" She looked at each in turn before continuing. "Cornelius, the answer to a wedding is no but only for now. We welcome you as a prospective Good Son and rejoice at our daughter's choice in you but I am sure you understand our thoughts and position at present?"

"Yes, ma'am I do." He said nobly. "I draw comfort from your concern for your daughter and for your kind words towards myself. But I promise you, as sure as Jupiter is our father in God, I'll be back to ask again ere this war is won."

"We would welcome such." She said, relieved.

"The matter's settled then, for the present anyway." Lucius announced firmly. "Now, we must let this young man on his way for he has his men to catch up with and a legion to join, but I would speak with you Centurion, before you depart. Daughter, you may have a few moments to say farewell, then I wish Cornelius to join me in my study."

Refilling his cup, Lucius strode for the door. Aemilia made for Cornelius but her mother stepped lithely past and grasped him by both arms kissing him quickly on either cheek.

"You do understand, don't you?" He nodded and smiled sadly as she continued. "Come home Cornelius! Come home safe to us! We love you; Lucius loves you and esteems you greatly but he will have his way, his daughters are his everything and he'll not see them hurt or heartbroken. Come home when this war's done and we shall have a wedding fit for all Rome to remember!" She kissed him on the brow and clutched his hands then with eyes close to tears turned towards the door.

Alone at last with Aemilia, Cornelius turned towards her and shrugged gently while chewing at his lip.

"I'm sorry my love, I tried."

Aemilia crossed the floor towards him, her sandals scuffing lightly on the tiled floor. She wrapped her arms around him and finally wept. He breathed in the sweet smell of her hair and scent of her perfume that wafted strongly from her heated skin. "Hush … hush now, come on, it'll be all right!" He said running his fingers through her hair and lifting her face to his, while pulling his scarf loose to dab gently at her tears. She was truly beautiful he thought, her angst seeming only to make her more so as she tried to hide her pain behind her pride. Her regal look and beauty amidst her tears tore at his heart and he muttered his apologies into her hair. She lifted her head and her lips sought his, kissing him gently; breaking from the kiss, she smiled sadly. He made to kiss her again and as she accepted, brought her hand up to hold his chin. Then before she eased her lips away, bit his bottom lip hard.

"What the …" He pulled back in shock wiping his mouth, as he tasted blood.

She smiled coyly. "That's for keeping secrets my love! Now come here and I'll kiss it better."

Shaking his head, he pulled her close where they kissed and held each other for a while, neither wishing to spoil the moment with words. Eventually Cornelius eased her gently away holding her at arm's length, taking a moment to study and enjoy her beauty. Her raven hair was gathered tightly into a high sprouting ponytail bound with silver ribbon and which cascaded to the base of her neck. Her skin had the olive hue of the Latin people and remained unblemished and firm with the freshness of youth. Her eyes, framed beneath long dark lashes were large and hazel in colour, her nose small and fine with perfectly shaped lips beneath, her chin delicate and rounded. Her frame was small verging on petite, with a narrow waist and small but shapely breasts accentuated by black fabric straps that crisscrossed them over her white gown then encircled her belly above her hips. Her legs, though covered by the dress he knew to be slender and shapely. Shaking his head in consternation at having to leave such beauty, he said.

"I have to go my love. Your father wants to speak to me yet and I've my Century to catch before nightfall."

Aemilia nodded as she fumbled with a catch on one of her necklaces. Undoing it, she laid the gold chain about his neck and leaned in close to fasten it.

"No Aemilia! I can't take that, it's your birthstone, your …"

"It's mine to give and it'll remind you of me when you're far away."

"But I've no gift to give you."

"Just come home Cornelius, that'll be gift enough!"

She kissed him quickly, then with eyes still wet with tears turned on her heel, scampering across the floor without looking back and disappeared from the room.

Cornelius looked down at the necklace and lifted it to examine it. The gold chain held two, thumbnail size but intricately wrought golden leaves set with rubies, giving the appearance of an exotic plant laden with red fruit. It caught the light and sparkled brightly. He smiled, then tucked it beneath his scarf and mail shirt his heart aching but never the less warmed.

Cornelius tapped assertively on the door to Lucius's study. A brusque 'Enter' saw him step forward and march smartly into the room. The air was musty with scents of parchment, ink and leather overlaid with cedar from the great desk that Lucius sat behind, it strewn with maps and scrolls. Lucius didn't look up, seeming engrossed in the largest map with his finger tracing over the black ink markings while he frowned and furrowed his brow as his mind worked through the information in front of him. Still without looking up, he began.

"What was said through there was necessary, not so much for you but for Aemilia's sake, I'm sure you understand!" It was a statement not a question.

"Yes sir."

Lucius continued to ponder over the map for some time before speaking again.

"You're marching north to join Flaminius at Arretium then?"

"Yes sir."

"So, we have Flaminius at Arretium in the west and Geminus at

Ariminum in the east and the damned Carthaginians breaking loose in the centre and devastating the Etruria plain. What do you think of that, Centurion?"

"Begging your pardon sir but strategy is not for the likes of me to comment upon, I ..."

"Well, I'm asking you to comment, Centurion!"

Cornelius was still reluctant but when Lucius raised his eyes and gestured him to the maps, he realised he had no option. Stepping closer, he scanned the map familiarising himself with the outline of his country and the major cities dotted upon it and the network of roads linking them. Putting his helmet down he leaned over looking closely, after some time he cleared his throat and ventured his thoughts.

"Hannibal has tricked us again sir. We expected to pin him against the sea either in the east or the west but instead, with his march over the Apennines he's now ahead of Consul Flaminius's legions with an open road to Rome unless we stop him."

Lucius cupped his chin in his hand. "Go on?"

"As you say sir, he's loose in the centre, taunting and goading us and laying waste to the countryside. Moreover, despite his unsecured position I think this is exactly where he wants to be for the moment as it serves a number of purposes for him. Firstly, he's re-supplying and re-conditioning his men, secondly, he's seeking battle in the open but again on ground of his own choosing where he can manoeuvre and use his cavalry to good effect. Lastly, he's demonstrating to all his current advantage over us."

"You mean rubbing our noses in the shit after defeating us twice!"

"Err ...yes sir! I hear he uses this prestige in seeking allies amongst the Gauls and disaffected Italian tribes. Those who aren't Roman he levies into his army else sends them on their way saying he has no quarrel with them, only with Rome. Subversion I think is the word for it?"

"Humph! And you would advise what?"

Cornelius swallowed hard and looked uncomfortable, he had no desire to share his thoughts with his superiors, prospective father-in-law or not. Realising however that Lucius was not going to let him away before he shared his thoughts, he committed.

"In my humble opinion sir, I think the Consuls should place cavalry screens and pickets into the field immediately. These to harass and worry the Carthaginians, keeping them from the sense of ease and supremacy they are enjoying at present. This distraction would let our people know we are neither idle nor mastered and allow time for the Consuls to join forces and shadow the Carthaginian army, pressurising them to battle when and where it suits us.

Hannibal likes the open plain for his cavalry. As you know, that suits our legions tactics too ... but, though I would rather have him in full view, where I can see him, I would like him with less space. If we pick our ground where he's constrained and we can bring our weight to bear I think we can break him!"

Lucius grunted and nodded sagely. "Aye, I believe you've the rights of it lad and I hear your father's wisdom in your words. Were that he was here instead of Spain, for your Uncle Gnaeus is very capable and was doing well enough there on his own. With good men, able thinking men, in short supply we can ill afford to spare him to Spain!"

Cornelius relaxed a little but determined to remain on his guard and to watch his words, as he was still very much politically inept and unsure of where the Generals of Rome opinions and alliances laid. Yes, there was a potential family tie between his house and that of Lucius through Aemilia but that did not necessarily mean agreement politically or militarily.

"So, you think the Consuls should attack in unison? A pincer movement? Box the Carthaginian in and destroy him as we did the Gauls at Telamon?"

"No sir, no, not quite."

"Hah! That's just as well then, for Flaminius couldn't even wait for Geminus after the elections. The hothead marched the moment his position was validated and without pause to observe the sacred rites and rituals required of a new Consul, hence you and others having to chase after him now!"

Again, Cornelius chose not to comment. Having heard the accusations of religious disrespect and despite his own strong piety, he saw logic to Flaminius's swift movements for he'd no doubt that the folk suffering and dying on the Etruria plain would welcome the legions like answered prayers, with blessings for the General that led them. It was one thing to maintain the moral high ground and observe protocols when safe behind walls far from the fight and quite another to face the depredations of a marauding army without support.

"Attack together yes but as one and lure the Carthaginian onto ground of our choosing. Open ground where he can't hide men but not so open that he can manoeuvre, then we use our greater numbers against them. Besides, I don't think Hannibal will fall for a pincer movement, his reconnaissance is too good and he too astute to allow that to happen."

"You credit him with much, Centurion."

Reluctantly committed now, Cornelius continued. "A grudging respect for my enemy is all sir; unfortunately, I've learned first-hand how he wage's war. Hannibal is no barbarian intent only upon destruction, rapine and murder but plans like us at campaign level. Thus, I believe that leaving our forces divided at this time will be detrimental."

"But at the Trebbia there was two consular armies were there not? A combined force such as you advise now, and we both know the outcome of that."

"Aye sir, only too well." He said lowering his head and frowning deeply.

"So why combine the forces then?"

"Sir ..." Cornelius hesitated. Lucius poured himself another wine and prompted him to continue.

"Speak freely Centurion, there's only you and I here."

"Well sir ... I, I believe we were ... mistaken in our actions at the Trebbia, we were tricked or rather cajoled into fighting when it suited the Carthaginian. He had everything prepared, his men breakfasted, oiled against the cold and well positioned with a large ambush laid, and us ... us led like lambs to the slaughter. He chose the battleground not us; he forced the action and the time not us, but we fell for it. Surprised and attacked in our own camp before dawn, then force-marched to the river, the men without breakfast and no food or drink. Some ... some didn't even have all their equipment. We forded the Trebbia amidst a hail storm, the icy waters up to our chests in places and then committed to battle almost immediately we were clear of the river." His voice thickened with emotion and anger as he recounted the day. "Shivering and chilled to the bone we were, hardly able to hold our weapons but we fought bravely never the less ... I've never seen such waste sir, good men so badly led!" He stopped himself suddenly fearing he may have said too much, then as if needing to be rid of the memory he continued. "We could have beaten them sir! Should have! For we had the numbers and the will but we needed to have been better prepared and properly arrayed but that day we were neither and thus paid the price."

Lucius looked thoughtful and sympathetically at Cornelius who wore his anguish and grief plainly on his features.

"So why return lad? When you could rest upon a duty and service to our city well rendered and with a Corona for bravery to add to it? Are you reckless? ... Do you seek further glory? ... Or do you just enjoy a fight? Do you see now my reason and trepidation for announcing a wedding?"

There was a long pause though Lucius didn't take his eyes from Cornelius. The younger nodded and cleared his throat.

"Sir, though I love your daughter dearly and wish only for her happiness, what kind of man would I be to stand by while my city and people go to war? If you'll be as honest with me as I've been with you, I think ... I think you would esteem me a little less if I were to resign my rank and stay home?"

When Lucius did not interrupt, Cornelius held his breath fearing he'd overstepped the mark before continuing in a steady, measured tone.

"Also ... also, I have vengeance to take for our fallen and for the injuries vested upon my father and ... and a blood feud to settle."

"A blood feud! With whom?"

"A one, Baldor Targa of Carthage."

When Lucius furrowed his brow and looked quizzical, he continued.

"It's a long story sir; suffice to say that we were once or should have been friends for he saved my life when I was but a boy. Since then, I've fought him at the Trebbia and the Ticinus where he would have slain my father."

"This Targa, he was responsible for your father's wounds?"

"Yes sir ... and I spared his life then ..." Again, Lucius looked lost and was about to interrupt when Cornelius carried on. "I had my father safe and Targa was left to face down my father's bodyguard, he would have died there but I couldn't leave him to such, I owed him my life so I gave him his."

Cornelius's face clouded his voice dropping low. "But that was then, not now ... now the debt is settled and he's like any other Carthaginian to me, better dead!"

"Finding one man amongst thousands will not be easy lad, more so when those thousands are trying to kill you."

"The Gods will throw us together again sir, for in the two battles we've fought we've already met this twice; the next meeting will be the last. He knows my legion and knows me from this."

Cornelius lifted his arm indicating the child's bracelet of brass and copper twists. "This was his; I won it from him the day he saved my life. And I'll know him by his height, his black plumed helmet and the twin falcata swords he carries crossed on his back ... and by the necklace I gave him in thanks for saving my life when we were boys." The words petered to a coarse whisper wrapped in bitterness. Lucius saw Cornelius's eyes stare unseeingly as if looking into the past. "And I will kill him!" He said with cold finality.

"See that you do lad, give no thought to quarter for I like not these strange portents and mystical scenarios."

The latch on the study door clicked loudly as if being lifted, then pushed slowly open causing both men to look up to see who ventured to disturb them without announcement. The door swung right back on its hinges yet no wind or draught followed it and no one ventured in nor stood upon the threshold. The two men stared at one another. Cornelius felt the hair on the back of his neck rise and a cold shiver tingle his spine. Lucius recovered first and clasping his hand on Cornelius's armoured shoulder said.

"The door is opening for you to march to glory. I sense greatness is to be laid upon your shoulders. Go well lad and may the Gods walk with you!"

Cornelius hid his hesitation and sudden sense of foreboding and straightened his shoulders then offered Lucius his hand.

"Thank you sir, for your faith. I will return ere this war's won to seek Aemilia's hand and your permission; I will strive to remain worthy."

"May the Gods guard your footsteps Cornelius, fare you well."

Chapter Three

Early evening saw Baldor and his cavalry unit back in camp. Tying his mount off at the horse line and removing his gear, he dried the sweat from the animal's coat and brushed out its tail and mane. Throwing a blanket over to keep it from a chill, he walked it down to the stream to drink.

It was a beautiful, still evening, the early summer warmth and longer days were encouraging the birds in courtship and nest building and he listened appreciatively to a Song thrush singing and whistling sweetly in the trees above the stream. After a long winter the countryside was coming to life, the ochre-coloured grass had turned lush green and the trees showed fresh new leaves and blossom. The sweet scent of meadow and earthy woodland combining with the thrush's song giving some comfort to his black mood.

He stroked the horse's withers as it drank, the animal quivered its coat then snorted and moved further into the small stream to drink some more. Warriors from his unit had also brought their mounts to drink, however none ventured close to talk and even Armaco kept his distance.

Angry with himself for his temper and hot words, he battled with his conscience concerning his orders and the way he'd handled the day, its trials and his men. Was he being unrealistic? Was he asking too much? Perhaps he could have handled things better with Armaco and he'd yet to see Andulas and hear his thoughts on the hanging of the Gaul.

Andulas and Armaco were seasoned warriors and both in early middle age making them more than fifteen years senior to Baldor in age. Both however, had turned down their chance of a more senior command choosing instead to serve as Hypolokhagos or Lieutenants to him, such was the esteem in which they held him. Andulas had given his own men, his tribesmen, over to Baldor's command and now these wild, Lingone Gauls made up most of the unit's numbers.

He swore beneath his breath for he'd not wished for the position he held, this of Captain of a mercenary cavalry unit, though happy to serve he wished no responsibility for others. However, Hannibal himself had decreed otherwise, for having witnessed Baldor's bravery in Spain he'd set him upon the promotion pathway, first to Hypolokhagos then to Captain after his successful storming and destruction of the Cenomani tribal fortress, Victumulae, earlier in the spring.

His mount raised its head from the water as another horse and rider approached, its inquisitive action drawing him back from his thoughts. He looked up to see Andulas leading his mount down towards the stream and him. The Gaul was as tall as Baldor though much broader across the chest and shoulders and where Baldor was swarthy skinned with short, black curled hair the Gaul sported a wrist thick, russet coloured pony tail that fell to the middle of his back and a broad, drooping moustache down past his chin. His features were large and coarse looking with ruddy cheeks like those of a peasant; his eyes though, were sharp and of the brightest green but narrowed now beneath a furrowed brow. Baldor took stock of the approaching man trying to guess his temperament from his look and carriage. His walk however was regal almost stately and as the steady, measured tread brought the man closer, Baldor could only guess at his mood and intentions.

"Hail Andulas." He said quietly.

"Baldor, Hail!"

Andulas paused a few paces away and gazed at his Captain as if anticipating his mood. There was an awkward silence between the pair. Normally good friends, each looked at the other with no idea of what to say, eventually Andulas spoke.

"What's done is done, the children are gone and the men hung. It won't happen again … let's leave the matter there?"

Baldor nodded slowly and chewed his lip. Andulas walked his horse the last few paces to the stream, leaving it to drink. He sighed heavily as he ran a hand over his face as if weary.

"Tomorrow's another day, eh?"

"Yes, we start again tomorrow."

"I've spoken to the men and there'll be no reprisals, no blood feud. Like you, I and most of the others aren't here to make war on children, we're not Romans to slay all."

"Thank you Andulas, I ..."

Andulas waved him to silence. "Tomorrow's another day."

Baldor nodded again and clasped Andulas on the shoulder then reached for his mount's bridle turning it away from the stream back towards the horse line. Tying it off and leaving it to crop the grass, he made his way through the vast city of tents towards his own. He removed his helmet as he walked, glad to be free of the heavy bronze helm and stretching his jaw as the tight cheek pieces released their grip on his face. Physically and mentally worn out and relieved at not having to face down an angered friend his thoughts turned to supper and bed.

Approaching his tent, he heard the soft, melodious sounds of a reed flute, the melody was slow and though a little sad in essence its beauty enthralled him. Stopping to listen he realised the sound came from his tent, furrowing his brow he eased the canvas door gently aside. His evening meal of cold meat, bread and fruit was already prepared and set on the small wooden table with his wine jug and goblet alongside. Sitting on a small campstool was Sulis, busy stitching and repairing his spare tunic whilst Lasairiona knelt on the floor leaning back on her thighs, her back to him playing the flute. He wondered at the pair sitting quietly together, seemingly content in each other's company and very different from when first brought to him as gifts for his victory at Victumulae. Sulis had been assigned his servant and the tamer of Lasairiona, she his slave by right of conquest and daughter to the Cenomani Chieftain Lugobelinos, whom Baldor had slain. Sulis had come with a stout stick with which to keep Lasairiona in line and a no-nonsense attitude to her work. Baldor however had forbidden any beatings and despite urgings from Hannibal, Armaco and Sulis, he'd declined to have Lasairiona sent to his bed. He'd been angry at first, wishing neither of the women, being more than content to look to himself and his needs, however he had to admit his quality of life had improved since; with his meals made, his gear cleaned and repaired and his larder kept stocked.

His reflection was interrupted when Sulis saw him and stood up. Nodding her head in respect, she gently pushed the flute from

Lasairiona's lips. The redhead put the flute down and also made to stand but Baldor stepped closer, gently pushing her back to the floor.

"Play! Play some more, if you will?"

When Lasairiona looked unsure, Sulis quickly urged her with hand signals to continue whilst she brought a chair for Baldor. Settling herself, Lasairiona began to play again while Sulis took Baldor's helmet then helped him unbuckle the harness holding the two, falcatas he wore crossed on his back. After hanging the helmet and swords from the wooden crosstree in the corner of the tent she returned quickly, bringing the goblet and wine jug from the table and poured him a drink. Knowing his needs, she waited as he downed the goblet without pause and held it out for her to refill, she then stood back but with the jug held in readiness. As the soft notes washed over Baldor and the harsh but potent wine hit his empty belly, he felt some of the anguish and tenseness leaving his body, taking the jug he waved Sulis to sit.

Lasairiona played the tune out then paused and looked at him for direction. On his third cup of wine, he stood making for the table and his meal while gesturing to the two women that they should also eat. Sulis produced two smaller plates and she and Lasairiona sat on the floor with their dinner. By the time Baldor finished eating he'd drained the jug and was seeking another, Sulis disappeared momentarily, returning with a larger clay pitcher from which she decanted more wine into the jug. Baldor tugged at the lacings on his leather corselet but finding the un-watered wine had affected his fingers, abandoned the effort and sat back lazily in the chair.

"Play! Play some more." He said loudly.

By the time darkness fell Baldor was slumped over the table from tiredness and the effects of the wine. Sulis lit the oil lamps then brought a bowl of water and a towel for him to wash and went to help him out of the corselet. Ignoring the water but accepting the help with the lacing he shrugged out of the tight leather skin then reached for the wine again bidding her once more to sit. Looking over the rim of his goblet from weary and wine-taken eyes, he watched Lasairiona as she continued to play. Her lustrous fox-orange hair hung long and layered past her shoulders, the dark colour accentuating the creamy whiteness of her skin. He noticed her shapely nose and pale pink lips so carefully pursed about the flutes tip. She kept her eyes closed as she played which allowed him to take in the rest of her body without her being aware of his somewhat lascivious study. Her neck was long and elegant and her shoulders though broad were not unfeminine. Her breasts were rounded and firm looking, and rose and fell gently beneath the constraints of her buckskin dress as she sought breath to play. The dress was gathered with a broad leather belt about her narrow waist giving an hourglass shape. The side split below her waist revealed legs that were long and shapely both of thigh and calf, ending in small feet for one so tall.

Enjoying the beauty and femininity before him and drink taken from the wine his thoughts turned lustful and to his manly needs. He'd become very aware of her femininity over the last few weeks but with much to do he'd had neither the time nor energy to dwell upon it. Now however, despite his drunken and weary state his mind and then his body became very aware of the beautiful woman before him. Reaching clumsily for more wine he almost knocked the jug over, swearing quietly and struggling to get up he slumped onto the table resting his head on his hands instead. Sulis rose and announced that his bed was ready should he wish it but again he waved her back to her seat while commanding loudly for Lasairiona to continue playing. Sulis dutifully returned to her mending leaving him to his licentious thoughts.

The next tune was equally sad and poignant and its beautiful though mournful melody took him back to the last woman in his life, Aiticia and the loss of her. Swilling another goblet of wine to the bitter reminiscence, he snarled at himself for what he judged to be his betrayal of his dead wife's memory and his lust turned to a cold, self-loathing. Pouring more wine but spilling most onto the tabletop his head slumped onto his arm as he neared inebriation. He knew no more until woken by a gentle shake from Sulis respectably urging him to his bed. Lasairiona was no longer playing and was instead, collared and chained to the tent post for the night. Just as she had been since arriving into Baldor's service.

Angrily shrugging Sulis off, he reached for the wine once more, his head spinning and his heart heavy.

"Let her play! Unchain her and let her play! Baal Almighty, woman! Must I suffer another monotonous night without entertainment?"

"I'm sorry sir; I thought … I thought you asleep!"

"Drunk! You thought me drunk is what you mean!" He snapped irritably.

Sulis didn't answer but unchained Lasairiona bidding her play some more then returned again to her mending. Baldor quaffed more wine, grimacing at the sour taste while his thoughts returned to the loss of his wife. He pulled at a leather cord around his neck and fished out a small, silver cameo from inside his tunic. Staring at the finely chased image of Aiticia's face, he traced a fingertip carefully almost reverently over it and felt his eyes fill and a stone-hard ache grow in his chest; he bit savagely at his lip. She had been beauty incarnate and the love of his life, his Goddess on this earthly plain but now she was gone, gone to ashes and dust and all he had left was this one image to remind him of her. Sighing deeply, he supported his head with his hand, his eyes bleary and senses fuddled, his thoughts a mixture of anger, bitterness, regret and sorrow. Outside, the camp had fallen quiet telling him the time was late, he noticed Sulis was asleep at her work, the portly woman breathed deeply and snored softly her head resting forward on her chest. Lasairiona continued to play though the notes seemed quieter than before and as his eyes lost their focus his head fell forward, when his hand failed to take its weight, he slumped across the table sound asleep.

A cold draught about his legs woke him just before dawn, along with an aching forearm long since numbed from the weight of his head. His mouth was desert dry and his head throbbed as if a demon were loose inside it with a hammer. As his vision focused, he saw one of his falcatas laid alongside him on the table. Rubbing hard at his eyes and shaking his head in an attempt to clear his senses he looked at the naked blade, this was not where he'd left it! Looking around the tent he saw the lamps had been turned down to a shadowy half-light and that Sulis was still hunched forward in her chair snoring softly, she remained fully dressed but a blanket had been wrapped about her shoulders. Shivering a little, he straightened up then felt the constraints about his shoulders and found that he too was wrapped in the bearskin cloak taken from atop his bed. Looking to the floor, he saw Lasairiona sound asleep amidst her own blanket with her flute to one side but with neither collar nor chain fitted or fastened. Half asleep, confused and more than a little drunk, he pulled himself unsteadily to his feet making his way with a stumbling gait towards his bed.

The following morning was his for leisure and he slept late; his company stood down as other detachments took their turn on patrol and their part in the devastation of the surrounding countryside. He woke gradually as the morning heat warmed the tent making the interior humid and stuffy, not wanting to get up he dozed fitfully until the sounds of the camp growing in volume finally pervaded his sleep. His headache had not eased its tempo of relentless banging and his stomach, which felt as if he'd swallowed a stone, griped and gurgled painfully causing him to belch. Grimacing at the bitter, acid taste of reflux, he retched and his mouth filled with vomit. Leaning then falling out of bed, he snatched up the bucket left for his night waste and emptied his stomach into it. Retching, hawking and groaning aloud, he sat back on the bed with the bucket between his knees and hands supporting his head, his skin prickling hotly and dotted with tiny beads of sweat. Swearing he would never drink again; he coughed and emptied the last of his stomach contents into the bucket then fell back on the bed breathless.

"Are you all right sir? Shall I call the physician?" Sulis called tentatively from beyond the curtain that divided his sleeping quarters from the main tent.

"Leave me be woman!" He snapped, then rolled himself in the blanket as the heat left his body, being replaced by a cold shiver. The sour stink of vomit mixed with the stale odour of his unwashed body and he wrinkled his nose in distaste. Forcing himself up from the bed, he wrapped a blanket about his nakedness and sought his washbowl. Supporting himself on the small table near the bowl, he hung his head and took stock of his condition and situation. His drinking was a problem of which he already knew and did his best to ignore. However, after what he remembered from the previous night and the unexplained appearance of his sword by his head it could well have been his last. Lasairiona, he had always judged was not to be trusted, for having slain her father and slaughtered her people he'd abhorred the idea of taking her into his service, likening it to sharing a den with a leopard. With difficulty, he recollected slipping into his drunken stupor and with Sulis already asleep, Lasairiona hadn't been tethered as usual, only she could have taken the falcata and placed it on the table. Why had she not buried it hilt deep between his shoulder blades in vengeance for her father and people?

His head hurt and his stomach was tender and raw, he felt terrible but worst of all he didn't understand, for he remembered only too well the curses she'd spat at him like hot venom as his men despoiled her father's house. He'd suffered her hatred that day, fierce and hot like a desert wind then imagined it slowly fermenting over the last few weeks into cold vengeance that when done would see him dead. No doubt her own demise would swiftly follow had she slain him, as his comrades would have in turn killed her but at least his death would have balanced the bloody scales for his actions at Victumulae. Shaking his head then groaning from the pain it brought; he dipped his head into the bowl. He came up a moment later gasping from the effect of the chilled water and blowing like a surfacing whale. Holding his breath, he pushed his head in again soaking his hair then running his fingers through it in an attempt to wash the dust and sweat from it. Persisting until he felt his hair and scalp clearer, and himself a little more alive, he reached for the water jug and quaffed half of it. He belched again as it hit his empty stomach; thankfully there was no sign of further vomiting. He stared into the polished bronze mirror fastened on the tent pole in front of him, running his hand over the untidy stubble covering his jaw and upper lip, he reached for his razor.

"Sulis! … Hot water! I need hot water now!" He shouted, and then held his head as his voice triggered more pain.

He felt ashamed at his physical state and the way he was conducting himself. What would Gestix have thought? The sudden memory of his friend and mentor hurt him further, as he remembered the big man's teachings to him from childhood through to when he'd buried him after the battle at the Ticinus River the previous winter. Gestix, though Gallic born had been like an elder brother, having returned to Carthage with Baldor's father after the first war with Rome and taken up residence with the Targa family. Present from Baldor's birth, he'd impressed onto him not only his formidable martial skills and language but also his philosophy on life, the meaning of loyalty as well as his devotion and reverence to the divine. Also, a fierce pride and sense of truth and honour that belied the label of barbarian given his people by the more conventional nations of the Mediterranean basin. The big man's death had broken Baldor's heart and almost his spirit, only the thought of bloody vengeance had nurtured him through the angst and misery, a vengeance against not only Rome but a particular Roman family; the Scipios.

His mind wandered to the Scipios and his thoughts darkened to wishful, grim images of the elder, the Consul, Publius Scipio, falling beneath the heavy blades of his falcatas to writhe in the bloodied dust before his head was hacked from his body. And the son, Cornelius, much the same age as himself, he too must die for his treachery and false words of friendship. Twice over, Cornelius and he had held the life of the other in their hand and friendship had looked to blossom, only to be dashed away by circumstance, leaving only a burning desire for each to kill the other. Baldor scowled, then feeling a hot, slippery warmth in his hand looked down and saw he'd gripped hard on the razor as the hate bridled his thoughts. As he relaxed and opened his hand the blood dripped freely and he stared at the red wetness. Placing the razor back on the table his lip curled back baring his teeth, like a dog guarding a bone from another. He made a fist and squeezed hard, the blood dripping quickly.

"I swear by all that's holy and by my blood that I'll kill both of you." He uttered in a gravel-like whisper. "The next time we meet there'll be no words to trade, no quarter to offer; only the edge of my swords will I give you. Aye, death will come to the house of Scipio for as you slew my brother, I will slay …"

His oath was interrupted by Sulis stepping tentatively inside his quarter with a bucket of steaming water.

"Your water sir; is there anything …"

Her voice tailed off as she saw his bloodied hand; quickly but calmly she produced a cloth from her pouch and wrapped it tightly about. Nodding his thanks, he turned back towards his washbowl. Sulis, surprisingly quick despite her portliness was there before him and had the bowl emptied into the night waste bucket and fresh hot water into the bowl before he could ask, she disappeared with a respectful nod taking the buckets with her.

He emerged from his quarter a short time later, his face scraped clean of bristles, hair washed, oiled, and hanging in loose black curls to his collar. He'd washed his body and anointed it with sweet smelling Hyssop oil and he felt and looked considerably better than the man who'd shambled to bed the night before. Sulis bade him sit then indicated to Lasairiona that she could serve his breakfast. Baldor watched carefully as the redhead set down a plate of fried eggs and fresh bread and ladled a coarse, brown porridge into a bowl alongside. She kept her eyes down as she worked but as she finished and stepped back, he reached out placing his hand over hers.

"Sit down … sit there." He said gently in Gallic while pointing to the other chair.

Looking unsure, she brushed her hair from her face while casting her gaze away as if hesitant to look at him.

"There, sit there … please!" He said again gesturing towards the other chair.

Lasairiona sat and this time looked him full in the face, her doelike eyes as cold and blue as sea ice but absent of malice. The pair stared for some time with no word spoken; eventually Baldor picked up the falcata and laid it in front of her.

"Why? … Why, am I not dead and you long gone?"

Lasairiona never took her eyes from him, her lips moved as if to speak but no words came out. He raised his eyebrows inviting her response, with no words forthcoming he took the lead and pointed again to the blade.

"I slew your father with this, so why am I not dead with it in my back? Your people … they live by blood feud do they not?"

"Because, Baldor Targa … because, you treat me well … for a slave."

"But your father? Your people? … Moreover you, a Chief's daughter, reduced to fetch and carry and living by another's leave, how's that being treated well? You were a free born woman and I know you to be fearless and proud … I don't understand?"

Lasairiona remained quiet as if gathering her thoughts, he saw her brow furrow slightly and the words forming on her lips.

"My father …" She said with a tang of bitterness. "My father was that in name only. He cared not whether his children lived or died, nor how they fared. He was cruel, greedy and tyrannical in his rule and my people followed him not out of loyalty or respect but from fear. He was fearless and brutal as was his brother, my uncle Magalus whom one of your comrades slew. Between them they held my people in thrall, though they rose us above other tribes owing to their prowess in war, that was all that kept him as Chieftain."

Baldor watched her face as she spoke seeking fabrication and falseness, seeing neither he probed further.

"But your child?" He asked quietly. "What of your child slain by my men? Surely that would incur blood feud between us?"

"Are you so keen to die, Baldor Targa?" She asked with a sad, almost bitter sneer. "Are you seeking or provoking a reason for me to slay you? It's as if … as if, you wished I'd forced that sword between your shoulders?"

It was Baldor's turn to be lost for words. Looking into her eyes he saw them moisten and mist over, she looked away and wiped quickly at them.

"The child wasn't mine ..."

"I thought ..."

"You thought because I cursed and attacked you, that the little one was mine? ... Cullen was my half-sister's child; he tried to defend me against the warrior who'd have raped me." Her eyes welled and the tears spilled quickly down her cheeks but she held back from weeping and drew herself up proudly forcing the words out.

"Yes, I grieve for the innocent, for the slain, for Cullen and I wish the death undone, for a child's death is a terrible thing but the little one was not mine, else yes, you would be crossing the river with the ferryman instead of talking to me now. In fact, I would have slain you long ere now, somehow ... but ..."

Baldor's surety and assumed control of the situation was shaken by her direct response, swallowing hard he tried to speak but Lasairiona continued.

"But I saw how you dealt with Cullen's murderers and ... and the man who'd have raped me and I am grateful for it ... most men would have condoned my treatment as just, for I was part of the spoils of war was I not?" Baldor was about to interrupt again but she carried on.

"After being given to you I was not ill-treated, you neither beat me nor forced yourself upon me and I am fed from your table with the same food as you eat! Yes, I do menial work but for a slave's position it could be much worse, for you saw what my father did to your people and your friend? Most would have vented their spleen on the daughter for the father's wrongs."

"I did not take this path to make war on women and children and I'm sorry for what you saw and suffered."

"Then I'm lucky!"

Lasairiona smiled briefly amidst her tears and her face lightened. Baldor had never seen her smile before and was captivated, her beauty further enhanced by the brief play of cheerfulness on her features.

"Sir! ... Sir." Sulis interrupted. "I beg your pardon but there's a messenger here from the General, he's asking for you immediately, if you please?"

Somewhat piqued by the interruption, Baldor rose and made his way to the tent door where he found the messenger awaiting him.

"What is it?"

"Captain Targa sir, the General requests your presence at his command tent; he asks that you come at midday and that you come formally attired."

"What's afoot courier?"

"I'm sorry sir, I know not. I only have the message; I was not privy to the General's reasons."

Baldor nodded and confirmed his attendance though he was loath to give up his conversation with Lasairiona. Turning back into the tent, he called for Sulis to fetch his helmet, good tunic, armour and cloak while he sought his formal parade sword and dagger.

Chapter Four

Baldor smoothed the folds from the scarlet tunic, quietly marvelling at the almost invisible repair where Sulis had made good the rent from the blade that had dispatched the former Roman owner. The material was of the highest quality and finely made, it felt soft and smooth on his skin and a welcome relief to the coarse woven tunic he usually wore. With the weather improving and growing hotter by the day he'd decided to take it for daily use, he saw no point in keeping anything for occasions as his life he mused grimly, could be measured in days not years anymore. If the Gods or rather the Fates smiled upon him and he survived the next raid or battle there would no doubt be more garments and armour to be had, so he would live for today. He fastened the belted girdle of white leather pteruges about his waist as Sulis offered up the front half of the ornate bronze cuirass to his chest, he holding it in place while she did the same with the back plate.

"Lasairiona! Quickly girl, push the pins in! Here girl! Here!" Sulis hissed, the pins held between her teeth, while nodding towards the barrelled connection points on the shoulders of the two bronze shells where the pins fitted to bind them together.

Lasairiona pushed the pins home and the two shells became one allowing the cuirass to rest upon Baldor's shoulders, Sulis pushed the final pins in on either side of the cuirass closing it completely around his ribcage and chest. He shrugged himself comfortable accustoming his body to the feeling and weight of the metal carapace, while the older woman teased the newly rumpled folds of his tunic straight. Sulis brought a long crimson sash next, his badge of office as a Captain, wrapping it over the armour taking it twice about his waist knotting it tightly above his groin. He picked up his black scarf and rolled it, wrapping it loosely about his neck covering the leather cord of his silver cameo and the gold chain of the ornate marble he wore. Sulis turned to the weapons belts hanging from the crosstree. Picking out the silver hilted spatha with decorated scabbard and tooled leather baldric, she laid them over his right shoulder leaving the lengthy blade to hang at his left hip. Another belt of black leather adorned with flattened bronze studs added over the top of the sash supported his dagger and purse, it filled to bulging with gold coins, finally she passed him his helmet.

Baldor gazed at the helmet, it was of burnished bronze and exquisitely ornate. Like his everyday helmet, it had a brim band and large cheek guards, this one however was much more elaborate. Like the rest of his attire, save the sword and dagger, it had belonged to a Roman Tribune slain at the Trebbia. Tucking the helmet beneath his arm, he ran his fingers over the cuirass admiring the tooled metal outline that portrayed an Adonis physique of broad chest and rippled stomach muscles.

He surprised himself with his thoughts and feelings; the robbed equipment was a good fit and despite his usual lack of vanity, he thought he looked good in it. He appeared older and more experienced and the quality bespoke him as a man of some wealth. His exultant thoughts faded to sombre feelings as he remembered railing hotly at Gestix after the Gaul had told him to strip and search two dead guardsmen and take anything of use. Yet here he was, dressed in the clothes and armour of a dead man and taking pleasure from it. He huffed loudly causing Sulis to look up expectantly, waving away her unspoken question he realised how much he'd changed since taking the warriors path almost two years ago. He wasn't the same man who'd lived quietly in Carthage, endeavouring to run the family business while enjoying married life; concerned only with cash flow, material orders and project deadlines, comforts of his woman and thoughts of children. Now, his concerns ran only to killing and in the last month to murder, for that was how he viewed this harrowing of the local populace.

"You were right again, Gestix." He muttered beneath his breath. "This soldiering has brought me no peace."

"Sorry sir, what was that?"

He turned to Sulis. "Nothing Sulis, nothing at all."

Smiling wanly, she passed him the bronze greaves, again courtesy of the dead Tribune. Shaped to the contour of the wearer's calf muscles and thus a more personal fitting item and though a little slack, he reasoned they'd suffice.

Finely attired, he ducked out of the tent making his way across the city of canvas and skin tents toward the command tent of Hannibal. The camp roads, horse lines, baggage drops, latrines and marshalling areas were laid out precisely, the rest of the camp however remained haphazard with tents and shelters holding to no row or pattern. Some men relied purely on their blankets and slept in the open by the fire while others constructed crude shelters from branches and fronds. Each regiment however held to its own area and thus there was little mixing between the races of which there was many; Carthaginians, Gauls, Libyans, Moors, Numidians, Ligurians, Spaniards and some Italian allies who'd already rebelled against their enforced alliances to Rome.

As he walked, his nose caught the appetising smells of the midday meal: the hearty, wholesome aroma of fresh bread baking and the salt-sweet tang of roasting meat. After their victory at the Trebbia, the men were living from the fat of the land and with no Roman interference since, had time and freedom to relax and enjoy it. Cresting a small but steep, scrub covered rise, he arrived in front of Hannibal's tent. Over a score of officers had assembled outside and were being served wine as they waited for the meeting to convene.

"Baldor! Baldor lad, over here, come stand with me!" Mago bellowed loudly while gesturing Baldor towards him.

Mago was brother to Hannibal and his leading General for the infantry regiments. Though a fierce fighter and recklessly brave he lacked his elder brother's sense of realism and careful planning, preferring to gamble all on strength and martial ability. His redeeming quality being that he knew his weakness and thus looked to his elder sibling for large-scale thinking and strategy. As much as he differed in personality to his brother, he also differed physically, being a bull of a man. Massively broad of shoulder and chest with arms of heavy corded muscle, his waist however, athletically narrow and supported on sturdy, oak limb thick, legs. Like most of his race, he was swarthy skinned and raven haired with a moustache and thick beard that covered his neck and face making him appear much older than his twenty-six years. When he and Baldor had first met, there had been animosity between them for each was as proud and fiery as the other and a squabble had looked to become a deadly duel. However, during a small skirmish, Baldor had risked his life to save Mago's turning their differences to friendship.

"Are you well Baldor? I haven't seen you of late." He said as he sought Baldor's hand, gripping and shaking it fiercely in warm greeting.

"Yes sir, I'm well thank you, my duties … have taken me far afield."

"All the more reason that we have a drink, tell some lies and laugh! … You do remember how to laugh don't you?" Mago chuckled as he baited Baldor, for he knew him to be staid and serious by nature. "Tonight! Come to my tent tonight and we'll dine, I have a brace of pheasants to share."

He laughed again when he saw the ever-ready excuses forming on Baldor's lips and added quickly but with a satirical grin. "And that's an order my friend!" He threw a heavy arm over Baldor's shoulder, shaking him in a show of rough camaraderie.

"Thank you sir, I would like that." Baldor replied with genuine gratitude.

An Adjutant stepped out of the tent ringing a small hand bell, quelling conversations and drawing everyone's attention.

"Gentlemen, the General bids you welcome. Come, please be seated within."

He gestured to the tent entrance and the flanking guards pulled back the cloth flaps allowing the men to file inwards. Within, a long trestle table complete with chairs filled the room, to the rear of it was Hannibal's personal quarters screened by a dividing curtain. As the men took their seats, the Adjutant filled the goblets set at each place with wine and allowed men time to settle.

"What's afoot sir? Are we preparing to move?" Baldor asked Mago.

The big man shrugged. "No idea and not that I've heard. There's no movement from the Romans as yet, they remain holed up and seem content to wait there, watching us lay waste to their land and folk."

Baldor nodded slowly and as Mago became involved in conversation to the man on the other side of him; he took the chance to study the faces around the table, mentally reacquainting himself with those he knew. The oldest man there was General Maharbal, in late middle age he was slight of frame and balding, with what was left of his greying hair cropped short to an olive-hued scalp. His eyes large and strangely warm giving him the look of a kindly grandfather, his goatee beard still held streaks of black amongst the grey and covered a very pointed chin, his bottom lip curved down to the left where an old wound had disfigured him. As undistinguished and un-martial as he looked, he was one of the finest commanders of light cavalry in the civilised world and his genius and mastery of the highly mobile Numidian cavalry had already cost the Romans dear.

The man next to him, General Gisgo was of similar age. He too was greying, though he retained a full head of hair. Falling to his shoulders it curled into elongated ringlets towards the ends. His beard, short and shaped along his jaw, rose slightly towards the centre of his bottom lip and again at the corners of his mouth but did not grow over his top lip. A thick, pale scar ran across the top of his mouth and off over his right cheek, testament to a sword slash many years before, the scar tissue preventing bristle growth thus the absence of a moustache. The old warrior was a pragmatist by nature and though his comments could sometimes be deemed over cautious, there was not a man in the tent that doubted his courage or his abilities. Both men had served with Hannibal's father, in the last war against Rome and with Hannibal since he'd taken command of the army in Spain at the age of twenty-six.

The man to Gisgo's side differed dramatically in age, colouring and creed, being in his late thirties, red headed and pale skinned; Sergatatonix was a Gallic warlord who commanded the Gallic forces allied to the Carthaginian army. He sat quietly with his arms folded seemingly deep in thought, he too decked in his finery with a gleaming coat of mail, his neck and wrists encompassed by heavy but beautifully fashioned gold torques. In front of him on the table was his helmet of iron and bronze. A high spire rose from the dome finishing in a small knob on the top, embossed onto the iron crown and peaks were effigies of mythical creatures cut from bronze sheet and riveted in place. It was beautiful to behold and it held Baldor's gaze until Mago's voice cut across the hubbub drawing everyone's attention.

"You there!" He called to the Adjutant. "Where's my brother?"

The Adjutant looked up from his ministrations.

"Patience is a virtue and manners a must, General. 'Please' would be polite!" He said cordially.

Mago's brow furrowed, about to growl a rebuke, the Adjutant smiled and chuckled.

"I'm right here brother, before your very eyes!" He raised his arms in an open gesture then bowed mockingly towards Mago.

"What the? ... Who? ... Hannibal? ... By the Gods, what's afoot man? What trickery's this?"

"A necessary ruse brother ... Gentlemen." He bowed politely to all at the table and brushed the long dark hair from his face.

No one at the table had seen through the disguise though in truth none were looking for it, brows furrowed as questions formed on men's lips. Hannibal however raised his hands for silence and made to explain.

"Gentlemen, we've done much slaughter hereabouts and as you know that's included some of the Galic population as well as Roman." He nodded respectably to Sergatatonix.

"No issue here General." The big man replied as he waved away the comment. "The tribes hereabouts are not my folk, nor kin to any here that I know."

"Thankfully no. However, I'm mindful of the death of my Good brother, Hasdrubal the Fair. He was slain by a Gaul for some slight or insult to his family, I will not live surrounded by bodyguards and thus will resolve to trickery."

"Baal Almighty Hannibal, you're as cunning as a fox! I didn't know my own kin. But is it really necessary? Surely, some personal guards are not too much inconvenience. And better than this mummery?"

"I disagree Mago. I can go where I will in this disguise and I see and hear things and men in the camp as they are. If I take guards with me, men will watch their words and behave differently and as I said earlier, I'm a harder target for an assassin to find."

"As you will brother." Mago chuckled and shook his head as Hannibal removed the wig and grey robe to reveal collar length black hair lying in large loose curls and a bronze cuirass on his chest. Hannibal was of slim build and clean-shaven like Baldor, though of more medium height, his swarthy skin denoting his Phoenician heritage. His eyes were large with pupils so dark they seemed black, despite this, they emanated a warmth and friendliness that along with his ready smile seemed to draw people to him. His armour and weapons were practical and less grand than those of his men, his only badge of rank being the purple sash around his waist.

"Gentlemen, I bid you welcome and ask Baal's blessings for you all." He said, raising his cup. The sentiment echoed back and the men drained their cups. Hannibal smacked his lips appreciatively and looked for a refill. "Where's that damned Adjutant got to?" He joked as he produced another two jars of wine. Refilling his cup, he passed the jars along the table. "Now, you'll be curious as to the reason for the summons? Well, there's still no movement from Flaminius; despite our best efforts, he remains within Arretium." He chuckled and rolled his eyes as the men laughed amidst calls of 'coward.' Raising hands for quiet, his tone turned serious. "He's no coward, believe me. I hear he's desperate to come teach us a lesson and show us our place!" The men's smiles and light banter changed to growls as Hannibal's comments focused their attention.

"What's stopping him then General? Is he waiting for Servilius to join him?" Maharbal asked.

"He may be? However, our scouts don't report Servilius heading directly for us but shadowing us from the east. Moreover, I don't envisage Flaminius waiting for him either; remember he departed Rome the moment his appointment was confirmed? I think he wants glory for himself. I'm told that like Sempronius Longus, Flaminius is intemperate in nature but it would seem with a little more restraint, at least for the moment. Still, we'll continue our attempts to draw him out, as I have said before, this Roman indecision, their impotence; it only helps us, for this extra time makes our men healthier and us only stronger. Also, our position here is favourable should either or both of them come for us, this open plain will fill them with a sense of comfort for their legions to manoeuvre in but as I have always said; I'll wager African pike against Roman pila and our cavalry against any."

The men responded with hearty 'Ayes' and banging of their cups.

Hannibal raised his hands for quiet. "Should they venture onto this plain and I pray to Baal Almighty they do, both of them. We will cut them to pieces for I've a plan that will see them undone."

The men looked on expectantly; Hannibal however just smiled and refilled his cup. "It'll keep for now, if they come, we'll be ready and you'll hear and see the plan long before, as always."

There were requests to hear it anyway but Hannibal was not to be drawn.

"Later Gentlemen, later." He grinned, tapping his nose with his forefinger and winking. "What I will tell you is, if Flaminius doesn't come soon, we'll head further south anyway, we won't tarry overlong."

He had to quieten the meeting again as the men grew vociferous.

"The second thing I wished to tell you is good … no! Excellent news and not something I'd envisaged to happen for many a month."

The men looked on eager to hear more.

"I have news that reinforcements are approaching from the southwest."

The men cheered and banged their cups on the table in appreciation, Hannibal held up his hands for silence.

"I believe they've landed at the port of Cosa and if the scouts estimate aright, number close to four perhaps five thousand, a mix of cavalry and foot."

An elated buzz started up as men spoke excitedly to one another, smiles and laughter breaking out along with calls for more wine.

"Who leads sir? Have you heard?" Maharbal asked when the hubbub died away.

"It's not clear as yet; the first scout was dispatched back to us before contact was made so to give us ample warning. The scouts recognised the Carthaginian standard and garb and without waiting to intercept the column sent the first galloper back."

Maharbal looked thoughtful then sceptical. "H'mm, I can't think who it will be? Barring the City's Sacred Band, all able-bodied men and Captains and Generals of note are already here with us."

Gisgo growled like a sleepy bear disturbed from its slumber. "I'll wager its some wet behind the ears popinjay relying on his father's connections in the senate."

"Gentlemen, gentlemen!" Hannibal chided playfully. "Should we not accept this gift for what it is? A bonus? Surely, you'd not look a gift horse in the mouth?" The two older men nodded sagely and managed half smiles. "Between us all I'm sure we can hammer any senate bred puppy into shape and if the men are soft city guards it matters not, for I have veterans here for to mould and make warriors of them."

Hannibal threw his arms about the shoulders of the two elders and laughed. "Does the potter ask where the clay comes from for his pots?"

"Fair enough sir." Maharbal agreed. "Forgive me; scepticism comes along with the need to piss in the middle of the night! Perhaps it's an age thing!"

"Speak for yourself old man!" Gisgo growled. "I'll stick with being sagacious!" He chuckled and raised his cup to his colleague and his General.

"Good news eh, Baldor?" Mago said as he punched Baldor's shoulder playfully.

"Aye sir! The best we've had for many a moon. They'll have enjoyed a quicker and easier passage than we had, by coming over the sea; the men and their mounts should still have some meat on their bones."

"True, true, my belly was touching my backbone when we crossed the Alps last winter and we could still suffer a moon or two more of this good living to bring us all back to peak condition. Think you then, what we'll do to the legions, when we're whole again."

"Yes, destroy them all … every last one!" Baldor said vehemently as he stared into his cup.

"They'll be here before dark." Hannibal continued, drawing the men's attention back. "Hence my request for you to turn out in your finery. They need to see us as triumphant, buoyant and confident, as first impressions are important. No doubt, full bellies will aid your demeanour so let's dine ere they arrive." He signalled to servants bearing platters of steaming meat and fish along with baskets of fruit and bread that they could begin serving.

****

It was early evening before trumpets blared a 'stand-to' announcing the arriving column. Lining the route through the camp to his tent, Hannibal had the Libyan pikemen ranked twenty deep, their pikes held vertical like an avenue of young trees.

The column marched in amidst rousing cheers from the camp, the leading horses stomping and bridling at the noise and mass of men. The cavalry, some five hundred strong were a blaze of colour in painted leather armour and brightly crested bronze helmets, the evening sun reflecting back from the spear points and the polished metal. Men and horses encompassed beneath a forest of bright standards and flags, their mounts well-nourished and fit looking, very different from those whom they came to join. The infantry regiments swaggered behind, the men travel stained and weary looking but their equipment well maintained, shields newly painted and the men themselves amply sustained. Hannibal and his officers waited outside his tent as the arriving command group dismounted, their horses taken by handlers. Hannibal noted the purple cloak of the foremost man who strode forward of the group towards him.

The man removed his helmet and with hand outstretched went to shake Hannibal's hand as his Adjutant announced.

"My Lord, Bomilcar Bodeshmun of Carthage."

"I bid you good evening my Lord and welcome."

"Thank you General. Your reputation and fame are well known to us all in Carthage, hence mine and my colleague here's desire to join you." He motioned to a younger man waiting by the horses. "General, may I present, Lord Sakarbaal Samilcar, youngest son to the sadly departed, Lord Hanno Samilcar and heir to that noble house along with his sister Serfina."

Hannibal stalled momentarily before he shook the younger man's hand. Behind him, Baldor groaned inwardly as he recognised Sakarbaal. His skin flushed hotly as the bad memories flooded back of; his slain wife, his home destroyed and his revenge slaying of Sakarbaal's elder brother and the crippling and later death of the second brother of the house of Samilcar. Now it seemed the younger brother had appeared, like a harbinger of doom to reopen old wounds. His gut heaved, reacting to the oily, nauseous feeling of his nerves approaching the raw. With all now ushered into the tent, Hannibal was busy with introductions of the two men to his officers and working his way slowly towards Baldor. He unconsciously edged backwards only to find a heavy arm thrown over his shoulder.

"Stay where you are, Baldor!" Mago hissed in his ear. "You've done nothing wrong and you've earned your right to be here if any man has! Raise your head and stand your ground, remember you're amongst friends!"

Bolstered by the sentiment, Baldor swallowed hard and raised his head as Mago stepped alongside him. Hannibal continued introducing his officers coming ever closer, the light banter and pleasantries filling the tent. Baldor's heart began to race and his skin flushed again, his throat tight then desert dry, making it difficult to swallow. As Mago's fingers gripped his arm reassuringly, he bolstered his resolve and faced front.

"My Lords; I present my brother Mago. General to my infantry divisions and my constant support since I took command of the army back in Spain."

Baldor kept his eyes front and held his breath as Hannibal stepped across Mago towards him. Hannibal's hand gestured to Baldor his only sign of hesitation being the clearing of his throat.

"My Lords, I present my youngest officer and Captain; Captain Targa. Despite his youth, a man of note and reputation for bravery amongst all here."

Bomilcar smiled thinly at Baldor "A weighty commendation for one so young, Captain T...."

"You!" Sakarbaal exclaimed, interrupting loudly as he stepped forward, lips curling back to snarl, his hand pointing accusingly. "You murdering bastard! They told me you were dead!"

The background talking ceased abruptly as men turned towards the outburst.

"Not dead Sakarbaal, not guilty of your brother's murder, and not a bastard!" Baldor's voice was menacingly low and firm as he stared unflinchingly at Sakarbaal.

There was a moment of pregnant silence as the two men eyed each other, the tension palpable.

Sakarbaal stepped closer to Baldor. "You lying son of a whore, Targa! General Hannibal, this man is a murderer! I demand you arrest him!"

"Over my dead body!" Mago growled stepping between the pair and pushing Sakarbaal backwards roughly.

Bomilcar also stepped in, jostling Mago as he did so. Baldor then thrusting Bomilcar roughly to one side sending him crashing into a table in an effort to confront Sakarbaal. Chaos ensued with accusing hands raised to point, everyone talking then shouting in effort to be heard. Bomilcar recovered his balance while glaring at Baldor through hate-filled eyes, his hand snatching for his sword hilt.

"Guards! Guards! To me!" Hannibal bellowed.

Four guards pushed quickly through the tent flaps drawing their swords as they came, the rasp of metal leaving leather and the sight of armoured authority having the effect of restoring order and men quietened quickly. Mago stepped back, hands in an open, halting pose and Bomilcar moved his hand away from his sword hilt.

"That's enough from all of you! I will have order here." Hannibal barked. He paused; waiting for the silence to take effect then lowered his voice, the tone however firm and cold as a sword blade. "My Lord Bodeshmun, General Mago, this matter concerns neither of you, mind it! My Lord Sakarbaal, you demand nothing, I command here sirrah! Captain Targa, I remind you once again of your temper! Lord Sakarbaal, this issue is over and closed, the law courts of Carthage have said so, I say so!" He glowered at the protagonists as if daring a retort. He stabbed a finger in turn at Sakarbaal and Baldor. "Not another word from either of you or anyone in this regard! Do I make myself clear?" Quiet but respectful agreement mumbled back from the pair and the rest of the room. As silence took effect, Hannibal changed his tone.

"Now, we have cause for celebration, our number has increased some five thousand strong, we have wine and good food I suggest we all partake of it."

Hannibal ushered the group to the table, he pausing only to dismiss the guards with orders for the new troops to be billeted and fed.

The meal proceeded without further incident the atmosphere becoming convivial as wine flowed and men relaxed, Baldor however found his appetite lacking and even his penchant for wine diminished as he quietly ruminated over the quarrel. The newcomers were placed near the head of the table, some distance from Mago and Baldor. Bomilcar appeared genial company to his host though Baldor did pick up a cursory but hateful look from him. Sakarbaal ignored him other than an occasional hateful look and Baldor detected a sense of unfinished business. Mago noticed Baldor's apathy to the feast and caught some of the casting looks from the others, pushing the wine jug at Baldor he muttered.

"Pay them no heed Baldor! ... Bodeshmun's a soft, senate bred, arsewipe and Samilcar, a wet behind the ears, boy! They're all just puffed-up chests and attitude; see if they crow as much when the fighting starts! Hah! I'll wager they're buggering one another!"

He hooted at his own jibe and swilled his wine. His mischievous look, and raised eyebrows from above the goblet rim finally drawing a smile from Baldor.

Chapter Five

A week passed and Baldor saw no more of Bodeshmun or Sakarbaal, they like him being allotted duties and patrols. The war footing atmosphere in the Carthaginian camp heightened as Hannibal took the initiative and stepped up his burning and deprivation operations, sending men yet further afield in a bid to prompt a reaction from the Romans. Meanwhile, the camp filled with slaves, riches, supplies and new allies that trickled in as the Latin and Gallic tribes sensed an impotent Rome.

Despite the wide swathe of slaughter and burning the legions in the east under Geminus were lethargic, moving southwards at only a snail's pace as if reluctant to close with the Carthaginians or perhaps waiting for movement or a signal from Flaminius. Flaminius and his legions however remained ensconced within Arretium, so with the days lengthening and the campaigning season stretching ahead, Hannibal decided he must force the action.

At a council of war, Hannibal advised his Generals and Captains of only ten more days in camp to complete supply stocks and bring the men up to final muster with training and mock fights before they marched. Both men and horses had regained some weight and condition from the good living but which now required a final honing before he loosed them upon the Romans once more. Ten more days he said, then prior to the summer solstice they would be on the march south. This march in the general direction of Rome would he was sure, force action from both Consuls. To ensure that it did, they would continue to 'trail their cloak' once more, baiting the Romans to come and stop them.

As the council broke up Baldor turned for his quarters, his mind full of preparation and work to do before they marched. He was just a hundred paces from Hannibal's tent when he heard his name shouted.

"Baldor Targa! … Targa!"

The tone was harsh and aggressive and he turned to see Sakarbaal hailing him. Groaning inwardly, he sighed deeply and turned back on his way.

"Targa! Targa, you murdering coward! Don't turn your back on me! What's the matter? Haven't you the guts to face me? … You and me Targa, just you and me, a fair fight … say where and when, if you dare?"

Baldor stopped and turned towards a forcefully approaching Sakarbaal.

"There's nothing left to say Sakarbaal, you heard the General, you know the ruling of the Court; the matter is finished, closed."

"The matter's closed when I say it's closed!" Sakarbaal retorted hotly, his lips curling back showing gritted, bared teeth.

"Go home Sakarbaal, let the matter be, leave me be!"

Refusing to be drawn into controversy, Baldor turned away again and walked on. However, with the evening breeze rustling through the nearby tree canopies, he didn't hear Sakarbaal's light footfalls come up behind him and was startled when a hand grabbed his shoulder and spun him around.

"Bastard!" Sakarbaal shouted as he swung a balled fist at Baldor's face.

Leopard quick, Baldor dodged the wild blow. Dropping his helmet, he blocked the following punch with his forearm. Sakarbaal closed quickly, trying to come under his guard. Baldor also stepped in, hooking his leg around the rear of Sakarbaal's ankle then pushing him backwards hard, sending him sprawling onto his back in the grass.

"For the love of Tanith! Go home Sakarbaal, I didn't murder your brothers!"

Sakarbaal leapt up from the ground in a cat-like, springing jump. Cursing loudly, he came at Baldor at speed while reaching for his sword. Baldor stepped in again, closing the distance while slapping Sakarbaal's hand fast and hard, away from the hilt and pushing him savagely away again.

"Don't be a bloody fool man, they'll crucify us both!"

Sakarbaal however, enraged beyond reason, snatched his dagger from its sheath instead. Baldor, faster than the rising dagger, surprised him by stepping towards him instead of away, while grabbing the dagger hand and Sakarbaal's throat.

"I won't tell you again!" He hissed through gritted teeth as he tightened his grip.

Feeling Sakarbaal's weight shift, Baldor pre-empted the rising knee aiming for his groin and turned sideways taking the blow on his thigh instead. Grunting at the impact, his fingers tightened on Sakarbaal's throat. His other hand twisted viciously around his wrist, breaking the dagger hold and drawing a yelp as the bone clicked then gave beneath his grasp. The dagger fell, while Sakarbaal threw his head back then side-to-side, shaking Baldor's hand from his throat. The pair separated and stood back apace, seeking an opening

Hatred, anger and pride had long overtaken sense and the pair clashed again, struggling and wrestling, hands grabbing and fists flying. Though their strengths were evenly matched, Baldor's uncanny speed and combat experience saw him gaining an advantage as he dodged Sakarbaal's blows while landing his own, his fast successive jabs forcing grunts from Sakarbaal and keeping him at a distance.

Realising he was losing the fist fight, Sakarbaal dropped low and charged Baldor, closing the distance and surprising him with the speed. Baldor went down heavily, the back of his head hitting the ground hard, Sakarbaal landing on top of him knocking the wind from him. On his back, dazed and breathless, he was vaguely aware of distant calls for 'guards!' and 'Hold! … Stop!'

Sakarbaal, recovering first from the fall, straddled Baldor's chest and grabbed for his throat. Baldor forced his head down trying to cover the vulnerable area. Sakarbaal's hands scrabbled around Baldor's chin seeking a hold and when a finger pushed into his mouth, Baldor bit down hard. Sakarbaal screamed as Baldor ground his jaw, biting deep into the flesh. Unable to pull his finger free, Sakarbaal's other hand clawed and scrabbled frantically towards Baldor's eyes. Baldor, his movements slow and senses sluggish from the fall, tried to fend the hands away. Excruciating pain exploded inside his head amidst light and dark flashes as Sakarbaal's hooked fingers poked and gouged his eyeballs, the soft tissue yielding beneath the pressure. Growling like a wounded beast, Baldor bit harder, his teeth crushing the bone and tearing the finger end off. Sakarbaal roared in agony as his hand was released. Baldor spat blood and the fingertip out while shaking his head attempting to loosen Sakarbaal's other handhold as it tore at the soft skin of his eyelids and upper cheek. The still clawing fingers and nails raked his face into bloody furrows as they dug deep, desperately seeking further purchase. Frantic to be free of the pain and drawing on his body's last strength reserves, he powered up.

The sudden upward thrust unbalanced Sakarbaal and Baldor threw him clear. Rolling his weight on to Sakarbaal, he head-butted him as he struggled and tried to rise and throw him off. Sakarbaal groaned at the impact that dropped him back almost senseless. Baldor's hands locked on his throat and windpipe, his fingers claw-like. Tightening his hold, he felt the cartilage beneath his fingers then it giving beneath his talonlike grip as he tried to tear Sakarbaal's throat out. Growling and roaring he gripped and shook his neck, his din mixing with the obscene sound of Sakarbaal's choking. Hot blood from his face wounds dripped onto Sakarbaal's causing his bulging eyes to blink. His legs kicked and his body bucked frantically as his airway closed down. His hand reached again, scrabbling, scraping and dragging over Baldor's face seeking his eyes or some means to slacken the vice-like grip on his throat. Maddened with pain, Baldor struggled not to surrender to it. Just as he thought he could bear no more, he felt the pressure leave his face as Sakarbaal's hand fell away, his body wilting. Baldor let go of him, rolling off and pushing him away. Gasping and choking, fighting to breathe, Sakarbaal rolled onto his side.

Baldor forced himself unsteadily to his feet, hands holding his bloodied face and eyes. Sakarbaal slowly raised his leg and eased onto one knee trying to get up amidst retching and choking.

"Targa! …" The words tailed off in dry rasp as his throat gave out.

Baldor turned on him again and kicked him hard in the upper thigh, the force knocking him onto his back again.

"Stay down! … Or I swear I'll kill you!"

Sakarbaal groaned loudly. Still gasping for air, he coughed and seemed to choke, the hollow rattle from his throat obscene.

"For the last time … leave it be!" Baldor managed to shout.

A moment later, a body crashed into him and a hard blow to the head sent him staggering backwards across the grass. Senses reeling, eyes and face bleeding, his vision blurred and balance gone, he staggered as if drunk. Trying to find his balance, he threw out his arms, hands grasping helplessly for support and finding nothing but air.

Looking through bloodied, bruised eyes, he saw a grey shadow approaching and turned towards it, hands outstretched seeking help. In the background, he could still hear frantic shouts of 'order!' and 'throw down!' He had no idea that the shadow was Bodeshmun coming at him with a drawn spatha. Confused, virtually blind and panicking, he raised empty hands in a halting gesture while blinking and trying to clear his vison of blood. He never saw the spatha thrust that drove between the pteruges seeking his groin but felt the searing, white-hot pain as the metal forced into his thigh then dragged out. Crying out in pain, his legs buckled and he fell heavily to his knees.

Instinctively, his hand reached under his tunic, groping for the wound in an effort to close it. The blood was hot and slippery and there was a lot of it. Thinking the large artery in his leg was severed, panic tightened his chest. Almost senseless and expecting a killing blow to follow, he raised an arm defensively over his head then heard Mago's voice above the din of the fight.

"Throw down sirrah! Else, Lord or not, I'll carve you in two! ... You! Take Captain Targa to the orderly's tent and send for my surgeon. You! Arrest these two, now!"

Suddenly, Baldor felt hands holding his firmly, reassuringly. Others gripped his ankles lifting him from the grass while mayhem and shouting continuing unabated around him. He was only dimly aware of being carried at a fast, bone-jarring pace back towards the tents. Moaning in agony from the rough passage, he felt the blood soaking his tunic around his waist and lower back. Deposited onto a bench in the orderly's tent, hands quickly stripped him of his armour, tunic and underclothing. Voices shouted above him calling for bandages, water and the surgeon, then a calmer, quieter voice trying to reassure him all would be well. Naked but for his boots, his hands sought the wound again, the clumsy fingers groping then pushing into the wound; he gritted his teeth biting back cries of agony. His hand was gently eased away and replaced by another's containing a cloth pad, while a tourniquet was applied above the rent. With his vision a mixture of grey, darting shapes washed in blood, his hands frantically clutched the air seeking someone, anyone to hold onto.

The orderly grasped the seeking hand. "Captain Targa! Captain Targa! Can you hear me? ... Captain, here?"

Baldor turned towards the voice his other hand locking vice-like onto the others. "I can't see! Baal almighty, I can't see!"

"We're bandaging your eyes for the moment Captain. We need to stop the blood flow from your leg first, that's the most important at present. Here, drink this."

Firm hands lifted and supported his head as he swallowed then gagged on the proffered bitter liquid they pushed to his lips. He choked and coughed at the taste, some dribbling down his chin as he struggled to swallow it all. They eased him back on the table as the surgeon arrived with rapid commands for the thigh to be washed, shaved and elevated, the tourniquet to be released at periods while the leg was stitched and dressed. Surrendering to the ministrations and succumbing drowsily to the vile tasting potion, he slipped into unconsciousness.

Having heard the commotion, Hannibal made his way to the tent doorway and the guards.

"What's to do, soldier?"

"A fight sir. General Mago has broken it up and restored order. He's arrested two men and the third is gone to the orderly's tent."

"Who was it? Gauls, Numidians?"

"Neither this time sir, it was our men …"

"Our men!"

"Yes sir, officers I believe."

Hannibal's face darkened. "Officers? Carthaginian officers?"

"Yes sir."

"Go! Find out who these brawlers are and have them brought to me and bring me a report of the injured man."

"Yes sir."

Hannibal heard raised voices approaching his tent and picked out Mago's gruff tones. Stepping back from the door he quickly seated himself behind his desk awaiting the men's arrival.

"General, sir!" The guard called from outside. "We have the prisoners as you requested. Permission to enter?"

No sooner had Hannibal acquiesced than Mago pushed forcibly through the tent flap growling curses and pulling, almost dragging two men behind him. Hands tied, they stumbled into the tent with the force of him pulling on the rope that bound both together. Seeing Bodeshmun and Sakarbaal, Hannibal was lost for words and just stared from one to the other. Seeing the hesitation Bodeshmun took the offensive.

"General, this is an outrage! We are not to be treated so! We …"

"Silence! Else I shut you up for good!" Mago barked as he cuffed Bodeshmun hard on the side of the head.

Bodeshmun stumbled under the blow then turned back on Mago snarling venom and curses. The guards joined the furore trying to keep the pair apart, the scenario dissolving into vociferous; jostling chaos. Hannibal banged his fist repeatedly on the desk.

"Silence! I will have order here!" He said firmly.

Bodeshmun tried to take control again. "General this …"

"Hannibal …" Mago cut in.

"I said silence! Damn you all!" Hannibal shouted, his temper breaking.

"How dare you speak to me so; I'm a Lord of Carthage!" Bodeshmun persisted while trying to step forward to Hannibal's desk.

Mago seized him by his neckerchief twisting it savagely drawing the scarf tight, throttling and pulling him backwards away from the desk.

Hannibal's face twisted in anger. "I said silence! … That's enough from all of you! General Mago, let him go!" He glared at each man in the room, then making a herculean effort to control his temper, pointed accusingly at Bodeshmun. "I dare, sir, because I'm the law here! This is a military camp! My camp! Now, you'll be silent until spoken to, else I'll have you gagged."

Bodeshmun's eyes widened, his mouth opened though no sound came out, a look of incredulous disbelief on his face. Hannibal let silence reign for a moment while making a conscious effort to control and calm himself. He spoke to two of the guards. "Loosen those bonds, fetch my scribe."

"Yes Sir."

Awaiting the scribe's arrival, Hannibal took the time to study the faces in the room. The guards were impassive awaiting their next orders. Mago simmered, brows knitted and face grim, his temper barely under control. Bodeshmun held an arrogant, contemptuous stare as he slackened the scarf while Sakarbaal coughed and massaged his throat while looking at the ground, his mind and thoughts elsewhere. Hannibal did notice a slight tremor in his body and shaking hands, which he did his best to hide.

The scribe appeared. Making a respectful greeting to Hannibal, he seated himself at a small desk to one side of the men and opened a wooden case containing a plate of smooth wax while taking a stylus in hand.

"Now!" Hannibal said, turning to the guard. "Tell me what you saw."

The man cleared his throat. "Not much sir, t'was all at distance see; first there was the young Lord there." He pointed to Sakarbaal. "I heard then saw him and another arguing then come to blows; I shouted to stop and would have intervened but couldn't leave my post. The other Lord here, he intervened or rather joined in the fight and put the other man on the ground."

"With what? Fists, blades?"

"Blade sir."

"Hannibal!" Mago cut in. "General " He corrected himself quickly. "It's Baldor, they've ..."

"General Mago, you can have your say in a moment." He said firmly, though cringed inwardly at the mention of Baldor. Remaining outwardly impassive, he looked at the guard. "Go on."

"General Mago intervened sir, telling all to throw down and stop."

"Did it stop?"

"No sir, not until General Mago physically intervened."

"Anything else?"

"No sir."

"Thank you. General Mago, is there anything you wish to add? Anything you disagree with?" Seeing Mago's temper rising he continued. "Just the facts General, as you saw it."

Mago cast a hard, cold look at the two prisoners, sneered and swallowed hard.

"No sir, the guard has the rights of it from what I saw; I think I was too late to really make a difference."

Hannibal looked up quickly. "Captain Targa, is he dead?"

"No sir, no! He's badly cut and half blinded, he's with the surgeon as we speak."

Seeing Mago's temper about to boil over again Hannibal turned quickly to Sakarbaal.

"And your side of the story is ...?"

Sakarbaal smoothed his throat, flinching at the contact then pulled himself upright and glanced around the tent then looked straight at Hannibal.

"It's true General, I attacked Targa ..." His words barely audible.

"Captain Targa, sirrah! Captain!" Hannibal snapped.

Sakarbaal lowered his gaze, his voice raspy and broken. "We had unfinished business sir, as ..." The words dissolved into a croak then nothing.

"No, I don't know!" Hannibal barked, finishing Sakarbaal's words for him. "I do know that this matter is closed! Finished! Baal damn you man; we've been through this!" Making a huge effort to bring himself back under control and lowering his voice he continued. "Who struck the first blow?"

Sakarbaal hesitated then looking straight at Hannibal once more, pointed to himself.

"Me ... General." He paused again looking awkward. Hannibal waited then gestured he should continue.

"Targa ... pardon, Captain Targa, tried to dissuade me from the fight but I would have none of it, sir ..." Hannibal pushed a cup of water at him, indicating he should drink. "I tried to strike him to draw him on; he pushed me away so ... I went for my sword."

Hannibal eyed him intently, waiting patiently as Sakarbaal relayed the tale.

"He knocked my hand away ... when I took my dagger to him; we fell to blows."

"He never once drew his weapon or made to?"

"No sir."

"And from there?"

"Lord Bodeshmun intervened ..."

"Aye! And cut the Captain down, while he was unarmed and ..."

"General Mago! Let the man speak." Hannibal snapped, Mago bridled but managed to hold his peace.

Sakarbaal quaffed more water, coughed and gasped for breath but continued; a slight tremor in his voice. "One of us would be dead now sir if it hadn't stopped ... and I think it would be me. The Captain is a formidable warrior."

"Hah! A grudging respect as well as honesty! Commendable qualities, my Lord Sakarbaal! Though come too late methinks?"

Sakarbaal said nothing though he did lower his head like a condemned man. Sensing he was finished, Hannibal turned to Bodeshmun, Mago however was not finished.

"Hannibal! For the love of Baal, let's have done here! These bastards are clearly guilty and by their own admission! Let's nail them to crosses and have done."

Hannibal glared at his brother, taking the time to bite back the sharp rebuke he felt rising on his tongue. Managing to keep his voice level, he said firmly. "General Mago … for the last time; hold your peace. You've had your say, now let the defendants speak." He turned to Bodeshmun.

"What have you to say for yourself, my Lord? How did you become embroiled in this ridiculous scenario? And more importantly why did you not stop it?"

"I stopped it by the only means possible, with force!"

"I disagree sir! General Mago stopped all of you and without the need to resort to blades."

"I refuse to brawl like some base born peasant …"

"General!" Hannibal snapped. "I remind you again of my rank!" He held up his hand to silence Mago who barely managed to hold back his retort to the insult.

"You could have summoned the guard. The fight was already drawing attention; aid would have come had you called rather than just intervened."

"It's not my job to police the camp! I saw my colleague attacked and went to defend him."

"I don't argue with you stopping the fight, it's how you stopped it!"

"What does it matter? Targa's a criminal; he should be crucified; my blow could be a mercy. If you cannot instil order in the men, then someone must."

Hannibal's hands knotted into fists, his lips twisting into a snarl, the anger pulling deep lines into his face, his eyes narrowing.

"Baal Almighty, my Lord! Your arrogance, ignorance and impertinence are unbelievable. You think yourself above all. You seem ignorant of the true facts surrounding Captain Targa and the Samilcars and your impertinent references to my staff, my camp and the command of it seemingly know no bounds."

The room fell silent except for the light scratching of the scribe's stylus in the wax as he noted all that was said.

Bodeshmun, realising he may have overstepped the mark, changed tack. "We've brought you five thousand men! We …"

"So far sir, you've brought me nothing but trouble!" Hannibal paused, his finger pointing accusingly at Bodeshmun then Sakarbaal. "Lord Sakarbaal condemns himself from his own mouth and you by the drawing of a weapon within the confines of camp and by attacking one of my officers."

Hannibal leaned back in his chair his face grim, his eyes flicking from Bodeshmun to Sakarbaal.

"I should crucify you both!" He said flatly.

"You would not dare! We're Lords of the City."

"I'll find you a higher, larger cross to suit your exalted station then, you arrogant bastard!" Mago spat.

Hannibal held up a hand to silence all and this time the room went quiet though the tension heightened. He glared at Bodeshmun.

"I dare much sirrah! Test me not if you value your life! If Captain Targa succumbs to his wounds, I promise you, as Baal is my witness, you will both die on the cross! Lords or not!"

Both men physically paled. Sakarbaal staggered slightly reaching out for the corner of the desk for support. Bodeshmun's mouth opened but no sound came out. Mago snorted but said nothing. Hannibal continued.

"However, … if he survives and an apology is given and …"

"Hannibal!" Mago spluttered.

Hannibal thumped the desk then held up his hand again for silence. "If he survives and an apology is given, then the matter is closed. We'll speak no more of it." He cast a warning glance at Mago. "Now! Guards, remove these two from my sight. The pair of you are confined to your quarters until I say otherwise. General Mago, back to your men."

Mago, the last to exit the tent turned back to Hannibal. Hannibal pre-empting his brother's ire raised a warning finger, his voice cold and hard.

"I know what you're going to say Mago and I warn you, don't venture there!"

Despite the warning Mago made to speak. Hannibal's face clouded, his jaw jutting forward, his eyes narrowing as he stood quickly, tipping his chair over as he did so.

"I'll not repeat myself or justify my decision, General! Leave it and me be! Now back to your men."

Mago glowered, his nostrils flaring, though he managed to hold his peace. Nodding his head in a perfunctory bow, he turned on his heel, though he did manage to slap the flap door hard as he left the tent.

Hannibal picked the chair up and resumed his seat, resting his chin on his fist he went over the scenario in his head. He growled into his fist then banged the table hard making the contents jump. Jumping to his feet, he hammered the table repeatedly before swiping the cups, wine pitcher and writing materials off it onto the floor of the tent following on by tipping the whole table over.

The guards, hearing the commotion stepped through the door, swords already leaving scabbards.

"Sir! … Sir, what's to do? Are you alright?"

Hannibal quickly recovered himself and stooped to begin picking the paraphernalia from the floor.

"I'm good, Dagon, good. I slipped and knocked the table was all. Here, help me if you will."

Chapter Six

Baldor awoke much later, senses fogged and confused, his mind slow to recall what had happened. His head pounded like a kettledrum and his eyes felt as if they were full of sand. His face was on fire as if burnt raw and his thigh throbbed dully. Trying to open his eyes, he encountered resistance and pain, seeing only blackness he began to panic. Sitting bolt upright, he groped his face, felt the dampened bandage covering it, and immediately went to tear it off. The movement caused acute pain and he groaned as he fought with the cloth. He tried to shout but his throat rendered only a dry croak. His words refused to form, tumbling out slurred and garbled as if he was drink taken. Fumbling with the bandage, he managed to pull it down and as the light hit his eyes, he cried again as new pain shot across the back of them. Lying back on the bed holding his hands over his face shielding the light, he groaned softly as he slowly recalled what had happened.

Tentatively opening his eyes again, he found his vision blurred and though he blinked trying to focus, it was to no affect. He felt his stomach knot then twist as he thought his sight might be permanently damaged. Fighting the terrifying thought of blindness, he felt rising in him, he tried to calm himself, beginning again to tentatively grope and assess his wounds.

His fingers traced lightly over his face, wincing as he found the furrows of raw flesh down his cheeks. His eyelids were swollen almost shut and the surrounding area too tender to touch. He slid his hand under the blanket towards his thigh. Finding himself naked, his fingers outlined the large and prominent bruise from Sakarbaal's knee then moved towards his inner thigh and the wound from the spatha. The wound was only a palm's width from his groin and remembering the amount of blood, most likely deep. Feeling the gut stitches that held it closed, an involuntary shiver swept over him at the thoughts of what could have been had the spatha blade been on target. Sore, bruised, and battered he cautiously continued his examination until gentle but firm hands eased his away and helped him up to a sitting position.

"Drink sir! Drink this and rest."

He felt the bandage being adjusted back around his eyes while someone else closed his hands around a cup then helped steer it to his lips. Recognising Sulis's voice he tried to respond with questions but slurred, incoherent words were all he could manage before he was gently shushed.

"All is well, sir. The wounds are treated and will heal but you must rest, that was the surgeon's orders! Lasairiona and I will care for you now."

Submitting to the ministrations and between swallows, he tried again to respond but the bitter herbs in the drink once more clouded his mind and tied his tongue. Listless and sighing deeply, he laid back on the bed slipping back into the black, empty void.

****

The days passed and between sleeping and eating he was kept prisoner in his bed by the two women. Any attempt to move seeing him scolded and fussed over, the need for his ablutions saw no respite with a pot brought to the bed instead. Objecting hotly for his dignity then finally resigning himself to his fate when the surgeon reinforced the women's urgings, he swallowed his pride and did as he was told. His eyes were no longer bandaged and his vison was slowly returning to normal, though when the sun shone the brightness hurt and to which the women quickly produced a strip of dark cloth. Blindfolded and naked bar a small loincloth, he fretted the time away while the women fed him, changed the wound dressings, shaved and bathed him while constantly checking the leg wound for healing and any sign of rot.

The surgeon returned daily to examine his charge and carefully sluice Baldor's eyes with fresh water, having him blink repeatedly as he did so. The torn skin of his face being cleaned and dried before applying a smooth salve of garlic and onion paste mixed with wine and cow bile. The surgeon sniffed, poked and prodded the leg wound, nodding sagely and mumbling as he worked. Satisfied, he urged Baldor up and as he swung his legs carefully over the bedside, had the two women support and aid him in walking a few steps. With nothing left of his pride, Baldor leaned on his servants and hobbled carefully around the tent, gingerly testing his bodyweight on his leg.

With word of his improving condition spreading, a stream of visitors began arriving, Armaco and Andulas being the first. Both warriors were ushered in but told by Sulis, firmly but politely, not to stay too long and not to weary her charge with un-necessary details of the campaign, he would be with them again soon enough. Armaco' s hot retort was stifled by a slap on the back from Andulas and a hearty laugh as he steered the short-tempered, limping warrior through to Baldor's quarter. Armaco was still bridling when Baldor stood to receive them.

"She's a mouthy fishwife that one, Baldor! You need to stamp your foot and show her who's in charge here!"

"What he means, Baldor is. Good day! How are you feeling? Are you recovering well?" Andulas smirked as he spoke.

"Yes, of course that's what I meant!" Armaco snapped. "Damned slaves, she needs a whipping I tell you! Remind her who's master here ... Humph, you look all right! Well, bar the mess of your face, though the ladies may find you more appealing now you look like a real warrior!"

Baldor rolled his eyes at Andulas then flinched as the bruises responded painfully to the movement. Turning towards the table and the light he had to shield his eyes from the glare. Armaco, seeing the damage in full continued.

"Baal Almighty, man!" He said stepping forward to run his fingers lightly over the scars and scabs covering Baldor's eyes, face and throat. "It looks like you picked a fight with a Harpie from the whorehouse."

"As I've told you before, I bow to your knowledge and experience of such." Baldor quipped, then smirked and gave a mocking bow.

Armaco snarled then smirked back. "Huh! The ladies like men with scars, which is why I get to choose the best in the house! You'll do all right now you look like a real man!"

"So, I'm almost as ugly as you then!" Baldor grinned and Andulas stifled a laugh.

Armaco glowered. "It's obvious the Lordling runt didn't damage your tongue any!"

Baldor laughed and slipped his arm over Armaco's shoulder. "No, my friend, that part of me remains whole, so watch out! Anyway, have you seen the state of my unfriend, Sakarbaal? I'll wager he came off worse than me?"

"I haven't seen him, though I've heard he can't speak or eat properly yet. Aye, you gave it to him I suppose, but you should have gutted the bastard and had done! Damned Lordling! City bred …"

"Armaco, leave it!" Andulas chided.

Unphased, Armaco carried on. "How long before you're back with us anyway? This Gaul here's driving me mad!"

Armaco was still mithering and complaining when Baldor offered a goblet of wine to each. Andulas pushed Armaco's cup towards his mouth signalling the wine should stop his tongue then turned towards Baldor.

"Well, I'll tell you Baldor, it's good to see you on your feet again. The men are asking for you, the unit is not whole without you methinks."

Baldor's smile and uplift was interrupted by Armaco again.

"Have you heard from the General yet and what he's doing with that pair of miscreants?"

Baldor stared into his wine cup. His tone uneasy. "No Armaco, nothing. No visit as yet and no word on what's to happen over the altercation."

"The bastards want crucifying!" Armaco snapped. "We all know the law and it's as simple as that! Damned Lords! They think we're all slaves to be beaten and belittled."

Baldor sighed and looked away disinterestedly.

"For Epona's sake, Armaco! Leave it alone, enough man!" Andulas interjected his tone short this time. "The General will see to it; justice will be done. Anyway, we're here to raise his spirits not dampen them."

Armaco nodded and raised open hands as if to say fair enough, though he continued to chunter beneath his breath. Andulas steered the conversation back to the men, relaying the lighter tales and goings on of troops with too much money and too much time on their hands and the usual mischief that followed with; women, wine and general misbehaviour. He raised smiles and finally laughter from Baldor when he told of one of the younger men being barred from the brothel in the camp as he was wearing some of the girls out.

"Brenner the bull, they've named him. Apparently, he's hung like one too! I was called by the Mistress to go and remove him after two of the girls were left so they could hardly walk and him still with coin to spend and seeking another!"

"Humph, walking's over rated anyway." Armaco chirped, poking fun at his crippled legs. "Real men ride everywhere."

"I think that was the problem!" Andulas said and all three burst into laughter.

"Aye, and before I forget." Armaco said. "Balaam, Harbro and Malo send their regards, they're on extended patrol otherwise they would have been around to see you. Balaam says you're to stop your apathy and languor and get back to the war!"

Baldor smirked at the comment as Armaco continued.

"Have you heard from General Mago?"

"He called when I was asleep, hence the fruit and wine." Baldor gestured to the laden table.

"The fishwife scattered him as well then?" Armaco chuckled. "That would have been a sight to see. Aye! He's a good one to have on your side all right; he damn near did for Bodeshmun they say. He gave him quite a few buffets to the head; the guards had to intervene to pull him away."

When Baldor's face fell again, Andulas advised that they best be going ere the 'good Sulis' dealt them a buffet or two to the head. Swilling their wine, the pair promised to visit again while wishing Baldor a continuing recovery amidst winks and nudges from Armaco, when he caught sight of Lasairiona as they departed into the afternoon sun.

****

Baldor continued to recover, his wounds healing quickly and cleanly. He exercised the limb lightly as instructed and kept faith with himself by continuing to limit his drinking. His appetite however had not returned to normal and his food intake remained minimal, he citing he was doing nothing active to warrant eating. Despite the women's urgings that he must eat to grow stronger, he only picked at his meals, which saw them summon the apothecary. With no solution found and Baldor complaining at the intrusion, before finally ordering the 'charlatan' out, the women remained perplexed. Thus, when the weather turned unseasonably and strangely very cold, he felt it and asked for his furs to be thrown over the bed. The plummeting temperatures heralded a hailstorm of unknown ferocity, sending folk running for cover and leaving the camp blanketed in white. On the back of the hailstorm, gale force winds arrived from the north, causing damage to shelters and tents and bringing with it a further increase of almost winter cold and misery, something neither heard of nor seen this close to the summer solstice.

Having shivered and shook for an extended period, Sulis felt his brow and finding it cold and clammy turned to Lasairiona and spoke quietly. Moments later the redhead stepped out of her dress and undershirt and naked as a babe, climbed into bed behind him, wrapping her arms over his shoulders and squeezing her body against his. Complaining from chattering teeth, he tried to pull away, grumbling this was an indignity he didn't need. He was still complaining as he felt the heat spreading from Lasairiona's body to his and finally warming his bones. As the shivering eased then stopped, he relaxed and fell sound asleep.

No longer used to sharing his bed, when he awoke it was with a start. He'd turned onto his back and Lasairiona's arm was now draped low over his hips, her breasts pressed against his arm, her leg entwined about his, her hair tumbling onto his chest. As he inhaled, he caught her scent, a soft musk of body oil on heated skin and despite his prior annoyance his stomach flipped and his groin began to ache. Trying to extricate himself only saw her snuggle closer and move her hands up over his chest to embrace him, mumbling softly she carried on sleeping. Forgoing his first thoughts of ousting her from his bed, he laid back in the darkness enjoying the warmth and her smell and for once in a long, long time feeling completely relaxed and somewhat comforted.

As the sun rose, shedding light and warmth into the tent, Sulis woke him with his breakfast. Lasairiona removed herself from the bed and collecting her clothes slipped out of his quarter into the main tent to dress. Unsure as to whether he was happy about her leaving or not, he noticed his maleness and saw that no matter what he thought, his body had its own ideas.

Hannibal arrived the following day and the pair sat at the table over wine.

"The surgeon tells me you're healing well Baldor and your women's care has been unstinting, a boon to your fast recovery?"

"Yes sir, despite my prior reservations it would seem I have two very good servants."

Hannibal smiled, looked as if he was about to comment then changed the subject.

"I was angry at the attack on you and thankful to know it to be no fault of yours. From those who saw it and from Samilcar himself I heard you tried not to respond, that you sought peace … This of blades … this is unforgiveable, one soldier attacking another!"

Baldor looked up at Hannibal expectantly, his breath held as he awaited the outcome.

"I've spoken to Bodeshmun and Samilcar, urging my utmost displeasure and they swear that it will not happen again. They will give you a public apology in presence of the command group. This controversy and fighting stops now."

Hannibal looked somewhat abashed as he finished speaking while Baldor looked at him askance, not believing what he'd heard. Hannibal read Baldor's look and pre-empted his response.

"I can't take further action Baldor! In truth, I cannot be seen to crucify two peers of the city … and after they brought in reinforcements, well …?"

"So, they go unpunished, sir?" His tone incredulous and piqued. "Damned aristocrats! Ordinary men would have paid with their lives, have done and for less!"

"There's the rub Baldor, they're not ordinary men!" Hannibal snapped.

Baldor looked as though he was about to argue then thought better of it. He gazed into his wine, grimaced and lowered his voice.

"Fair enough then sir, it is what it is. I'll accept the apology and do my best to keep away from them; I'll not antagonise the situation further."

"Thank you Baldor, I knew you would understand. Moreover, think on it, only the Gods know how long they will last. There's another battle coming and perhaps the Lord Baal may release us of their burden and take them onto himself?" He rolled his eyes and gave a whimsical smile. "Between you and me, as long as they leave me the men they brought, I care not! Now, how long before you're able to return to duty? Your men are operating well under Armaco and Andulas but I'll be happier when you are whole again and back in charge and … I miss you!"

Baldor coloured under the sentiment and stuttered his answer that he should be riding within a few days.

"Excellent! We're nearly ready to move, Baldor. I've already briefed the commanders whilst you have been laid up, so hence after your health, the second reason for my visit." Hannibal lowered his voice and leaned across the table towards Baldor, beckoning him closer. "I hear Flaminius can finally bear our taunting no more and is pushing his command group into mobilising from Arretium." He smiled and chuckled. "It's taken a while longer than I thought. As I told you, he's known for his bullish intemperance just like Longus, though it appears with more restraint. Anyway, it would seem that he's coming for us, the race is on."

"The race sir?"

"Yes." Hannibal smiled mischievously. "I think, that they think we'll march on Rome? However, with no siege train and Consular armies to our rear and flank, we'd be foolish to do so, but here's the rub, they dare not presume we won't head for Rome, as the road lies open. So, they have to either bring us to battle or cut us off before we can reach it."

"So, we could have Flaminius on our tail and Geminus trying to cut us off?"

Hannibal smiled again and chuckled lightly as he answered. "Yes, and seeing as how they haven't joined up and don't appear to have any plans to do so; we'll destroy them one by one."

Hannibal paused to refill the cups then produced a folded parchment map from his tunic. Spreading it across the table, he weighted the corners with the wine pitcher and spare cups

"However, when we march it must be quick. Flaminius and his legions could swing westwards and make good time on the Via Aurelia or even over the plains for that matter, trying to place themselves ahead of us." He traced his finger over the road then directly down the map from Arretium towards the Carthaginian camp just to the north of Lake Trasimene. "They can move fast for they've no extended baggage train such as we have and giving credit where it's due, they're good infantrymen." He flashed a smile and raised his eyebrows.

"Geminus could follow the Via Flaminia and attempt to either block us or join Flaminius? Either way, I don't want them to catch up until the timing and ground suits us. So as always, I want to be sure of our route and know where I can bring either one or both to battle. Though I would hazard a sack of gold shekels that it will be Flaminius we meet first … and I'm not a gambling man!"

Hannibal paused and took a drink

"As you will expect I have reports coming in all the time from our scouts and with the maps we've made since, a good idea of the terrain. However, I would like to go look for myself, would you be fit to ride with me in a few days or so?"

"Yes sir! I'm almost whole again. It would be an honour."

Hannibal waved away the sentiment. "Can you find your archer friend? … The Nubian? Kushite?"

"You mean Malo sir; he's Nubian, he rides with Captain Balaam's troop."

"That's him, the hunter! Bring him also!"

"Yes sir, I'll see Captain Balaam."

"Excellent! The three of us and Ducarius."

"Who sir?"

"Ducarius is Chief of the Insubres a local Gallic tribe, he'll be our guide. My mapmakers and I have already spoken with him via an interpreter, so I've a good idea of the land hereabout. I want him to take us further afield, hopefully by the time we return we'll have a better idea of what lies ahead. As well as your company I'd appreciate your services to translate for me, shall we say three days hence?" Hannibal poured more wine into both cups then gestured for a toast. "Your good health Baldor and Flaminius's demise!"

"Thank you sir, Flaminius's demise!"

"Business done Baldor. So, stop calling me sir and tell me of your women!"

As Baldor coloured, Hannibal sat back in his chair and laughed.

The surgeon returned to examine Baldor's leg, the older man mumbling to himself as he unwrapped and pressed the area around the wound. Hearing no pained reaction to his ministrations, he declared soberly the stitches could be removed. The tiny but carefully hooked blade he produced sliced through the gut stitches almost on contact and as the skin relaxed, Baldor felt more ease. The surgeon produced a pot of cream and began rubbing it into the skin of the wound and surrounding area.

"What's that?"

"A concoction of honey, beeswax, olive oil, royal jelly, pollen and bee propolis sir, I learned of it from an Egyptian physician. It will nourish the skin and ease where the stitches have come out. Apply it, as you need to keep the skin supple. I'll leave the jar with you."

"There's no need; that will suffice, thank you."

"General's orders sir, you're to have the best care that I can give and he's to pay for it."

"But! …"

"It's no good arguing with me sir, those were his orders, and I but follow them. Now, you may continue exercising the limb lightly but don't go at it like most of these fool soldiers here and think it's going to be good immediately! Now, let me see your eyes and wounds to your face"

Again, he mumbled and tutted as his fingers traced over the scabs on Baldor's face. Some had already shed the dried crust, showing new, lighter coloured skin beneath, the deeper gouges retained the scabs but to which he declared were healing well.

Baldor exercised his leg throughout the afternoon easing some of the tightness, stopping only when the muscle began to ache, pleased with his progress he called for wine. Sulis brought it to him on a tray along with his jug. Procrastinating for a moment, then ushering her back into the main tent he called for two more goblets, filling them himself, he offered one to each of the women.

"Thank you … thank you both."

The women, somewhat surprised and unsure only took the goblets at his urging.

He raised his goblet in salute. Bemused, the pair smiled and sipped the wine though he did notice a lingering look from Lasairiona across the top of her cup. He asked that three places be set for dinner and sent Lasairiona out with coin to find and purchase two more chairs, some cushions and throws.

Slipping on a clean tunic and covering it with a short hunting cloak, he took his place at the head of the small table as the two women placed the meal before him, then at his behest joined him for the repast. He shared the wine and refused another jug adding water to his cup instead, his promise to curb his drinking holding, at least for the moment.

He cleared his throat and looked at each woman in turn.

"Ladies, again I thank you for your care. I would not have recovered as quickly as I have, perhaps not at all without your devotion. From now on we all eat from the table, everything I have I will share, we have I think become a family of sorts." Pushing his plate to one side he upended his purse onto the table, the gold and silver coins clattering into a glinting heap under the light of the oil lamps. Dividing the heap into three, he pushed a portion at each woman. "Yours to do with as you see fit, tell me when you need more."

The women looked on somewhat incredulously at the money and not believing what they were hearing, their status suddenly elevated from spoils of war to seemingly equals with their former master.

"Will you play the flute for me, Lasairiona?" He asked.

While Sulis cleared the table, Lasairiona settled Baldor in his chair with his leg elevated onto a stool then fetched her flute. Settling on the floor, she began to play, the melodious but haunting tune reminding him of the hills and forests from which she came. His eyes wandered over her body as she played. She, with her eyes closed and lost in the music, perhaps also thinking of her homeland. Again, he noticed her skin, unblemished, pale and smooth as alabaster. Her finely sculptured features and pale pink lips. Long, yet elegant fingers moving dextrously up and down the flute teasing forth the sound. Her fox-coloured hair cascading in thick tresses onto her shoulders, her breasts rising and falling as she played and her long legs tucked under her. She was he decided, beautiful.

Sulis interrupted his pleasant reverie as she pulled up a stool to one side of him and producing a distaff began teasing the wool from it, twisting and spinning it into yarn, she smiled as she hummed and rocked gently in time with the music. Lasairiona continued to play until Baldor began to slump in his chair and at which point Sulis disappeared only to return bearing a tray laden in readiness with; hot water, fresh bandages, powdered acacia bark and the cream the surgeon had left. Helping a drowsy Baldor to his feet, Lasairiona ushered him to his sleeping quarters and towards his bed, Sulis following with the tray. Placing it on the stool by the bed, she bade Baldor goodnight, departing with a coy smile to Lasairiona, which Baldor didn't see.

The late evening was warm and the air stuffy in the small room where the sun had warmed it with the last of the day's heat. Baldor removed his cloak and let Lasairiona help him out of his tunic and boots, sitting him back on the bed propping his back with cushions, he naked but for a loincloth. Having become used to her ministrations he didn't object when she eased his legs open and knelt to closely examine the thigh wound. She washed the area then dabbed it dry.

"It looks well, sir." She said while gently pressing the skin. "The stitches have done their work and the ointment is putting suppleness back into the skin. The physician told me to reapply it as you require." She un-stoppered the ointment and began spreading it over his inner thigh, her touch firm and somewhat lingering, he not objecting. She finished up and placing the jar on the tray stood to go.

Baldor also stood. Placing his hand on her arm stopping her and gently taking the tray from her, setting it back on the stool. She looked at him without a word as he took her hand and steered her back towards the bed. Feeling his own breath quicken he noticed her chest lift and her eyes flutter as she looked down as though shy. Lifting her chin, he quietly marvelled at her eyes, large and blue as sea ice but this time strangely warm. Her breath was coming in little gasps, his heart beating fast as he leaned towards her face. They shared a hesitant look for a moment before he tilted his head and kissed her gently on the lips. She didn't pull away but closed her eyes and kissed him back, this time for longer. His fingers stroked her face and ran through her hair as he gently pulled her face to his to kiss her once more but this time longer and deeper. Neither spoke a word as he moved his lips to her neck, kissing below her ears onto her shoulders, she gasping a little. Smelling the soft musk of her body oil, his stomach knotted as his groin stirred into life. She eased the straps of her dress from her shoulders letting it fall to the floor, slipping off her sandals she lifted the under shirt over her head dropping it alongside and stood before him naked.

He'd noticed and seen hints of her beauty over the last few weeks, felt it's affect as she'd left his bed, now seeing her stood before him unadorned he swallowed hard as she took his breath away.

Reaching for her hand, he pulled her gently towards the bed.

Chapter Seven

The City of Arretium June 217 BC

The dying rays of the early June sun blazed through the window, adding further heat to the already stifling room and blinding Cornelius causing him to shade his eyes. Secretly glad of an excuse to stand back from the table, he placed his helmet under his arm while quietly sipping his wine, watching and listening to his superior officers arguing with Consul Flaminius over what action to take.

As a Centurion, he felt uncomfortably out of place amongst the Legates, Tribunes and Prefects and others of high rank clustered around the table in vociferous exchange with Flaminius as to tactics, Hannibal and how and where to stop him. He knew he was only present owing to his father's and Flaminius's friendship and as he watched the meeting descend from logical argument to heated, incensed diatribe he wished to all the Gods that he was somewhere else. Flaminius's fist banging the table and his raised voice brought him sharply back to the present.

"These Carthaginian savages are shaming us in front of all; they're rubbing our noses in the shit! Surely, you can all see it?" He glared around the table. "Well, I'll suffer it no more! We march now and bring them to battle here on the plain!"

"Sir, we concede, agree that Hannibal needs to be stopped but we must have support from Consul Geminus before taking him on! It ..."

"Geminus is making no move towards us and the west that I've heard! We've received no messages of support from him!"

"Have you requested any?" The Legate snapped. "I mean, with respect sir, have you requested any?"

Flaminius glowered at his Legate. "Am I to go cap in hand to Geminus? I ask you again, why has he not ventured westwards? Why has he not blocked the road to Rome? He's in front of the Carthaginians, we can easily attack their rear, we could box them in between our two forces but I have heard nothing, nothing!"

"Sir, with respect, our messengers are being intercepted and killed, perhaps his also? As you know, Hannibal dominates the plain."

"Aye, damn you, he does! And for the moment perhaps. But not for much longer, mark my …"

"Sir, please! Hannibal has already made us look foolish by stealing a march and bypassing us but to chase him down without support is inviting disaster!"

Flaminius flushed scarlet. The colour accentuating the thick white scar running from beneath his eye down his cheek to his lower jaw. As he turned towards the accusing Tribune, the sunlight reflected from his balding head, the rays shimmering off the beads of sweat that dotted his pate like morning dew. His eyes narrowed to slits as he stood back from the map table, his hands bunching into fists, lips twisting into a snarl.

"We march tomorrow for I will delay no longer! Hannibal must be stopped and by the Gods, I will stop him if no one else will! He's not some demi-God! He's not invincible! What are you all afraid of? If he's so able, so confident himself, why then has he not attacked us?"

There was a pregnant silence as men looked at their Consul or down at the table. Cornelius, reluctant as he was, found his voice.

"With respect sir, it's because it doesn't suit him." Came out in rush.

The men turned towards Cornelius.

"Centurion, I remind you, you are suffered here only out of respect to your father!" A Tribune said curtly.

"Is he Tribune? Is he?" Flaminius snapped. "He's fought Hannibal this twice and been recommended for a Corona Civica, so rank aside I think that entitles him a voice. I might ask what it is you have committed to this war, so far."

The Tribune looked abashed and lowered his head; Cornelius cringed inwardly not wanting to add more diversity to the current argument.

"You were going to say, Centurion?" Flaminius asked flatly.

Cornelius cleared his throat, seeking to bolster his resolve.

"Consul, Gentlemen, I can only speak from experience. Hannibal is no fool; we will be the fools if we judge him so." Flaminius quickly shouted down the grumbles of outrage. "He may appear rash by placing himself between ourselves and Consul Geminus, a dangerous move you may think? But I think he has reason for it."

"Then educate us Centurion, we're all ears." The Prefect sneered, causing some amusement amongst the group.

"I said that's enough!" Flaminius growled. "I've heard your bleating arguments for days so let him speak. The last time I looked, we were all freeborn men! ... Go on, Centurion."

"I believe ..." Cornelius cleared his throat again. "I believe; he would have liked us to combine our forces and attack him on the plain where he has room to manoeuvre and strength in cavalry to maximise on it."

"But that's perfect ground for our legions Centurion, you do know that?" The Legate quipped, a light note of sarcasm still evident.

"Yes sir. And I agree, the plain suits our legions also, but we cannot move at the speed of his cavalry and our own have proved ineffective against his so far."

The grumbles and complaints grew louder and more incensed; again, Flaminius quietened them by banging on the table.

"This is a council of war, now let him be heard! ... Centurion ..."

Cornelius swallowed nervously. "As you know, we haven't taken his bait but by delaying and procrastinating, by doing nothing, we've only fed the myth of his superiority and invincibility."

The grumbles, angry and in some cases enraged uproar began again. After barking for order and quiet and then hammering the table until he had complete silence, Flaminius himself fronted the questions, his tone terse.

"Well Centurion, you've told us what we are not doing, or doing wrong. What would you advise?"

Cornelius glanced around the room at the sea of angry faces. Colouring under the stares, he swallowed hard and then as if resigned to his fate committed.

"I would start by harassing him sir, immediately! Attack his foraging parties, his water details, and his patrols, anywhere and anyway I could. Small but decisive actions are all we need. Prod him! Sting him! Make him bleed! Hit and run if need be! However, we must remove this sense of ease he and his men have enjoyed for too long. Show our people we are still potent ..."

"Hit and run, boy! Are we bandits now that we must ambush and murder and then run?" The Legate chided.

"Yes sir, exactly that! Because that is the last thing, Hannibal will expect. He's waiting for the usual all out legion strength, the heavy frontal assault in our usual style."

"That style has served us well enough in the past; it beat them in the last war and carved us an empire here in Italy!"

"I don't deny it sir. Nevertheless, we need to change the way we are doing things, at least for the present. We're predictable to the point that he knows what we'll do and how, before we do it ... put the boot on the other foot for a moment and ask yourself, do we know what he's going to do? For certain!"

The rising babble and ranting in the room stopped suddenly as men paused to consider, the silence that followed only proving the point.

Flaminius cupped his chin, looking thoughtful.

"And after these raids and skirmishes, what then?"

"While we occupy him with that sir, we counter-march, around and past him!" Cornelius's enthusiasm grew with the telling and he stepped up to the map again, his finger tracing his words. "Swing wide to the west coast and the Via Aurelia ..."

"Why so far to the west, Centurion?"

"To get safely past him sir, we can afford the time I think. His columns, encumbered with the slaves, beasts and baggage will be slow moving even on the plain. As you know, we can comfortably march twenty-five miles a day on the road. Just three days' sir and we can be in front of him on the edge of the plain, five days would place us outside Rome if ...."

"Yes Centurion, I can count!" Flaminius snapped as his irritation peaked.

"Yes sir, beg your pardon sir. However, if Consul Geminus were to approach down the Via Flaminia we can join with him and bring Hannibal to battle where the plain narrows, else block the road to Rome."

"Humph! If Geminus moves from the east? If he will meet us at the edge of the plain? If he will meet us outside Rome, and I say if! And if we turn tail and run! That's a lot of 'if's' Centurion and I don't like the turn tail and run idea."

"Not turn tail sir, box clever! Play Hannibal at his own game!"

"Why not try and trap him between us?"

"Because sir ... because, Hannibal will never allow it to happen, he is ..."

The uproar drowned Cornelius's words; this time Flaminius hammered his dagger hilt on the table to gain silence.

"So how do we fight Hannibal then? No regular tactics, no pincer movement, no wide-open plain? Pray tell me Cornelius, for I profess to being confused."

"We counter-march sir and join up with Consul Geminus. Be it on the edge of the plain or in front of Rome. From there and perhaps most importantly, we select the ground for battle, where we can see Hannibal clearly, no chance of another ambush, no great space for his cavalry. We funnel him towards us and then use our weight and power against him, and then we destroy him."

There was silence as the group digested the plan, even some nodding heads and thoughtful looks.

The Legate cleared his throat. "I think the Centurion has some measure of it Consul, it seems sound advice given that ..."

"Given that what?"

"That we should join with Consul Geminus, sir."

"And you also hold with this idea of a counter-march and then bringing him to battle?"

"Yes sir, I think the Centurion, despite his advocacy of Hannibal's genius has some credence in what he says. Though I disagree with marching as far as Rome and squandering men in raids and skirmishes, we are Romans not barbarian tribesmen, we fight in the open!"

"But Legate, sir, it's ..."

"You've had your say Centurion, now let him speak." Flaminius said, though not unkindly. "Legate?"

"I think we should bring Hannibal to battle before he leaves the plain and before he's too close to Rome, if I may?"

The Legate gestured towards the map table; Flaminius nodding his assent. The group closed around the table once more. The Legate pointed to the map and the area around Lake Trasimene, for the first time during the meeting, his voice had an excitement about it and a sense of purpose.

"We know Consul Geminus is somewhere south of Ariminum. If he's close enough to Perusia he could march towards and around the south side of Lake Trasimene and block the road to Rome as the Centurion suggests or he could follow the road along the northern edge of the lake towards us." His finger traced his words on the parchment. "If we can join with him, we could fight Hannibal at the base of the hills there?"

With interest kindled, the men pored over the map, studying the options.

"If we have our back to the hills that limits him for his Punic tricks and ambushes and see, the plain narrows there, restricting his manoeuvres."

The Prefect committed. "I think it would favour us if Geminus came along the south side of the lake, if we join him there we have our backs firmly to Rome, the men will fight all the harder then, I'm sure?"

Flaminius raised his hands for silence.

"I've heard you all out and my decision is thus; firstly, we need to march, the sooner the better! Secondly, I'll concede that we try again to make contact with Geminus; otherwise, we're blind to his movements. Dispatch fresh messengers now, asking Geminus to march to either the north or south of Lake Trasimene and to keep us informed of which. Meanwhile we will circumvent Hannibal as the Centurion advises. We march in the morning, issue the orders!"

"Sir, what about raiders? Skirmishers?"

"No Cornelius, thank you but no, we are Romans not savages and bandits."

****

Despite the early summer and the lengthening days, cockcrow was still some time away, darkness still shrouded the land as Malo, and Baldor collected their mounts from the horse lines. Riding across a quiet, torchlit camp they approached Hannibal's tent just as dawn became a faint, grey smear in the eastern sky. With the trumpet still unsounded, no one stirred other than sentries adding wood to the braziers or shuffling between guard posts. As the dew formed, it brought a sharp drop in temperature and like the sentries; both Baldor and Malo were heavily cloaked from the chill. Drawing rein in front of Hannibal's tent, Baldor noticed movement in the shadows and looked up to see the outline of a mounted man.

"Sir?" Baldor asked into the gloom.

The man motioned his horse forward and Baldor seeing the figure was much taller and broader than Hannibal, grabbed for his swords. Malo, a heartbeat quicker than Baldor already had his blade clear of its scabbard when the figure growled in Gallic.

"I'm Ducarius ... the General said to await him here."

Ducarius walked his mount into the torchlight and Baldor moved his hands back from the hilts. "It's all right Malo; this man is our local guide ..."

"This man, Baldor, is Ducarius, Chief of the Insubres." Hannibal interrupted as he stepped through the tent door; both men quickly saluted and made to dismount out of respect.

"Good morning, Gentlemen! Don't dismount for me; let's be on our way as we've some ground to cover. Methinks it'll be dark before we return."

"Yes sir."

"Sir."

"Allow me to acquaint you all. Ducarius! This is, Captain Baldor Targa of Carthage and Malo of Nubia ... a country to the southeast of my homeland." He added when Ducarius looked bemused. "Baldor, can you explain?" As Baldor relayed the information, Hannibal continued. "Shall we?"

He walked the few paces to where his own mount was tethered and threw his riding blanket over it, fastening the girth strap before swinging easily onto its back. Dressed no better than his men, he lifted his scarf to cover his mouth and nose then adjusted his weapons before motioning his horse and the men southward. "Lead on Ducarius, south as discussed."

The sky was still a pale pink-blue wash hidden behind the eastern hills as they reached the camp's perimeter with the plain ahead still in semi-darkness. The air was cold and clear, the grass smelled fresh and damp and as the birds sensed the new day the dawn chorus began. As usual, the blackbirds led and though their singing and whistling was sporadic at first, before long each song was answered until a cacophony ensued with thrushes, larks and warblers all contributing.

As the sun pushed above the distant hilltops and spilled a pale orange glow, the blue haze faded to clear light showing patchy white mist that boiled and steamed from the small ponds and watercourses that dotted the sward. With the light brightening quickly, Hannibal waved them from a trot to a canter and as the horses stretched into the pace, the men settled themselves for the long ride.

It was midmorning before Hannibal signalled a halt then pointed towards a small copse where they could rest up with some cover. They walked the horses, allowing the animals' time to ease their muscles and regulate their breathing before the men hobbled them. Stretching and rubbing stiffness from their own limbs, they sought wineskins and a bite to eat. Hannibal spoke quietly to Baldor.

"Your leg, it's good?"

"Yes sir, a little stiff but no problems."

"Nothing a sultry redhead couldn't massage out then?" He clasped Baldor on the shoulder and laughed softly; he laughed again when Baldor gave a rare smile and replied.

"I guess not, sir!"

Malo glanced about warily, motioning the others to silence and to remain still then quietly disappeared, slipping deeper into the bushes. They waited in silence, hands hovering near sword hilts, listening. A pheasant squawked somewhere in the distance and a peacock seemed to wail an answer, other than that it was silent. Malo returned moments later, appearing noiselessly out of the scrub.

"Don't go through that way sir, there's a small pond full of ducks and waterfowl. They're quiet at present but if they lift, anybody within a dozen stades' will know we're about."

Nodding ascent, Hannibal gestured them all to sit. Gulping some wine, he fished a folded parchment from his purse, straightening the creases he laid it in front of them

"Ducarius, over to you." He said in hushed tones while gesturing to the map.

The Gaul took a moment to familiarise himself with the sketch then rang a heavily ringed finger over it. Looking between Hannibal and Baldor, he explained.

"By midday we should be on the edge of the plain. To the east is the road towards the lake and Perusia, to the southwest is the road to Rome."

After Baldor translated, Hannibal pointed to the map.

"Baldor, you and Ducarius ride east and scout the road leading to the lake, Malo and I will continue southwest in the direction of Rome. I surmise Geminus will try to cut us off if we march that way and with

Flaminius to our rear; I need to be sure we can't be trapped and pinned by terrain. Ducarius, how long to reach the lake and return here?"

Baldor translated and the Gaul glanced at the sun while stroking the thick plait in his beard then sighed deeply.

"With hard riding, we could be back here by dusk."

"Very well, meet us back here by dark tonight, we'll camp here. Malo, any objections or thoughts on the campsite?"

"Only that we keep back from the water sir, other than that it's good, we can remain in cover and see anyone coming from any direction."

Hannibal gathered up the map and taking a final sip of wine rose and made to mount, pausing only to hold his fist to his heart and dip his head towards Baldor and Ducarius.

"The Lord Baal keep you both."

"And you sir." Replied Baldor as both men dipped their heads in respect. "Malo! Amun's blessings keep you!"

The Nubian flashed a smile of bright white teeth then threw himself over his already departing horse.

Baldor and Ducarius were already at the campsite when Hannibal and Malo rode in at dusk, Malo having looped them around to avoid the waterfowl. Baldor jumped up to take the bridle of Hannibal's horse as he dismounted.

"We were beginning to worry sir; you've been gone a long time?"

"Aye, we went further than I anticipated but it was worth it. I know now that we don't want to venture that way. As the plain ends the ground rises steeply to hills before turning into a narrow river valley, we rode as far as we could down it until we saw the road leading back into the hills again. Not a place we want to be with two consular armies chasing us, if we were bottled up in there ...." Leaving the rest unsaid, he dismounted and stretched his back then clasping Baldor's shoulder asked. "Tell me you have better news?"

"I'm not so sure sir. The road leaves the plain towards the east and passes through some low hills down to the lake. It skirts the water's edge with heavily wooded hills rising away from it to the north and west and then continues on, rising back into the hills again at the eastern side of the lake. Its beautiful country though, blue water and lush forest, but no flat area for manoeuvre."

"Beautiful, eh? I think you're becoming a romantic, Baldor!" Hannibal winked and laughed, slapping Baldor's back roughly.

Baldor smiled at the sarcasm and continued speaking his thoughts aloud. "It could be a fine place to live sir, there's fresh water from the streams and Ducarius says there's good hunting in the forest and plenty of fish in the lake."

"All it needs is a beautiful redhead to come home to, eh?"

Malo sniggered and tried to hide his laughter as Baldor coloured, which only made Hannibal worse, laughing at Baldor's discomfort he said.

"We'll go visit this beautiful country in the morning then, for I'm keen to take a look for myself, if we leave here before first light we could be back to camp before dark."

The men shared a cold supper of dried beef, olives and flat bread washed down with wine, after which, Ducarius and Malo bedded down leaving Hannibal and Baldor to converse quietly over the map. The pair hunkered down, enjoying the last of the day's light and warmth.

"From memory Baldor, if we follow your road after it leaves the lake, we have more hills to pass through before we reach the east coast. Geminus is over there somewhere and we still have Flaminius in our rear." Hannibal looked thoughtful. "Hmm, time for a change of tactics methinks. As you know, I wished to fight both Consuls together on the plain here but seeing as that doesn't look likely we'll destroy them singly. For if we have to move through hills and valleys, I only want one enemy to contend with at once, what think you?"

"Agreed sir, I'd be happier with one Consul gone and if that's to be the case, why don't we just go south, I know you don't like the terrain but it seems eastwards is no better?"

"Maybe, however it keeps us away from Rome."

Baldor looked surprised. "Why, keep us away sir?"

"A few reasons Baldor, firstly; we need to destroy the Roman field armies before approaching Rome, without the legions the senate's resolve will be weaker and they will have to listen to my demands. Secondly, as we have no siege equipment it would be starvation rather than assault that takes Rome, so no legions coming at our back makes for an easier life. Lastly, and as you know, despite their bluster and foolishness these Romans are hard fighters, I can only imagine their resolve would stiffen further if we face them with Rome at their backs."

Baldor absorbed the lesson and nodded. "And eastwards sir, what lies that way, apart from Geminus?"

"Apulia! … Apulia, I'm told is rich, fertile country. If we attack that, they will come seeking us, I'm sure."

"But this Etruria plain was the same and yet they haven't come for us, despite our depravations."

Hannibal looked thoughtful and chewed his lip.

"True. Perhaps time Baldor, just a little more time. If we continue to goad and humiliate, the Romans will succumb to their Latin pride and fight us." Hannibal smiled and swilled wine from the skin before passing it to Baldor. "Time for sleep my friend? We are on the way again before first light."

The cold woke Baldor before anyone else stirred. With the warm evening, he'd laid on top of his blankets and being exhausted had slipped into a deep sleep, now he was damp with dew and stiff with the cold. It was still dark and dawn some time off, but in a bid to warm up and ease his aching limbs he began preparing the horses for the morning ride. Before too long the others joined him and after another cold breakfast, consumed as they worked, they were on their way before dawn broke. Ducarius took the lead, guiding them eastwards across the plain towards the still, night blackened hills and the dawn breaking behind them. The sun was rising fast as they galloped towards it, the light changing through a spectrum of a grey-blue to burnt pink-red and then to pale orange. The brightness intensified as the sun climbed higher peaking the hilltops, the men having to shade their eyes as it lit the plain.

"How much further Baldor?" Hannibal asked above the noise of the pounding hooves.

"By the time the sun is clear of these hills, sir, we'll be almost through them and the lake is just the other side. There, look!" He pointed to the sky through the hills. "That white cloud is mist rising from the water beneath."

As the horses reached the base of the hills, the sun was hidden again and the shadows fell once more. Following the winding dirt road through them, they rode into a murky grey-light and a giant white cloud of mist hovering just above the lake and road, and hiding the tops of the trees.

"Hold!" Hannibal called, raising his hand for all to stop.

The party drew rein and stared into the whiteness. The mist boiled and swirled over the water's surface like steam from a cooking pot, before drifting across the road in thick, white patches. With the sun's heat warming it; the haze drifted and wafted on the thermals enveloping the trees and forming a vapour roof in and above them. The contour of the hillside appeared occasionally through gaps in the haze though the ridgeline remained hidden from view. Hannibal motioned them forward again walking their horses along the waterside through the mist. The visibility and temperature dropped again and water droplets began to form on both men and horses.

"Baldor, ask Ducarius if it's always like this? Every morning? Does he know?"

After a lengthy exchange, Baldor turned back to Hannibal.

"At this time of year, sir it's very common, he says. The mist tends to drift as you see it now, drawn off the lake towards the forest and on up the hill. It will be like this until the sun is higher and the heat burns it off. By mid-morning it'll all be gone."

Hannibal nodded very slowly. Deep in thought, he looked this way and that, watching intently as the white vapour tumbled through and over the treetops, one moment exposing them, then just as quickly closing and obscuring them from view. He motioned the party off the road into the forest. In the trees, the air was chillingly cold and the light dimmed to a dark, grey murk owing to the thick canopy and the tendrils of mist drifting through the branches. Moisture dripped like light rain from leaves and limbs. The ground sloped, steeply in places, though the footing remained good but thickly carpeted with the previous autumn's leaves and old pine needles. Keeping adjacent to the road, the men walked the horses for some distance, the smell of damp foliage, leaf mould, timber and tangy pinesap accompanying them. Hannibal signalled them back out onto the roadway.

"Baldor, show me the road where it enters the hills again."

"Yes sir. Ducarius!"

Just before mid-morning, the group, having followed the road as it skirted the lake, reached the gap in the hills leading away from the water. Following the rising road, they rode out of the mist into a clear morning and the warming sun, Hannibal turned his mount to look back over the lake. The mist cloud still lay blanket-like over the lake but at its edges, near the road, it seemed to stir and flow like water, across the road into the trees, then picking up speed seemed to wash up the hillside to vaporize across the hillcrest.

Shortly, the vapour began to thin and develop holes, exposing views of the water and trees, the sunlight shining into the holes making them larger. As the sun warmed the watching men's backs, the mist began to disappear. The view was beautiful; the water reflecting the azure blue of the morning sky, its surface, undisturbed by wind was mirror-like with only the odd ripple from a rising fish to mar it. The forest was green and lush with bright new leaves and spring growth, the trees a mixture of pines, firs and giant broadleaves; they grew close together as if competing for space on the hillside.

"Romantic or not Baldor my friend, you were right, it is truly beautiful."

The men remained at their viewpoint for some time enjoying the heat and the view; no one spoke, words being unnecessary for such a rare moment of beauty and peace.

Hannibal gave orders to break camp the following day. The huge, slow column heading southeast across the plain towards the hills and Lake Trasimene. With a strong vanguard and rearguard in place and the main army, baggage and camp followers safely in the centre, he gave orders to destroy everything and anything they couldn't carry and that may be of use to the enemy.

"Well, we'll see what the Romans do now I suppose?" Armaco said as he reined alongside Baldor, while looking back at the columns of smoke rising steadily into the sky. "We're raising enough hell back there to …"

"I know and I pity the people, this isn't war."

"But necessary all the same Baldor, it's …"

"A means to an end? We've had this conversation Armaco and Baal knows I'm only pleased to be spared the job."

Armaco remembered the terse diatribe at the farmhouse and fell silent. Feeling awkward, he looked back at the warriors riding behind and then in his usual brash style came back at Baldor.

"We'll have to agree to disagree then? For I hate the Roman bastards! And to me they are reaping what they have always sown, misery and death!"

"I've no love for them either and hate them every much as you do, believe me. They're not all Romans though, Armaco, these are farming folk not …"

"Captain Targa, Captain!" A messenger called as he cantered up the side of the column. "The General requests your presence sir."

Chapter Eight

Dawn was still a grey smudge in the east when the cornu blared across Arretium. The brassy notes echoed back from others across the city and within moments, the place stirred into life. Like worker bees exiting a hive, legionaries spilled from barrack blocks, houses, temple yards and tents; all shelters being necessary to house the huge overspill of men encamped within the walls. They busied themselves helping one another into their armour and collecting gear then forming into their centuries that quickly and efficiently made ready to join the marching column. Cavalrymen led their horses out into the light, the horses whickering and skittish from the buzz of excitement and tension emanating from the men. Above it all, Centurions barked and shouted while Optios pushed and coerced tardy and tired men into tight formation. Before the sun was above the city walls, Flaminius, his colour party and command group led an ordered column through the main gates southwest towards the coast and the Via Aurelia.

Outriders had disappeared before first light, scouting well ahead. Cavalry screens at turma strength followed but riding only two miles distant from either side of the column, the remaining cavalry followed behind Flaminius and his command group. Velites were also deployed in loose order on either side of the column but only half a mile distant from it, again to act as screens and missile troops giving added protection to the marching men. Flaminius it seemed was taking no chances. The infantry marched behind the cavalry vanguard and Flaminius's command group, the legionaries arrayed in order of battle, Hastati, Principes and Triari.

Once clear of the city, each century's vexilla was unfurled and as the men settled into the day's slog, bawdy marching songs started up. With the men in good spirits the Centurions encouraged the singing and the march continued at a good pace and without incident until midmorning when dark smoke clouds were seen rising in the southeast.

The smoke was spreading over a huge distance. As far as the eye could see, hundreds of grey and black pillars of it rose towards a cloudless sky. With not a breath of wind on the plain, they gained height before a high-altitude breeze caught them, coalescing all into a giant cloud that hid the sun and covered the land like a corpse's shroud.

A mounted scout appeared from under it, him and his mount racing across the plain at full gallop a grey dust trail rising in their wake. Whipping the horse for extra speed, he made for the front of the column and Flaminius. The horse was wet with sweat and lathered white with spume, its hind hooves slipped and slid on the grass as the rider pulled it to a vicious, abrupt stop.

"Sir, sir! Hannibal has fired the plain! He's destroyed his camp and marched southeast!" His mount wheeled about and whickered, tossing its head and causing the scout to lurch in his seat. "He's driving our folk before him, sir else slaughtering them if they resist!"

The man was wounded, his tunic bloodied and hacked away at the shoulder revealing a deep gash and a steady flow of blood that coloured his arm scarlet to the wrist and spotted his leg and the horse's flank.

Flaminius listened and quietly fumed, his face displaying the anger and hate seething within him.

"He's burning everything in his path, sir! The buildings, grass even the trees and bushes are ablaze! The un-ripened crops are being trampled as they march and any animal they can't catch or use they slaughter! He's destroying everything!"

The man slumped a little, his balance awry as blood loss and the fast ride began to take its toll. His eyes rolled and flickered; Flaminius shot out a steadying hand to support him.

"You were almost caught?"

"Yes … yes sir, we were ambushed by Numidian cavalry, they appeared out of nowhere, I'm the only survivor of my patrol."

Flaminius nodded slowly. "Anything else, trooper?"

"Hannibal's covering his advance with large rearguards of cavalry sir, both light and heavy, they're formidable sir."

This time Flaminius's face twisted into a snarl and he growled. "Maybe trooper! We'll see." He turned to his officers and snapped his commands. "Get this man to the surgeon! Bring the column about southeast."

A chorus of objections sprang up from the command group.

"Enough! Damn your eyes, I've heard enough!" Flaminius balled. "We're being humbled and despised by these savages. We'll chase this barbarian down now! Do you hear me?"

Reticent and disjointed, low voiced 'yes sirs' came back as Flaminius glared at his commanders as if daring further retorts.

"Now! We should catch him before he turns east at the hills towards Lake Trasimene, I want him brought to battle before he's off the plain."

The orders relayed down the column and like a giant bronze scaled, serpent it slowly flexed, curving and swinging eastwards. Men eyed one another and looked at the smoke rising directly ahead of them now, it was obvious to all what was happening, a fight was coming and sooner rather than later. The singing ceased and the mood changed to that of caution and apprehension, chatter amongst the men barked to silence as the Centurions and Optios enforced discipline.

As the morning wore on a light breeze sprang up, almost unnoticeable at first but strong enough to push the smoke back towards the advancing legions. Forming an iron-grey roof over their heads and blotting out the sun it hid the blue sky, the day suddenly transformed from early summer to what seemed like autumn fog. Billowing and rolling in banks and heavy with ash and debris, the smoke descended upon them stinging eyes and burning throats. Men pulled scarfs over mouths and noses to prevent smoke entering their lungs and to evade the sickly, sweet stink it brought with it, the stench of burning bodies.

The mood of the men changed again to that of anger as the column passed the first of the devastation; buildings afire, animals slaughtered in the field or deposited in streams and waterways, and bodies of folk dead where they lay. The column had to slow its pace as the visibility reduced further and while the cavalry and Velite screens were called in closer so to maintain contact. Despite the lack of sunlight, the temperature in the smoke was oppressively hot, almost furnace like, the men sweating heavily beneath their armour and scarves so it was a welcome relief in the afternoon when the breeze strengthened and the smoke dissipated into patches and clouds.

As early evening arrived the smoke had all but gone. Driven away on a strange, unseasonable wind that now howled and blew like a winter gale across the plain, whipping up voluminous dust clouds and dust devils. The column marched on; the pace adjusted up or down as visibility allowed; horses mules and men lowering their heads to their chests against the blow. The men's low-voiced curses ceased as they were choked and blinded by dust and stung with grit that caked on sweat-damp skin or found its way beneath armour and clothing. The heat though did not lessen, remaining oven-like even when the sun dropped in the western sky. As men sought water and rest from what had been a harrowing day's march, in front of them was no sign of the Carthaginian army.

Gaius found Cornelius taking a report from his Optio regarding the men's status.

"They're tired and footsore sir but only two injuries to note; a twisted ankle and a knee. Once strapped though, neither will keep the pair out of action. Morale is good, after what the lads have seen today, they're spoiling for a fight; for payback."

Cornelius nodded, looked thoughtful but made no comment other than to thank the Optio, his sombre visage only lightening when he saw Gaius.

"Gaius! How was the march?" He smiled at the sight of his friend though he couldn't hide his trepidation at the day's events.

"I'm good Cornelius, you know me? This was just a stroll for us old hands." The pair clasped and Gaius produced a wine skin from his other hand. "Shall we? It's a little harsh but it'll settle the dust and wash the smoke out of your throat. I'm keeping the Falernian till we've seen these Carthaginian savages off."

Cornelius's smile faded and Gaius punched him playfully. "What's the matter? All that soft living in Rome left you with taste only for the good stuff?"

Cornelius cast a glance around him then dropped his voice to a tight-lipped whisper.

"That Falernian may have to keep for a while Gaius."

"What?" Gaius frowned darkly as he shoved a small but full cup at Cornelius. Cornelius threw the liquid down his throat in one and dragged his hand over his mouth.

"Surely you can see what's happening?"

Before Gaius could lower his own cup and reply, Cornelius continued.

"We're being led by the nose, again! This was not what we planned, what we agreed?"

"Whoa lad! We planned and agreed nothing; we do as we are told." Gaius countered.

"But I explained! Flaminius listened, agreed, the plan was to …"

"Plans change; you know that?"

"Yes, but it's not us changing them, it's Hannibal."

"Well, we're countering his move is all?" Gaius refilled the cups as he talked.

"Are we? Do you honestly think so? All I see is; having previously forced us to about turn he's now forcing us to change direction."

"I grant you he turned us but I think he's in trouble now …"

"How so?"

"Well, he's heading east and therefore towards Geminus, we could catch him between us."

Cornelius gave a bitter laugh. "It'll never happen!" His voice rising as he shook his head. "He's leading us like lambs to the slaughter; he'll trap us and cut us to pieces, mark …"

"Hush man!" Gaius pulled Cornelius to the side and out of any earshot. "Gods' above lad!" He hissed. "Keep your voice down; they'll crucify you if they hear that!"

Cornelius shrugged. "Either way then? Crucifixion or Hannibal, the end's the same."

"Come on Cornelius, this is not like you! We're not beaten; Jupiter knows it hasn't started yet!"

"I'd welcome the chance to fight, Gaius but not on Hannibal's terms because as long as he dictates the time and ground, he'll beat us every time."

"Steady on lad, he's not that good; he's a lucky General is all."

"No! He is that good; he's been changing the rules and turning conventional warfare on its head since he took over the Carthaginian army in Spain."

"Yes, yes! I've heard all that too." Gaius sighed, removing his helmet and running his hand over his head then wiping the sweat from his eyes. "It will be all right you know, this time things …"

"Will be different? By Jupiter! I wish I shared your optimism. But I tell you this, I sense another set up!"

"Another set up?"

"Yes, he's prodded and poked and pushed, just as he did with Sempronius before the Trebbia and now we've taken the bait." Cornelius shook his head gently and looked away, his eyes fixed trancelike. When he spoke, it was as if talking to himself. "Gods above! It's as if he knew we were ready to move. I need to talk to Flaminius, make him listen."

"What? Hold up there!" Gaius placed a hand on Cornelius's shoulder. "Steady on lad, we're Centurions, not Tribunes! It's not for the likes of us to advise on strategy."

Cornelius downed his drink again and handed the cup to Gaius, his eyes still staring, vacant, his mind elsewhere. Turning on his heel, he headed away.

"Cornelius! ... Cornelius, for the love of Venus, man, think about this! You can't just march in there demanding to see the Consul."

Cornelius stopped suddenly and turned back; this time he clasped Gaius on the shoulder.

"I'll find you tomorrow."

****

The Carthaginians camped on the edge of the plain, their eastern flank nestled safely against the hills, the road to the lake just in front of them. Strong skirmish parties were deployed to the army's rear, just in case Flaminius pushed on after dark in a bid to catch and surprise the Carthaginians in camp. Scouts disappeared eastwards, riding hard towards the lake and far beyond, with instructions to report immediately, any sightings of Geminus and his legions marching westwards. Content with his preparations, Hannibal called his commanders to a council of war.

"Gentlemen, I bid you good evening and ask Baal's blessings upon you all. Come sit." He beamed at his men, his manner jovial and relaxed. "Come, come, I'm hungry, you must be! Let's eat."

As usual, Mago sought Baldor out and steered him to the table and seats together, the big man, like his brother, at ease and happy. Baldor caught sight of Sakarbaal and Bodeshmun as they filed into the tent, the quick but cold-eyed stare from Bodeshmun reminding him that though the altercation may be closed officially, hatred and payback remained unsettled issues. With all seated and food and wine before them, Hannibal called a blessing from the Gods for both the repast and men, then with wine in hand drew their attention to a map board secured to a trestle. With an atmosphere that was more feast than council of war, men relaxed as they watched and listened to their young commander demonstrating and explaining his plan as he ate, he laughing and encouraging them as if describing a coming game. Despite his upbeat manner, he constantly rubbed his right eye and occasionally shook his head as if trying to clear his vision, questions on his affliction were waved away, 'dust and tiredness was all', he said.

"We move before first light tomorrow. I want us through the hills here." His finger followed the road on the map. "And past the lake into the Cortonian hills before dark tomorrow, we'll make camp there tomorrow night." He circled the area in charcoal. "We must move quickly! I don't want Flaminius catching up with us until the following day. The scouts tell me the smoke has slowed his march and though he's pushing his men hard they shouldn't be able to catch us till then, Baal Almighty, willing."

"Do you think he'll assault us in the hills, sir? From what you say he's more intelligent than Longus?"

The light laughter in the room cut off as Hannibal became very serious.

"We're not going to give him that option, Sergatatonix; we'll destroy him by the lakeside while he's marching."

A hush fell over the room, men stopped eating and drinking their eyes fixed on Hannibal.

"Tomorrow we'll follow the lakeside road and camp in the eastern hills as I've said. The camp however will contain only servants, slaves, some guards and a token force, a regiment or two of crack infantry. However, we'll light many fires to look as though we are all in camp, should any Roman scouts come looking."

"And the rest of us brother? ... Pray tell?" Mago quipped.

Hannibal paused to drink his wine and rub again at his eye. "The rest of us will be in the forest waiting." Seeing questions forming he held up his hands for quiet. "See here? The road follows the lakeside along its western and northern edges; the forest skirts the road all the way along it and back up to the hillcrest behind."

Mago chuckled. "Ha! You're going to hide an ambush party in there, like we did at the Trebbia?"

"No brother, I'm going to hide a whole army in there! All of us, cavalry and infantry."

There were sharp intakes of breath and looks of disbelief. The atmosphere in the room suddenly charged, palpable with excitement, wonder and tension. Again, men sought to question or comment and again Hannibal raised his hands.

"Bear with me Gentlemen, all your questions and comments I will hear as always but please hear me out, then you're welcome to your say!" He paused as if waiting for the silence to affect and sipped at his wine, his eyes scanning the men's faces. "Right! As discussed, I want the camp set up on the eastern hills before dusk tomorrow. The army will march to the camp then past it, backtracking but out of sight, on the blind side of the hill from the lake, back into the forest. We'll lie up in the forest overnight" He smiled and looked at Mago. "All of us this time brother and I promise you, it won't be as cold as the last time you laid in wait in the moonlight!"

"I thank the Gods for that mercy then brother. After that last time, at the Trebbia River there, they had to sew my balls back on!"

The men laughed as Mago continued his diatribe on the perils of frozen anatomy until Hannibal tapped his goblet and called for order.

"The forest is thick enough to hide us from sight and where it isn't, I'm counting on the morning mist rising off the lake for extra cover."

"Mist sir?"

"Aye, I've seen it and been told that the lake exudes thick mist every morning at this time of year."

"Won't it hide the legions then, sir? And what risk do we run of a battle in the mist?"

"Very little risk for us, General Gisgo! For a start, I have you and these other fine men here at my back! Flaminius may not want to place a wager on the outcome though!"

The men laughed and cheered and banged their goblets on the table, Hannibal smiled and quietened them again.

"As I said; very little risk. The legions will be in column on the road with the lake on their immediate right and the forest and us on their left, all we need do is charge out of the trees and hit them in the flank, there's no difficult manoeuvres to make this time!"

The men were silent for a moment as they pondered what they'd heard.

"Baal Almighty! They're penned in, sir? On a narrow road between us and the lake?" Maharbal grunted.

"Yes." Hannibal said with a slight smile on his lips.

Men eyed each other and the conversation began in earnest, excitement and tension filling the air in equal mix. Hannibal continued.

"Yes, penned in General! Only silence and timing are the key factors to our success here." The men began to interrupt and again Hannibal gestured for silence. "The timing is relatively easy, we wait till the legions are through the hills and arrayed along the road, in fact, almost at our camp before we close the door at their rear. Trumpets and noise of the contact can then release the rest of us out of the trees to attack the column. Alternatively, if they are strung out on the march and the front of the column reaches our camp first, then the token infantry force can hold them until we see the end of the column and close the trap, either way it works. With little room to move, a token force is all we need to hold them in front of the camp."

Hannibal's tone changed slightly becoming more serious, his smiles replaced by a more solemn look.

"Silence however!" He held his finger over his lips. "Silence, is the critical element and therefore the worry factor to the plan! If they see or hear us before they're all arrayed along the road, the trap will not be complete. Our men have to watch and listen while remaining hidden as their enemy marches past, their enemy in some cases, less than a stone's throw away and completely unaware. They must ... must!" He rapped the table to emphasise his point. "Curb their battle fury! It will not be easy but it's imperative to the trap's success. Therefore, urge ... no, enforce upon your men! No noise or movement until battle is dictated by either the front or rear of the column. Am I clear on this?"

The men, deep in thought, nodded acknowledgement. Hannibal, sensing their need for questions finally opened the floor.

"A whole army sir! And silence! Is that possible?"

"Yes, General Gisgo. With discipline and care, we can make great slaughter! The Romans will have no room to form battle lines and even less time!" Hannibal's eyes lightened again and the corners of his mouth teased into a grin. "We'll hit them like a hammer upon an anvil and can be in amongst them before they know what's happening; I surmise the weight of us coming forward may even be enough to drive them off the road into the lake!"

"Cavalry sir? You said cavalry as well as infantry?"

"Yes, we'll use cavalry to close the trap, horses and men make for a more effective barrier than men alone. I also want a smallish, flying troop of cavalry that I can direct, as I require, to attack certain positions in the column such as rallying or strong points or anywhere that we see order trying to come out of chaos. Also, a reserve unit of two thousand infantry for the same purpose. We'll place more cavalry in our centre, again to use their weight and impetus to cut the column in half, the rest of the army will be an alternate mix of heavy and light infantry units. I do this so we hit their column at different strengths all along it; this has to cause buckling inward or swelling outward, as heavy troops contact light and vice versa. We may struggle in places if our light troops contact their armoured veterans but surprise is a potent weapon and don't forget speed. However, and here's the rub! Both actions are in our favour as they'll cause fragmentation and openings. Then ... then we'll be lions loose amongst sheep, not wolves, methinks!"

Hannibal rubbed his eye and nibbled some chicken while the group conversed amongst themselves, questions forming. There were calls for cup refills as the heat remained oppressive and the men looked to slake their thirst while mopping sweat soaked brows.

Twilight faded into darkness before all questions were answered and theories and scenarios discussed but eventually with all concerns abated and the men settling, Hannibal closed the council.

"So, we must be about our business early tomorrow gentlemen, have your people on the move at first light. Remember, we sleep with the animals in the forest tomorrow night, so I'm for my bed now while I have it. I'll bid you all goodnight and Baal's blessings upon you."

As the group filed out of the tent, Baldor held back, happy to let Sakarbaal and Bodeshmun get away. Seeing Hannibal was alone and gathering up his maps and scrolls, he made his way over.

"Sir, may I ask? Are you well? Your eye, does it ail you?"

Hannibal looked up and around the tent and seeing no one, beckoned Baldor closer.

"Thank you for your concern Baldor, I'm fine though my eye is paining me."

Up close, Baldor saw Hannibal's eyelid was thick and swollen and the bottom rim of the eye red and sore looking, yellow mucus oozed from the corner onto previous secretions, which had dried to a crust.

"Have you something in it sir? Dust or …"

"No, nothing so simple. The surgeon examined it and advises there's nothing to find, he believes it a malady or affliction from when we passed through the Arno marsh."

"It's troubled you that long sir?"

"Yes, on and off. Now it's worsened." He cast a glance around the tent again. "Between you and me Baldor, though Mago knows already, I may lose the sight from it."

"No!"

"It's no matter Baldor, an eye is just an eye and I have another!" He smiled and laughed a little. "Anyway, Philip of Macedon and Antigonus the 'one-eyed' survived well enough! Old Antigonus survived into his eighty-first year and even then, it was a javelin that slew him!" He chuckled lightly. "Baal grant I may live so long!"

"But surely they can treat it, sir?"

"They've tried salt rinses and an ointment made from the Aconitum plant but to no avail; it appears I've left it too long before seeking treatment."

Baldor's expression was grave; Hannibal threw an arm around him.

"Come on, it's only an eye!"

"How can you be so accepting sir? It's …"

"It is what it is, Baldor! Nothing can or will change it, so I must accept and get on with it. At the end of the day, I'm neither dying nor crippled and I thank Baal Almighty for that mercy. I am I think, a lucky man. Anyway, the thought of a patch or a cloth across it will only make me appear grimmer; my visage may frighten the Romans as much as my army? Hannibal the one-eyed. Yes, that has a ring to it!" He chuckled lightly.

"It won't worsen further? If the sight goes, that will be it. Your health will not fade?"

"Not according to the surgeon, the price of my neglect is the eye and that will be it."

Hannibal undid his neck cloth and rolled it loosely before tying it across his eye; he picked up his helmet, fitted it, and turned towards Baldor. "There, do I not look grim, like Philip? Is it enough to scare the Roman children or must I grow a beard as well?" He laughed and looked in the bronze mirror. "I like it! However, I've a way to go, to catch you up on scars! Do they help with attracting the ladies, Baldor?"

Baldor coloured a little then laughed. "I don't know sir, I do know I could have done without the pain of getting them, ladies or not."

Hannibal smiled. "I like to tease you Baldor and I see your sense of humour is returning, once over you would have rebuked me for it."

Baldor coloured again, cringed inwardly at the memory of his sharp reproaches, then smiled.

"Forgive me sir; I was somewhat intemperate in my youth."

"Aye, I remember." Hannibal laughed heartily and slapped Baldor on the shoulder. "Intemperate in my youth!" He repeated to himself shaking his head and smiling. "And you are now, how old?"

"Almost twenty-two summers sir." Baldor laughed at his own satire.

"It's good to see you smile and laugh my friend, for life can be precariously short in our profession, a drink?"

"Yes sir, thank you."

"Enough of the 'sir' Baldor, remember what I told you when it's just you and I?"

"Yes, Hannibal."

Hannibal smiled and gestured Baldor back to the table as he poured two cups of wine. "So, my friend, battle is almost upon us again and if my plan works there will be much slaughter. I want you and your troop with me for this fight, to be the flying troop I mentioned."

Baldor looked up from his drink, his eyes wide. "You do me much honour Hannibal; I hope I prove worthy?"

"You will and I know it! Your actions at Victumulae last spring demonstrated such and that's why I ask it. I need Mago, Maharbal and Gisgo to close the trap at either end and smash the column in the middle. I'll use you and your men as a surgeon uses his knife, to cut out the dangerous parts that I see, such as rallying points, colour parties, even Flaminius himself! Will you be my knife Baldor? Will you help me rid the world of this malady that is Rome?"

"I will and I'm honoured to be asked. I'll report to you tomorrow eve along with my men?"

"Yes, I'll save you a bed in the forest." Hannibal smiled and raised his cup in salute; he drank then lowered it, his manner growing more serious. "This will be a hard fight Baldor, for men trapped like rats are wont to fight like them! And I'll be sending you in amongst the most desperate!"

"I welcome it! My men are I think a tempered, moulded unit now. We'll cut these fiercest rats out from the column for you."

"Thank you. You'll have your two seconds, your comrades alongside?"

"Andulas and Armaco, yes!"

"Good! See that you do, for I sense that pair are guard dogs where you're concerned. Moreover, I wish to safeguard the right to take another drink with you when this fight is done. I also ask … ask for Baal Almighty to watch over you …" Hannibal held up his hands quickly, silencing the retort already forming on Baldor's lips. "I don't ask that you pray or that you pray with me! However, I do ask, that you accept the blessing for what it is, the care and thought of one man for another, for his friend?"

Baldor pressed his lips tight together as if deep in thought else holding back a hasty reply. He gave a wry smile and nodded.

"I thank you sincerely for your thought, your kindness and concern. You do me much honour as an officer but most of all as a friend. The blessing is welcome and though I remain an unbeliever, I ask your God for the same for you."

Hannibal looked as if he would venture further on the religious question then nodded and poured more wine.

"To victory, honour and safe returns Baldor!"

"And your health sir!"

Chapter Nine

Cornelius approached Flaminius's command tent at a brisk pace. His direct and purposeful stride caught the attention of the guards and prompted a defensive reaction, both sentries coming sharply to attention and crossing their pila in front of the entrance.

"Hold! State your business!"

As anxious and hot-tempered as he felt, Cornelius realised his approach was unacceptable and thus held back the sharp rebuke rising in his throat at the disrespect to his rank. Slowing his pace, he held up a hand and announced.

"Centurion Scipio to see the Consul, if he so pleases?"

One of the guards lowered his weapon and stepped through the tent doorway, the other remaining attentive but now less threatening. Cornelius busied himself removing his helmet, the action as much to mask the awkward waiting as prepare for an audience. Thankfully, the other guard reappeared quickly and with a notable change of attitude and tone, announced the Consul would see him now and that he may enter.

Composing himself, Cornelius pushed through the tent folds. A servant ushered him through to the inner tent and the Consul's private quarters. Stepping through as the servant announced him; Flaminius himself greeted and gestured him forward.

"Cornelius! Welcome, come, come!" He snapped his fingers at a nearby slave holding a tray filled with silver goblets, who stepping forward, bowed his head and offered Cornelius a drink. "Gentlemen, may I once more introduce Centurion Cornelius Scipio." Most of the men remained nonchalant or looked down their noses until Flaminius reminded them. "The son of my friend and former Consul; Publius Scipio."

With greetings and salutations suddenly more enthusiastic, Cornelius bowed his head and held his fist to his heart in salute.

"What brings you to me, Cornelius? All is well with you and your men?"

"Yes sir, err … undoubtedly yes, and thank you. Sir, I must speak with you urgently, on matters of great importance."

Flaminius gestured to the men about him then back to Cornelius. "Speak freely then Cornelius, you're amongst friends here."

Cornelius cleared his throat. "Consul, if I may, these matters are for your ears alone."

"Oh, personal issues?" Flaminius lowered his voice and turned away from the group. "I trust all is well with your family and …"

"Err … thank you Consul, yes, no, that's not … I must speak to you on matters military."

Flaminius looked confused. "Why then, speak away! As I said you're amongst friends here."

"Consul I, I fear, I cannot."

Again, Flaminius looked perplexed, glancing between Cornelius and the group of men in the tent, and then reasserted himself.

"Centurion, if it's not family or personal issues that brings you here but matters military, then these men have the right to know."

Cornelius had the momentary look of a startled rabbit. Then clearing his throat, marshalled himself, straightening his back and raising his head.

"Consul, sir. With the greatest of respect, we must cease this pursuit of Hannibal now! It's …"

"Cornelius, enough." Flaminius interjected quickly though not harshly.

"No sir, not enough! For the love of the Gods, we …"

Flaminius's face twisted into a scowl, his knuckles turning white as he gripped his wine cup.

"You forget yourself Centurion, I …"

"Sir, with the greatest respect, I do not! I beseech you; halt this column now before disaster strikes!"

Flaminius spoke above the grumblings starting up from the men as his temper gave way, his voice booming across the tent like thunder on a rising storm.

"By Jupiter! That is sedition Centurion; I could have you crucified for such! … Damn you man! Have you lost use of your wits?"

Taking a deep breath Cornelius retorted, his angst overriding decorum and sense.

"No Sir. Nevertheless, it's plain to see what's happening, surely? … Gods above! A fool can see …"

"How dare you, Centurion?" Flaminius stepped forward quickly the wine sloshing from his cup, his face colouring in anger and spittle spraying from his mouth from the incensed response. One of the men placed a cautionary hand on his shoulder, which was angrily shaken off. The hand however seemed to give Flaminius pause and he hesitated, waiting a moment, as if to compose himself and his words. "By Jupiter! You overstep the mark, Centurion! Both as an officer and as the son of my friend, whom you do no great honour! Now, you will remove yourself from my presence and take your … your cowardly mithering with you!"

Cornelius looked aghast at the accusation and seemed to wilt. Flaminius sensing capitulation pressed his advantage and continued.

"I said go now!" He pointed to the door. "Don't make me call the guards to have you removed forcibly. Go now and hold onto the only dignity you have left yourself, that of your family name. Do not! I repeat, do not! Cast further aspersions on what is a noble house."

Flaminius turned his back and walked back to the table leaving Cornelius dallying in the middle of the floor. Embarrassed and dumbstruck he saluted Flaminius's back and turned towards the tent door.

It was much later in the evening, just before lights out when Gaius found him. The stalwart Centurion shouted his greetings as he breezed into Cornelius's tent to find him at his desk, head in his hands. Cornelius jumped up as he entered trying to raise a smile and appear affable; the charade however was wasted on Gaius.

"What in Jupiter's name's wrong lad? Your father, is he well?" Receiving no response, he continued. "Amelia? … Your mother? She is …?"

Cornelius raised his hands and shook his head. "No, Gaius, no they are fine, thank you for your concerns. All is well on that front, It's me, I am it seems the master of my own misery and demise."

Gaius's face fell and he shook his head as he began to speak. "Please tell me you haven't been to see Flaminius? That you ..."

"Yes, to seeing Flaminius and yes, I have all but ruined my career and good name."

"Oh, for the love of ..."

"Please! No lectures, no more please! My head hurts ..."

Gaius pushed Cornelius back into the chair and sat down heavily in the other. "Have a drink!" Noticing the reluctance and disinterested look on Cornelius's face, he added. "That's an order not a request!" Sensing petulance from Cornelius, he continued. "I've had my rank long before you and I command the right-hand century so that makes me your senior, now drink!" He filled two cups and pushed one across the table towards Cornelius. "Now, tell me how much damage you've done."

It was dark when Cornelius finished relaying the debacle and Gaius whistled softly.

"I'm amazed you're sitting here telling me this, most Consuls would have arrested you and sentenced you to the cross! For the love of Venus man! Have you gone barking mad?"

Cornelius gazed blankly into his cup. "Maybe? The Gods above know. We'll know for certain one way or another when we march."

"Forgive me if I don't hope you're right in your assumptions."

The pair stared at one another, their expressions grim, Cornelius downcast by his actions and thoughts and Gaius suitably concerned. Gaius collected himself and sought to allay the apprehensions.

"You could be wrong you know?"

"I pray to Jupiter and Mars that I am, for then it's only me who will suffer the consequences."

"It'll be fine!" Gaius sounded assertive. "We're ready this time and Flaminius is no fool, his actions at Telamon and after have proven that, and the men, they like him, respect him."

"Agreed! I too hold the Consul in high regard, I just think he's badly advised and mistaken in this."

"Well, think on lad! He's not untried; he helped defeat the Insubres at Clastidium some five years ago! He's very able and is showing caution still, and at the end of the day we need to bring these Carthaginian savages to battle sooner rather than ..."

"Agreed! But that's not the point!" Cornelius banged his fist on the table in frustration, his voice rising with worry and anger. "Yes, we need a battle but it must be one that we can win! Jupiter knows we need a win! And the only way to do that is on our chosen ground and at our time! For the love of the Gods can no one see it! Are you all blind?"

Cornelius put his head back in his hands. Seeing that reasoning wasn't working Gaius turned his tack to force again.

"Now listen to me Centurion and listen well! There are some wise heads among Flaminius's staff and we both agree he's no fool either?" When Cornelius didn't respond, Gaius prodded him hard making him look up. "You could be wrong in your thinking!" Cornelius gurned his lip and went to interrupt but Gaius carried on, his tone bordering on aggressive. "But whatever happens in the next few days, whether you can control it or not, you can and will control yourself! You have a duty to the men under your command, they look to you for leadership and part of that is displaying confidence in them, yourself and our commanders. So, man up, Cornelius Publius Scipio! Be the Centurion and the man I know you to be! As you well know, soldiering is not all victories and parades but it is up to us, our duty, to try and make it so!"

Cornelius lifted his head as Gaius continued, his voice lowering and his tone moderating.

"Tomorrow's another day Cornelius and things usually look better in the morning, get some sleep eh? Enough chafing and worrying for now."

The following dawn, bleary eyed, footsore and aching the legionaries emptied from their tents as assembly sounded. Despite the semi-darkness and usual foot soldier grumbles, they efficiently armed themselves, dismantled tents and prepared breakfast while their officers moved amongst them chivvying and hurrying. As Cornelius formed his century, he and his Optio went amongst the men checking all had eaten and were prepared ready for the march, along with ample supplies of food and water, the hard lesson learned at the Trebbia still fresh. Before the sun cleared the horizon, the column moved off, leaving Engineers and a cohort of legionaries to destroy and fire the camp and to catch up with the column later in the morning.

****

The vanguard and the first supply wagons from the Carthaginian camp were on the move eastwards before dawn broke; the need for speed outweighing the risk of accidents and lost equipment in the gloom. The tortured creak from an ungreased wagon axle as it passed Baldor's tent dragged him from his slumber, he opened one eye and scanned the tent. The oil lamp had burned low and now sputtered erratically having not been extinguished from the night before. The exhaustion from love making with Lasairiona seeing it ignored, both lovers content to fall asleep in the other's arms, energy spent and sleep calling. The fierce heat of the evening had not abated with the coming dawn and the pair had discarded the bed sheets to the floor, body heat being more than enough to keep them comfortable. Lasairiona was still asleep, head resting on his chest, her fox-orange hair in glorious disarray and her arm laid over his waist. He caught the scent of her perfume, a sweet, fruit odour with tinges of freshness that reminded him of the forest. He sighed softly, enjoying the smell and the velvet like feel of her skin. Reluctant to move he trailed his fingers through her hair, admiring the softness and the dark orange-red of the tresses. She stirred beneath his touch, breathed deeply as if inhaling his smell then snuggled back into him, her eyes still closed.

"We have to go." He said softly.

He heard Sulis moving around in the main tent. Having packed most of their belongings the previous evening she was busy preparing breakfast, he heard the small milling stone grinding wheat to flour for the morning bread and gently shook Lasairiona again.

"Come, we have to go." He said gently. "Breakfast and then we must be on our way."

She snuggled closer and kissed his chest and throat.

"No! Tell them to go away; they can have their war without you!" She kissed him again but then slowly eased herself from the bed.

Standing naked as she sought to untangle the sheets from the pile on the floor, he quietly admired her body, her frame toned and Amazon-like, her skin strangely white compared to his olive hue. Swinging his legs over the bed, he found his tunic. Slipping it on, he headed through to seek breakfast, the night's exertions having left him hungry and thirsty but also strangely relaxed. He felt good, his body ached a little but it was a pleasant, soft ache, he smiled as he bade Sulis greetings for the day. Lasairiona appeared behind him wrapped in a sheet, seeing Sulis fully dressed and working, she disappeared reappearing moments later in her dress and pulling a comb through her hair.

The three sat for breakfast and Baldor outlined the plans.

"Take the tent down and have everything ready to go, two of my men will be here shortly with a wagon and will load it. Can any of you drive the wagon? I need the men."

Sulis shook her head. "Until now I've only ever been a ladies' slave, sir. I've no experience with horses."

"I'll do it; you sit with me." Lasairiona smiled at Sulis and Baldor nodded.

"The column will move all day, no stops; the camp will be in the eastern hills at the edge of the lake tonight." He cleared his throat. "I may not see you till tomorrow evening … I'll find you there."

Lasairiona looked up sharply, her eyes widening. "Battle is coming tomorrow?"

Baldor didn't answer immediately; looking down at his food then back at the women and managed a smile. "I'll find you tomorrow night, let's leave it at that."

He pushed some olives and warm bread into his mouth, swilled it with the hot, honeyed water and rose from the table. As the women went to rise with him, he gestured them down. He pulled on his calf length boots and slipped his mail shirt over his head then fastened the skirt of pteruges about his waist. Shrugging the heavy metal skin into place on his shoulders, he fastened his waist belt holding his dagger and purse. The twin falcatas rattled as he fastened and adjusted the straps across his chest pulling the weapons tight into his back, the hilts standing clear of his shoulders. Hearing the rumble of hooves coming close, he took his helmet from the weapons tree and moved to the door.

"Captain! Captain Targa!"

He pushed through the tent door and was met by Armaco, Andulas, and his unit. "Good morning, Gentlemen!"

"Good morning, sir."

"Morning sir." Echoed back. Both men struggling to hide their surprise at Baldor's pleasant demeanour.

Armaco tugged on the reins of the horse he was leading, moving it forward for Baldor to mount. As he swung onto its back, Lasairiona exited the tent. Some of the warriors looked discreetly away, Armaco however, casting a knowing look at Andulas, as if to say, 'told you so!'

Couldn't restrain himself. He did nevertheless manage to sound sincere.

"Good morning, my Lady."

Andulas looked away and Baldor glowered. Armaco somehow maintained a serious and respectful look, the mischief however, clearly visible on his face as he continued. "A fine morning, my Lady!"

Lasairiona gave a small nod of acknowledgement along with a wry smile and took hold of the bridle of Baldor's mount. Stroking its cheek, she settled the animal as it raised and lowered its head. Turning towards Baldor, she spoke softly in Gallic. Her hand hovered over her heart as she finished the blessing and Baldor nodded. He replied in Gallic with words that were barely audible, though Lasairiona smiled and demurely dropped her head. He looked as if he was about to ride on when he leant down and hooking his fingers gently under her chin, raised her head and kissed her full on the lips. He smiled warmly at her then kicked the horse on. As the horses settled into the walk Armaco pushed alongside, Baldor turned towards him.

"Say just one-word Armaco and I'll kill you." He laughed and moved the troop up to a trot.

****

By midmorning, the legions were pushing on at double pace as Flaminius called for speed. A huge grey-white dust cloud rose in their wake choking and blinding the wagon drivers, servants and the rearguard following behind. Expecting to sight the Carthaginians at any time across the open plain, Flaminius pulled his scouting parties back and closed the column to tight formations. Cornelius quietly fretted at the unrelenting pace; his memories haunted from the forced march to the Trebbia, his discomfort growing when he saw the scouts recalled. Though he did reason, no one could hide on the plain and with the hills still some distance away, he tried to calm his fears. By midday however, looking to where the road turned east and disappeared into the hills, they saw rising dust and flashes of light from armour and spear points as the Carthaginian rearguard slipped from sight. Flaminius became excited at the sighting and ordered the scouts released again and the pace maintained. His commanders however, advising that by the time they reached the hills it would be too late for battle and as the terrain was closing in, caution would be advisable.

They concurred with releasing scouts but advised of easing the pace, as it was clear they wouldn't catch the Carthaginians before tomorrow. Flaminius, frustrated and agitated chafed at the advice. Looking from the hills then back to the column he assessed for himself, the time and pace required to reach them, then watching the legionaries as they marched past realised the advice was sound. With the sun almost at its zenith and heat risen accordingly, the men were cooking in their armour, the horses' lathered white with sweat and the rising dust choking all and clinging to any drop of moisture. There was no singing now, the precious breath needed to maintain the pace and carry equipment. Most legionaries had removed their helmets in a bid to ventilate, leaving them to hang from their necks; their faces flushed red and streaked with sweat that coursed through the cloying dust.

Flaminius thumped his thigh hard, his horse jumping forward at the sudden movement. "Damn them! Damn them to Hades!"

"Beg your pardon sir?" The Legate asked, having to shout above the din of pounding feet, hooves and jingling harness.

"We should have marched during the night! It would have been cooler and we'd have caught them ere now!"

"I respectfully disagree sir; the men were exhausted last night and would have been in no shape for a fight. I wouldn't have liked to hazard a night march either; this plain would be hard to navigate after dark being so flat and featureless, we could have easily blundered into the Carthaginians else lost our way. We should catch them tomorrow; their march will slow through the hills. I would let the men rest sir and out here in the open is good."

Flaminius glowered and spat, wiping the dust that stuck to his lips. He looked at the men and saw the Legate was right; grim faced, heads down and signs of exhaustion showing, they needed to rest.

"Very well, call a halt, we'll camp here. Send scouts forward and have them report back before dark."

"Yes sir."

The Legate turned to relay the orders to the command party and officers scattered to their units. A trumpet wailed signalling a halt and within moments the column stopped. The noise of the march replaced by sounds of heavy breathing and gasps of air as men sucked the precious commodity into their lungs as if ambrosia. Centurions barked at men who wilted or lowered their shields while they waited for the camp's work details to be issued.

****

In the early evening, Hannibal dispatched squadrons of light and heavy cavalry back north westwards as far as the hills bordering the lake and edge of the plain, seeking signs of Roman scouts or vanguard. If required, they were to hold the Romans off from further advance at least until dusk, after which they could retire. It was a surprise to find the Romans camped on the plain well short of the hills. Leaving a strong party of horse in place to watch, the rest returned to camp to report their findings. Hannibal was delighted with the news; this allowed additional time to feed and provision his men before moving them into position in the forest before nightfall.

The Carthaginian column had marched around the northern end of the lake, setting up camp in the eastern hills while remaining visible from the road skirting the lake's edge. The camp was set up with tents and shelters erected and cooking fires burning, giving the appearance of the whole army bedding down for the night. However, as soldiers reached the camp in the early evening they were fed, watered, and provisioned with breakfast, then discreetly marched onwards over the hillcrest. In cover of the ridgeline, they about turned and marched back westwards on the blind side of the hills and entered the forest from the rear. With the long summer evening and the light good, the manoeuvres were simple and with no alarms coming from the cavalry rearguard watching the Roman camp, there was no urgency.

Hannibal went among the men as they passed through the camp, encouraging them to eat as they went while exchanging greetings and a word with those he knew. He dispatched units in the order he required, filling the forested hills with regiment after regiment in a mix of heavy and light, cavalry and infantry. Catching sight of Baldor's troop arriving he made his way across to him.

"Well met Baldor! I trust your day has been a pleasant one. See your men are fed and then wait for me by my banner." He pointed across the camp to the standard in front of his tent. "I'll see the last of the units into position and then join you, from there it's a quick ride over the hill to the forest then we can bed down for the night." With that, he was gone, chivvying another unit back westwards.

Baldor led his men to where the quartermasters and cooks were distributing food. Joining the queues, the smell of roasting lamb, chicken and goat and baking bread assailed his nostrils and set his stomach rumbling. He cast his eyes over his men as he waited; their mood was jubilant with an air of jaunty confidence clearly apparent. And why not, he thought; they'd beaten the Romans twice in the field and laid waste to their country without reprisal. These would be 'masters of the middle sea,' these sons of the 'she wolf' had not withstood the test of arms against the 'Lions cubs,' yet they had not sued for peace? He wondered at that, their losses should have seen them at least seek terms but here they were, with new legions raised, new Consuls appointed, seeking battle again. Still deep in thought he received his food ration then made his way to a quieter spot to eat. Armaco and Andulas sought him out and hunkered down beside him. Armaco struggled to settle his legs, having to use his hands to pull them into place, though he could ride well enough, walking was laborious and strained and sitting difficult. As ever, the warrior never complained of his injuries or the difficulties he suffered, though he complained of everything else and that made Baldor smile.

"You look happy, Captain!" Armaco smirked as he tore meat from a chicken leg.

Baldor grinned and shrugged. "Why wouldn't I be? The day has gone according to plan and we are ready for tomorrow, I have you and Andulas for company and good food to eat." Seeing Armaco gulping then swallowing his food to reply, he pre-empted him. "And sleeping alone for a night will be a welcome change and perhaps grant me some rest, satisfying a lady till daybreak is tiring."

Armaco's one eye went wide, his mouth hung open, his look that of a stunned mullet.

A thump of hooves and a rider approaching them stalled the conversation. The rider pulled up in front of Baldor.

"Captain Targa! The General sends his respects and asks that you join him in overseeing the final troop depositions now, you can return for your men and bring them on later."

Baldor got up quickly and unhitched his horse's reins from the rope line. "I'll see you both back here later; see the men are fed and provisioned for breakfast and ready to move."

He slapped both men on the back in farewell but as he passed Armaco, he snatched the chicken leg from his hand. Armaco grabbed at Baldor's meat laden fist and missed, trying to get up he lost the plate, tipping his supper onto the floor.

"Damn you boy!" He shouted, amidst flecks of food and a shaking fist. "Captain or not, you're not too bloody old to slap!"

Baldor pushed the chicken between his teeth as he mounted. "I'll need this to keep my strength up!" He pulled his mount around, the animal stomping and whickering eager to be off. "You're becoming old and slow my friend!" He laughed; gave a mocking bow then tore a mouthful of meat from the bone and turned to the messenger. "Take me to the General"

Andulas roared with laughter while Armaco growled in his throat. Reaching down, he snatched a discarded bone from the ground and threw it after Baldor. "I don't know what's worse? Him, happy or him bloody miserable? Damned striplings, a cuff around the ear wouldn't go amiss!"

Andulas chuckled. "Well, you shouldn't bait him." He reached for Armaco's plate. "Here old man, let me replenish your supper."

"Old man! Hah! You can give me ten years!"

Andulas chuckled again and nodded. "True, true! Perhaps I can also give you some wisdom!"

"If I had another bone, I'd be hurling it at you! Damned Gauls! Damned Captains!" Seeing Andulas laughing again then wiping watery eyes, his mouth turned up at the edges and he started to laugh himself.

"Ahr, you're all bastards!"

"Good Evening Sir." Baldor called as he reined in alongside Hannibal.

"And to you Baldor, have you eaten?"

"Yes sir, thank you."

"Good ... good." Hannibal stared fixedly as he spoke. Watching the troops deploying into the forest he passed a wineskin across to Baldor. "All going well tomorrow, we'll destroy Flaminius and his legions. Our men's morale is high, they're well fed and prepared and with surprise on our side the dice roll is loaded in our favour." Taking the wineskin back, he took a drink. "This terrain suits our warriors Baldor, the Gauls are used to the uplands and the Spaniards too are at home with forest and hill. Our Libyan pikemen we'll place in front of the camp as a strong screen as they will be of no use in the forest here; hopefully the sight of them will encourage the Romans onward, thinking they will see battle on flat ground below the camp."

"Can we tempt them that far sir?"

"I pray to Baal it will be so. Furthermore, if we can keep our men in check, in cover and silent, I believe we can slaughter the Romans almost to a man."

"It all hinges on silence and surprise sir?"

"Exactly Baldor! The rest is done for us; the forest is dark to hide in and dawn should render thick mist from the lake to add to our cover. With tired, dozy legionaries who don't expect a fight until mid-afternoon, the stage should be set. I've assumed their column width of eight or at maximum ten men abreast, so that's the whole road width taken up. Calculating that frontage and some spacing between units, against the distance from where the road exits the hills and follows the lake to our camp, almost the whole Roman army will be strung along it before we slam the gate shut in their rear."

"Their whole army sir?" Baldor asked, shaking his head in disbelief.

"Their whole army Baldor! We have the ground right, our position right, the enemy's position right, all we need is disciplined silence."

Baldor nodded and mopped the sweat trickling from his scalp down his face. Hannibal glanced at him and smiled.

"I don't remember heat like this since I left Africa and Spain but I pray that it persists. All we have to do is sit and wait in the forest shade while the legionaries sweat and eat dust along the road. If Flaminius continues the pace he has, we can add tiredness to their discomforts." He chuckled lightly. "It all adds up to advantages for us."

"Yes sir, and for once the hardships are all theirs!"

"Aye! Let them hasten to their doom. If this plan works as well as I think it will, there will be one Consular army less to concern us."

"And Geminus sir? What of him?"

"Pay him no heed for the present Baldor; he's still to the east and no threat yet, however when we do meet him, we will serve him the same fare as Flaminius receives tomorrow."

"Begging your pardon sir but are you, we, not being over confident? The very sense you warn us against."

"Ah Baldor! As honest and forthright as always."

"I mean no disrespect sir."

"None taken and here's the difference, I seek council, I ask, we plan, all of you have your say. We choose our ground and the time and then vary our tactics to suit; it appears these Roman Consuls do neither? They just come bravely on without a thought or care it seems, so I will use trickery, the land and their own brashness against them.

Moreover, think on. These new legions, so recently raised, have had no time for men to earn or learn trust of others; they have no fighting history. Inversely, you and your men, you'd trust each other with your lives, have done?"

"Aye sir!"

Hannibal smiled. "Hence my confidence Baldor, methinks we tip the scales in our favour?" He gestured, weighing imagined cups of a scale with his hands. "I think we have it all; good men and officers, sound tactics, respect for our enemy and ..."

"And we have you sir! That tips the scales well in our favour."

Hannibal inclined his head and smiled. "Thank you, I'd wager gold coin that the Consuls don't hear such loyalty."

Part 2

The Red Lake.
The trees came alive, the earth shook and
the water became blood.

Anon

Chapter Ten

Baldor halted his mount at the forest edge and looked back over his company stretched out in a thin, snakelike column behind him.

"All accounted for Baldor." Andulas said as if reading the others thoughts. "All are well fed, watered and victualed for the morrow, as you commanded." Baldor smiled and nodded then urged his horse on into the darkness of the trees.

As the late evening sunlight turned to shade beneath the canopy, so did the fierce heat, replaced by a cooler but heady pine scented aroma mixed with rich earth and leaf mould. His mount shied from the different smells then stepped quickly as its footing changed from hard, grassed hill to soft, springy needles and leaves. The bright colours of the warrior's tunics, helmet crests and painted shields turned to greys and monotones as the light faded with their advance deeper into the forest. The trees were a mixture of pines, spruces and firs as well as broadleaf oaks, ash and beech, their thick leafed canopies blotting out the sun but for chinks of light filtering through the branches in long golden shafts and lighting small areas of the gloom. The dust the horses kicked up swirled and danced in the light and as the men passed through the light beams, they momentarily regained their colouring before changing back to grey as they entered shadow again. The men let the horses pick their own way through, weaving between trees as flat ground gave way to hillside that sloped gently down towards daylight and the edge of the lakeside road.

To the men's left an infantry regiment was already settling down, the warriors sitting or lying on the forest floor with their equipment. Some looking to sleep, others still conversing in low whispers else checking weapons and harness. Baldor led his men down towards the forest's edge but halted them some fifty paces back, keeping them in shadow and screened by a crop of ferns that sprouted boldly from the forest floor. Dismounting his men and leaving Armaco to settle them, he and Andulas inspected the ground in front of their position, checking for potholes, rocks or ditches where a horse could break an ankle or fall and lose its rider. The ground, although sloping towards the road remained even and devoid of obstacles other than the trees themselves.

"It's good Baldor! We can make speed quickly and without risk, we can hit the legionaries apace and hopefully before they have chance to form battle lines."

Baldor nodded and pushed through the waist high ferns then dropped onto his belly, crawling the last few paces to the edge of the trees. Peering cautiously onto the road, he glanced right and left then beckoned Andulas on. Andulas joined him, also on his belly.

"Look at the road." Baldor pointed. Hannibal's right, it's only wide enough for eight, maybe ten men to march along and they'll need more space when they have to turn to face us and fight. Gods above! They'll struggle to form a defence; we'll hem them in and cut them to pieces! They've no space to manoeuvre and nowhere to go!"

"Aye, if we catch them unawares, we should be able to sweep them off the road into the lake."

Baldor looked at the road running parallel to the lake mentally assessing distance. If Hannibal had calculated aright, it would be a killing ground, with the small beach or the lake's shallows the only place to run to, the lake itself being too wide to swim. He caught Andulas's eye and gestured backwards with a flick of his head.

Slipping back through the ferns Baldor stopped suddenly, his hand snatching for a falcata hilt, his eyes on the forest floor watching. Andulas, following closely in his steps bumped into him.

"What the …?"

"What in Baal's creation is that?" Baldor's finger pointed to a grey-black, spiked ball on the ground. "A moment ago it was moving, on legs! Now it's stopped and become a ball?"

Andulas moved alongside then chuckled; slipping on a glove, he bent down to the spiky effigy and carefully scooped it up.

"It's a furze pig or forest hog, they're harmless but as you can see, you have to handle them carefully." He tapped the spikes with his finger. "Here, let me show you."

The pair stepped clear of the ferns and Andulas gently set the hog down a pace or two away, he motioned Baldor to sit and be silent. The hog never moved, after a while Baldor picked up a stick and went to prod it. Andulas gently knocked the stick away and held up a halting hand and whispering. "Wait!" A further period of silence finally produced movement and the ball slowly uncurled changing to a more elongated shape, a long twitching snout appeared. Sensing no immediate danger, legs appeared and the hog seemed to right itself then set off at a wobbling gait. Slipping on his own glove, Baldor followed, the moment he touched the hog, it reverted to a spiky ball. Holding it tentatively, he turned the small animal over for a closer look. The hog however remained tightly balled.

"You've not seen one before, Baldor?"

"Never! Though I've heard tales of similar creatures, only much larger with longer spikes that live in the forest in Africa, the gold merchants use their quills as receptacles for transporting gold dust."

"Humph, we just bag our gold dust and eat the hogs if the winters are hard."

"How on earth do you eat such?"

"Carefully!" Andulas smirked then laughed when Baldor caught the jest. "Seriously, after you kill it, you wrap it in clay and bake it; it tastes fine! A bit like chicken."

Taking a last close look at the creature Baldor set it down among the ferns. "I hope it's gone by tomorrow; else it may be crushed as we attack."

Andulas wondered at his friend, so concerned over a small creature whilst on the morrow his own life was to be hung in balance.

After relaying the terrain information to Armaco, Baldor worked his way around his troops checking all were settled and comfortable as possible, with the horses ready and near to hand. He exchanged a word or two with those he knew and smiles and handshakes with those he did not. Although finding it difficult, he noticed the positive reaction of the men by way of smiles and brightened eyes as he recalled a name or wished them well.

The leafy canopy speeded darkness and he looked through the trees down towards the road seeking the last of the fading light as a guide back to the front of his men. Settling himself next to Andulas and

Armaco, he rolled in the needle and leaf bed making himself comfortable and smiling at the soft snores emanating from Armaco, he already wrapped in his blanket sound asleep. Andulas offered him a wineskin; Baldor swilled a mouthful.

"Do you think this will end it tomorrow, Andulas? If we destroy them, surely, they must sue for peace?"

"The Gods alone know that." He said taking the skin back and drinking. "I do know them to be a resilient people though, they seem to bounce back from defeats and raising new armies seems to hold no issue for they are many. Why? ... Would you seek home and a little peace? Call an end to this soldiering?"

"If I could fulfil my vow for vengeance, I could enjoy the peace I think. For when I gazed at this beauty today, these hills and forests, this blue lake, I wanted nothing more than to enjoy it."

"And home?"

"Home Andulas?" He sighed. "No, not back to Carthage. I'm long done with Carthage." His words reflecting his sadness.

"You're more Gaul than Carthaginian anyway methinks, Baldor Targa." He chuckled. "Gestix, your friend? Your brother? He has instilled much of us upon you."

Baldor's teeth flashed white in the gloom and he laughed lightly. "Aye, I think you've the rights of it, and were that he was here to share this wine with us."

Andulas raised the skin in salute. "To your friend! May Epona bless and keep him." He drank and passed the skin to Baldor.

"To Gestix, son of Teutorix, son of Catutigernos of the Boii, my friend and brother." He tipped a mouthful of wine on the ground then drank.

There was silence for a while as the men swapped the skin between them. Sensing Baldor's mood moving to the melancholy, Andulas spoke again.

"So, not home you say, where to then? Epona, granting life."

"Well." He cleared his throat. "Well, a long time ago you offered me a home, the chance to live with your people; I wonder if that offer is still open? If it is, I'd not need asking again."

"The offer's there for as long as you draw breath and Epona knows it would make me a happy man. Our friendship was forged out of blood and bravery and I do not forget it, you risked all for my folk that day. A hearth and a home are the least we can offer in return."

"Well at least you wouldn't have to find him a bloody woman, Andulas! Your women folk are safe methinks." Armaco growled from his blanket.

"I thought you were sleeping!" Baldor chided.

"What! With you two gabbling like old women! Go to bloody sleep or talk quieter!"

Ignoring the grumbles, Andulas continued. "And that offer is open to you too, Armaco. A home and a good Gallic woman would do much to improve that temper of yours methinks. Some buxom, big titted blonde, to cook your supper, wash and mend your clothes and whelp some brats upon."

"The Gods save us from more of his ilk; Andulas, don't encourage him to breed."

Armaco muttered something they couldn't hear and Baldor laughed. Andulas however turned serious.

"Armaco; like Baldor you're my friend through blood and bravery, so a hearth, a home and a good … no, a fine Gallic woman for you when this war is done. And my word upon it, as one brother in arms to another."

The dark shape that was Armaco sat up.

"You're offering me a home? … Me? … Why would you do that?"

"Because you're a good man! And my friend" There was a long silence. "We can't soldier forever and if we win tomorrow and gain peace? Would you come?"

"Yes, yes I would … and I thank you for your offer." He rolled back in his blanket and muttered. "Someone will have to show you both how to hunt I suppose."

Baldor laughed quietly. "Steady Armaco, you were almost gracious before."

"Go to sleep boy, we've a battle to fight tomorrow!"

"Plenty time to sleep if we are killed … how do you do it through, sleep like that? You just roll over and next thing you're snoring like a hog."

"It's easy, when no one's yapping in my ear."

"Armaco's right Baldor, we should sleep. Dawn will not be long coming for the nights are short this time of year. We can't dice or knuckle bone in this murk so best to bed."

The birds woke Baldor; or rather, the tapping cadence of a

woodpecker seeking grubs in a tree bole pervaded his sleep. Cold and stiff, he was about to pull his blanket closer but found it very damp. Sitting up quickly and discarding the soggy cover, he rubbed vigorously at his limbs trying to put warmth in them. Looking around in the gloom, he saw tendrils of mist drifting through the branches, the visibility came and went and the light fluctuated, fading and brightening a shade or two. The mist was here! Patchy but here! He heard light footfalls behind him and turned to see Hannibal and Ducarius weaving their way around the still slumbering men towards him.

"Good morning, Baldor."

"Good morning, sir."

"We have a good day for it, the mist is playing its part and Ducarius thinks, will thicken a little yet. Flaminius is breaking camp and will be on the move soon, wake your men and then take breakfast with me." He waved a small bag before sitting down.

Baldor went amongst his folk, quietly urging them up and to breakfast. Slowly, men woke with yawns, coughs, moans and breaking wind, officers hissing and growling as they reinforced the need for quiet. All around, men were waking, rearming and breakfasting, the forest floor covered with equipment and warriors, an army of almost fifty thousand men hidden in the trees. He made his way back to Hannibal and was offered bread and dried meat with watered wine, Hannibal shared around what he had, including Armaco, Andulas and Ducarius in the repast.

"Are you ready, Gentlemen?" He asked between mouthfuls.

"Aye sir." Came back from full mouths.

"All's done now; everyone in position; briefed and ready. We can do no more; the die is cast it's in the hands of the Gods now and the strength of your sword arms. However, we can enjoy a leisurely breakfast while we await the good Flaminius and seeing we've time to wait I'm for a nap, wake me Baldor, ere the Romans are sighted."

Hannibal took a last drink and wrapped his cloak about him snuggling down into the leaf carpet.

Time slipped by and as dawn came full the mist thickened just as Ducarius had predicted. It drifted in patches through the trees, sometimes thicker than winter gruel other times wispy and gossamer like, hiding and exposing men as it passed. Heavy with moisture it gradually soaked the waiting men, dripping from their armour and saturating tunics and skin. The temperature however rose quickly, the air becoming hot and moist, the ground steaming in places. The mist haze motionless one moment before moving off upwards following the contour of the hill. With all noise forbidden men fretted, unable to talk to their comrades or sharpen weapons to keep their thoughts occupied many fell to praying. Hannibal slept on.

****

The Romans had breakfasted and broken camp before dawn then formed column. The vanguard, a mixture of Velites and Equites were already well through the hills leading to the lake before the sun skirted the eastern hill summits. The first legion followed on with Flaminius, his colour party and staff and some ten turmaes of cavalry coming next, followed by the second legion with the two auxiliary legions close behind. Flaminius had scattered cavalry turmaes throughout the column thinking to add strength and flexibility whilst on the march, his archers he left in the rear but forward of the final turmaes of cavalry, these to shepherd all.

Cornelius led his century, his eyes casting about in the murk, his mind full of Carthaginian ruses and traps and his heart heavy with the thought. Gaius stepped alongside interrupting his glum reverie.

"Good Morning Cornelius, Juno's blessings upon you!"

"And on you."

"Are you ready for it? We've a bit of a march first as Hannibal's camp is at the top end of the lake on the rise. A stretch of the legs will warm the lads up nicely and then we'll take these Carthaginians to task, though I don't think we'll see battle till midday at the earliest?"

"Do you think he's waiting up there? At his camp?"

"Where else could he be?"

Cornelius shrugged. "Jupiter knows, what I don't understand is; why he would exit the plain and move into the hills when he has such good strength of cavalry."

"Maybe he thought he could be through the hills to Apulia before we caught up with him?"

Cornelius looked thoughtful. "Maybe, but he's always so thorough; this doesn't make sense to me?"

Gaius shrugged and forced a smile. "On the other hand, he may have miscalculated or perhaps he's content where he is? Anyway, local knowledge says there's room for battle at the foot of the hills below his camp."

"Aye! But not nearly enough to manoeuvre as is his want and this is not good cavalry country!"

"Well, I surmise he's going to take us on there, his rear is protected by the hill and his flanks are easy to secure, so it's still a strong position for him, cavalry or not."

"True, but why would he let us come at him head on, Gaius? He knows we're superior in heavy infantry and butting heads like that is our trait, these two things put him at a disadvantage."

"A commander can't have it all you know. Anyway, perhaps he's over confident. As I said, maybe his timing is wrong; perhaps he was slow to march with all that baggage ...''

"No, there's something not right, I can feel it."

"Steady lad, he's not infallible and we've marched fast, I think we may have caught him. Perhaps he's chosen to make a stand now as he doesn't know where Geminus is?"

"We don't know where Geminus is!"

"Shush lad!" Gaius hissed as he cast furtive glances about them. "Put that vine stick under your arm and lift your damn head. Come on! Set an example to your Century. Hannibal is not a God, just a man! And all men are fallible, maybe this time he has it wrong? And see, we're wide awake, well prepared, breakfasted and the men's morale is high."

Cornelius gave a slow smile then grinned.

"That's better lad! That's the Cornelius I know!"

"You're a good man Gaius. Thank you. I appreciate ..."

Cornelius was interrupted by a cavalryman reining in alongside, the horse sidestepping and stomping as it adjusted its gait to that of the marching men.

"Begging your pardon sir but the Consul requests your presence; he's to the rear of the first legion. If you'll follow me sir, I'll take you to him."

Cornelius extended his hand to Gaius, the pair each grasping the other firmly.

"Go well Gaius, victory and honour. I pray that Juno keep and bless you." His other hand clasped over his heart as he spoke.

"And you lad, look to your men and yourself, mind it! Juno bless and keep you also and may Mars be your shield! I'll find you when this is done … for that Falernian!" He gestured quaffing from a small wineskin and smiled.

Cornelius managed a quick bow of his head then jogged after the departing horseman.

As the road exited the hills towards the lake, the giant mist cloud was visible, laid like a thick white shroud just above the water's surface. Where it met the land, it seemed to take life, swirling and flowing slowly across the road before drifting upwards into the trees and thick enough to screen the sunlight to a milk-coloured murk. Cornelius used the column of men as a guide through it as he trotted after the messenger. Reassuring himself there would be no battle yet, he passed the Standard-bearers and cornicen players at the front of the second legion then the cavalry units and the Consul's command group. Flaminius himself was resplendent in bronze cuirass, red tunic and white leather pteruges. The white horsehair crest of his helmet adding height to his stature before cascading tail-like, half way down his back, stark against the crimson of his war cloak. His mount, as white as the winter snows stepped proudly, its head nodding and tossing as it walked. Cornelius took a big breath, as much to calm his nerves as to replenish his lungs then fell in alongside Flaminius's mount.

"Greetings of the day sir. Centurion Scipio reporting as commanded." He had to shout above the rumble of hooves and rattle and creak of harness.

"Ah, Cornelius! Good morning to you. You're well?"

"Yes sir, thank you sir."

Flaminius beckoned Cornelius closer. "Come! Walk alongside me, here take hold." He gestured to the mounts tack. "I would talk with you."

Grasping a corner of the riding blanket, Cornelius bit his lip and spoke quickly. "I'm sorry sir, sorry for my outburst. My misgivings had the better of me. I ask your forgiveness and forbearance."

"Granted Cornelius!"

"Thank …Thank you sir." He gabbled, taken aback by the quick clemency. "I swear I will mind my tongue in future. Though I'm told I am my father's son in that I speak plainly, however it seems without a modicum of his wisdom."

"Enough Cornelius! Your apology is accepted and the matter done with. I've sat at your father's table, you, and him at mine. I want no bad blood between us. You are young and thus I understand or rather will make allowances for what has gone before. Wisdom, they tell me comes with age!"

"Thank you, sir."

Flaminius waved the thanks away. "What make you of this heat? It's just after dawn yet it feels like midday."

"I know not sir; it is passing strange for sure; I've not experienced the like before this early in summer."

"High winds one day, insufferable heat the next. And now a soaking in this mist to boot! Is this not a soldier's lot?" He laughed lightly. "Now! Your Century, it's ready? You're ready? For I think we will see battle by midday."

"Yes sir, all ready. What did the scouts report on Hannibal's numbers and troop positions?"

"Scouts? No! No, need for scouts this morning lad. Some local folk came into camp last night and told of Hannibal's movements."

Cornelius groaned inwardly at the mention of no scouts but lesson learned, he choked back his reply. Sensing the apprehension, Flaminius added.

"These folk are trustworthy Cornelius, being known personally to one of the Tribunes, who hails from these parts apparently."

Cornelius nodded, somewhat relieved.

"They tell us Hannibal's established a huge camp on the Cortonian hills at the head of the lake; he's marshalled his heavy infantry divisions in front of it and set his banners." Flaminius glanced down at Cornelius and smiled. "We've caught him, Cornelius! By Jupiter, we've caught him! He's making a stand ere we overtake him on the road. He's also deployed light troops at the foot of the slopes while blocking the road adjacent to them with his African pikemen where the land widens. I say this ends today! We have him just where we want him, boxed in between the lake and his camp, with no great space for manoeuvre or tricks, and Jupiter knows; our men are confident and spoiling for a fight. His light troops we can sweep aside easily, the pikemen will break when the legionaries get in amongst them and disrupt their formation thereby letting our cavalry in and I'll wager legionary against Libyan mercenary any day."

Cornelius looked up, questions forming on his lips.

"I know what you're thinking Cornelius; his heavy infantry may come down to support the pikemen? Pray that they do! For it'll save us advancing up the slope to reach them … but we will if we have to! Roman grit, determination, and we being the better men will see these barbarians off. We'll hit them like a hammer on an anvil, a Roman fighting on his home soil will put paid to Spaniard, African and Gallic savages fighting for loot. What say you?"

"What of his cavalry sir? Where's he placed them? That's his arm that I fear."

"Hah! Fear not then! His cavalry along with some infantry were seen slipping over the hill before dark, eastwards towards Perusia. We think he's sent them as a probing or screening force for fear of Geminus coming up in his rear."

Cornelius's heart lifted. "Is Consul Geminus marching to meet us sir, have you heard?"

"Yes, we finally received a message from Geminus; it arrived just before first light this morning." Cornelius's sudden reassurance was short lived as Flaminius continued. "He's advancing towards us but too slowly to affect the outcome today!"

"Should we not delay then sir, wait a day or two?" Cornelius was careful in his tone, enquiring as if an apprentice to his Journeyman.

"No lad, I'm set upon this, I have the Carthaginian where I want him and as I said, this ends today. Geminus does help us though; he's dispatched four thousand cavalry under the Propraetor, Gaius Centenius towards us or rather towards Hannibal. With the Carthaginians taking the easy route eastwards past Trasimene and towards him and Apulia they can block him."

Cornelius felt an unsettled nagging in his subconscious; this wasn't like Hannibal, taking the easiest road! When had he ever done that? Masking his concerns from Flaminius and keeping his tongue between his teeth the other continued.

"It's a Roman Consul's duty to advance and engage the enemy and though I like the man not, I can no longer doubt his resolve to his responsibilities. He's sending a good man in Centenius, I know him of old and he's not unexperienced in the ways of war."

With the supportive comments and the knowledge of the departing, Carthaginian cavalry and the advancing Centenius, Cornelius brightened and wondered if maybe Gaius was right, had he read too much into this whole affair? Was he affording Hannibal too much credence? Did his experience of defeats have him conjuring unbeatable

Carthaginian demons? This time it seemed Hannibal would be forced to fight on somewhat unfavourable ground and without his cavalry.

"That must have given Hannibal some unease then sir? For him to dispatch his cavalry before battle? If he's not sure what's happening and who is where, it can only unsettle him and help us?"

"My thoughts exactly, Cornelius!"

****

Baldor loosened his scarf using it to mop his face and brow, unsure if it was moisture or sweat as the air was unnaturally hot for just after dawn. He glanced at Armaco then Andulas, both sat with heads bowed and mumbling prayers, Andulas gently rubbed a bronze effigy of Epona between his fingers as he chanted softly.

With his own piety long gone, his only observance remained his dead wife and friend and he pulled the silver cameo bearing Aiticia's image from under his shirt. Gazing at it, he looked away quickly, thoughts and remorse of his amorous liaison with Lasairiona fresh in his mind. Feeling disloyal and shamefully guilty, he kept looking at the image then looking away not knowing what to think or say. In the end, he gently kissed the still warm metal then pushed it back in his shirt. Seeking a prop to focus upon, he slowly drew a falcata and holding it to his chest quietly intoned his thoughts to Gestix.

"Brother, keep me strong this day. Help me to lead well and be a good man. If this is to be my last day, I rejoice in that I will see you sooner. I will strive for vengeance on those who took you from me, help me to be brave and wise just as you were. Victory, honour and vengeance brother, may Epona keep you."

As he opened his eyes, he found a messenger a pace or two away.

"Sir, the Roman vanguard is advancing up the road with the legions following on." The man saluted and moved on to relay his message further.

Baldor knelt next to Hannibal and gently shook his leg while speaking quietly. "Sir … sir! It begins."

Hannibal woke with a smile and seemingly instant recollection of the situation.

"I take by the silence that all is well, Baldor? Our guests expect nothing?"

"So far sir, yes."

Hannibal stood and looked around at the men scattered thickly about him, some had risen to their feet in readiness, others looking to do so. Catching the men's attention he motioned them back down, as others looked, he repeated the gesture, adding a finger across his lips intimating they pass it on; soon the eager warriors were settling back onto the ground.

The tomb-like hush seemed deafening. The tension rising, becoming tight as a drawn bowstring. When the distant rumble of hooves and jingle and creak of harness filtered through the trees, the air seemed to become charged. Men strained their ears, listening for any change in the approaching noise that would announce the trap rumbled or battle joined further back down the road. The sound however remained the same, only growing in volume. Soon, the cadence of marching feet added to the din as the Romans came ever closer. Sweat oozed from men's pores and not just from the heat. Some stared wide-eyed down towards the road trying to peer through the mist. Others fidgeted, tightening their grip on spear shafts and sword hilts or adjusting shield straps. Officers watched their men like mother hens, guarding for any premature movement while watching and waiting for the signal to attack, the tension palpable. Down on the road the Romans marched purposely on, blissfully ignorant of their enemy laid only four score paces away.

Hannibal edged forward of his troops, crawling on his belly closer to the road amidst cover of the forest ferns affording him a better view of the passing Romans. Producing a tiny abacus from inside his tunic he beckoned Baldor alongside and intimated he should keep watch while he counted and summed the passing men.

Chapter Eleven

The Roman vanguard of Velites and cavalry had long since passed Hannibal and Baldor's position and the coloured beads on the abacus now resembled heavily strung necklaces. The thump of marching feet and the rattle of spear shafts, metal and the hiss of men's breath was very loud as the column pushed by at quick pace. The stink of sweating men drifted up through the trees mixing with the mist and the smells of the forest. The Carthaginians continued to watch and wait. The tension lifting a notch higher as men silently stressed and fretted. Nerves balanced on a knife's edge, ready for the first shouts that would begin the chaos and battle to join. The waiting was always the worst, the time when bladders seemed overfull, bowels felt watery and weak and guts churned and heaved as if with the flux. Baldor, his breath coming in short, sharp breaths and sweat dripping from his chin watched Hannibal calmly sliding beads across the wires as he counted the passing centuries and turmaes. As he blinked and rubbed his eyes clear of the stinging, salty moisture, Hannibal glanced up at him and grinned while gesturing he breathe deeply, be calm and relax. Nodding, Baldor swallowed hard and settled alongside to watch as the first legion passed and yet more beads move across the wire. Waiting was bad enough but counting and watching the enemy numbers grow stronger with each passing moment seemed acute agony, verging upon madness.

A gap appeared in the column just after the first legion and as the pair strained their necks to see who came next; Flaminius himself rode into view followed closely by his bodyguards, command group and then more cavalry. The officers were a blaze of colour beneath dancing horsehair plumes and feathered, helmet crests. Their bronze plate body armour burnished and shield faces newly painted, their crimson and white, tunics showing little signs of campaign wear or dirt. The cornicen players marched by in gleaming mail coats, helmets and shoulders draped with silver-grey wolf skins. The vexillifers followed wrapped in leopard skins, their blood red standards denoting the legion's name, number and SPQR the 'senate and people of Rome' in golden letters. Hannibal's fixed gaze changed to intent examination as he nudged Baldor and pointed to the Consul.

"Baal Almighty! There he is Baldor!" He whispered sharply. "There's our would-be nemesis! My, my, he looks fine does he not? We're obviously important enough for him to dress for the occasion and us, just simple soldiers!" He chuckled lightly as he slid more beads along the abacus rail. "So, he's going to be well forward in the column, after the van and the first legion but in front of the rest, mind it for me."

"Yes sir."

The noise increased as more cavalry passed with clopping hooves, jingling harness and snorting horses adding to the din, the strong odour of heated horseflesh wafting up into the trees. The mist thinned a little as the sunlight grew stronger, more of the road appeared, and though the brightness did not pervade the trees, the secreted men subconsciously hunkered lower to the ground. Some supply wagons creaked by, then another standard appeared with associated musicians and leading Centurions.

"Look Baldor." Hannibal whispered, nodding to a pole standard displaying a wild boar and marked, Legio Secunda. "The second legion methinks? That's your adversary's legion, isn't it? Young Scipio?"

"Aye sir and Baal grant I find the bastard for I still have scores to settle!"

Hannibal noticed the ice in Baldor's voice and turned to look at him.

"Take care Baldor! Though I doubt not your puissance as a warrior or skill with a blade, hate is a powerful driver and can lead a man to mistakes when he sees only what he wants and not what is."

"Yes sir, I'll mind it. I've been told similar before and it's good advice and well to be reminded of it."

Baldor peered at the passing men for a long time, seeking the familiar face of his sworn enemy but with distance, the churning mist and helmets donned it was near impossible to tell one man from another. He looked back at the abacus and saw yet more beads had transferred to the right and felt his guts heave and a hollow feeling in his bowels.

'How much longer? Baal Almighty, how much longer?' He thought. It was serving well that the trap had not been sprung as Hannibal wanted to envelop the whole Roman army but it was detrimental to the nerves and Baldor quietly begged for battle to start. As the tail of the second legion passed, Hannibal quietly summed the beads then turned to whisper.

"Just under nine thousand legionaries Baldor, plus the vanguard and the cavalry. Altogether I make that almost fifteen thousand men or roughly half the Roman army past this point, I'm happy for battle to commence any time now."

"Will you give the command sir? Let the hounds loose?" He asked anxiously.

"Not yet! Seeing as how we've remained quiet this far, we'll give it a little longer and let the trap door close on the Roman rear if we can. That way we have them all, no one escapes!" A wolfish grin spread over his face, his head nodding in quiet satisfaction. Hannibal placed the abacus in a bag and turned back to watch the Romans. The ominous silence continued and Baldor fretted further, chewing his lip and fighting the need to piss.

Baldor's mental relief was not too long coming, though the action started slowly enough with sporadic shouts and screams from back up the road. The Roman column seemed to fall into sudden disorder as some men stopped to listen causing commotion in the ranks, while others marched on colliding and stumbling into them. Optios stepped out from the column seeking clarification on what was happening. Baldor glanced at Hannibal and saw he was already on his feet and waving to his trumpeter. The signaller cleared his throat, lifted the trumpet to his lips, and blew a long wailing note. It was quickly repeated by more trumpets and war horns; the vibrant notes cascading as they rose and fell through the forest. The Gallic carnyx joined the cacophony, their brassy, primeval notes blowing long and hollow, sounding chillingly cold through the trees.

Men jumped up from the ground as if magically sprouted. The air suddenly alive and deafeningly loud with war cries; shouts and whoops as the secretive, carefully stored lethal energy found terrible vent. Like hounds loosed from the leash, the first wave of men leaped and ran down the forested hillside towards the road, their blood lust up and desperate to find release.

Down on the road the legionaries stared, gawped and looked about, seeing nothing. They'd heard the sounds of fighting in the distance but it was now drowned by a growing roar and the thunder of thousands of feet crashing through undergrowth in the forest to their left and above them. They could only hear and imagine what was bearing down upon them. Staid veterans were already turning towards the trees, dropping marching packs and anything they didn't need to be encumbered with and raising shields while calling comrades to close up.

Centurions and Optios rushed down the narrow sward between the column and the forest, calling signallers to sound battle order and men to close ranks and left face. Legionaries jostled one another as they hefted their shields trying to find space, some tripping and losing balance as they were pushed by other ranks. The men nearest the lakeside were forced off the road, stumbling or falling down the verge towards the water, pushed by their comrades nearest the forest who were panicking and seeking space. All, desperately trying to form a shield wall against the attack that was growing louder and closer by the moment.

The first javelins arced out of the trees, followed by showers of arrows, loosed from an enemy still unseen. The whistle of javelin shafts and the whoosh of wind over feathers announced the Carthaginian missile storm to the disrupted column. The clatter of projectiles as they bounced off or shattered against the legionary's shields and helmets sounded like tree branches rattling together in a storm. With no cohesive roof of shields, the missiles found and slipped through gaps, glancing off helmets and armour but also finding flesh. Bodies fell, men grunting and screaming transfixed by arrows and spears. Commanders shouted themselves hoarse trying to instil order but couldn't make themselves heard above the din of the missiles and a very audible but still invisible enemy.

The whir of slings loading up was followed moments later by the whine of released bullets and stones, this salvo accompanied in flight by some hand axes and fighting spears as men's battle rage overtook their senses. Just back from the treeline, the first fleeting shapes appeared in the shadows.

Shields lifted overhead against the incoming missiles, opening gaps for the slingshot. Coming at close range at an accurate and deadly, horizontal trajectory, it raked the outer ranks like a deadly winter hail. Blood spurted high in the air as lead bullets, the size of bantam eggs, pummelled flesh and bone to red pulp. Legionaries hit in the face had their heads burst open like rotten fruit. Unprotected knees and ankles were smashed knocking the legs from under the men, putting them down or where they couldn't fall in the tight press, collapsing against their comrades. The slingers also loosed at the mules, who fell braying and dying else bucking wildly if hit by a glancing shot. Some ran out of control trying to escape their pain and collided, along with their cargo into the rear of legionaries, further disrupting the ranks. The horses, unprotected and a large, easy target, also died beneath the whining death, the bullets driving deep into soft flesh, the larger, rounded stones breaking bones. The animals whickered and reared wildly in fright and pain, throwing riders and bolting, else collapsing to crush their rider if he was too slow to move.

Optios, Centurions and trumpeters, being the closest to the trees bore the brunt of the slingshot and most died where they stood. Any that remained alive being swept off their feet and killed as the Carthaginian host burst out of the mist-shrouded treeline like Hade's Harpies. The trees seemed to come alive as thousands of men hurled themselves at lightning speed across the few paces of grass between the forest edge and the road, trampling the Roman dead and wounded underfoot.

The remaining Centurions, trying to maintain calm in front of their men bellowed to close ranks as a second wave of javelins rained down. As the attackers hit the column, war cries and screams suddenly turned to a loud grunt as the Carthaginians smashed into the Roman ranks at the run. Flesh and bone burst and broke as it absorbed the crippling impact and suddenly men were face to face with their enemy. Shocked and somewhat panicked, the legionary's ranks buckled under the impetus of the attack. Many were knocked off balance stumbling and falling into their comrades, while men shuffled together trying to form a shield wall and find space where there was none.

Owing to the varying terrain in the forest and degrees of steepness, undergrowth and in some places a streambed, some of the Carthaginian units pushed ahead of others. Therefore, the attack, although a total surprise, arrived un-coordinated hitting the Roman column with heavy but sporadic hammer blows that came fast and hard. Howling for blood, their faces twisted in hate, the charging warriors came on; the attacks coming so quickly that in most places the Romans had no time to launch a retaliatory volley of pila. Some were hurled at almost point-blank range just before the attackers reached the column, most however were thrown down as legionaries reached for their gladius, the more useful weapon at close quarters.

The Roman column buckled and swelled, twisting and constricting like a giant serpent on the move as it absorbed the varying impacts of the incoming human wave. With no space or cohesion, legionaries went down like nine pins as the weight of the attack increased and struck home. Some Gauls, so infused with adrenalin and battle madness hurled themselves at the raised shields using their bodies as battering rams. Some smashed through, tumbling and scattering the defenders, allowing their comrades to flood into the gap hacking and killing. Others were solidly repulsed where an unyielding defence had managed to form; these dying beneath the stabbing gladius's and falling to be stamped upon as the Roman line pushed forward desperately seeking space to fight.

However, with no organised battle line the column was disintegrating, chopped into small groups of desperate men trying to hold off the Carthaginians. To the Romans, it seemed there was no end to the enemy numbers as the forest continued to spew men by the thousands. They flowed and swirled in and about the column, battering it like a rogue tide against a slowly collapsing sea wall.

At the command group, Flaminius dragged on the reins halting his horse and looked back over his shoulder. His officers, trying to do the same broke ranks as men turned their mounts to see what caused the commotion back down the column. Heads turned quickly back to the forest, hands grabbing sword hilts as the rumble of thousands of feet, breaking branches and a cohesive, primeval roar announced the Carthaginians to this part of the column.

"Form up! Form up!" Flaminius bellowed as he snatched his gladius from its sheath, holding it high as a rallying point. The first javelins, arrows and slingshot flew out of the trees. "Shields up!"

Cornelius, still walking alongside Flaminius's horse couldn't see anything. Confused, he was drawing his gladius when the flanks of Flaminius's horse buffeted him sideways as the Consul forced it about to face the forest. Horses screamed wildly as missiles found their mark, some collapsing under smashed legs as lead bullets struck home else their flanks feathered with arrows. Others whickered and stomped wild-eyed in fright, some reared as the forest's edge filled with men rushing headlong at the column whooping and yelling their hate. As the range closed, individual faces became terrifyingly clear with; snarls, bared teeth, scars, tattoos, narrowed eyes and looks that promised death. Chaos ensued.

Cornelius stepped bravely in front of Flaminius's mount, reaching for its bridle trying to hold and calm it as it stomped, whickered and tossed its head. The horse reared as a slingshot hit it above the eye spraying hot blood and grey-pink slime over Cornelius. The bridle torn from his hands as the horse pirouetted then collapsed onto its back legs, he having to jump clear of the animals fall. Flaminius jumped off the dying beast and tumbled down the small incline towards the lake. Cornelius raced after him, slipping and sliding over the grass shelf in his haste. Finding his balance, he helped Flaminius to his feet and back towards the road.

"Cornelius! Have them sound battle stations! Form the men ..." His words cut short as a huge Gaul jumped down in front of them, a double-handed axe raised high to strike. Cornelius, lightning quick, thrust his gladius into the Gaul's bare chest, the man's impetus driving it deep. The Gaul collapsed as the blade ruptured his heart, Cornelius heaving the wilting body to one side while aiding Flaminius back over the grass step.

Back on the road, Cornelius glanced about quickly, up and down the column seeing only chaos and shock with no sign of order. The forest was still gushing a steady stream of warriors and the Roman column buckling under the force and driven sideways off the road toward the lake.

Baldor, seeing the attack go in, donned his helmet and turned seeking his mount. Hannibal's hand gripped his shoulder.

"Wait you, Baldor! Remember I said I wanted your men to use as a surgeon's knife?"

"Yes sir."

"Here's what I want you to do. Stay in cover of the trees and take your men in the direction of the camp, stay parallel to the road but not on it, mark you! I don't wish you to become embroiled in the fight."

Baldor stared at him. "What sir? ... Why?"

"Find Flaminius for me! He's forward of us as you know, past the second legion and the cavalry, so you've a way to go. Don't deviate or become involved in anything along the way. Your objective is to capture Flaminius, nothing else! Do you have it?"

"Yes sir!" Baldor nodded as he fastened his chinstrap and gestured for his horse to be brought. Whistling shrilly at Armaco and Andulas then lifting his arm quickly had the pair turn to the troop and call to mount up. Taking his mount's reins, he threw his leg over its back. Hannibal reached for the horse's bridle.

"Take Ducarius with you and send him back to me with your results."

"Yes sir."

As Baldor took up the reins, Hannibal continued to hold the bridle.

"Capture him Baldor, if you can? A Roman Consul as a prisoner would be a weighty bargaining chip. Take minimal risks though! Kill him if you can see no other way or if needs must, for I want you back here safe. Baal Hammon protect and keep you!"

"Yes sir, thank you sir!" Baldor grinned, his face now squashed tightly between the cheek guards of his helmet.

It was agonisingly slow going as the horses crossed the wooded slope. Forced to thread the trees over soft, uneven ground covered in leaves and needles, the animals stepped warily. Some stumbled causing whinnying protests and soon the small column had lost any cohesion as riders let the animals pick their own way, slanting up or down hill, as long as they moved forward. In places they had to climb higher to pass above groups of waiting warriors which Hannibal had left in reserve, leaving the way clear to the road should they be called to the fray. The din of battle below was not so loud now, the noise somewhat muffled by the trees, reducing it to a dull drone of men's shouts and clashing of metal. Horses whickered as they picked up the stink of blood and the taint of men's fear as they stood by fretting anxiously, wishing either to be down amongst the action or for it all to be over and the madness to stop.

Baldor dispatched Ducarius and another man, Bōdashtart down to the road seeking the Roman cavalry and the Consul's command group. He, racking his brains as to how he would carry out the attack and hoped for capture, once their quarry was found.

They continued onward for what seemed an inordinate amount of time, Baldor fretting that they'd bypassed Flaminius else the man was already down, wounded or dead from missiles as the trap closed. Waving his men on, he pushed his mount downhill to the treeline and the two men, asking anxiously for a report only to be told that no cavalry had been sighted, only legionaries. With an effort, he calmed his fears and forced his mount back up the slope to his troop. Coming across another reserve infantry company, he queried the Captain on the whereabouts of the Roman command group.

"They're ahead sir, further along the road but no too far, we saw them ride past but a short while ago. The lads to the left of us are fighting against their second legion, Regulars sir, not Auxiliaries, if that's any help?"

"Yes, Captain. Thank you, that's reassuring. I was concerned we'd come too far."

"No sir, you'll find them shortly. Baal go with you sir."

"And with you, Captain."

Before long, a loud whistle came from Ducarius and as Baldor looked down, he signalled, cavalry!

Baldor acknowledged and intimated they should continue onwards and watch for the Consul. Looking ahead into the trees, he saw more reserves, this time cavalry. The ground was so steep to their rear that he saw no option other than to pass in front of them; he dispatched a rider to the command group seeking permission to pass. Within moments, his rider waved them forward while pointing to pass in front of the waiting men. Closing his troop up best as the land would allow, Baldor cut across the waiting cavalry's front. Passing the commanders and Standard-bearers, he looked up and waved his thanks to see stony stares by way of return from Bodeshmun and Sakarbaal. As Baldor scowled back, Sakarbaal looked away, while Bodeshmun glared at him, his lip twisting in a snarl before he spat contemptuously. Baldor's men could not fail to notice as most were looking up at the waiting ranks above them. Taken aback, Baldor just gawped. At a loss as to how to respond, his embarrassment and awkwardness was saved by a quick thinking Armaco, who forced his mount alongside and between the parties, making a show as if escorting his Captain while muttering quietly.

"Shite doesn't rot quickly Captain, they'll keep! But now's not the time."

Quietly fuming Baldor turned away, his features struggling to hide the hot anger rising within him at the insult. The horses walked on and suddenly Baldor snatched at the reins trying to turn his horse back. This time Andulas put out a cautionary arm.

"Leave it Baldor! Please? Armaco's right; now's not the time."

"Gods above, I'll endure no more! This ends now, orders or not."

Seeing Armaco about to argue and shout Baldor down, Andulas spoke quickly and quietly.

"Please Baldor! Another time? We have orders to carry out, a battle to fight. Who knows what could happen if you challenge them now? Will their men join in? Will we end up fighting ourselves instead of the Romans?"

"This is insufferable!" He hissed from behind gritted teeth. "First they attack me and now they insult me!"

"Yes, they have! But we've a saying; Baldor, revenge is a dish best served cold!"

Perhaps hearing echoes of Gestix in Andulas's words, Baldor choked back a retort. His face twisting with the effort, he let his horse walk on. There was a pregnant hush amongst the small group, Armaco and Andulas content to let silence diffuse the situation and Baldor using it to cool his temper.

The troop walked on passing more impatient, agitated infantry reserves and also noticing the mist was thinning quickly now. Sunlight appeared at the treeline by the road and raised the light level in the forest as it broke through the canopy scattering golden beams of light. Another whistle had Baldor look down to see the two men wave then point out towards the road, signalling they'd found Flaminius.

With excitement replacing his anger, he halted his troop. With all thoughts of Bodeshmun and Sakarbaal suddenly gone from his mind, he urged his mount down to the two men to look for himself. The battle noise increased dramatically as he reined alongside, the stink of blood, shit and body offal suddenly strong in his nose. Following his men's directing, he looked across a mass of pushing, seething warriors, gaudily plumed helmets and rising and falling weapons. There was only one Roman left mounted where the men pointed. The man's sword arm rising and falling as he stabbed and parried at the swirling mass about him while forcing his horse about. Baldor squinted.

"That's not him! Flaminius has white plumes in his helmet!"

"Not the mounted man sir, look there!" Bōdashtart pointed further to the right.

Baldor looked again but where Bōdashtart pointed was suddenly filled with fighting warriors.

"Where damn it? I can't see him!"

"Wait a moment sir, the fighting ebbs and flows, especially around him. His officers are trying to screen and protect him but our lads are giving them a hard time. Trouble is, we only have light troops in this sector, heavies are what's needed to break through their cordon."

Baldor continued to watch, his frustration growing. Time slipped by and sweat ran from beneath his helmet stinging his eyes else dripping off his chin, the delay doing nothing for his nerves.

"Are you sure you saw him? This isn't just a cavalry turma that's hard pressed?"

"I saw him!" Ducarius cut in sharply. "He's over there." He pointed again into the heaving mass.

Once more, the three waited. When the mounted Roman was finally dragged from his horse, the agitation had Baldor speak again, his tone brusque.

"He'd be hard to see in this press, what makes you so sure it's him?"

"I'd know Flaminius if he were in disguise." Ducarius growled, his eyes not leaving the fighting.

"How so?"

"Because of the scar on his face." Ducarius drew his finger across his cheek demonstrating to Baldor.

"You know him?"

"You could say that! He slew my father and brother at Telamon, eight years past. I gave him that scar! Now I'll take his head!"

Baldor was surprised at the information and about to confirm the orders were for Flaminius to be taken alive when Ducarius pointed again. The fighting had abated slightly as men were forced to pause for breath and suddenly Flaminius was visible. Dismounted, sword and shield in hand he directed his men in defence, readying for the next attack. His armour and helmet were splattered in blood, though whether it was his own was impossible to say. Baldor saw the scar; it was quite prominent. Turning towards Ducarius, he found him raising his spear and pushing his horse past him.

"Ducarius! Wait!"

"I'll wait no longer! He dies today!" Howling like a wolf, he kicked his mount hard, sending it leaping forward out of the trees.

Baldor turned quickly to his troop and signalled them to advance towards him. Men and horses came down the slope in no orderly fashion, horses slipping and sliding on the needle-strewn ground and whinnying in protest, the men laid backwards across their mount's haunches trying to maintain their balance. With the road only paces away and their own men still in front of them there was no space to mount an effective charge. Thinking quickly, Baldor ordered a funnelling column.

All was action as men hefted shields and raised fighting spears and without further pause, Baldor shouted for the attack. The signaller blew his horn in loud undulating notes as the horses burst out of the trees, war cries and whoops splitting the air. The fight in front of them seemed to pause momentarily as men looked over their shoulders; the Carthaginians that weren't engaged began pushing and stepping to one side clear of the oncoming horses. Baldor grimaced as some warriors, too slow to move, were knocked to the side else went down, trampled beneath the hooves of his men's ragged charge. The required speed to break through the Roman cordon taking precedent.

Suddenly, they were on top of the Romans, the battered cordon breaking apart in the face of the oncoming horseflesh. Legionaries would have stood their ground in the face of the horses but the men around Flaminius were dismounted cavalry not trained infantry and their only thought was to flee from the approaching charge. Baldor found his first target as a Roman turned and raised his shield. The man was either tired or most likely unused to fighting on foot and he opened his guard too wide, Baldor's spear took him low in the stomach. Having learned from experience, he didn't strike the man hard, letting the speed and impetus of his travel do the work instead, before twisting the spear quickly so it didn't lodge in the man's body. The man staggered backwards from the force as Baldor passed him, seeking his next quarry. Another Roman stepped in front of Baldor's mount, his sword raised to slash the horse's face. Baldor threw his fighting spear at him, the short distance saw the heavy weapon thud into his shield and the force push him back off balance, before he recovered, Baldor drew a falcata and cleaved his neck.

Most of his unit had broken through the cordon, the warriors sawing cruelly on their mount's bits, forcing the horses around, back at the scattered Romans. Baldor, being the furthest through the ring of men, found himself assailed by a handful of them. Throwing down his shield, he drew the second falcata while forcing his horse in a tight, fast circle, using its weight to scatter the swarming Romans as he chopped downwards with both blades. Everything became a blur. The Romans pushed aside else spun away as his horse's forequarters or rump hit them, his blades felling any who stepped close. Free of adversaries again, he looked about seeking Flaminius. Baldor's men had done their work well as very few Romans remained inside the cordon, though battle still raged on the edges of the now misshapen circle of Flaminius's bodyguard. A horseman forced past him, its rider kicking its flanks hard urging speed, Ducarius!

Baldor looked to where the man was headed and saw Flaminius, his white helmet crest swirling as he battled another horseman. Using his shield as a weapon, he stepped back from his adversary and backhanded the shield into the horse's face. The animal whinnied in pain, twisted its neck away and stumbled sideways, the rider losing his balance at the unexpected move and falling prey to Flaminius's gladius. As Baldor urged his mount forward, Ducarius, roaring his battle cry was already attacking Flaminius. Flaminius ducked under the wild thrust of Ducarius's spear and would no doubt have killed him as he rode past, if he'd not been distracted by Baldor bearing down on him. Baldor approached head on. Flaminius sidestepped, left then right trying to keep Baldor guessing as to which side of his mount he would go. However, with both Baldor's swords in play it mattered not which way Flaminius stepped and Baldor aimed straight for him.

Flaminius, seeing the sword in Baldor's left hand jumped to the right side of the horse at the last moment, seeing no shield he'd presumed Baldor's right hand empty. Instead, an upswept sword met him, battering his shield and knocking him down with the force. Baldor dug his knee into his mount's flank, forcing it tight about so he could close with Flaminius as he rose. The Roman though was a doughty fighter and instead of standing, rolled then scrambled away seeking space to stand and fight. Baldor pushed the horse after him, it whinnying as he forced it to sidestep, hoping to batter the man with the animal's flanks. Flaminius gave ground as Baldor attacked, his eyes glancing over his shield rim, the gladius to the side ready to stab. Baldor's horse whinnied loudly and he felt it shudder then falter. It took a step or two more then collapsed on its fore legs; lurching forward, he managed to jump clear as the animal fell on its side. Landing lightly on his feet he saw a javelin lodged in the animal's chest and another Roman closing on him quickly. Ducarius hurtled past him again heading for Flaminius.

Baldor turned to meet his new adversary. The man came on, eyes peering over his shield. Baldor stepped towards him, keen to finish the fight and return to Flaminius before Ducarius could slay him. Battle still swirled about them, however, as Flaminius's bodyguard had gone down under Baldor's cavalry attack, the heavy fighting was moving away to the left and right as the Carthaginians sought more to kill. In the immediate area now, there remained only Flaminius, Ducarius, Baldor and this last Roman. Baldor flexed his arms and swung his falcatas confidently inviting the Roman forward. The Roman came on bravely then stopped, his shield lowering a little.

"Baldor? Baldor Targa?" He shouted above the battle din.

Baldor stared at the man's eyes peering over the shield rim, his face still hidden. He glanced at the man's gladius and right wrist. Recognising a brass and copper twist bracelet his lips curled back into a snarl.

"You! … Cornelius!" He spat as he launched himself forward, both swords in play, one battering the shield the other engaging the defensively held gladius. Blades clanged and tinged while the other thudded dully against the wooden shield, Cornelius using it to push Baldor away as he bore down on him. Neither spoke. Baldor saving his breath as he'd been taught and trying to keep his anger in check as he'd been warned. Cornelius, under pressure from the determined onslaught too busy fending both blades away. The men fought forwards and backwards as advantage was gained then lost as the other counter attacked. The only sounds from the pair being grunts and gasps for breath. Baldor, still relatively fresh and unencumbered with the weight of a shield constantly pushed Cornelius making him use his to fend him off. Cornelius, having marched and previously embattled was tiring, the weight of the shield and the enforced, continual movement sapping his strength. Baldor sensed it and bore down harder.

Narrowly fending Baldor off again and pushing him away hard, Cornelius gasped from punished lungs.

"Baldor! For the love of Juno! … Enough!"

Baldor took advantage of the pause and distance, wiping the sweat off his face with his forearm then pointed the blade at Cornelius.

"This ends now, you bastard! … No more false words! No more treachery, only death!"

Spitting the words, hot as molten metal, he came at Cornelius again, both blades battering and hacking and despite good defence, Cornelius was forced to give ground. Back he went, a step at a time, the twin falcatas driving him off the road towards the grass verge and lake. His shield rim was chopped through and the face splitting under the repeated attack. Shards of painted wood flew off as Baldor hammered it relentlessly while holding Cornelius's attention with his other blade. Cornelius stepped back again, then lost his footing as he stumbled over a body. Baldor, taking quick advantage hooked the gladius from his hand with a twist of the falcata.

With his gladius gone, Cornelius stepped away seeking space and a moment, his chest heaving. Desperately scanning the ground for another weapon, he didn't see the sward edge and lost his footing and balance, falling backwards off the road onto the small beach. The drop was only a cubit but he landed heavily, his remaining breath knocked out of him. Hearing Baldor jump down onto the beach, he rolled away, trying to put distance between them but was inhibited by his shield. His boots scrabbled and slipped in the small stones as he tried desperately to regain his feet before Baldor closed on him. Baldor attacked him at the run hammering the shield with a herculean blow that broke it in two.

Cornelius stepped back again, his shield arm numb from the blows and he breathless, this time Baldor stumbled amongst the stones. Seizing the moment's respite Cornelius threw down the ruined shield and snatched for his dagger. The pair stared at one another, chests heaving as lungs sought precious air. Baldor's lip curled into a snarl as he hefted both falcatas and advanced. Cornelius, recognising his doom shouted desperately.

"Is this it, Baldor? Is this where it ends? You take back the life you gave!"

Baldor stopped, though he pushed one blade out in front of him and lifted the other behind his head parallel to his shoulders. His nerves on the raw, he screamed his response so hard his head hurt.

"You ask that! … Your father slew my friend! You … you, tried to slay me when all was done that day at the Trebbia!" Cornelius tried to answer but was shouted down. "You die now!"

Cornelius glanced to the lake only a pace or two away as if contemplating escape. Realising he'd no chance of swimming in his mail shirt he shrugged and threw the dagger down.

"Do what you will Baldor, though Jupiter knows, I bear you no malice." He dropped heavily to his knees and looked up as Baldor stepped closer; falcata raised. A prayer slipped quickly across his lips. "Juno, mother of us all, accept your son …"

"Fight you bastard!" Baldor threw a falcata down alongside Cornelius. "Stand up and fight!"

Cornelius just closed his eyes and carried on his prayers.

Baldor roared like a wounded bull and kicked Cornelius in the chest knocking him into the dirt. Groaning in agony as he rolled in the gravel, he slowly pulled himself onto his knees, coughing and gasping for breath.

"Get up and fight, damn you!" Baldor roared and kicked the falcata towards him again.

Cornelius ignored both the blade and Baldor. His hand, shaking a little, moved under his neckerchief and clasped the pendant hanging from his neck. His eyes took on a distant, vacant look. He smiled slightly; whispering something Baldor couldn't hear then raised the bauble to his lips.

Frustrated at the situation, his senses still heightened to battle fury and his temper frayed, Baldor felt his rationale snap and he stepped towards Cornelius.

"It ends now!" He shouted and raised his falcata high for the deathblow.

Chapter Twelve

Before Baldor could strike there was a deep grinding rumble like one mountain crashing into another and the earth shook. The ground moved beneath his feet and his vision lost focus as the near distance heaved and quivered as if aboard a storm-tossed ship. Quickly lowering his blade, he sought balance as the small stones vibrated and shifted like marbles beneath his boots.

The shaking stopped though a low rumble continued and he glanced about wondering if he was dreaming. Battle still raged unabated above him on the road, with no sign of a lull or that anyone had heard or felt anything except the chaos and noise of battle. Looking down the beach however, to where others had also carried the fight to the water's edge, he saw they too had halted. The combatants stood back from one another watching warily. Weapons still ready but the warriors bemused, heads casting around cockerel-like, as they listened and watched nervously. He looked down at Cornelius, who with eyes now wide open also stared about him.

The sound of water rushing over stones turned his head to the lake where he saw the water receding as if drawn back by the pull of a riptide. Back it went, dragging and peeling the gravel away with it, tearing it from the muddy bed as it receded, the noise like that of a giant bucket emptied of pebbles. Exposing the bed for some four-spear lengths, it left some small fish flipping and jumping amongst the black mud and weed. The air had the smell of rotten eggs; he hadn't noticed it before with the stink of battle strong in his nostrils. He stared at the water; it had stopped rolling back and now held itself, suspended, while it built and heightened like an ocean wave frozen in time before it breaks. It rose higher, reaching the height of a fighting spear then as the crest curled, fell forward with a crash that shook the earth again and sent the water hurtling back at the beach.

Quicker than the telling, the water thundered up the beach like a tidal wave, all white foam and tumbling power, carrying stones and rocks in its midst. Cornelius was swept off his knees and disappeared beneath the torrent; surfacing again, he was rolled and tossed in the surf like a broken doll. Baldor stepped back quickly but was defeated by the water's speed and knocked forcibly off his feet. Holding on grimly to his one falcata, he was tumbled over and over, the wild rush of the water loud in his ears, stones hitting him and his body scraped and battered hard along the stony beach. Deposited roughly at the edge of the water's power, he dragged himself slowly to his feet. Coughing and hawking water, he watched as it receded again, settling back to its normal level as if nothing had happened. Cornelius too had survived. Like Baldor, he was shaken and bashed bloody, with myriad cuts on his arms, legs and face. Seeing Baldor still armed and coming towards him, he took the initiative.

"See Baldor! See! … The Gods, the Fates, they don't wish us to kill one another!"

Baldor coughed and spat. "To Hades with the Gods and Fates! I care not what they wish!"

Suddenly and as if in response, the ground shook again, this time more violently than before. Baldor lost his balance and fell onto one knee but stood again quickly. Both men looked at the lake and though it shimmered like a nudged soup bowl, there was no greater movement. A loud reverberating rumble like distant thunder in the mountains sounded and the earth shook again.

"Are you sure Baldor Targa? … Are you?" Cornelius yelled.

This time Baldor was disconcerted, his battle fervour had cooled and he was shocked, physically and mentally. Unsure of what to think he just looked about. Wiping water and dirt from his eyes, he saw the battle along the road had not lessened in ferocity and the men on the beach ahead of him were fighting fiercely again. There were less of them standing than before with broken and dead bodies washed up and laid like debris all along the new, high waterline. The fight had moved back to the water's edge again and to where it seemed the Romans had tried to flee, bodies already thickly littering the shallows and staining the water red.

Had he imagined the shaking, the noise, and the water? Had he dreamed it? Had the Gods or the Fates intervened? Bemused and soaked to the skin, he saw Cornelius approaching. Snapping from his thoughts, he brought the falcata up into defence mode. Seeing Cornelius still unarmed and just looking at him he lowered the weapon. Both men stared at one another. Again, it was Cornelius who found his voice.

"The Fates have tied us together, Baldor! As if brothers from the same womb. Destiny is at play here, the Gods watching, playing with us even. How else do you explain that?" He pointed to the lake and then the mountains. "Are we not unlike Achilles and Hector before the walls of Troy, when Apollo came between them?"

Baldor stared at Cornelius. A long, searching look. Perhaps again seeing the soaked, half-drowned boy he'd rescued while both were children and which seemed an eternity ago now. The moment was broken when more legionaries spilled onto the beach a stade or so away, followed by Carthaginian cavalry who chased and hacked at them, killing many and chasing the rest into the lake and slaughtering them there.

Baldor snapped back to reality.

"I think you'd better go Cornelius, while you still can and before I change my mind."

Cornelius glanced about warily then backed slowly away, watching and listening.

"For what it's worth Baldor, I didn't plan or wish your death that day at the Trebbia. Those arrows were not my doing."

"Just go, Cornelius."

"It's important that you know Baldor, important to me!" Baldor looked away, disinterested. "Listen to me, damn you!" He shouted. Baldor turned and stared back at him. "I could not, cannot, wish you dead! Remember that! ... May your Gods bless you and keep you always, Baldor Targa."

Cornelius bowed his head quickly then turned to run. As he did so, Armaco appeared on the grass just above the beach his horse shying at the drop to the shingle below.

"Baldor! Baldor! ... For the love of Baal, man! Are you alright?"

Baldor just raised a hand in recognition and mute reply. Armaco, seeing Cornelius running kicked his horse on over the lip to the beach and after him, hefting his spear.

"Armaco! Leave him! Let him go." Baldor bawled.

Armaco reined up. "What the …?"

"Let him go … Just let him go, it's a long story."

Armaco snarled then shrugged. "Bastard won't get far anyhow, there's nowhere to run. We have them Baldor! Caught like rats in a trap and they're dying like flies!"

Baldor seemed to snap out of the trance like state he was in and came alongside Armaco grabbing hold of his mounts tack.

"Get us up onto the road Armaco. I need a horse and I need to find Flaminius."

Armaco began to reply but was shouted over as Baldor urged him back onto the road. Armaco growled but kicked the horse onwards, driving it back up over the ledge onto the road, Baldor holding and running alongside, the horse whinnying in protest at the climb.

The fighting had moved off, further up and down the road. The immediate area left thickly carpeted with bodies, horses, scattered weapons and a wagon with a dead mule in its traces. A few men still moved amongst the carnage, crawling or trying to sit up, gasping and weeping as their life force gave out. Some horses thrashed on the ground, trying to rise and whinnying pitifully. Others stood quietly else limped on injured legs. Blood pooled thickly, bright and stark against the grey road and the grassy sward. Severed limbs, guts and shit added to the carnage and the stink. High above, the first of the carrion birds glided lazily in wide circles.

Armaco reined in and Baldor cast his eyes over the slaughter. Both men taking a moment to catch their breaths.

"Did you see Flaminius? Is he down?" Baldor queried, as he continued to scan the dead.

"He's down alright! That's what I was trying to tell you. Ducarius killed the bastard and took his head."

"Damn it!" Baldor grimaced. "The General wanted him alive. Where's Ducarius?"

"I don't know, I think he turned back into the forest."

"But we have to report back to the General, he'll want to know all!"

Armaco shrugged. "You know these bloody Gauls! He'll be heading home to nail Flaminius's head above the door of his hut, else boiling it down to make a piss pot. Plunder or heads, it's all they're interested in … bloody barbarians!"

"I wouldn't let Andulas hear you say that!"

Armaco huffed and shrugged. "He's different; he's a cultured barbarian and my friend!" He grinned. "Anyway, what was that all about, down on the beach there?"

"Later. Come on, we'd best get back into the fight, there are still Romans to kill. Look, there's a spare horse over there."

Baldor caught the horse and picked up a spear and shield from the ground, the pair riding along the road to the edge of the fighting.

The battle was turning to massacre. The Romans, unable to form any cohesive defence being cut to pieces. Trained to fight in line and to protect one another they'd suffered terribly as the Carthaginians decimated their ranks; herding them like sheep to the slaughter. Small knots of resistance still fought on as legionaries stood back-to-back selling their lives as dearly as they could, no quarter offered and presently none being asked. Baldor and his troop could not close with the remaining Romans owing to the mass of warriors in front of them and could only watch as the Roman ranks thinned and died.

As the mist finally burned off with the mid-morning sun, the extent of the slaughter became apparent. As far as the eye could see, like some grim harvest, the ground was covered with dead, nearly all of which were Roman. The surprise and ferocity of the attack combined with the lack of space having had the desired effect. The fighting had moved to the foot of the hills below the Carthaginian camp and with a blare of trumpets their heavy infantry began advancing down to screen the camp and close the trap tighter. Seeing fresh troops advancing in good order and closing ranks to form a solid wall of shields, the legionaries seemed to take on a new desperate energy and the fighting intensified again. Similar to cornered rats who've recognised their demise, the Romans fought back like demons against the Libyan pikemen, trying to break their formation and for a while, the Carthaginian push stalled and even gave a little ground.

However, as the fear driven adrenalin waned, the legionaries, bone weary of a battle that had raged without respite since just after dawn began losing their ferocity. The forced march, surprise ambush and a morning of continued fighting was taking its toll and their resilience was fading. Exhausted men made mistakes and reacted too slowly while the Carthaginians, sensing victory and spurred on by bloodlust, hurled themselves back at the Romans. When the Carthaginian heavies joined the fight with a savage roar, men broke.

Some threw their weapons down calling at last for quarter. Others turned to the forest, deciding whatever lay in there was less frightening than thoughts of surrender or being caught between the pikemen and the heavy infantry to their front or the massed warriors to their rear. The first few broke towards the trees followed soon by an exodus of men clinging to faint hopes of escape and salvation. Seeing the Romans scattering, the Carthaginians turned on them with yet more vigour, giving chase and cutting down those who'd surrendered, desperate not to be cheated of the chance to slay them all.

In the forest, the Romans encountered the unbloodied reserves and were surprised again. Though their flight was checked for a while, desperation seemed to imbue them once more with almost superhuman strength and they burst through the reserve's lines, though not without further heavy casualties. Scattering like chaff on the wind and losing themselves amongst the trees and scrub, the Carthaginians raced after them, baying like hounds on the hunt.

Down on the road the legionaries that remained whole began throwing down their weapons and again seeking surrender. The killing however, as always, was not easy to stop and men were butchered where they stood while begging for quarter. Baldor, at the rear of the warrior mass turned his mount and troop about face, his stomach sickened.

"Andulas!"

"Yes sir!"

"Roll call please. Let me know the butcher's bill."

"Yes, sir." Andulas turned his mount and rode back down the column counting heads. He was back at Baldor's side very quickly causing Baldor some alarm. His face however creased into a smile.

"All present sir, a dozen lightly wounded and three that are sore hurt but will survive."

Baldor let out a sigh of relief.

"Are they able to ride or do they need help back to the orderly's tent?"

"No sir, they're mounted and following at the rear. If you wish to take us back to the General, I'll detail them off to the orderly, no point in dragging them along."

"Yes, of course Andulas, back to camp with them."

Baldor led his men back down the road to where he'd left Hannibal. It was slow going owing to the thousands of bodies littering the way and at which the horses shied, stepped over or walked around. With no great urgency now, Baldor didn't chafe at the progress and turned a blind eye as his warriors stopped to loot the dead of an espied precious object or weapon before remounting quickly and following on. They passed some prisoners being secured and herded and the first of the clearing parties stepping amongst the carnage, stabbing and thrusting here and there, as they dispatched wounded Romans. The first orderlies were arriving and moving about the dead and dying, seeking any injured Carthaginian that drew breath and needing help. Baldor noticed they didn't seem to be finding much work; a study of the field showed the majority of the casualties to be Roman. It seemed very much like a great victory for the 'Lions brood' and with what he could discern, at a small cost.

A commotion down at the lakeside drew his gaze. Numidian horsemen swam their mounts while stabbing spears at what looked like bobbing fishing net floats. A closer look found the floats to be Roman heads, the fleeing legionaries having run into the water in an attempt to escape only to realise it was too far to the other bank to swim, though some were trying. Most were just trying to stay afloat and out of reach of the laughing horsemen while calling for mercy. The pleas were ignored as the Numidians turned the slaughter into a game. Wagers being argued and placed amidst whoops of delight and laughter as they herded, chased down and stabbed at the swimming men. Some archers and slingers were also joining the sport and taking shots at the Roman swimmers furthest out from the shore. Bodies littered the beach hiding it from view, more floated in the shallows, drifting like discarded rubbish, bumping gently together and colouring the water darkest red.

Crows and ravens were arriving, drawn by the smell and sight of blood, alighting now to stalk around and onto the bodies of the slain. Charking their flat, baleful cry they squabbled and flapped at each other as if there was not enough feeding for all, Baldor noting grimly that presently there were more bodies than birds. Their pitiless, ebony eyes sought out the easy morsels of soft entrails, eyes and broken body parts; iron-grey beaks ripping and pulling at them with ruthless efficiency. High above the battlefield the kites circled, having followed the ravens they awaited their turn at the bloody feast.

The stink of body offal, emptied bowels and death was already strong and by late afternoon no doubt would become a cloying, nauseous stench, which in turn would bring wolves and wild dogs as the light faded. Men groaned and cried as Baldor passed, some calling for their mother or for water, others begging for death, some holding their hurt while coughing and spitting blood.

Baldor found Hannibal on the road and busy directing, ordering and organising men for various duties.

"Baldor! Praise be to Baal you've come through the fight and I pray unscathed?" His eyes swept over Baldor seeking wounds or damage.

"Thank you sir, I'm well. Superficial cuts and bruises is all, no real harm."

"Excellent! Your wellbeing adds lustre to our victory." Hannibal came to take Baldor's hand and shake it. Smiling, he looked past him into his troop his eyes searching. "Flaminius? Did you find him?"

Baldor began to answer but Hannibal interrupted. "I haven't seen Ducarius, did you send him back?"

Baldor's head dropped. "I'm sorry sir, Flaminius is dead. I tried to reach him; in fact, I did but was then engaged by another. When I sought him anew my men told me he was dead at Ducarius's hand and his head taken."

"And Ducarius?"

"Gone, I believe sir, along with the head, though I know not where."

Hannibal looked disappointed though only briefly. "It matters not, dead will do! You've survived the fight and we have a victory almost as great as the Trebbia. My thanks to you and your men, to all here. And to Baal Almighty for this day."

Baldor's men broke into cheers, which were quickly taken up by others; warriors rattled swords on shields and began chanting Hannibal's name.

That evening, citing weariness Baldor politely rejected Hannibal's invite to dinner with himself and his officers and turned down requests from Andulas and Armaco to attend the victory feast. Ignoring Aramco's lewd jibes regarding his woman interest, he sought his tent and peace, his mind full of the day's events and the strange scenario played out between Cornelius and himself. Having spoken to a number of his men just after the battle, he'd heard from some who'd also experienced the earth shake and heard the rumble. One or two had even seen the lake retreat and return. Most however, if heavily engaged in battle had heard and seen nothing, thinking like others that it was noise from cavalry. So, he wasn't imagining it. What he'd seen and felt did happen! Despite his lack of belief in the divine, he did wonder what was at play; was it the Fates? The Gods? The only thing he was sure of was; it was something he could neither explain nor understand.

Having rubbed down his mount, he made his way to his tent. Receiving a warm smile and a courteous bow from Sulis as she took his weapons and shield, he was surprised by the passionate hug from Lasairiona and somewhat moved when he felt her warm tears on his cheek. Kissing him fiercely, she disappeared back into the tent. Shrugging out of his blood-flecked armour, Sulis took it away for cleaning. Slumping into his chair, he gave a sigh of relief, his body aching and battered and his head full of thoughts. Sulis returned, along with a stool for his feet and a bowl of hot, rosewater and towels so he could wash. Lasairiona reappeared, composed and placing his wine jug on the table. After pouring his drink, they left him with the promise of dinner and a bath. After washing the dried blood from his face and hands, he relaxed into his chair, quietly contemplating his survival while trying to calm his battle fraught nerves. Sipping his promised 'one' jug of watered wine, he wondered in turn at his broken vow to slay Cornelius.

His musings were interrupted when Lasairiona called him to his bath. The women had secured a large wooden, horse trough, it now filled with steaming water and scented with oil, all no doubt looted from a Roman manor or farm. Alone with Lasairiona in his quarter of the tent and suddenly aware of his aches and sores, he surrendered willingly as she removed his boots and helped him out of his tunic and into the bath. Sighing contentedly, he sank into the warmth though flinching slightly as the hot water flowed into the deeper gashes and cuts on his arms and legs. Lasairiona laid a hot cloth over his eyes and scars that still striped his upper cheekbones, while the oil-scented steam relaxed him and induced sleep. She washed him from head to foot, examining the cuts from the battering at the beach and removing any dirt and grit. However, her careful ministrations in his groin area, purposely left until last, brought him back to wakefulness as his maleness stirred into life. Lasairiona, pretending indifference to his state proffered more wine, advising his dinner was ready when he was. Holding a towel in readiness, she was caught off guard when he gestured for a hand up, only to find herself pulled quickly into the bath alongside him. Shrieking in mock alarm she tumbled on top of him, water and wine splashing and slopping onto the floor as she was drawn into his embrace, his lips seeking hers, she by no means tardy in response.

****

Bomilcar yawned and ran his hand over the three-day stubble on his cheeks and jaw then stroked his goatee beard thoughtfully, his thin lips forming a smile.

"A good day Sakarbaal! Minimal casualties for us, the Romans broken and harried to the four winds and we've nearly a hundred prisoners to sell as slaves, the Gods have been kind." He chuckled and nudged Sakarbaal as he threw more wood on the fire then looked around for his Adjutant. "Ah, Milos, there you are, I trust that's good wine you're fetching this time and not some local peasant piss?"

"No, my Lord, though it's black as Hades my nose tells me this is a good wine."

"And like as not, I hazard your nose has been in it?"

"No, my Lord, I ..."

"Hah! You'll say anything but your prayers man! Bring it here and let us sample this Roman ambrosia. Did you hear me Sakarbaal?"

"Yes! ... Yes, a good day, Bomilcar." Sakarbaal said quietly over his wine cup.

Bomilcar sipped then smacked his lips appreciatively, drank some more and nodded to himself.

"Now! What ails you man? Why so morose?"

"Nothing, no! ..." When Bomilcar continued to look at him searchingly, Sakarbaal lowered his voice to a whisper. "Just today, the battle, it was harder than I thought, the noise, the smell. I swear I was close to vomiting."

"Ah! Your first battle?"

Sakarbaal cast furtive glances at others sitting close by, they thankfully lost in their own conversations and not hearing.

"Yes." He said in a hushed tone.

"It'll become easier, you'll harden to it and you fought well! You didn't shrink from the fight?"

Sakarbaal shivered beneath his blanket but managed to keep his voice steady.

"I tried to do my best. It's ... it's just I can't get the stink out of my nose."

"Killing can be a dirty business. Here, give your face a wipe." He threw a wet cloth to Sakarbaal. "There's still blood and Baal knows what mess on your chin and neck and there, on the top of your tunic." He pointed to show where. "It would I suppose, have been better to return to camp and wash the blood and sweat off and rest but I wish to be up and doing in the morning. Any Romans still in the area, and I guess there will still be plenty, will want to move quickly. They won't expect us this far from camp so we may catch them napping at first light, hence my decision to camp here in the woods. More prisoners to sell would be good!"

Sakarbaal finished the purposeful, almost agitated rubbing clean of his skin and tunic, nodded then drained his wine. He held a small bag of herbs to his nose and sniffed hard, his eyes once more staring absently into the fire. Bomilcar nudged him again, shaking him from his apathy and pouring more wine into his cup.

"Get that into you, then let's sleep, it's not long before dawn comes again." He gave a long yawn. "I know its summer but I've never known days so long!"

Sakarbaal pulled the blanket tighter around his shoulders and edged closer to the fire. It wasn't cold but with the sky hidden by the tree canopy and the forest itself black as a winter's night, the flickering yellow flames were a comfort and helped drive the day's demons away. Bomilcar swilled the last of his wine and made to rise, Sakarbaal however did not want to be alone so searched for a subject to keep the conversation going.

"That noise, that rumble today, like the mountains were hollow or breaking inside? And the ground shaking, did you feel it?"

Bomilcar nodded slowly. "I heard the noise; it was strange and nothing that I can say I recognise but the ground shaking? I thought that to be caused by the horses, there were hundreds of us!"

"But we weren't moving at speed, not like a great charge of horseflesh! That, I could perhaps understand?"

Bomilcar shrugged and stretched.

"I don't know Sakarbaal and right now I'm too tired to care. We're alive and well and growing richer by the day so let's forget about the noises and the battle and sleep. I'll see you at first light."

Rising and picking up his blankets Bomilcar turned from the fire seeking a sleeping spot. Sakarbaal however, his nerves still raw with memories of spraying blood, severed limbs, decapitated bodies and body offal, was far from tired and sought to talk further, anything was better than being alone in the darkness.

"Do you … do you think Targa will have survived the day? He was pushing forward towards the fighting when we saw him."

Bomilcar stopped and spun around at the mention of Baldor, his mouth twisting into a hateful snarl, his face catching the reflection of the fire glow. Turning into the lee of the flames, the glow was replaced by dark shadows that moved over his cheekbones, chin and brow like black paint. His eyes suddenly alight and smouldering in the darkness like fanned coals. He looked about the vicinity of the fire before answering, seeing no one close by the words came out cold and hard.

"I pray to Baal the bastard has!" Sakarbaal looked up quickly, his mouth gaping in surprise. "So, I can kill the baseborn, peasant myself!"

"But we agreed, we promised the General …"

"I know what we said and I don't care a jot for a promise made under duress. A promise such as that is no promise at all, what choice did we have? That or the cross? I'm going to kill Targa for me having to apologise in front of others!" His voice rose as his anger came to the fore; he checked himself dropping it to a harsh, thunderous whisper. "I apologise to no man, I'm a Lord of Carthage not some bastard, merchant's son or simple soldier to be told when and how to doff my cap! Targa will be entering Hades as soon as I see my chance." Sakarbaal didn't answer but just stared at Bomilcar. "Surely you must want him dead and gone? Vengeance for your brothers, pay back for your hurts?"

"I've given my word …"

"Then un-give it!" He hissed.

"I'm no longer sure I'm right in what I think? My second brother, though he died from Targa's hand did not blame him nor did the Court find him guilty."

"Courts can be bought!"

"What!"

"Surely you're not so innocent to think justice always prevails?"

Seeing the shocked look on Sakarbaal's face told Bomilcar that was exactly what he believed.

Sakarbaal changed tack, his voice despondent.

"He could've killed me if he'd wanted to, that day when I attacked him. He had the right; he was defending himself. Baal knows I did my best but he was faster, surer than I, in a different class, a far better warrior …"

"Till I make him a dead one!" Bomilcar spat the words. "Think as you wish Sakarbaal but I'll have my honour back when I send him to Hades. I'll finish what I began; that upstart whelp won't see the end of this campaign alive."

"I want no more trouble with Targa, Bomilcar I'm here to fight for my city and that's sufficient, Baal knows I'm finding that hard enough!"

"Very well then, I'll deal with it. Seeing as you lack the backbone."

Sakarbaal's eyes flashed in the firelight as he raised his head to stare at Bomilcar, his brow creasing into a scowl, his eyes narrowing.

"It's no good casting me filthy looks, you may be able to forgive and forget but I won't."

"It's not that! I didn't say I forgave or that I'll forget." Sakarbaal snapped.

"Keep your damned voice down!" Bomilcar growled as two warriors passed close by, blankets in their hands. "Well, you won't mind when I kill him then."

"I think we should leave it; the Romans may do it for us anyway and that way we can't be implicated!"

"I don't want the Romans to do it! I want my …"

"For Baal's sake, Bomilcar!"

"Don't raise your voice to me boy!"

"Boy!" Sakarbaal jumped up dropping the blanket, his shattered nerves releasing his temper, his hand reaching for his sword hilt.

Bomilcar however was too fast for him and as one hand slapped Sakarbaal's away from the hilt the other back handed him hard across the throat. Sakarbaal instinctively reached for his throat and lowered his head as he gagged and gasped for breath. Bomilcar pushed him backwards over the log he'd been resting against a moment before. Stepping over the log and the sprawling Sakarbaal, he fastened a vice-like hand around his windpipe.

"Don't ever come that tone with me, boy! And if you try to take a blade to me again, I'll kill you! Do you hear me?" His hand tightened further as he spat the words.

Sakarbaal's mouth opened and closed like a landed fish but no sound came out. When he managed a perfunctory nod, Bomilcar finally let him go.

"Now! Get out of my sight, boy!"

Sakarbaal struggled to his hands and knees, his breath laboured and noisy between harsh gasps and coughs. Pulling himself to his feet, he picked up his blanket and slunk off into the darkness.

Chapter Thirteen

Cornelius eased the window shutter slowly ajar and scanned the fields and forest's edge below the village. Looking into the blue shadows of dusk his strained and weary eyes darted from forest edge to the hill, to valley and the plain beyond then back to the trees seeking any movement, anything that might betray Carthaginian cavalry still in pursuit. Seeing nothing, he stood back from the window and removed his helmet. He cuffed sweat and caked dirt from his face, flinching as his hand scraped over raw, bloodied skin. He sneezed for the umpteenth time since entering the stable, the movement of his men having stirred up the straw dust, which now floated and danced in the lamplight. He sniffed hard to clear his nose, the smell of the dry, fresh straw strong in his nostrils. With no relief, he blocked one nostril then blew hard, doing the same for the other, using the back of his arm to wipe his nose, removing his neck cloth he dabbed his eyes as the salty sweat stung them causing him to squint.

Pursued from the lake, he and the men around him had ran and skirmished all afternoon and into the early evening to evade the Carthaginian cavalry who'd chased them down like hunted deer. Having seen men slaughtered as they ran with no quarter given, else dying from wounds or exhaustion as they fled; he too was approaching breaking point. A slight tremor in his hands and an occasional quiver in his voice betrayed the steely resolve he endeavoured to portray for the sake of his men. The physical exertion and light wounds he'd suffered he knew he'd recover from. The horrors he'd experienced he felt he could manage and in time perhaps forget but the nagging doubts haunting him, adding mental torture to his exhausted body asked the questions; why would no one listen? Will no one ever learn that Hannibal will never be conventional or predictable? Shaking his head and chewing hard at his lip, he took another long drink.

The rough, local wine they'd found in one of the house cellars was harsh but potent and he felt his body ease a little as he drank. With the edge off his nerves, he decided enough was enough and he firmly stoppered the pitcher placing it to one side, reasoning he was going to need wakefulness and his wits to find a way clear back to Rome. He was almost oblivious now to the whimpers and gasps emitted by the wounded men scattered on the straw, makeshift beds and floor of the stable that now passed for a field hospital. Taking shelter in this small hamlet on a hill, a would-be haven come refuge, only the strongest and fittest or perhaps luckiest men remained whole, making for a mixed collection of legionaries, unhorsed cavalrymen and Velites. Settling himself on a pile of woolsacks and picking at the bread and cheese he'd found in one of the house larders, he heard an Optio calling him as he entered the stable.

"Here, Optio. Report?"

"All's quiet sir. There's no sign anywhere of Carthaginian cavalry now. As you can see, dusk is falling and I hazard a guess they'll be seeking their camp and victuals."

"Aye, I think you've the rights of it." He replied, his tone bitter. "It seems the coming darkness is the only thing that'll halt their bloodlust. How many men do we have, Optio?"

"Around seventy able-bodied, sir. These, plus the injured make for around ninety men sir, though I've seen others heading this way."

"Others?"

"Aye sir! I saw them from the house roof. Three small parties exiting the woods, mostly Triari I think?"

"I didn't see anyone?"

"You wouldn't from here sir, they're coming in from the north."

"From the north! How in Jupiter's name have they ended up northwards?"

"The Gods alone know sir, though when we broke and scattered, I guess men went any which way they could. And it's the direction the Carthaginians are least likely to look."

Cornelius nodded. "How many men, Optio? ... Approximately?"

"I would say each party is close to century strength, sir or thereabouts?"

For the first time since leaving the battlefield, Cornelius felt a surge of hope. They were still in dire trouble but with greater numbers, their chances against enemy cavalry patrols were improving.

"Anyone of higher rank than me, Optio?" He asked hopefully, wishing to have the burden of command lifted from him.

"There's a Centurion with one of the parties sir but that's all! ... Oh! Sorry sir, no disrespect sir!"

Cornelius waved the comment away and clasped the Optio on the shoulder. "Bring them here as they arrive, let's see what our strength totals then, we can plan from there."

"Yes sir."

While he waited, Cornelius walked amongst the wounded, helping with bandages, slings and supports making men as comfortable as possible. The seriously wounded had died in the forest along the way, these men, though badly hurt were not so much bleeding heavily as suffering from broken bones, dislocations and painful but staunched wounds and utter exhaustion. He'd ensured all had received water, and what food was obtainable had been shared around all. His head was full of what to do next.

The door creaked open and the Optio stepped in followed by a Centurion. Cornelius's face lit up.

"Gaius?" Cornelius looked anxiously past the dried blood spatters, dirt and sweat on the man's face. "Gaius! Thank the Gods! You're unhurt?"

"Aye, it's not my blood." He gestured to the blood encrusted mail shirt, and then wiped his face with a brown stained hand. "Jupiter knows it was a close-run thing though, they're formidable, I'll warrant! And yourself, lad?"

"I'm fine ... thank you." However, the tone of his voice said otherwise. "As you say, a close-run thing." As the pair stepped forward amidst hand shaking and backslapping, he cast Gaius a pensive look that said, there's more to it.

"What have we got, Cornelius? How many men? What state?" Gaius signalled to those behind him to settle in and eat, then let Cornelius steer him to a quiet corner. As the pair sat, Cornelius offered food and drink.

"I'll take another drink Cornelius but we ate as we ran, we may have taken a damned beating but I refuse to fight or die on an empty stomach." He managed a smile then pushed his head closer as Cornelius beckoned and lowered his voice to speak.

"I've seventy able-bodied men and around twenty wounded, the wounded can march and fight to some degree. I think we should keep moving now darkness has fallen, it'll give us a head start before the Carthaginian cavalry come hunting us in the morning."

Gaius swallowed the watered wine and smacked his lips appreciatively as if it was nectar, then replied in low tones.

"Have you a local who can guide us?"

"No … no, the village was deserted when we arrived, they'd have heard and seen the fallout from the battle and fled. I can't say I blame them; we could have easily been Carthaginian warriors converging on them."

Gaius swallowed then belched. "What you say about moving makes good sense but without a guide we could easily become lost. I estimate we've come some twelve maybe fifteen miles from the battle and most of that distance was spent fighting as we went. I hate to say it Cornelius, but I think the men need some time to rest and then march at first light."

Cornelius's heart sank a little, if Gaius deemed the men needed rest, things must be bad. As if sensing the others concern's, Gaius continued.

"We could waste time and precious energy blundering in the dark. Let the lads rest then we can be up and away at cockcrow. The Carthaginians will be back at camp and even if they leave at first light, we'll still have a head start. With time and daylight lad, we can give them a bloody nose if they come calling! What think ye?" He managed another smile as he finished. Cornelius nodded though he didn't seem convinced, Gaius continued. "There's also a chance more men will come in through the night, with a stretched-out battle like that, men will be scattered everywhere. The more strength we have, the harder target we become and believe me, victorious warriors are tender of their skin straight after a fight and will seek softer targets not well-armed, well-disciplined ones, which is what we'll be in the morning."

Cornelius smiled at last. Gaius drained his cup and rose. "Come on, grab your stick and we'll settle the lads and check the sentries, then snatch some sleep."

Cornelius's face fell at the mention of the vine stick, his Centurion's badge of office.

"I've lost it Gaius, either in battle or in the lake … I'm sorry, I …"

Gaius's face betrayed that which he managed to hold back from saying regarding the disgrace of losing the stick, the hesitation was not lost on Cornelius. He went to speak again but Gaius cut him short.

"There's more than that been lost on this field, lad. In the scheme of things, it pales to insignificance. Come on!"

As Cornelius tried to speak, Gaius shushed him and steered him towards the door.

The pair conducted weapons checks, settled the men and inspected the sentries. Their spirits rose as more small groups of men came in, most of which were again Triari, who perhaps being heavier armed and more experienced had fared better?

Making their way to settle and rest, Gaius sensed a hesitation or a concern from Cornelius, more than just the frayed and weary nerves from battle. Steering him to a quiet corner of the stable block, he picked up an oil lamp and a small bench, lifting them into an empty stall gesturing Cornelius to sit. There was a strong smell of straw, horses and leather but the straw floor covering was clean and thick as if just changed. The lamp lit most of the stall but left the bench in shadow. Gaius poured another cup of wine. Pushing it into Cornelius's hand, he glanced back down the stable ensuring no one was near before pulling the stall door to, leaving it ajar so he could see if anyone approached. The bench rocked and creaked as he sat alongside his friend, keeping his voice low, he asked.

"How bad was it, Cornelius? Do you want to talk about it or just forget it?"

A long silence followed, Cornelius fidgeted with the cup and shuffled his feet, staring into the corner of the stall. His mouth opened then closed again, his eyes closed then opened wide, his brow furrowed as he grimaced. Just as Gaius was about to prompt, Cornelius sipped the wine and cleared his throat.

"He was there Gaius, Baldor Targa!"

"You saw him?"

"I fought him!"

"What! All those men, a battle strung out for miles and the pair of you cross paths again! For the love of Venus! What's going on?"

"Aye, what were the chances of it?"

"Did you kill the bastard?"

"No ... no!" Shaking his head gently he lowered his tone, a sad smile playing on his lips. "Jupiter knows I tried or rather, tried to stop him killing me!" He swallowed hard.

"And?"

"I thought I was a dead man, Gaius." He paused as emotion stole his words. "I ran into him while he was trying to kill Flaminius and …"

"And?"

"We fought tooth and nail across the road …" Cornelius paused again as the words caught in his throat.

"And!" Gaius snapped.

Cornelius flinched at the tone and Gaius lowered his voice. "Pardon me lad, go on."

Cornelius's voice was low and raspy as he began again. "He's terrifyingly good with those twin swords of his. He came on as … I imagine, Achilles would? His attack was faultless and …" Gaius waited as Cornelius stared blankly into the darkness. "And try, try as I might, I couldn't hold him. He chopped my shield to matchwood then hooked the gladius from my hand …"

"Go on lad."

"I stumbled off the road onto the beach by the lakeside, he threw me one of his swords and bade me fight some more …"

"Cocky bastard!"

Cornelius seemed to sink on the bench, his features morose his voice a low whisper. "Maybe, Gaius but he is that good. In truth, I'd had enough, he'd fought me to a standstill and I knew … I knew I couldn't beat him."

Gaius was about to interrupt again but held his peace as he saw Cornelius wilt and his eyes mist.

"To my shame I gave up … I thought my end had come. I fell to my knees and my prayers. He seemed hesitant to strike because I was unarmed but I told him … have done! Finish it!"

Cornelius clamped his hand over his mouth stifling a cry as a tear slipped down his face; his body quivered as he wrestled his emotions. Gaius placed a hand firmly over Cornelius's forearm, his other arm slipping over his shoulder gripping him tightly and pulling him close. He spoke quietly. "Come on lad, let's have it all out, eh?"

Cornelius wiped his eyes, sniffed hard and cleared his throat.

"He hesitated again … but then, as if needs must, he raised his sword, I … I saw the anger and hate … I. Mother of the Gods, I thought my end had come!" His tears fell profusely and he lowered his head, his breath coming out in stilted gasps. He took a moment and cleared his throat then firmed his voice. "Then … just as he was about to kill me, the earth rumbled and shook." Gaius furrowed his brow as if lost. "Did you not hear it? Feel it?"

"I heard a rumble and felt the ground shudder but I thought it was their damned cavalry, there were hundreds of them milling about."

"No Gaius, it wasn't cavalry."

"But …"

"No, the earth shook and the lake water drew back …"

"The lake drew back?"

"Yes, like a falling tide only very fast. It drew back, exposing the bed and forming a wave that built like those off an ocean beach, then came thundering back up the shore knocking both of us off our feet. We and others fighting on the beach were dashed along the ground by the torrent." Gaius's eyes went wide and he went to speak but Cornelius carried on as if to rid himself of the tale. "After the wave swept us along the beach the water receded again and then went back to normal. And there he was, battered and wet as I but still armed and coming to finish what he'd begun."

Gaius shook his head in dismay.

"Then the earth shook again and the mountains seemed to rumble as if hollow. It gave him pause; it was uncanny, eerie! I asked him then. Was he so sure he was to kill me?"

"And … what then, lad?"

"He lowered his sword and told me to go. Go while I could and before he changed his mind. He even called one of his men off when he sought to ride me down as I ran. I don't know what to make of it all, Gaius. I do wonder, is it …?"

"The Gods intervening, playing!" Gaius finished for him. "What else could it be?" His eyes wide and head shaking in disbelief.

"Like Apollo coming between Achilles and Hector when they fought before the walls of Troy? The co-incidences, Gaius there are so many!"

"Jupiter Almighty lad! You know me not to be superstitious or a believer in portents but …"

"I'm sorry I wasn't braver, I should have fought on, I …" He blurted, his voice dry and raspy, his body shaking, the tears falling again.

Seeing Cornelius still struggling with his emotions, Gaius pushed the wine cup to his lips bidding him drink.

"Hush lad!" He said quietly but kindly. "You fought and I've no doubt, fought bravely. You'd do the very best you could, that I know. You asked no quarter, that's brave enough for me." He smiled; trying to lighten the conversation then punched Cornelius on the shoulder in rough camaraderie. "You and this Targa are making it an interesting war!"

The Romans passed the night without disturbance, exhaustion masking the horrors of the day and allowing for much needed rest and sleep. Before dawn broke, men were awake and preparing for the march. Still tired, aching and sore but with food and drink in their bellies, and strengthening numbers, they stood a greater chance of survival should they encounter Carthaginian cavalry again. Just as Gaius had forecast, more survivors had slipped into the village overnight, arriving in small groups and taking the combined total to just over four hundred men.

The assembling column assumed tight formation and was readying to move off with lighter troops in the lead, the injured in the centre and the heavier Triari bringing up the rear.

"Slight change to the usual order of march, Cornelius. You take the lead and as discussed push southwest. I've scattered three Optios through the column and I'll bring up the rear. If we're going to be hit, it'll likely come from behind, I reckon the Triari will make for a good rearguard and give the bastards pause. However, they may ride around us and come for the rest of you? If they do, you've only two choices. If there's cover nearby; trees, rocks anything that'll break them up and you can reach before they close on you, use it! If you're caught out in the open …"

"Close ranks, sir. Form square."

"That's it, lad! If they've bypassed us, we can then close on them and support you. As long as we don't panic and we work as a team, we can get out of this. Questions?"

"None sir. I'm just waiting on the last scout coming back, the rest are all in with nothing to report."

"Which way did he go?"

"Southwest, sir."

Gaius chewed his lip and glanced at the brightening sky. "H'mm, our route and the safest methinks. I call that we move off anyway. We can't dally, dawn's coming quickly and we should be moving."

Cornelius looked a little doubtful. "Shouldn't we wait till he comes in, sir?"

"Usually, yes. But let's take a gamble lad, it's the safest route and we need to be gone, agreed?"

"Agreed sir." Cornelius was also desperate to be moving, anything was better than waiting; he felt every pace south-westward gave them a better chance of survival. Gaius offered his hand and Cornelius shook it.

"Lead on lad."

Cornelius led the column out across the open fields outside the village. The sun rising behind them chased the last of the shadows, the brightness lifting the men's spirits a little, they too, happier to be on the move. However, the column's rear was not clear of the village when trouble came. The missing scout burst out of the treeline a mile or so away, running hard and stumbling as he came, casting furtive glances over his shoulder to the forest behind. An Optio saw him first and sent word to Cornelius. The scout also saw the column and began shouting and waving his arms then pointing behind him. His shouts were incoherent but his speed and meaning were clear enough.

Supressing his fear, Cornelius bellowed for the men to halt. Seeing most of the column was still within the village, he called an about turn.

With shouted commands having to suffice in the absence of a trumpeter and his right hand drawing fast circles in the air, he dispatched a runner back to Gaius who was still ensconced in the village with most of the column and rearguard.

As the column manoeuvred, Bodeshmun's cavalry were spilling from the treeline and racing across the meadow towards it.

"Juno, mother of all, help us!" Cornelius muttered, his heart pounding, his skin all of a prickle as he heard the frenzied whoops and yells of the horsemen. He gauged the speed of the oncoming cavalry and distance back to the village; the legionaries were going to lose the race! Seeing the scout speared as he ran, he called fresh orders.

"Outer ranks! Shields up!" Drawing his gladius, he trotted along the column as the men hefted their shields. "Keep moving, keep moving! Stay together! Shields up! We fight as we go! Hold the formation!"

The cavalry were almost upon them and some javelins began to fall, clattering and thumping into shield faces. An uncoordinated and ragged volley of pila answered and a few mounts went down or riderless, then the cavalry were alongside. Men shouted a mixture of battle cries and screams of fear while horses whickered and shied from the big shields thrust at them. Legionaries died as spears stabbed over shield rims else found gaps as the jogging ranks inadvertently opened up, their bodies targets for the probing spears. Men stumbled and fell to be trampled by their comrades as the column kept up its fighting retreat. The cavalry didn't have it all their own way, the legionaries speared, tripped or hacked at the horses, killing them and unseating their riders, else dragged the riders to the ground to be butchered when they ventured too close.

Some Velites, unused to fighting cavalry at close quarters, panicked and peeled away from the column hoping to make the safety of the village. A few became a handful, which became a mob. Cornelius shouted himself hoarse trying to maintain order, even beating some of the fleeing men back into line with the flat of his gladius in a bid to keep them together. An Optio stepped alongside, bravely dropping his shield and holding his staff like a barrier as though heading off frightened sheep. Seeing authority, the panic slowed, men closing up once more and turning back on their attackers. Then the Optio went down with a spear through his chest as a horseman cantered past, the spear bursting out of his back such was the force of the thrust. Cornelius, recovering his balance from the horseman's drive, stepped alongside and catching the man on his shielded side, forced his gladius under it, the point puncturing the leather armour and entering below his ribs. Twisting the blade quickly as he'd been taught, he turned back to his men as the man crumpled and fell from the careering horse.

However, the tentative rally was undone and panic ensued as the column began to disintegrate, the swirling cavalry forcing into gaps shattering it and wreaking havoc. As the Velites tried to flee, veterans bellowed to 'stand and fight' while the horsemen whooped as they slaughtered. Panic became terror as men fell or slipped on the blood-slicked grass, knocking others over as they tried to step clear of the horses and swords of the riders, blood sprayed like warm summer rain dappling horses and men.

Cornelius had no shield and as the formation shattered, he sheathed his gladius and snatched up a fallen spear pushing in alongside a small group who'd had the sense and guts to stay together. The men shuffled their way back towards the village; spears protruding like hedgehog spikes keeping the horsemen away. The bodies of the Velites and those who'd ran littered the grassy hill.

The outer buildings of the village helped save the column as the road funnelled between houses offering cover for the Romans and obstacles to the horsemen. Having to ride around houses, walls, drainage ditches and swiftly overturned carts, forced the Carthaginians into small groups, slowing their momentum and breaking up the attack. Gaius and the rear of the column had already assumed defensive positions, he dashing from group to group organising and reinforcing where he saw the need. Men grew braver now they had cover and dodged around obstructions circling and mobbing the separated cavalrymen like dogs bringing down wild boar. Horses were tripped and speared in the narrow lanes; the fighting vicious as men and animals came close. Horses stomped and reared, wild-eyed in fear. Men fought hand to hand, spears replaced by swords, daggers and fists. Blood sprayed house walls and slicked the cobbles, bodies littering the road and filling gutters. The stench of blood, opened bowels and body offal overpowering in the tight space.

As the fighting turned to stalemate, a long wailing drone from a war horn sounded the recall and the horsemen looked to extricate themselves from the killing zone.

Chapter Fourteen

The morning following the battle at the lake saw Baldor's troop placed under overall command of General Maharbal and dispatched in great force to seek out Roman survivors. The body count on the field totalled some two thousand five hundred Carthaginian dead with many wounded amongst the lighter armoured troops. However, with fifteen thousand Roman dead by comparison including the Consul, his Legates, Tribunes and many Centurions and Optios, it was deemed a great victory at light cost. The remainder of the Romans to be hunted down, slain or taken prisoner, it mattered not which. The prisoners already taken amounted to thousands, many of which were auxiliaries. These, being non-Roman, Hannibal dismissed to their homes saying he'd no argument with them, only the 'would be mistress' of all, Rome. The Roman citizens however, he would sell into slavery.

With the infantry left scouring the field for weapons, armour and booty and the unenviable task of disposing of the dead, the cavalry fanned out in all directions seeking survivors. The trails were easy to follow with bodies marking the way, strewn thickly to begin with as the badly wounded expired quickly from fighting at the run. The bodies thinning out as the distance from the battle grew and the lightly injured or stronger men continued to make their escape. Occasionally they encountered a large number of dead, usually in a clearing where the fleeing men had been caught in the open. Having sensed escape and hope, only to see it dashed, the fighting had been particularly fierce as the Romans made a last stand against their pursuers. Here the Carthaginian losses seemed heavier as Roman desperation fuelled savagery. Despite the casualties and the heaped bodies of both men and horses there was no sign of any Romans surviving, only hoof prints being found leaving the scene, off to hunt down more sons of the 'she wolf.'

Seeking dead legionaries and blood trails as waymarkers the searchers followed the signs of human carnage. Stepping their mounts around and through the slaughter, they encountered and scattered packs of wild dogs, these seemingly brave enough to venture out in daylight for the easy pickings. Huge flocks of carrion birds soared skyward at the horses' approach, squawking and charking in bitter protest, leaving their feast only at the last moment to circle tight and low, alighting once more as the horses passed by. The incessant buzz of flies accompanied the riders everywhere, billowing in thick black clouds like a desert sandstorm mobbing the living as well as the dead. The sickening stench of rot was already rising from the bodies beginning to bloat in the fierce summer heat, forcing men to fasten scarves over their noses and mouths.

The mist, like the previous day, burned off in the mid-morning sun making tracking the retreating Romans easier. With visibility improving, Maharbal split his cavalry regiments into smaller groups and sent them in different directions, the order however being to stay in good numbers, a minimum of two companies being the requirement. Though the Romans had fled, it was estimated some thousands were still at large and armed, though no doubt scattered in all directions. Balaam reined in alongside Baldor. His arm outstretched in greeting.

"Hail Captain, will you ride with us?"

Baldor smiled and shook the proffered hand. "Yes Captain, we will, and gladly!" He bowed his head raising his fist in salute to Harbro and Malo riding just behind Balaam. "Brothers! It's good to see you both and hale I see; the Gods be thanked."

"It's good to be seen." Quipped Harbro. "The alternative has little appeal!" He laughed heartily and pushed his mount toward Baldor. "Baal bless you lad, it's good to see you well too ... and doing well!" He gestured to Baldor's men. "You're a bloody miss though."

When Baldor looked quizzical, Harbro continued, albeit lower voiced. "With you promoted and gone the Captain gives me and Malo all the grief instead!"

Baldor laughed and Malo smiled, bowing his head in salute. The Nubian as always said little, though Baldor trusted and knew him to be as sincere as any of his old troop comrades.

"Captain! Hypolokhagos; Harbro and Malo. Allow me to present my Hypolokhagos' Armaco and Andulas."

The pair pushed their mounts forward exchanging handshakes. Armaco and Balaam, being formerly acquainted, managing to joke albeit in lower tones but within Baldor's earshot, about keeping boy's aright in matters military. Baldor taking all with good grace.

"All right! Before we start swapping spit, we've Romans to find, we'd best get to it!" Balaam snapped. Assuming overall command, he led off. Baldor looked to Harbro and smiled as they fell in alongside each other. Harbro chuckled lightly when Baldor muttered.

"Nothing changes I see!"

"No lad! Not with him. He's good though, knows his business, you know that! Bear with him if you will, though you both now carry the same rank, he's worth a listen."

"No argument there, friend. Life's hopefully teaching me humility and respect as well as cooling some of that hot temper of mine!"

"Not too much though Baldor, I owe my life to your temper." He smiled. "I won't forget that day in the forest in Spain. You gave all you had; you risked all, especially your life."

"I was glad to do it, though I doubt I would have succeeded without Malo's help, he slew many with his bow."

"Aye, true enough but it was you who took action, on your own and before all, when no others would move. Now it's our turn to watch your back, so ride up front and keep an eye on that old dog …. Captain, sir." Harbro smiled as he flicked his head towards Balaam and slapped the rump of Baldor's mount, driving it forward.

The company pushed on without incident, the legionaries they encountered laying down their weapons. Baldor having them roped together and escorted back to camp by a handful of warriors. Similar scenarios repeated throughout the afternoon. The Romans, with battle madness cooled and with hope of life, seemingly content to surrender without a fight. These too were escorted back, though at the cost of warriors from the cavalry troops.

All was progressing well, with no hard riding or fighting until the first scout galloped back advising of a sizeable village ahead and from which was coming sounds of heavy fighting. Balaam and Baldor called their men to order while dispatching Armaco forward with the scout to ascertain who was fighting and in what numbers. The mood in the column changed dramatically as men sensed battle once more and weapons checks began in earnest.

Balaam called a halt and moved the men into the trees while awaiting the scout's return. The warriors were silent, eyes watching frontwards only the odd snorting or shake of the head from the horses and the slow drone of flying insects disturbed the quiet. At the sound of approaching horses men's ears pricked up, then Armaco and the scout drew rein in front of Balaam and Baldor.

"Report!" Balaam snapped.

"The village is some ten stades' ahead sir. Battle is joined …"

"Aye! But who man? How many? Baal Almighty, must I look for myself?"

"From what we saw sir, maybe two or three centuries of legionaries. Mainly Triari by the looks of them, still well armed and disciplined. They're fighting off cavalry in similar strength to us. Our men are faring worst; it's no place for cavalry, there's no space. Many horses are down; the fighting's heavy."

"No infantry for support?"

"Not that I can see sir."

Balaam digested the information, his mouth twitching between chewing his lip and snarling. "Baal Almighty! What kind of fool attacks a defended village with cavalry and no infantry support? Have they lost use of their wits?"

"They keep withdrawing, reforming and attacking again sir. They're probing on all sides of the village."

"Maybe! But without infantry they're pissing in the wind!" What do you think Baldor? How …"

"Sir, there's more …"

Balaam turned back, as this time it was Armaco who spoke.

"Go on."

"The cavalry are led by Bodeshmun and Samilcar, I saw Bodeshmun's banner, a silver horse on a red field."

Balaam hooted and looked at Baldor. Who said nothing but looked thoughtful.

"That's the bastards that attacked you, isn't it?"

Baldor nodded.

"Hah! There's divine retribution then. Pompous, puffed up, city arsewipes! Leave them to the Romans, why risk our necks for the likes of them? Give them and the Romans time to slaughter one another and then we'll mop up what's left."

"What about their men though? Do they deserve to die for their commander's foolishness?"

Balaam shrugged and grimaced. "Your decision then, Baldor? I tell you though, if it was me they'd wronged, I'd leave the bastards to the Romans."

Baldor nodded slowly. "Aye, it's true, I owe them nothing but ill will and blood but ..."

"But your honour's getting in the way of your common sense?"

Baldor whipped his head around a rebuke forming. "Steady Captain." Balaam cut in before Baldor could speak. He smirked and raised a placating hand. "No insult intended; I just know you remember? I'm not saying you're wrong but would they do it for you? For us? With the hatred they seem to bear you?"

Baldor shook his head slowly and sighed. "I doubt it very much, Captain."

Balaam shrugged. "There's your answer then."

"But I'm not them!" He said quietly. "I'll not stoop so low. I care not one jot for them ... but their men; I cannot leave them and keep clear conscience."

Balaam swatted casually at a fly. "Think on, Baldor. The Romans are entrenched and may outnumber us; we're guessing at numbers, there could be more of them in the village. We're down eighty men after those we've sent back with prisoners and if the fighting's to be hand to hand with us dismounted, mayhap?" Balaam hawked and spat, wiping a gloved hand over his beard. "Not good odds, lad and they have the advantage."

Balaam looked intently at Baldor, whose emotions played across his features as he wrestled his conscience and thoughts.

"I need to see this for myself."

When Baldor swung his shield from his back, Balaam turned to his men and rapped orders.

"Stand to!"

Horses bridled and stamped as men hefted shields and spears.

"Captain!" Balaam turned as Baldor placed a cautionary hand on his forearm. "This is my conscience, my choice. What you say is correct, I owe them nothing. If you don't think this right, hold your men here."

"What? Stand by, while you fight! I don't think so! I care not a fig for those men down there but you and yours, that's different. I made you boy! I'll be damned if I'll see you lost now! Gestix wouldn't like it!" He waved the column on.

Baldor smiled at the sentiment then had to kick his mount after Balaam to catch him.

Covering the distance to the village quickly, the cavalry halted again inside the treeline on a hill overlooking the valley and the village on the opposite hill. Shouts and the clash of arms could be heard in the distance. The horses stepped and stomped the forest floor as they sensed men's tension, the riders trying to settle them while staring into the distance trying to ascertain how the situation was unfolding. Another scout appeared, this time pointing to the edge of an adjacent wooded hill and advising he'd found a small group of wounded warriors from Bodeshmun's troop.

Balaam flicked his head at Baldor and both turned their mounts back through the trees. Exiting onto the hill but below the ridgeline, they led their men to the wood the scout had indicated. Halting the men back in the trees, Baldor and Balaam dismounted and walked into the rear of the wounded men's camp. Most were laid down else propped against trees for support, it was quiet but for low moans and whimpers, an orderly and his assistant moved between the men bandaging wounds and strapping limbs.

"Who's in charge here?" Balaam growled.

Men looked up in fright until they recognised Carthaginian garb.

"That'll be me sir." A man spoke quietly. "Hypolokhagos, Baraak Saldaar."

Using a tree trunk as support, he struggled to his feet. Holding one arm across bandaged ribs, he dipped his head by way of salute. With one knee bandaged and his leg splinted, he stumbled slightly as he sought his balance.

"Captain Balaam and this is Captain Targa." Balaam announced curtly as he looked at Saldaar then towards the village and scowled. "What's the situation?"

Saldaar chewed his lip and took a moment to gather his words. "Two companies of our horse attacking the village, sirs. There are good numbers of Romans ensconced within, including Triari."

"How in Hades name do you expect to take the village with just horse, man? You need …"

"Infantry support sir, yes." Saldaar lowered his head not deigning to look Balaam in the eye. "They were leaving, marching out when we attacked. Trouble was, most of them were still out of sight within the village."

"Why not wait till they were all in the open, away from the buildings? You could have slaughtered them piecemeal then!"

Saldaar cleared his throat. "That wasn't my decision sir; I'm just a Hypolok …"

Balaam waved the man to silence and turned to Baldor.

"I trust you've a plan Captain? Else we try and pull Bodeshmun's troops back and bottle the Romans up till we can call up infantry support to winkle them out?"

"I have a plan but we may be able to improve upon it."

"Say on."

"Hypolokhagos Saldaar! Have you seen any archers in the village?"

"No, not that I've seen sir and they'll also be short of javelins by now I'll wager."

Baldor nodded and looked at Balaam. "That means we can get closer in relative safely and then burn them out. Methinks with the weather we've had, that thatch will burn like tinder. This way, they lose their cover and if they try to escape in the smoke, we'll have them in the open?"

Balaam was already shouting for the men to come forward, for Malo and his bow, and for javelins to be bound with cloth and a fire made.

Dry leaves and grass produced ready kindling and soon a small fire was ablaze. The added dry wood crackled loudly as it burned fiercely, producing incredible heat but little smoke. Branches were cut into torch lengths and blankets and cloaks cut into strips to bind about arrow shafts and javelin necks. Before long, the wood was leaving glowing red embers, which were transferred into small mess tins, one for each troop.

"Nearly ready Baldor! ... Harbro! Mount the men up, then move them out."

"Hold Captain! Hold a moment."

Balaam reined in, holding up his hand halting the column.

"One more thing sir." Baldor ventured. "As you say we're not great in numbers, so along with our surprise attack a little trickery may also help even the score."

"I'm all ears lad!"

"What if we split into two troops and approach from different sides, while making much display of banner waving? If we use cover and gaps in the hills to appear then disappear, we could perhaps mask our numbers, leaving the Romans guessing as to how many we are; that may give them pause. Then we start our fire raising?"

"Aye, it's worth a try. Send a messenger to this Bodeshmun though and let him know our intent before he throws more of his men into the mess!"

"We'd better send a man of some rank then; otherwise, he's not likely to listen."

Balaam's face twisted in anger, his horse stomping as he dragged on the reins. "Harbro! You go on my behalf, tell … ask this halfwit Lordling to retire until we can drive these Roman bastards into the open."

"Sir."

As the company split into two, Balaam called to Baldor then reined in alongside, shouting above the jingle of harness and rumble of hooves.

"Here's my two shekels worth, whoever reaches the village first sounds their war horn. The other to respond with two blasts if they're also in position. We don't move until we hear the two blasts. Do you have it?"

"Yes sir!" Baldor shouted as he wheeled his mount about hard, the animal whinnying in protest then springing forward as he kicked hard on its flanks.

The distance was covered quickly, the country being gently rolling hills and small copses. Baldor halted his men within the treeline of a small wood and took a moment to study. The main village sat on top of the hill with some overspill houses and gardens built on to the outskirts as the village had expanded. The place lacked a palisade but the houses and outbuildings clustered tightly together, the roofs almost touching. Armaco pushed alongside Baldor. Smiling grimly at the prospect of a burning, his smile faded as he saw many bodies and horses marking a trail from the plain back up the hill to the first houses.

"All the fighting's within and I can't see Bodeshmun's banner, maybe they're about finished?"

Three long blasts of a horn carried across the valley, followed moments later by three more.

"That's the recall! Harbro must have persuaded Bodeshmun to

retire?"

Armaco grumbled then spat. "Damned amateurs! Wasting men's lives!"

Horses began spilling from the lanes around the houses, streaming downhill and away to loud jeers from the Romans. As the horses fell back, some Romans appeared and began collecting up spent javelins.

"Bastards are still keen to fight then!" Baldor said quietly.

"Why wouldn't they be? With warriors served up piecemeal for them to slaughter like …"

A loud, undulating blast blew across the paddock from the other side of the village silencing Armaco and sending the Romans scurrying back to cover.

"Signaller, two blasts! Standard-bearer to me! Light up … light up!" Baldor's mount stomped and whinnied, tossing its head as a warrior ran across the front of the horse line with the fire pot, pausing momentarily as warriors offered cloth shrouded spearheads into the flames. Baldor trotted his mount along the line of men.

"Not too close lads! Watch for javelins coming back at us! Once your spear's thrown pull back and let the fire do the work!" Raising his fighting spear, he pointed to the village. "Forward!"

As the line pushed forward, horses surged and bridled wanting to be away from the fire and smoke.

"Hold the line! … Hold the line!" Armaco bellowed.

On the other side of the village, an arrow arced across the sky trailing a plume of smoke, followed quickly by others headed in different directions, all disappearing from sight into the village.

Cornelius saw the arrows fly and cupped his hands to shout.

"Gaius! They're going to burn us out!"

Gaius peered over the barricade and saw arrows landing in the thatch.

"Every third man there!" He roared; pointing to a line of legionaries positioned behind a garden wall. "Find buckets! Put that thatch out! Move!"

Men ran in search of buckets while others began hauling water from the well.

"Ladders! Get up there and tear that thatch down!"

"Sir! Sir! Over here." Gaius ran to where the man pointed. "They're coming again sir, there are more of them this time and these are fresh troops."

Gaius ground his teeth, his lips curling into a snarl as he saw the line of warriors advancing, all bearing burning spears or torches. He looked back to where his men were trying to extinguish the flames, which were already taking rapid hold high in the thatch. A shortage of ladders and buckets and the inability to spare more men from the barricades, plus the rising wind was making it a fight they couldn't win. He waved Cornelius across to him.

Cornelius saw the advancing cavalry as he came alongside. "They're on the other side too Gaius, all carrying torches and burning spears as well!"

"How many?"

"Hard to say sir, probably too many."

"Sir!" A voice hailed from the front barricade. "I think there's more of them behind the hills too."

"How many?"

"Can't say sir, we've only caught glimpses of them."

"Cornelius! Any javelins or pila left?"

"A handful, that's all!"

Gaius's face was grim. "Some bastard's thinking! They'll standoff and watch, until we either fry or try to run."

The Carthaginians cantered to just within range for throwing the heavy fighting spears and loosed. Some javelins flew from the barricades killing two riders, the rest wheeling safely away after their spear was thrown.

Most of the spears landed purposely high in the roofs; those reachable from the ground being pulled out and extinguished by the defenders. The fire spread quickly in the thatch. Bone-dry, it crackled then roared loudly as the wind fanned the flames higher. Blackened and burning debris swirled on the rising heat, thick brown smoke blowing in all directions as the wind whipped it about. The few buckets of water made no difference and as the fire took hold, heat and smoke drove men back and away.

"It looks like they've caught us! This fire will drive us out and in the open ground they'll cut us to pieces!"

"Maybe, Cornelius but we're not done yet." Gaius waved his hands in a halting gesture. "Leave it! Leave it to burn lads! We can't control it so save your energy."

The men dropped buckets and picked up their weapons, Gaius

nudged Cornelius. "Go and check the other side of the village see if they're still standing off and let me know."

"Yes sir." He arrived back moments later. "They're not moving they're just waiting."

"Aye, they're not daft. New troops have brought a smarter head." Wiping his eyes and coughing from the smoke, Gaius pulled Cornelius away from the increasing heat. "We've a moment before this fire drives us out so here's the plan; we march out, the moment we're clear we form a testudo and make for the trees."

"That'll be difficult over this broken ground."

"What choice do we have?"

Cornelius shrugged then had to shield his face as the smoke billowed low, bringing a wave of heat and covering them both in hot ash. Gaius coughed as the smoke caught his breath and he and Cornelius stepped further back from the heat. He hawked and spat.

"At least we have the Triari, they're steady. If we hold our nerve and make the trees we'll have a chance."

Cornelius nodded. Offering his hand to Gaius the pair shook hard, and then called a 'stand to.'

The legionaries spilled onto the meadow; some formed a small skirmish line while the testudo formed behind them. The Carthaginians, seeing the manoeuvre were already advancing quickly towards them.

"Move it! Move it! Lock those shields!" Gaius bellowed while dressing the milling lines of men.

The Carthaginians bullied their mounts for speed, racing to catch the Romans before the formation closed tight.

"Close up there! Steady lads! Steady!" Cornelius shouted as he checked and sealed the rear ranks.

"Skirmish line, fall back! Move!" Gaius bellowed as he too fell back.

Just before the first horses came within javelin range, the skirmishing line assimilated into the testudo and the shields slammed shut. A few stray javelins clattered onto the wooden wall as the Carthaginians drew rein.

The horses, almost at the gallop whinnied and shied as reins were hauled back, some animals sliding on the grass, others peeling away to the sides of the solid, rectangle of wood and men.

"Keep tight! ... On command! ... Ready! One, two! One two! ...

Keep moving." Gaius called time while risking a peek over a shield rim. The men, picking up on the cadence of their feet punctuating it with staccato grunts.

The Carthaginians wheeled about, powerless to press an attack or break the juggernaut as it headed for the trees.

"Andulas! Shadow them, if they break open …"

"We'll have them sir!"

"I'll be back; I have an idea." Baldor kicked his horse towards the village lashing the reins on either flank as he sought more speed.

Inside the testudo, men sweated and panted, the heat and stink from the close packed bodies stifling the air. Hands slippery with sweat gripping shield straps and spear shafts. Loud grunts; the rattle of shields, spear shafts, and the thump of feet adding to the horror of the dark, confined space. Cornelius, tucked in at the rear of the formation felt the panic rising, tightening his throat as he struggled to breathe, keep time and order as they marched on.

One or two javelins were hurled low at the legionaries' feet managing to injure or trip some. However, the moment of chance as a man fell was too fleeting, as the veteran Triari stoically closed ranks and marched on. The fallen Romans becoming prey to the frustrated horsemen with no quarter given.

Like lions trying to bring down an elephant the Carthaginians darted in, worrying and harassing the testudo, seeking gaps then thrusting with spears. More men fell from the outer edge of the formation to be speared on the ground, any regaining their feet, were ridden or hacked down by low swinging spathas. The ranks however, instantly closing up again before the gaps could be exploited. Despite the losses, the Romans held tight, knowing if they could make the treeline there was a chance of escape.

As Andulas wheeled away from hurling a last javelin, he saw Baldor coming out of the village urging his horse into a gallop.

Baldor jumped down from his horse before it stopped, while unslinging a coil of rope from his shoulders and pointing to a long, thin log tied behind his mount. He threw the rope to Andulas.

"Quick! Tie this off on the timber, then low across your horse's chest! We go together and keep the log low. We drag it through them as far as we can, it'll trip and break them up. Be ready to jump clear as the horses will likely go down with the force."

"Aye, sir!" Andulas grinned as he quickly tied the rope and

remounted.

Baldor threw himself back over his mount, it stomping then whinnying as he forced it on again.

"Go that side of them!" He pointed. "Don't let the log come up too high, just take it to them."

"Sir!"

The testudo pushed on. Gaius risking occasional looks over the shield rims, barking orders as to direction and keeping them on course. Seeing another horseman pass in front of them didn't perturb him, as the Carthaginians had not relented their attack. He didn't see the trailing rope or the timber in the high grass and urged the men on towards the trees.

"Keep tight! Nearly there lads." His voice hoarse and gravelly as he shouted above the 'Huh, huh, huh' of the men.

The men's grunts were also hoarse as they struggled for breath but suddenly strengthened in volume as they heard the trees were close. With a chance of survival, adrenalin pumped harder and men's throats tightened again, knowing open battle would commence anew once the formation split.

Baldor looked back, gauging the distance of the testudo from the log and the rope slithering snake-like through the grass behind him.

Andulas too was watching and matching his speed to Baldor's and the rope. The rope lifted a hands breadth above the grass as it tensioned. A shrill whistle cut over the din as Baldor drew Andulas's attention, his hand indicating to go. With their mounts in the opposite direction to the Roman advance, the horses would take the coming force on their chests.

The testudo stomped on as Baldor and Andulas kicked their horses forward lifting the timber from the grass. Riding down either flank and hauling the ropes, the log bounced and thudded over bumps and tufts as the horses gained speed. Just before the timber collided with the testudo, a cry of alarm went up. The shout however, came too late and the timber smashed into the legs of the front rank, shattering shinbones, knees and breaking ankles. Men were snatched off their feet, crashing into comrades, stumbling and falling amidst bodies and shields as the front of the wooden leviathan went down then began bursting apart.

Chapter Fifteen

The force of the testudo momentum pulled hard on the rope and snatched Baldor's horse from its feet. Baldor jumped clear as the animal reared, twisted about and hit the ground hard, hooves flailing. It, wild-eyed and whinnying pitifully as it was dragged across the grass. Andulas managed to stay mounted though his horse was also hauled backwards with the force.

Gaius went down in the chaos, crushed by the men behind him who could not stop. The front four ranks of the testudo disintegrated into a sprawling mass of tangled bodies, shields and weapons. The fifth and sixth ranks bunched up then fell into those in front as men went down like scythed wheat. Behind these, others tripped and fell as their forward impetus continued. Seizing their chance, the Carthaginians attacked as the Romans tried to regain their feet, javelins and fighting spears decimating the now open ranks. Legionaries struggled to rise or find balance, some standing on their comrades, others caught in shield straps, dying men and others struggling to be free.

The first men died quickly. The air, misting red as bodies, faces and throats absorbed the javelin shower, grunts and screams rising above the noise of horses and the clash of metal.

Gaius heaved a dead legionary off him, trying to rise he dropped low as a javelin whistled past where his chest had been a moment before. Seeing total chaos and the remains of the testudo fragmenting, he realised it was every man for himself. Trying to haul a shield from a dead man, he was forced to give up and roll away to avoid a cavalryman's stabbing spear. As the man stepped his horse around the bodies seeking the Centurion, Gaius rolled again and snatched its tail, using it to pull him to his feet. The horse staggered backwards under the unexpected load pitching the rider forward and off balance. Gaius stepped alongside pushing him off, the man landing atop the dead legionaries. Quickly drawing his gladius, he stabbed the sprawling man in the throat. The horse, regaining its balance stomped forward, desperate to be clear of the mayhem, blood and bodies, finally bolting as it found firm ground.

Gaius spied Cornelius, separated and on his own.

"Cornelius! … Cornelius! Over here!" Seeing Cornelius looking about, he raised his hand beckoning him on. Cornelius ran towards him.

With the fight breaking into small open actions, the two Centurions stood out in their distinctive helmets and phalerae belts and horsemen began turning their attention towards them.

The pair came alongside just as the first cavalryman attacked them. A back handed slash across the horse's mouth from Gaius's gladius sent it rearing then crashing to the ground. Cornelius stabbed the warrior as he landed. The horse kicked and thrashed to regain its feet, its tossing head throwing blood and broken teeth from its ruined mouth.

Cornelius's head jerked like a cockerel, not sure what to do or where to go. His feet feeling like they were rooted to the ground.

Gaius seized his shoulder. "Come on! This is lost."

"Where? … The men …"

"We're dying here Cornelius, look!"

Cornelius saw only a handful of legionaries remained on their feet. Some fought savagely on while others threw down their weapons seeking surrender. These being slaughtered where they stood as the Carthaginians paid back for the frustration and dead comrades. Momentarily clear of attackers, Gaius gestured uphill towards the trees.

"It's our only chance."

The pair ran. Cornelius shocked at the speed at which a solid formation had collapsed and the resulting carnage felt as if he was wading through water. Struggling to co-ordinate his movements, he ran woodenly.

"Come on! If they catch us, we're dead!"

The hill punished their lungs as they climbed, the trees seeming as far away as ever. Gaius pushed Cornelius on while pausing to turn and see if they were being followed.

"Go on! … Go, I'm coming!" He urged.

Cornelius turned to look as he ran. A moment later, he fell headlong as his foot caught in a wandering briar root. Gaius saw him go down. Coming behind him and seizing him by his dagger belt, he snatched him up from the ground pushing him onwards, stumbling and running uphill towards the forest.

"Run lad! Run! ... Into the trees!"

Hearing hooves closing behind, he drew his gladius and turned to face a pursuing horseman who came on with a wild whoop. With no shield or spear, he was vulnerable and would have to rely on speed and agility to evade and kill his opponent.

The rider dug his heels into the horse's flanks forcing a whinnied protest and an increase in speed up the steepening hill. He adjusted his fighting spear, held overhand to stab down at the Centurion who stood his ground beckoning him on and roaring his hate. Gaius stepped quickly from side to side forcing the rider to adjust his aim. The rider, seeing a determined defence surprised Gaius by hurling the fighting spear then quickly drawing his sword. Dodging the spear forced Gaius to one side, allowing the rider to turn the horse broadside on and engage him with his sword. The animal's flanks slammed into Gaius forcing him backwards as the rider's sword slashed down, the blow aimed at decapitating the Roman. Gaius parried savagely, slapping the blade away amidst a hideous screech of metal. The rider kneed the horse sideways hard pushing Gaius backwards again. The push uphill sent him stumbling, preventing any attacking blow as he sought balance. The rider, seeing his advantage flicked his wrist and stabbed the blade downwards but missed Gaius's face and throat, piercing the top of his left shoulder. The mail rings ruptured under the savage thrust but slowed the blade's travel before it forced through the leather undershirt into the flesh. Gaius grunted with pain but stabbed upwards, under the man's shield into his leather corselet. The momentum of the horse forced the gladius through the leather and deep into the man's vitals. The warrior gasped as the blade punctured his lungs and found his heart, he sagged and folded forward over the animal's neck as the horse stomped on; the gladius wrenched from Gaius's grip.

Grabbing his bleeding shoulder to hold the wound closed he glanced about. There were no more riders nearby and his adversary's mount had pushed on, the warrior falling from its back a few paces onward, the animal trotted on then stopped. With his gladius gone, he thought of catching the horse then abandoned the idea, realising that with both he and Cornelius mounted on it they'd no chance against the less burdened Carthaginian cavalry.

Cornelius had reached the edge of the forest and was frantically calling him towards the relative safety of the trees. He tried briefly to wrestle the gladius from the dead man's body but it was stuck fast. Cursing the pain in his shoulder, he ran towards Cornelius leaping and blundering through scrub and briar heading for the forest edge.

The Roman bodies littered the field, most were dead though a few still knelt or dragged themselves along the ground holding their hurt, a few rider-less horses stood around, testament that the Carthaginians had not had everything all their own way. Baldor pulled his mount around in a tight circle seeking further adversaries and found none, just his comrades finishing off the wounded and dying.

"Over there Captain!" Baldor looked to where a warrior shouted then pointed. "Two of them sir! Centurions by the look of their panoply, disappearing into the tree line, one's hurt but still running."

Baldor kicked his mount in the direction the man indicated and seeing the Romans, drove his mount hard up the long incline, the warrior following but still some way behind. Baldor's horse, tired from the morning's ride, battle and now being pushed uphill, laboured. Its hooves throwing up dust and divots as it crossed sheep tracks and rough pasture. Losing sight of the fleeing Centurions, he halted the horse at the edge of the trees and scanned the ground, seeking a blood trail for the direction the men had ran.

In the forest, Cornelius helped Gaius along, the pair making noisy progress as they stepped on dry twigs and blundered through bracken and undergrowth. Cornelius, seeing blood on Gaius's shoulder and the ruptured mail held up a restraining hand, halting them both. Breathing hard from the uphill run, he snatched the scarf from his neck making to bandage Gaius's shoulder.

"Leave it lad, there's no time, come …"

"The blood, Gaius …"

"It's nothing, come on!"

"We're leaving a trail, look!"

Gaius peered back the way they'd come and saw the blood, bright and stark against the brown leaf carpet still covering the ground from the previous autumn. Looking at his arm and the quickly dripping blood, he grimaced.

Cornelius's eyes went wide with fear as he heard a horse enter the trees and muffled shouts from the rider.

"Damn it!" Gaius spat. "Give me your gladius lad, I'll hold them while I can, now go! … Go!"

Feeling like a stag before the hounds and looking as though he was about to bolt, Cornelius bit his lip and shook his head.

"No! … No!" He hissed. "I will not!"

"Do as I say! Go! There's no sense in us both perishing here!"

When Gaius tried to push him away and snatch his gladius Cornelius twisted to one side, deftly forcing the scarf over Gaius's arm binding it tight.

"We'll both die here Cornelius! Leave me!" He growled.

In answer, Cornelius seized Gaius by his phalerae belt and tried to pull him along. "Come on!"

Gaius stumbled from the pull but didn't move further, he shook Cornelius's hand loose. "Go lad! As Senior Centurion, I command you to go!"

Seeing the determined look on Gaius's face, Cornelius drew his gladius and calmly stepped around him, putting his back to him, facing the sounds of the oncoming horsemen.

"Damn you, Cornelius! Do as I command!" He hissed.

"You wouldn't leave me." He said, his voice quivering. "If this is where the road ends, it'll be for both of us, stand or run, you choose? But Mars as my witness, I'll not leave you!"

"Oh, for the love of Juno!" Gaius looked down and shook his head slightly.

The sounds of more horses entering the wood saw Cornelius draw his dagger as well while quietly but quickly mumbling his prayers.

"Jupiter, damn you boy! You reckless, brave bastard! Come on then!" His good arm seized Cornelius turning him back the way they'd been running.

The pair dodged between the trees further into the gloom running hard, the sound of the pursuing horses crashing through the undergrowth not far behind them. The trees grew closer together along the top of a small escarpment then stepped away down the hill, opening out as the steep gradient spread them wider apart. With the light penetrating the canopy, ferns, briar and blackberry had taken hold and covered the forest floor. Dodging around the undergrowth, the pair hurtled down the hill without slackening pace. Gaius stumbled on an unseen root then slipped on the dry leaves. He crashed into Cornelius knocking him down as well, the pair rolling and sliding down the hill amidst grunts, dust and leaves before coming to rest where the ground flattened into a small clearing.

Cornelius was up first hauling a protesting Gaius to his feet.

"Damn you, Cornelius!" He panted; the breath knocked out of him. "Leave me, I'll run no more! For the last time, give me your gladius and go!"

Cornelius gestured for silence and hearing the sounds of pursuit were now distant, he smiled grimly and snatched Gaius's harness dragging him onwards. The pair careered further downhill, half-running, sliding and swerving between trees and brambles then jumping a stream that cut deeply across another small clearing, Gaius cursing vehemently as they went. Cornelius paused again, shushing him to listen, both men blowing hard their lungs and legs punished. The noise of the trailing horsemen was still evident but more distant now as the steep country slowed their pursuit. He also noticed the makeshift bandage was soaked in blood and once more leaking down Gaius's mail. With the wound worsening and both of them approaching the edge of their endurance, he sought a place to hide.

Wiping sweat from his face and taking a deep breath, a stench of rot and filth caught in his nostrils. Sniffing hard, he glanced around the small glade seeking the source and saw a 'D' shaped hole burrowed into the bank beneath the exposed roots of a large beech tree. Twigs, dry grass and debris littered the holes entrance and as he moved closer, the stench grew stronger.

Gaius was becoming listless as the blood loss took its toll on his body and he was physically wilting, though the fire in his eyes and grim look still spoke of savage defiance. Cornelius squatted at the hole's entrance, peering into the darkness assessing whether it was deep enough to fit a man into, he gagged as the stench intensified. Satisfied that it was just large enough he grabbed Gaius again.

"Come on! In there, we can't run anymore."

"What?" Gaius queried, though his voice was low and lacking the command of before.

"It's a Badger's sett I think, going by the stink and those scratch marks on the tree roots. Let's hope he isn't home! Squeeze in backwards; feet first, I'll hide your trail once you're in."

"What? ... What about you lad? ... I told you, leave me."

Cornelius ignored him, steering him backwards and pushing him down towards the hole.

"Take your helmet off … quickly!"

Gaius fumbled the strap with his good hand and Cornelius took it, hurling it deep into the hole.

"Hurry! Hurry! We don't have much time, they're coming!"

Gaius groaned when his arm dragged as he wriggled backwards, feet first into the confines of the sett. Soil from the top of the burrow fell on his head and down his neck into his tunic sticking to his sweat soaked skin as he squeezed his shoulders deeper into the recess.

"Right back! As far as you can go!" Cornelius pushed and shoved Gaius as best he could, finally using his foot against the good shoulder forcing him in like a cork in a bottle, deep into the hole out of sight. He heard Gaius gag then retch. "Shush!" He whispered. "I'll be in the briar, don't move till I come for you."

Not waiting for a response, he rearranged the leaves and twigs at the entrance and scanned the ground for signs of blood. Finding a bright red smear, he scuffed leaf mould over it then covered it with leaves ensuring the dry sides stayed to the top. The horses were closer now, he heard the rattle of harness and whinnies of protest as the animals were forced downhill at speed. Men's voices carried clearer, telling him their pursuers were not far behind. Stepping back, he checked the ground again for signs of disturbance and anything that might betray men had passed this way and then ran towards the briar that grew bush-like beneath the trees.

Throwing his gladius and helmet deep inside the foliage and stepping carefully, so not to flatten the unruly blackberry runners, he dropped to his knees and with difficulty lifted the spreading tendrils over his head, pushing deeper into the bush. Barbs tore his skin and hooked and pulled at his tunic as he crawled amongst the plant's roots then flattened his body onto the forest floor. Laid under the briar canopy, he prayed it was thick enough to hide the colours of his tunic as he scraped old leaves over the helmet plumes hiding it as best he could. The pollen and dust from the disturbed leaves swirled about him, dancing and swirling in the narrow shafts of sunlight; he clamped his hand over his mouth and nose, frightened the powder would bring on a sneezing fit.

A horse entered the clearing, its pace slowed now to a walk. It plodded across the ground with dull thuds and a slight rustle of disturbed leaves. Cornelius's heart hammered in his chest. His punished lungs desperate for air that he fought to inhale, in small gasps. Soaked in sweat, his tunic clinging to his skin, his face dripping the salty liquid onto the cool, strong-smelling earth on which he lay; he heard another horse arrive and two men conversing. The horses didn't move, he could only surmise the riders were studying the ground seeking the pair's tracks. Unable to see more than an arm's length in front of him, he listened as they talked. Not understanding, he listened to their tone trying to detect excitement that may reveal they'd found the trail.

Frightened to move, he laid corpse like, his heartbeat thumping drum-like in his ears. Sweat ran off his brow into his eyes forcing him to squint, more ran off his top lip, bitter in his mouth. He watched absently as a spider walked slowly across the ground in front of him before effortlessly ascending a heavily spiked stem. Wishing he could be that small, he closed his eyes and mouthed a silent prayer to Jupiter, offering a sacrifice of a prize bullock if the God would see him clear of his plight. Another horse arrived then more diatribe; his ears pricked up and his eyes opened wide when he heard the name, 'Baldor.' The horses walked on and as best as he could tell, spread out, two heading further downhill, their hoof beats quietening, one remained, moving about close by.

Baldor walked his horse about the clearing, he looking intently for signs of passage amongst the leaves and bracken while glancing at the briar. His nose wrinkled as the stench of rot assailed his senses; he looked about and saw the hole, yawning blackly from under the tangle of beech roots. Walking his horse across to it, it shied from the smell and he pulled his scarf over his nose and mouth while backing the horse further away. He turned his attention back to the briar patch. Walking the horse around the perimeter of it he found no sign of footfalls, broken stems or anything indicating a man had passed that way. He probed one or two places with his spear then backed the horse away as the other riders returned to the clearing.

"Nothing Baldor! We've cut across the hillside and there's no sign of anyone down there, it's as if they vanished into thin air. Have you found anything?"

"No Armaco, nothing."

"What in Hades name is that smell?" Armaco and the other horseman clamped their hands over their noses."

"I don't know; it's coming from that hole under the tree." Baldor nodded in the direction.

Armaco coughed and growled. "Some stinking animal hole likely, what a stench!"

The three men eyed the clearing, Baldor dismounting and walking again to the briar squatting to peer into the profusion of green leaves and red-purple, thorn-heavy, runners. He thrust his spear into the leafy profusion again.

Armaco walked his mount across and scanned the ground.

"You're right Baldor, there's nothing here; no blood, no broken stems, no disturbed leaves … Baal knows where they've gone?"

"Would they've had time to back track and follow the stream bed we crossed?" The other warrior suggested.

"It's worth a look." Armaco said, turning his mount back towards the stream."

The pair moved off but looked back again when Baldor didn't join them, he still probing the briar with his spear.

"Come on Baldor, there's nothing in there."

"My gut tells me different Armaco. I don't know what it is but there's something about this briar I can't explain."

"We don't know where they are Baldor but there's two of the bastards and Centurions to boot! Please come with us while we search the stream bed, it's some way back and we shouldn't separate over that distance."

Baldor looked thoughtful then nodded and walked back to his mount. The three riding back the way they had come.

As the hoof beats grew quieter, Cornelius dared to breathe deeply. He still didn't move, his ears straining, listening, trying to be sure that all three men had gone. He lay for some time, hearing nothing but the odd rustle of leaves and creaking limbs in the tree canopy as the breeze stirred it. He looked at his forearms and the myriad cuts on his skin, the blood had dried on some but still oozed slowly from others that had gone deep. He was just about to push himself backwards out of the briar when he heard hoof beats again then a long drone of a horn followed by a shout.

"Come on Baldor, the recall's sounding."

"Just one more look Armaco, then I'll leave it."

Cornelius flattened himself again as the hoof beats came close then stopped. He heard the soft thud of a man dismounting and then footsteps pushing into and crushing the briar. Wishing the ground would swallow him up, he held his breath as he heard the spear slashing and probing through the leaves.

The search continued for what seemed to Cornelius like eternity. His hand wrapped around the gladius hilt as the probing spear point twice came within a cubit of where he lay, the long, bright head burrowing half deep into the soft soil in front of him. He heard the sound of a horse arriving again.

"Baldor! For the love of Baal! Come on! There's nothing down here."

"There's something Armaco! Something I can't explain and bothers me about this briar ..."

"Come on! A man couldn't get in there, not without leaving signs."

Baldor stopped probing and nodded. "I guess you're right, I just can't explain what keeps pulling me back to this place, it's like I'm drawn to it."

"Come on, we'd best get back, we have more than a few injured to see to and there'll be other Romans to catch and kill ere the day's done."

Cornelius wasn't sure how long he lay before moving out of the briar. The foliage was so thick that he couldn't see anything and thus must rely upon his ears. He'd already made two attempts at extraction and both times heard noises he couldn't explain and thus remained ensconced in his leafy prison. The light was fading before he finally crawled cautiously into the open dell; he peered all around ensuring no one was watching. Dragging himself to his feet, he stumbled and limped trying to find his balance while rubbing chilled and stiffened muscles as he made his way towards the hole.

"Gaius! Gaius!" He hissed into the hole. He had to turn away from the stench and call again before he received an answer.

"Get me out lad! I can't move; I'm jammed solid!" The voice was muted from the confines of the hole and also weaker than before.

Cornelius held his breath and lay down next to the hole, extending his arm in as far as he could reach, his fingers straining and clutching in the air.

"I can't reach you Gaius, can you push towards me?"

"No, my legs are numb and I can't move my arms much."

Cornelius undid his baldric and flicked the end down the hole; it took a number of tries before Gaius grasped it.

"Hold on tight and I'll pull you out."

Setting his feet either side of the hole he leaned backwards hauling on the baldric. Slowly, a little at a time, hand over hand, the belt came back to him as Gaius was dragged up to the surface. Hauling him clear of the hole, he saw that beneath the filth, he was ashen. The bleeding had stopped but then started again from the exertion of the removal, the blood mixing with the dirt and the remains of vomit where Gaius had purged from the stench. Cornelius gagged again and Gaius managed a small laugh as he rolled onto his side.

"Catches you, doesn't it? I can honestly say I can't smell a thing anymore."

Cornelius smiled wanly and began checking Gaius's wound. "Give me your scarf, I'll bind it again, then we need some water and to get as far away as we can before tomorrow."

"My legs, lad, I can't feel them at all." He began rubbing his thigh with his good hand.

Cornelius finished binding the wound and turned to help, rubbing briskly, trying to force heat and circulation back into the cold and cramped muscles.

"That was a close call, eh?" Though he tried to sound nonchalant, Gaius detected a tremble in Cornelius's voice.

"Aye too close! I told you lad; you should've left me ... are you all right?"

Cornelius ignored the comment. "Yes, yes I think, no ... I'm sure Baldor Targa was one of the horsemen. I heard his name mentioned."

Gaius just stared.

"Someone ... someone kept coming back to where I was hidden, again and again ... like they couldn't let it go. I think it was him."

Part 3

The Reckoning

Chapter Sixteen

"What? ... No! He can't be. There must be a mistake."
"I'm sorry sir, it's no mistake I've seen him. He's over there, half way up the hill, he went after the two Centurions."

Baldor set off apace towards the hill, Andulas in his wake and Armaco following on his horse. As they drew close, they found Harbro crouched on the floor and a group of warriors gathered around. Baldor pushed through the men then stopped abruptly as he saw the body. Lost for words, he just stared. Harbro looked up.

"He's gone lad. He was dead when we found him."

Baldor looked at the gladius lodged deeply in the leather corselet and the huge bloodstain caked around it. He growled low in his throat as he squatted alongside Balaam's body and stroked his eyes closed. Seeing blood dripping onto Balaam's corselet, he looked up and saw Harbro was bleeding from his shoulder.

"What? ..."

"A spear. The bastard was quick, but in the end, not quick enough. It's worse than it looks; the Roman mail underneath my leather corselet saved me, it seems they are good for something!"

"Make sure it's seen to Harbro, no more bad news eh? Enough for one day."

"What now sir?" Andulas asked quietly. "It would seem you are in charge of ..."

"You men! Down here now! Secure these prisoners and we'll be gone."

The bellow cut Andulas short and saw the gathered men turn to see a handful of Romans stood to one side under guard and Bodeshmun waving his arm in summons.

"Move! We haven't all day!"

Baldor stood quickly and turned towards the shouted command, a fierce snarl twisting his mouth. Sense and reason left him, his mind suddenly darkened. His temper boiling over with hate for the losses and injuries to his men, the death of his friend and for the previous wound and insults he'd suffered. Reaching for a falcata and stepping quickly down the hill, he made for Bodeshmun. Armaco, seeing Baldor's anger guessed his intention and forced his mount across his path, adjusting the horse's stance as Baldor made to side step.

"Hold Baldor!"

Baldor ignored him and pushed past the horse.

"Sir! … Captain, wait!" Armaco called as he turned the horse again.

"Baldor wait ..." Harbro called.

"Baldor! This is not the time." Andulas shouted.

"Captain!" Malo added to the halting calls.

The men's voices faded behind him as he increased his pace while throwing Andulas's restraining arm from his shoulder. Bodeshmun saw him coming and though not recognising him, recognised the bared blade and intent and drew his own. As the distance between the two men narrowed, warriors stepped in to keep them apart. Pandemonium broke loose as men pushed between the pair calling for a halt and peace. Baldor, cursing and struggling with Andulas, Harbro and Malo, as all three tried to hold him back, bellowed.

"Bodeshmun! You vainglorious bastard! These deaths are your doing! … You die here! … Unhand me!" He screamed at the men holding him back. "Bastard! … Bastard! Good men are dead because of you!"

Bodeshmun, finally recognising Baldor, smiled grimly, pointing his sword while beckoning. "Come Targa! … Come, I can add you to the offal!"

More men joined those holding both adversaries back and despite threats of dire retribution kept them restrained. The hullabaloo of shouts and pushing only stopping when a horn sounded. As men fell quiet and turned to see, Armaco, still mounted, pushed forward blowing hard on the horn. Harbro took the initiative and command.

"Captain … my Lord!" He addressed both men firmly. "We have wounded to tend and our dead to collect before a lengthy ride back to camp. I suggest you put your endeavours into that and air your grievances to the General, not here."

The two antagonists lessened their struggles and men eased slowly back allowing them to lower their weapons. The tension remained highly charged for a moment as the pair glared at each other. Only when Baldor sheathed his falcata did calm return. Cautiously, the warriors turned once more to their wounded and preparations for the ride back to camp. To one side of the scuffle, standing alone and quiet, Sakarbaal watched.

However, when Bodeshmun's first action was again the securing of prisoners and not the needs of his men, Baldor erupted again. Quicker than the men previously restraining him, he ran at Bodeshmun, drawing both falcatas as he went. Bodeshmun, seeing him, drew his falcata and dagger and also went to the attack. This time men stepped wide of the drawn blades, deigning not to be caught between the warring pair. The two met amid a clash of blades and shouts. Both were lightning quick, swords and dagger stabbing and thrusting, bodies twisting this way and that. Bodeshmun ducking under a swipe from Baldor's falcata, he swerving to one side as Bodeshmun's dagger sought his belly. Men looked on in awe at the weapon mastery, speed and footwork as the grim dance went forward and back across the grass.

"Do we try and stop it again?" Andulas asked Harbro.

"How? They're as like to kill anyone getting in their way. I'll lose no more men today."

"I'll stop it!" Armaco growled and kicked his mount forward towards the fight while snatching his helmet from the hook on the horse's tack. Stepping the horse in and around the men as they growled, thrusted and parried, he swung the helmet hard by the chinstrap, smacking Bodeshmun on the back of his head. "Enough!" He bellowed while forcing the horse between the pair as Bodeshmun crumpled and Baldor went to land a killing blow. "Enough Captain!" He carried on forcing the horse in front of Baldor, using it as barrier. When Baldor raised the weapon to him, he shouted again. "Captain, enough! For the love of Baal enough!"

With Bodeshmun down, unconscious and the horse pushing him away, Baldor finally lowered his blades. With his anger still hot, he snapped orders.

"Kill those prisoners! If they're so damned precious to him, they can die here."

"Captain, they're valuable, we ..." A warrior protested.

"Kill them!" Baldor screamed. "Unless you wish to join them! Now, see to our wounded." He looked down at the still unconscious Bodeshmun. "Then tie this offal on his horse, we're leaving here."

There was a brief moment of silence as Bodeshmun's men realised Baldor was taking sole command, then cries for mercy as the Carthaginians began slaughtering the prisoners. The bloodletting was quick and brutal; blades hacked, stabbed and slashed at the unarmed men, killing them where they stood. Any that managed to run were ridden down. As the slaughter stopped, an eerie silence descended and all eyes turned to Baldor.

Fighting his own demons of anger and shock at his actions, he snapped his orders. "Harbro, Malo, bring Captain Balaam's body. Andulas, marshal our men, Armaco see to Bodeshmun's men and his wounded we saw back in the trees."

He turned to see three warriors were already hefting Bodeshmun on to his horse and tying him there. With all underway he finally sheathed his blades. The long ride back to camp was a quiet one, other than relaying information, Andulas and the others kept their distance from Baldor, even Armaco was silent.

Late evening found the column safely back in camp, Baldor saw the wounded into care then dismissed his men for rest and food. Requesting a meeting with Hannibal and taking Bodeshmun and two guards with him, he waited his turn to report. The sight of a bound and gagged Bodeshmun drew some curious stares from others also waiting to offer their reports.

It was almost dark before Baldor was granted admission and Hannibal, like others, stared in shocked disbelief as Bodeshmun was pushed into the tent. Bodeshmun mumbled into his gag and Hannibal signalled that it should be removed and his bonds untied. Frowning sternly at both men, he pointed to each in turn, his tone sharp.

"I warn you both now, before any of you say anything, the time is late! I'm weary and will suffer no more of personal disagreements. This had better be worth my time. Captain Targa! Seeing as how you're holding sway you may begin, I warn you, Lord Bodeshmun! Not a word till he's finished!"

Baldor took a moment to clear his throat and calm his anger.

"General, I charge this man with gross negligence to the cost of men's lives, not least that of Captain Balaam."

"What? Captain Balaam is dead?"

"Aye sir; thanks to this man's folly."

Bodeshmun bridled but managed to hold his tongue.

"Explain Captain and quickly."

Baldor relayed the events of the skirmish outside the village and the casualty numbers. Hannibal's face clouded though he said nothing. As Baldor finished, Hannibal turned to Bodeshmun his face darkening.

"And your side of the story, my Lord?"

Bodeshmun claimed he was about to withdraw and call up infantry support when Baldor and Balaam had intervened and pressed the attack, after which Baldor had attacked him. Hannibal silenced Baldor with a stern look and a pointed finger as he went to interrupt. Seeing the argument would degenerate into supposition and lengthy diatribe, he went to his desk and seated himself. Snapping both men to attention in front of him, he took control.

"My Lord. Attacking a fortified position with a cavalry unit without infantry support is tantamount to madness. Why you didn't just bottle them up and send for support is beyond me. As I have heard, your foolishness has cost me dear in men and a veteran Captain, both of which I can ill afford to lose. Until I deem otherwise, you will report directly to General Maharbal and do nothing without his authority. Do you understand?"

Bodeshmun flushed, grimaced and went to speak; Hannibal cut him short.

"Don't dare to argue, sir! Officers have been crucified for military failings such as this. Do not try my patience." Bodeshmun glared and his mouth twisted but he held his peace. Hannibal turned to Baldor. "Captain Targa." Baldor swallowed hard as Hannibal tuned a baleful stare on him. "It would seem your actions brought a satisfactory conclusion to this mess; however, it should have stopped there. What in Baal's name did you think you were doing attacking a fellow officer in front of the men? Accusations of military incompetence are brought to me, not made an open brawl in the field!" Hannibal slammed his fist on the desk making the paraphernalia jump. Baldor paled at his General's temper. "What if the men had taken sides? What then? A bloodbath!"

"I'm sorry sir."

"Silence!" Hannibal hammered the desk this time. "I could crucify you for this! You know the law better than any; one soldier is not to attack another!"

Baldor felt his stomach heave and his heart racing in his chest; another nervous swallow prevented any answer.

"You save yourself only through your good military actions; your personal behaviour remains a disgrace, a damned disgrace! You too will report directly to General Maharbal and do nothing without his command."

Hannibal took a moment to calm himself, the silence and tension in the tent palpable. Finally, trusting himself to speak rationally, his voice lowered but the tone remained firm. "Both of you are under camp arrest until we move or I deem otherwise. Should either of you break this curfew I will have you crucified without further thought. Lord or Captain, I care not, is that clear?" Without waiting for an answer, he called for the guards. Two large warriors quickly appeared in the tent.

"Take these men out of my sight, escort them to their quarters." He glared as Baldor and Bodeshmun saluted before being ushered out by the guards.

****

"There's only farming folk down there that I can see." Cornelius stood up from his prone position beside the tree as he spoke. Helping Gaius up, he slipped his arm across his back and into the armpit of his wounded shoulder. "We'll have to risk it; your wound needs proper attention and you need rest."

The two Centurions slipped out of the trees making their way slowly across the meadow towards the small farm, Cornelius supporting Gaius who leaned heavily on him. As they came close, Cornelius saw the buildings were blackened from partial burning. Their presence was noted and people disappeared quickly from sight. Just before they reached the main house a big man, carrying a levelled spear stepped in front of them.

"Who are you and what do you want?" He growled as he brandished the spear.

"We're Romans, the same as you. Survivors of the last battle, my friend needs help."

"You're a long way from Rome, boy, and we're Umbrians, not Romans!"

"Please! My friend needs help."

"Begone! We want nothing with you!" The man gestured with his spear.

"For the love of Juno, my friend needs help!"

"What help did we have from you when the Carthaginians passed through killing and burning? Where were you? . . . Go!" He snarled.

"I'll pay! Please! Just help my friend."

"I said go, before I take this spear to you!"

With Gaius almost unconscious and both of them exhausted, Cornelius was in no state to argue or fight and he had no doubt of the big man's capacity for violence.

"Just give us some water then … please!"

"I said go!"

Cornelius fished in the purse on his belt with one hand while supporting Gaius with the other. He groaned inwardly when he found his coins almost all gone. The soaking at the lake or the hurried pursuit had opened the flap; all that remained were some copper asses and a silver denarius. He thrust the coins at the man.

"Here! Here! It's all I have but give us water and we'll be gone."

The man looked as if he was about to spear the pair and take the coins when a woman appeared behind him.

"Bring them into the house, Petrino and fetch some water."

"But Mistress Adrianna …"

"Do as I ask, Petrino." She said firmly. "These men need help."

Petrino's lip curled into a snarl that he directed at the two men, then reluctantly lowered the spear.

The timber outbuildings in front of the house had burned to the ground, a dead cow, all bloated with the heat and swarming with flies lay in the courtyard. The house had also been burnt leaving only the stonewalls standing. The pantile roof had collapsed blocking the doorway with fallen timber and debris, leaving just a small area above the gable supported by precariously thin, blackened timber trusses.

When Cornelius looked bemused, Petrino growled and nodded.

"Round the back."

A small offshoot at the house rear remained roofed and thus habitable. The room stank of smoke and burned wood, the white walls all soot blackened. Cornelius lowered Gaius onto a wooden crate, the only item of furniture remaining it seemed.

"Thank you! Thank you, lady." He mumbled while watching the man returning with the water.

As Cornelius helped Gaius drink, the woman stared at the blood-crusted mail and his white, dead looking pallor. Removing the scarf, she looked at the wound and sniffed.

"The wound needs stitching but the scarf has kept it clean. Take his mail and shirt off, how long ago did this happen?"

"Yesterday … today … I don't know. Our men were slaughtered; we were hunted, we've run for miles, I …" Cornelius gabbled, his nerves on the raw.

"It's all right, it doesn't matter." She said quietly. "Your friend has lost a lot of blood and needs to rest. I have some healing skill, but I need your help."

Cornelius helped Gaius out of his mail and leather undershirt, he listless, quiet and compliant to the ministrations.

"Petrino, fill that pot with water and set it to boil. Flavia, fetch my box of ointments, clean linen, needle and thread … today girl!" She said, clapping her hands for urgency.

Cornelius sat behind Gaius, propping him up as his body went limp. His eyes flickered.

"Gaius! Gaius! …" Cornelius shook him. "Gaius!" He felt his chest tighten as panic took hold.

Adrianna put her fingers to Gaius's neck while shushing Cornelius. "Quiet! … It's all right. I can feel the thump of his heart in the vein here; it's weak but steady. As I said, he's exhausted from loss of blood and needs to rest. I'll work as quickly as I can."

Adrianna fished in the box while shooing Flavia to fetch more wood for the fire. Producing a small mortar and pestle, she tipped some coarse, dark brown powder from a jar into the mortar and began grinding it. Cornelius watched, his other arm encircling Gaius's chest keeping him upright.

"See if you can get him to drink. Here, this will help bring him around." She passed a small glass phial over. "Put it under his nose."

Cornelius did as he was bidden and a moment later Gaius twisted his head away from the phial and his eyes flickered.

"What is …?" Cornelius asked.

"Hammoniacus sal, sharp smelling crystals. Here, I need to get this into him." She talked while tipping a few drops of water into the mortar making a brown liquid. "Tip his head back"

Adrianna offered the mortar to Gaius's mouth and tipped the liquid in. He gagged and spilled some over his chest. "Drink it … drink it, I know its bitter but it will help." She stroked his throat helping him swallow.

"What is it?" Cornelius asked.

"Opium, from the poppy flower. It will sedate him while I stitch his wound. Hold him steady and still. Flavia! Is that water hot?" Rinsing and then filling two bowls with the hot water, she tipped a fine metal needle and shears into one and clean linen swabs into the other. Washing her hands with the remainder, she began cleaning in and around the wound. Gaius didn't flinch from the pressure or the hot swabs and she pinched his cheek, again to no response. "I hope I haven't given him too much."

"How much should you give him?"

"Less than I give a horse, I suppose."

"A horse!"

Adrianna shrugged. "My medical skill is with animals, I never professed to be a surgeon." Cornelius chewed his lip and said nothing. She pressed around and below the wound. "It's deep but I don't think its cut into any bones or damaged organs, blood loss is the main worry, and he will need rest." She snipped one or two pieces of ragged flesh away tidying the wound edges, and then threaded the needle. "I use silk." She said as she began lacing the skin. "It's cleaner than horse hair or animal gut, so there will be less chance of a reaction and bad humours as the wound heals."

"Thank you."

"Thank me when he wakes up and grows stronger."

"You think he won't?"

She shrugged. "As I said, my skill is with horses." She tied then snipped off the thread. "I've done my best. All you can do now is let him rest and pray to Hygeia for his recovery. Flavia! Fetch some straw and pile it in the corner there, find a blanket or cloak to throw over it."

With the rough bed made, Cornelius and Petrino lifted Gaius onto it; Adrianna checked the wound then turned to Cornelius. "Come, eat! We don't have much but you are welcome, the Carthaginians took almost everything we had but we found some cheese they missed and the grain pit went undiscovered so we have bread."

****

Baldor found an anxious Andulas and Armaco awaiting him in his tent.

Both stood as he entered. Seeing the guard turning away, Armaco found voice.

"Why the guard?"

Baldor relayed the audience with Hannibal. There were sharp intakes of breath from the two listeners. Seeing Armaco about to launch into an angry diatribe, Baldor held up his hand to silence him.

"Some wine, eh?"

Lasairiona filled the cups as Baldor outlined the outcome of the meeting and for once Armaco had no jibes to make. "We're all stood down then?" He muttered from his cup.

"Yes, until General Maharbal requires and commands us." Armaco was about to expound his thoughts but Baldor continued. "It's my fault; I shouldn't have attacked Bodeshmun ..."

"You should have gutted the arrogant bastard." Armaco got in quickly; Andulas gripped his forearm and shook his head signalling he should be quiet.

"No, Armaco." Baldor replied quietly. "The General is right; the fight could have turned his men against us." Andulas squeezed harder on Armaco's arm preventing any retort. "If I had just left it and placed my report of his incompetence, Captain Balaam's death and our losses it may have been enough to see him removed."

Armaco snatched his arm back. "Just killing the bastard quietly would have done it."

"Armaco! Let it go!" Andulas snapped.

Baldor gently shushed both men; clasping Armaco on the shoulder for further affect, he lowered his voice to a hoarse whisper.

"I'll kill the bastard, don't you worry, but I will pick my time and place and no one will know."

"Just blade him in the next battle, no one will see. I've heard bad officers are sometimes gotten rid that way."

"No, I'll kill him face on, I want him to know it's me that ends his days." Baldor growled.

"Just blade him! He's dangerously fast and good with ..."

"Do you doubt I can kill him face on?" Baldor's voice rose in anger, his lip twisting.

"No, I'm not! I'm saying be careful!" Armaco snapped back, quite bewildered at Baldor's temper.

"Enough!" Andulas growled as he glared at both men. Neither had heard Andulas raise his voice in anger and the shock silenced both. "Keep your voices down and stop bickering like children. Baldor, all Armaco, and myself are saying is be careful. We saw how he fought and it seems he's as fast as you are and as skilled, so yes, pick your moment if you must but carefully. Armaco, keep your tongue between your teeth."

Baldor nodded slowly. "I'm sorry, sorry for my temper." He clasped each man's shoulder. "Thank you both for your thoughts and concerns, I'll mind it and I will be careful."

"See that you do, he's not worth being crucified for." Armaco got in quickly.

Baldor managed a smile at his friend's tenacity and Andulas just shook his head. "And they say us Gauls are the barbarians for our bickering and blood feuds! Epona save us from the pair of you!"

"I just need to protect him from himself!"

"Armaco, just shush!" Andulas placed his finger on Armaco's lips.

Armaco held up both hands and nodded slightly, Andulas taking the chance to push another cup of wine at him.

The following morning, Baldor dressed in his parade armour and made his way to the fields by the camp edge where the dead were being cremated on large pyres. A separate pyre to one side of the larger, communal ones supported Balaam's body, it washed and wrapped in white linen.

"The lads thought he deserved a place of his own." Harbro said, gesturing to the men gathered about it.

Baldor nodded. "I can't believe he's gone; I thought … I thought …"

"You thought he was indestructible? We all did, they don't come any better than him. He was a hard man but a fair one and a good Captain."

Baldor nodded. "I know." He said quietly, trying to keep his emotions in check.

"He thought a lot about you, he saw your potential."

Baldor managed a sad smile. "I think I made him angry most of the time, trying his patience."

"That's youth for you Baldor." Harbro smiled. "We've all been there; he saw past it, knew what was in there." Harbro thumped Baldor's heart lightly. "Come, Elysium is calling for him, give your blessing and we will send him on his way."

As the pyre took hold and the flames roared on the wind, Baldor's eyes smarted and the tears fell. Growling low in his throat, he mumbled a promise of vengeance. Another good man gone to the Gods. Another vow, another death to repay.

Later that afternoon Harbro appeared at Baldor's tent, a falcata and finely tooled leather baldric in his hand.

"Can you spare me a moment or two, Captain?" He asked as Baldor ushered him to a seat.

"Only if you'll take a cup of wine with me?" He chuckled and pushed a cup at Harbro, who took it up, smiling.

As the pair settled, Harbro raised his cup. "Captain Balaam."

"Captain Balaam." Baldor echoed and the pair drank.

"I've sorted the Captain's affairs, Baldor. His funeral fund has left us a goodly amount to see his memory feasted, the rest is to go back to Carthage to his wife and children."

"He had a wife and family?" Baldor shook his head at the surprise.

"Aye, so it would seem."

"You didn't know either?"

"No, I'm as surprised as you. From the first dates on his will, he has a son at least your age and a daughter a year or so younger."

Baldor shook his head and smiled. "A wife, daughter and a son. Who'd have guessed?"

"We'll have the feast tomorrow; will you bring Armaco and Andulas with you?"

"I will. Have you stories to tell? You knew him best of us all?"

Harbro chuckled. "Aye, I think I can entertain you all for a while. Anyway, there's more. He's left me his helmet, horses and war gear but he left you this."

Harbro laid the falcata and baldric on the table. Baldor just stared.

"For me? … Why would he …?"

"He liked you Baldor, esteemed you greatly and perhaps you reminded him of the son he doesn't see."

Baldor looked at the sword. The handgrip was ivory with gold wire twisted through it affording a good grip, a horse's head wrought in gold forming the curve of the handle. The cross guard remained practical in bronze but was decorated in intricate swirling patterns. Sliding the blade from its scabbard, he saw it was finely wrought, and as he expected, carefully maintained. He shook his head again.

"That's Balaam, Baldor. Always full of surprises. There is one last thing. My promotion has been confirmed this morning. I'm to take over the troop; the General has made me Captain."

Baldor beamed a smile and stood raising his cup.

"Hail Captain! May you live long and prosper; your God's blessings be upon you."

Putting the cup down, he placed his hand over his heart and bowed his head.

"Thank you Baldor, and you." Harbro raised his cup in salute.

****

A week had passed since Cornelius and Gaius arrived at the farmhouse. Gaius was much recovered with Adrianna's care and up and about, though he tired easily and still slept a lot. Adrianna explaining to Cornelius that it was normal; his body needed the time and sleep was a great healer.

Petrino ignored the two men, responding only to his mistress's commands until Cornelius asked about the old horse he had seen in the paddock. The big man erupted.

"You're not having that! If your friend is well enough, begone! Leave us be!"

"That's enough Petrino!" Adrianna snapped. "The horse is not yours; these men have done nothing to us, so ..."

"The Romans did nothing to help us either when the Carthaginians passed through! Where were they? They left us to fend for ourselves! Now they've had your help and want the last animal you possess!"

"One old horse is not going to restore my fortunes, Petrino." She said with a sad smile.

Petrino just growled and threw his arms in the air then walked off.

"Take the horse, Cornelius. It's too small to pull a cart and too old for much else but it may see you home."

Cornelius reached behind his head and undid Amelia's jewel.

"Mistress Adrianna, this is the only thing of worth I possess at present, please take it as payment for the horse and your kindness." He pressed it into her hand.

Adrianna looked at the gold and the rubies that caught the light.

"This is a lady's jewel, your woman's jewel I imagine?"

"It was, is, she gave it to me to …"

"Then you best keep it Cornelius, a gift given in love should be kept." She went to pass it back to him.

Cornelius closed his hand over hers. "Without your care, mistress, Gaius would not have recovered so quickly, perhaps not at all."

"He was hurt and I won't see anyone suffer … keep it." She said, trying to return the necklace.

Cornelius held her hand firmly closed. "Lady, you have suffered much, your people, your house, and your livelihood gone. The jewel is mine to give and I give it willingly for your help. I'm sure my betrothed will understand. It won't restore your fortune but it will buy you a better horse and at least you won't starve."

Adrianna smiled and kissed him gently on the cheek. "You could buy yourself two fine horses with this."

"We need to be gone and I daren't risk being seen dressed like this. Not everyone will be as accepting as you, selling us to the Carthaginians would appeal too many."

The following morning saw the two men depart. Gaius, despite his protests mounted on the horse and Cornelius leading it by the bridle. Adrianna pushed a flask of water and some bread and cheese into a bag, passing it to Cornelius.

"It's not much but it will see you most of the way back to Rome."

Cornelius smiled and bowed his head. "Thank you Lady, Juno bless and keep you."

Chapter Seventeen

Cups, plates and wine jugs flew across the tent as Bomilcar swiped them from the table. Growling and cursing, he kicked the table over then smashed the chair with a heavy downward kick, his servants cowered in the corner of the tent as their Lord's temper vented.

Stopping for breath, he glowered around the tent.

"Clean this up then get out there and find me replacements!"

The servants and slaves scurried to collect the broken crockery and furniture from the floor, while keeping their eyes down and away from their Lord as he prowled the tent. With the clear up complete, the servants removed themselves.

"You!" Bomilcar snapped his fingers at the last departing servant. "Send in Hephaestus."

The man bowed low. "Yes, my Lord."

Shortly, a tall, broad man stepped into the tent. "You sent for me, my Lord."

"Aye, come! We'll walk and talk, tents have ears." Bomilcar led the way outside. Lowering his voice, he began. "I have a task for you to organise, however it must not implicate me, you or any of our men in any way."

"My Lord?"

Steering Hephaestus away from the tents and people, Bomilcar quietly expounded his plan as they walked. Hephaestus stopped suddenly and stared at him; his eyes wide.

"Well man!" Bomilcar growled, impatient at Hephaestus's delayed reply. "What's the problem? Baal knows it's not difficult!"

"But my Lord, this could lead to murder and ..."

"So! ... I'm not asking you to do it, just arrange it!"

"But won't it attract suspicion, an enquiry? I've heard yourself say that Targa is or was a favourite of Hannibal."

"That's why I can't attack him openly but he will know no peace until I can kill him. Here!" He pushed a small leather bag at Hephaestus. "I'll even pay the low-life for the service. I don't want to know any details, neither do you, what we don't know can't implicate us. We'll know when it's done as I am sure there will be an enquiry and I will no doubt be a suspect. Hence the need for total secrecy and for me to be well away from here, do you understand?"

Hephaestus looked uneasy, Bomilcar seeing it rounded on him.

"It's a simple task, you only need be careful."

"But my Lord ..."

"Damn you man! ..." He paused to lower his voice and bridle his temper. "You've lived easy and well from my employ all these years now do as I command, else begone." When Hephaestus still looked uneasy, Bomilcar growled. "Go! If you won't do as I command but bear in mind your wife and family reside at my pleasure on my estate in Carthage."

Hephaestus paled as he grasped Bomilcar's meaning, clearing his throat he answered. "It will be as you command my Lord."

A cold smile and sneer teased Bomilcar's lips.

"That's better! I'm sure my employ has been easier on them and you than your previous life as a ragged-arsed, Greek mercenary."

"Yes, my Lord."

"Well! Do as I command and carefully if you value your hide and those of your family. Remember, no trace, no mistakes ... go!"

"Yes, my Lord." Hephaestus pushed the bag into his tunic and turned to go; Bomilcar placed a restraining hand on his arm.

"And while you are about it, throw my Lord Sakarbaal out of his quarters. Tell him to make his own way, at his expense instead of mine, I don't keep dogs that don't work or question my orders."

"Yes, my Lord."

"What? ..." Sakarbaal stared at Hephaestus and the soldiers who'd began removing his belongings.

"I'm sorry my Lord. As I said, I'm following orders from Lord Bodeshmun, I am to remove you and your belongings from his retinue, and you are to find your own way."

Armistaar, Sakarbaal's second in command reached for his falcata hilt.

Hephaestus saw it and snatched at his own, his other hand raised in a halting gesture.

"Hold sir! Hold! This is a lawful command that I do." Hephaestus's men stepped back quickly from their work, hands dropping to sword hilts. Hephaestus spoke quickly across the tension. "There is no need for bloodshed and if you attack myself or my men, I am sure Lord Bodeshmun would see you crucified."

Sakarbaal placed a hand on Armistaar's shoulder and spoke quietly. "Let them be, we are better gone from here and him."

Armistaar moved his hand away and the tension eased, the soldiers returning to emptying the tent, depositing the belongings outside on the grass.

****

Cornelius and Gaius had travelled for two days across meadows and farm tracks, away from Adrianna's house and the Carthaginians, south-westwards towards the Via Aurelia. Following the sun for direction, they'd avoided farms, homesteads and people, keeping to hedgerows and small copses for cover. With the weather still dry, they had slept in hedges and drainage ditches, fugitives in their own land.

Cresting a small rise early on the third day, Cornelius pointed northwards into the heat-hazed distance and the grey-white ribbon of road just visible at the end of a wide expanse of forest. "At last! If we make the road it will be easier going and we can go openly, we may even pick up some help from patrols."

"Aye but let's get through that wood first." Gaius nodded to the track leading into the trees directly in front of them.

"I think we should go around it?" Cornelius pointed north again.

Gaius shook his head. "If we do and at our pace, it could put a day on our journey. We then have to double back south again."

"Better that than risk bandits in the wood. We are ill prepared to take on such."

"I think we should risk it; I imagine such as they will have scattered with all the upheaval."

Cornelius looked uneasy. "Your wound still needs time and we only have one gladius between us and a dagger apiece."

"And my vine stick!" He chuckled. "Let's risk it lad, I think we'll be all right, we have a duty to reach Rome as soon as we can and report."

"I'm sure others will already have done that; we've been delayed a while."

"All the more reason we should push on quickly."

Cornelius shrugged. "Fair enough, perhaps you're right, the scum will have scattered."

The pair pushed on following the track towards the trees, though Gaius had Cornelius pass him up a short but hefty branch, which he slipped between his thigh and the horse. He winked at Cornelius.

"Just in case, eh?"

The pair made good time through the forest, the trees giving shade and a welcome respite from the fierce heat. However, unlike the road, the woodland track was narrow, it twisted and snaked, avoiding fallen trees, hillocks and low boggy areas. The wood was still, no wind stirred the high canopy, the only noise coming from the birds as they flittered ahead or away as the men came close. Blackbirds chirped loudly in alarm then settled back on the track after the pair had passed, seeking insects where the men's footfalls had disturbed the leaves. A woodpecker abandoned his noisy assault on an old trunk as the men approached, quietly watching from above as they passed beneath him.

It was now late afternoon but the broadleaf canopy was prematurely diminishing the light, Cornelius stopped and pointed through the trees, his lips creasing into a smile.

"There! There's the road, look! Past that big oak, through the gap."

Gaius however had also stopped, looking down at his mount's hoof but listening. When Cornelius stepped back to take the bridle he whispered softly. "Check the front, left hoof lad and take your time."

"What?"

"Just do it." He muttered.

Cornelius ran his hand down the horse's leg and crouched to lift the hoof. "What's the matter?" He whispered as he scraped at the inner hoof with a small stick.

"I might be wrong but the birds have stopped singing, it's gone very quiet."

"Evening's almost here?"

"Maybe but I don't hear any pigeons roosting, the finch's and blackbirds have disappeared. It's all gone quiet, too bloody quiet."

Cornelius carried on the hoof inspection and then a cuckoo called close by. "There you go." He said, breathing a little sigh of relief.

Gaius growled. "When did you last hear a cuckoo call this late in the season, egg laying finished long since!" His hand slid towards the branch beneath his thigh.

Cornelius began to rise. Suddenly a man appeared from behind a large tree and ran at Cornelius's back, a club in his hand. Cornelius heard the approaching footfalls but before he could stand and turn, Gaius swung his stick across hitting the attacking man hard in the jaw. The man fell to the side but knocked Cornelius off his feet. He heaved the dazed man away while snatching his dagger from its sheath and stabbed him quickly, twice in the ribs. The man grunted and stayed down. Gaius pulled the horse around, as three more men appeared, one off to the right and two others behind, all rushing to close on the two Centurions. A heavy boot hit Cornelius in the ribs before he could rise, the force rolling him over, the new assailant following and landing another vicious kick. The other two bandits, one with a sword the other with a short spear, attacked Gaius.

The man attacking Cornelius roared as he stepped quickly after him, swinging a two-handed, lead-weighted club trying to smash his head before he could rise. Cornelius; though winded and badly hurt from the kicks, held onto his dagger as he twisted and turned fast across the ground avoiding the quick but crude club blows. The man tried to stamp on his legs while swinging the club one handed at his face. Cornelius kicked at the man's ankles but missed and had to use his arm to block the incoming club strike, he yelped loudly as the blow smashed his forearm. The bandit, sensing victory stepped closer while raising the club for another strike to finish the fight. Cornelius rolled towards him, growling as his damaged arm momentarily took his weight and sat up, surprising him and forcing his dagger, hilt deep into the man's lower belly. The man stalled, groaning loudly, the club falling from his hand as he tried to hold his hurt. Cornelius tried to pull the dagger free but it only came halfway out, twisting it, he forced it deep again. The man screamed and staggered forward then collapsed to his knees, blood soaking his tunic, the dagger hilt and Cornelius's hand. Cornelius tried to get up and gasped as his ribs objected.

Gaius was holding the swordsman off with his branch, the sword thankfully having little in the way of an edge. The horse, untrained to battle whinnied in fright and stepped about trying to escape the fight. Its erratic movements and the nearby trees forced the spearman the same side as the swordsman, spoiling his attack. Unable to close with

Gaius the bandit speared the horse instead. The spearhead went deep and the animal gave a high-pitched whinny, rearing and pulling the spear from the man's hand. As the horse stumbled and lurched, Gaius lost his balance. Teetering wildly, his flailing stick hit the swordsman in the face sending him staggering backwards, his mouth and nose a burst of blood. Gaius fell from the horse as it collapsed, losing his branch and grunting loudly as his wounded shoulder hit the ground hard, his hip banging off an old tree stump.

Cornelius had managed to gain his feet and stepped over Gaius's legs towards the two bandits, gladius drawn, and his broken arm tight against his side trying to support his ribs.

The swordsman, dazed and spitting blood and teeth, wiped his eyes. Seeing the outstretched gladius and Centurion's garb, he glanced quickly at his comrade who'd snatched a dagger from his belt. Cornelius moved the blade point threateningly from one man to the other as he advanced. The dagger man, recognising a man who knew how to use a blade, stepped backwards then turned and ran back into the trees. Cornelius stepped quickly at the swordsman who swung his blade wildly at him. The crude stroke missed and left the bandit's guard and belly exposed. Cornelius thrust the gladius into him, twisting it as he'd been taught. The man screamed as the blade forced through his gut and out of his back and he dropped his sword. Cornelius snatched the gladius back out then stabbed again. The man collapsed to his knees and Cornelius stabbed him again and again.

"Bastard! … Bastard!" He screamed as he turned the man's chest and belly into bloodied flesh.

Gaius meanwhile had gained his feet and snatched his dagger and vine stick from his belt. Seeing Cornelius finishing the swordsman, he advanced on the two injured bandits Cornelius had fought, and who now crawled slowly across the ground trying to escape. He smacked each hard on the head with his stick. When both were unconscious, he limped back towards the dropped, lead-weighted club, picking it up; he smashed each man's head to a pulp.

"A blade's too good for the likes of you!" He growled as blood, grey jelly and shards of bone flew from the repeated blows. Out of breath and dizzy, he looked around for Cornelius. "Are you all right lad?" He shouted when he saw Cornelius holding his ribs and leaning heavily on his gladius, it stuck in the forest floor. "Cornelius!"

"I'm all right Gaius." He gasped as the pain in his chest stole his breath. "I think my ribs and left arm are broken but I'm all right, you?"

"Aye lad, I'll survive! My shoulder's on fire and my hip's not too good but I'm all right."

"Bastards! Scum! What did we have that was worth taking?" His tone incredulous.

Gaius checked the horse; the spear had gone deep and the animal had bled out. He picked up the saddle blanket, food bag and the water flasks.

"We both walk from here, I guess. Let's have a look at you." He limped across to Cornelius and helped him straighten up. Cornelius groaned loudly, his good arm automatically holding his chest. "You did well lad, three of the bastards! If we take the belts off these pigs, we can strap your chest and make a sling for your arm, that'll help until we can find some proper care. Let's see your arm." Gaius gently fingered Cornelius's forearm, making him wince and curse softly when his fingers found the break. "It's a clean break but it needs aligning, it'll hurt while I move it into position but it's better done now."

Squatting down and groaning sharply as his hip objected, he found two dry sticks, which he measured against his own forearm, snapping them to size. Next, he unlaced one of the dead bandit's sandals then knotting the laces, he gestured to Cornelius. "Hold your arm level."

Cornelius offered his arm. He groaned loudly and gasped for breath as his hand and wrist sagged.

"Here, I'll lift your wrist; you'll need to hold it while I splint it. I'm sorry, this will hurt."

Cornelius cursed under his breath and growled low in his throat as Gaius moved the arm to align the bones. Sweat broke out on his brow and he swallowed hard trying not to throw up.

"Won't be long lad." He said as he bound the sticks parallel on the arm with the laces. "You'll have to hold it there; I need to strap your ribs before we sling your arm."

Pulling the leather belts from the dead bandits, Gaius used two to strap Cornelius's chest and the third as a sling. Cornelius saw Gaius's shoulder wound had bled again but on examination found only part of the skin had opened up. Gaius cut a piece from his tunic and stuffed it under his mail shirt and over the wound. Pulling the spear from the horse, he tried it as a walking staff.

"It'll do, it will take a bit of weight off my hip. Come on, the road is not so far. I'm sorry; I should have listened to you and gone around the forest."

Cornelius waved the comment away. The pair set off again along the track towards the road, their pace slow, each helping the other along.

****

The trumpet call for the cavalry to assemble drifted over the Carthaginian camp. Within moments, Andulas and Armaco were at Baldor's tent.

"What's afoot Baldor? Are we on the move?" Andulas asked.

"Any orders from the General?" Armaco growled.

"Nothing, we remain stood down unless called."

The three men stepped outside the tent into the dawn.

"That's a lot of horse assembling." Andulas said as he watched men and horses forming troops then growing into regiments.

"Aye! A lot alright." Armaco said as he mouthed numbers, his head nodding gently as he counted. "Something big is going down, more bloody Romans likely?"

"Surely not! We've just given them a thumping."

Baldor shrugged. There was silence for a while as the men watched. "Unless … unless, Geminus has appeared from the east?"

A messenger galloping his horse towards Baldor's tent interrupted the men's thoughts. The man drew his horse up hard in front of them.

"Captain! Captain Targa?"

"Yes soldier, what is it?"

"Captain Sir! Orders from the General. Assemble all your horse immediately and join the regiments under General Maharbal." The man pushed a bronze token stamped with an 'H' into Baldor's hand.

"What's to do?" Baldor asked as he took the horse's bridle.

"Roman cavalry sir, about four thousand strong heading this way from the east."

"Geminus's cavalry?"

"We think so, sir. There's no infantry just cavalry. General Maharbal is to intercept them, if we leave now, we have time to catch them in the hills southeast of the lake."

"Thank you soldier. Tell General Maharbal we will be with him very shortly." Baldor released the bridle and the man saluted and pulled the horse about. "Gentlemen, assemble our men here, fully armed and victualled." Andulas took off at the run, Armaco limping along behind him. Baldor ducked back in the tent. "Lasairiona! Sulis! I need my war gear, now!"

****

The two Centurions stepped out of the forest and weaved their way around the stumps of the trees that had been cleared a quarter-mile either side of the road; ensuring bandits could not come close without being seen. Gaius looked northwards and saw two travellers making their way south.

"Here! … Here! We need help … over here!" He shouted and waved. "Come on lad, let's get a spurt on." The travellers had stopped, seeking the direction of the call. "Here! … Over here!" He waved his arm in the air again as they stumbled on towards the road. The travellers pointed, looked in the direction of the shout and then seeing the pair took off at the run southwards.

"Wait! … Wait! For the love of Juno wait!" Cornelius shouted loudly, making his head hurt. The travellers ran on. "You useless bastards! Wait!"

Injured, weary and having to step around stumps and scrub the pair stood no chance of catching the travellers and they slowed their pace, watching as they fled down the road.

"You can't blame them lad, we could just as easy be bandits from this distance. At least we are at the road."

Stepping over a shallow ditch, they set foot on the road and Cornelius's spirits lifted slightly. Walking on the paved surface was easy compared to the woodland track and with a good, all round view the pair relaxed and concentrated in helping the other along. Shortly they caught sight of a waymarker.

"How far to Rome do you think?"

Cornelius shrugged. "I've no idea; I only know we are walking southwest."

As they approached the white stone pillar, Gaius limped ahead and stood in front of the marker then turned, a smile creasing his face. "Guess?" Cornelius was too tired to care and just shrugged. "Only twenty-three miles! That's not too bad!"

"What? In the shape we are in. That's almost a good day's march if we were fit."

"Come on Cornelius, we're alive and free, aren't we? There's a lot of lads back at the lake who would happily swap places with us."

The thought sobered Cornelius and he straightened his back. "Yes, yes you are right. The Gods have been good, we have got this far and the rest should be easy." His eyes misted and his face twisted as he tried to hide his emotions. "I'm sorry Gaius, I should ..." His tears fell coursing through the grime on his cheeks as he broke down. He cuffed them away, sniffed hard and tried to speak. Gaius limped towards him and put his arm over his shoulder.

"It's all right lad, it's all right. It's not been easy. It's been a hard few days but we're nearly there. Come on, if we walk until dark that'll eat another mile or two up and make for a shorter day tomorrow."

Stopping just before dark, they stepped off the road again seeking cover and lying down amongst the old stumps and scrub. Gaius passed some bread.

"Eat it up lad; it'll stop the worms nibbling your guts. We should be in Rome by tomorrow night and enjoying a proper meal."

Cornelius tore at the hard bread and chewed. "What do we tell them Gaius? We've survived and our men haven't, shouldn't we be dead?"

"Others will have survived too; we won't be the only ones and Jupiter knows we have the wounds to prove how hard we've fought."

"I don't know how I can face my family or Aemilia's family; this is our third defeat!"

"Hey! We're just Centurions, not Consuls. We don't plan battles or campaigns." He passed the water flask. "Get some sleep eh? We'll be on our way at first light."

Cornelius nodded, gave a wan smile and stretched out gingerly trying to find comfort for his ribs and arm. The evening was warm and the smell of the grass and scrub pleasant, listening to the birds evening chorus and the crickets and cicadas whirring and clicking, he fell asleep.

He was awoken by the dewfall, the evening's heat long gone and replaced by a sharp cold. Exhausted, he'd slept soundly though his body ached all over and as he moved, his ribs and arm announced their displeasure, the pain snatching his breath away. Stifling his groans, he whispered into the half-light for Gaius.

"I'm here Cornelius, wet-arsed and bloody frozen but I'm here!"

Cornelius slowly got to his feet and helped Gaius up, he having to use the spear as a staff and Cornelius's good arm. Both men were damp with dew, chilled and keen to move on, hoping movement would put some warmth into them and perhaps loosen up their body's stiffness. They had just passed the twenty-mile marker when they heard the drum of hooves in the distance behind them.

"A patrol?" Cornelius's face lit up.

"Coming at that speed and this early, it has to be but let's just step off the road and watch first."

Cornelius's face fell. "You don't think they could be Carthaginians, do you?"

"No, no I don't but we aren't taking any more chances. Come on, back in the scrub." The pair shuffled off the road and laid down, watching. The thunder of hooves came closer. "That's a fair few horses coming this way."

"A turma?"

"Could be." Gaius carefully parted the grass and looked back down the road. "Jupiter, Juno and Mars be thanked! They're ours!"

Both men struggled to their feet, helping one another and waving at the oncoming horsemen. They weren't seen at first, then spears suddenly raised and the formation turned and swelled from column to line across the road. Both men raised an arm and edged slowly out of the scrub. The Decurion held up a halting hand and the horsemen slowed then stopped a spear's throw from the two men.

"Who in Hade's name are you?" He bawled. "Out here on the road, now! Where we can see you."

Gaius left his spear and the pair stepped onto the road showing empty hands.

"Centurions' Scipio and Laelius from the second legion. Who in Hade's name are you?" Gaius snapped back.

"Decurion, Marcus Quintus Herminius." The man peered and then walked his horse forward. His eyes widened at the state of the pair. Seeing Gaius's vine stick, he looked again, past the grime, blood and makeshift bandages and recognising the phalerae harnesses, he saluted. "Begging your pardon Centurion but we had to be sure, the Carthaginians are roaming everywhere." The pair lowered their hands. "You're survivors of the battle?"

"Aye."

"Can you ride?"

"I doubt it, I think my hip is cracked and Centurion Scipio's ribs and arm are broken."

The Decurion looked thoughtful. "We passed a cart a mile or so back, heading this way. We'll commandeer it and get you back to Rome on that. When did you last eat or drink?"

The Decurion stood the troop down to await the cart and food and watered wine were found for the pair. Gesturing them to one side and lowering his voice, he asked.

"How bad was it?"

"Bad enough." Gaius answered while biting lumps off some dried meat and a fresh loaf, stuffing it into his mouth and swilling wine. "They cut us up on the road by Lake Trasimene and hounded us through the forest. We fought a defensive action at a farm the following day but they slaughtered us. Some locals helped us with care, food and a horse, but we were ambushed yesterday in the forest by bandits. At least three of the bastards won't trouble anyone again!" He growled and flicked his head back towards the forest.

The Decurion shook his head gently. "I'm sorry; you've had it rough all right."

"Aye, time for pay back methinks. What news from Rome?"

"Consul Geminus is recalled ..."

"No loss there!"

The Decurion raised his eyebrows at Gaius's sharp retort. "He dispatched his whole cavalry arm towards you, surely they ...?"

"No idea! We never saw any cavalry."

"You don't think they've been ..."

Gaius shrugged and took another drink. "Who knows? But cavalry moving through hill country without infantry support ..."

"But that's a sizeable force, upwards of three maybe four thousand men?"

"Hannibal has just chopped thirty thousand men to bloody ruin, a few thousand is a lot less of a challenge ... who's the new Consul?"

Marcus chewed his lip. "Geminus is relieved of his command and the senate has appointed a Dictator instead."

"What?" Gaius stopped chewing and looked askance at the Decurion. Cornelius seemed to wake from his apathy and just gawped.

"They've declared crisis and handed Dictatorial power to a senior senator, Quintus Fabius Maximus."

Gaius was about to expound his thoughts on senators when

Cornelius squeezed his arm and cut in. "He's a soldier at least; he served in the last war against the Carthaginians."

An approaching trooper halted the conversation. "The cart's approaching sir."

When the cart arrived and the owner advised of his new obligations and his outrage quelled, the pair were carefully loaded amongst the cargo of bales of cloth. Cornelius quietened the man's grumbles when he offered to pay recompense for the inconvenience and any damage to the goods, once they reached Rome.

A mile or two down the road, the Decurion edged his mount near to the cart. "I'll leave ten men with you as an escort and ride ahead to place my report. It'll take you another day to reach Rome at the pace of the cart, is there anyone in Rome I can inform that you are on your way home."

With food in their bellies and the gentle sway of the cart, Cornelius was already asleep and didn't hear, Gaius answered. "Go to the house of the former Consul, Publius Scipio and tell them their son is safe and on his way home."

The Decurion's eyes widened and he stared at Cornelius. "He's … he's …"

"Yes, he is."

The man recovered his surprise. "And yourself sir? Who can we notify for you?"

Gaius just shook his head gently. "No one … no one, Decurion don't worry about it."

"Very well sir. Decurion, Marcus Quintus Herminius at your service, safe journey."

****

Bomilcar waved the messenger away and had his signaller sound assembly. Warriors appeared from their tents, strapping on mail and making their way to the horse lines.

"Hephaestus! Here." Bomilcar waved the man over to him. "We are joining General Maharbal to intercept Roman cavalry coming from the east."

"Yes sir, I'll have your horse brought."

"Just a moment! In here quickly" He beckoned Hephaestus into the tent and dispatched another servant for the horse. After checking every

231

corner of the tent and ensuring all the servants and slaves were out, he pulled Hephaestus close and spoke in a low whisper. "If I'm being summoned, there is a good chance Targa has been also. They think we are at least a day away from contact with the Romans so you stay here and make sure he is gone. If he is, now is the time for the plan we discussed. See to it!"

Hephaestus looked uncomfortable but a cold stare from Bomilcar had him nod his head and mumble. "Yes, my Lord."

"No trace to me, you or anyone in my retinue, do you have it?"

"Yes, my Lord."

"His people dead or sold, it matters not. His possessions gone but not sold where they may be seen and traced."

"Yes, my Lord."

"Well see to it then … Where's my horse?"

Chapter Eighteen

A day and half of riding saw Maharbal's column southeast of the lake and their camp. His men and horses, secreted now in the forest were more numerous than the trees. Warriors had dismounted resting their mounts while snatching a bite to eat and drink out of the midday heat. The infantry contingent, happy to lay their weapons down after their tireless trot behind the cavalry drank and ate sparingly, ready to up and go on command. General Maharbal summoned his commanders to a briefing in a small clearing, his Captains squatting in a circle around him as they ate. Maharbal scratched his plan on the forest floor with his sword blade.

"Our scouts advise we are less than half a day from contact with the Romans. They're coming on apace from the east with their scouts well ahead of them."

"They're learning then, sir." A Captain quipped and raised a murmur of laughter.

"Aye, they are." Maharbal gave a little chuckle while removing his helmet and mopping his baldhead with his scarf. "However, I have a plan to put to you. A short ride from here the track leads into a deep valley. By the time the Romans reach it, it will be late afternoon and I think they'll make camp there where their men can stay together rather than be spread out along the track."

"Are you thinking of a night assault sir?" A Captain asked.

"No, I would rather catch and fight them in the light."

"But if their scouts are as active and far out as you say, they would have ample warning of us."

"Not if we remove and replace their scouts with ours." The group looked on with acute interest. "We've been watching and their scouts are operating singly and are clumsy, so much so that we've already exchanged …" He chuckled again. "Some of them with our own men."

Some chuckles and light laughter came back from the group at which he smiled but waved to silence.

"We think, if we keep our distance and just use hand signals, we may be able to fox them and lure their main body on or at least give them a false sense of ease.

The hills rise on either side of the valley floor but there are smaller hills directly in front of these forming a defile between them, large enough to hide men and horses." Men leaned in close as he scratched on the floor. "Here's my thoughts. If we split into three columns, the first with myself as a large blocking and holding force to continue east and meet the Romans head on in the valley. The other two columns to approach from the north under Lieutenant General Himilco and south under Lieutenant General Hanno, both positioning themselves in the hill defiles either side of the valley …"

"We box them in General, on three sides?" Himilco asked.

"Aye, that's my plan."

"What of timing, General and signals?" Hanno cupped his chin as he stared at the scratching on the floor.

"Once my column has contact, yours and Lieutenant General Himilco's men will hear the din and can attack."

"What if we are late arriving in the defile, sir?"

"Attack as soon as you are able."

"Will that not jeopardise you and your men, sir?"

"No, the track narrows as it exits the valley; we'll be arrayed there, we have enough men to hold the Romans until your columns come up either side."

"Could they try and outflank you sir?"

"I doubt it, I'm told the hills are steep and horses could only go slowly and singly along sheep tracks, so we could easily counter any movement coming that way. Furthermore, I plan to use Captain Tercero and his five hundred, Spanish infantry that we have with us as support." He nodded towards a grizzled, black bearded, man who smiled back. "They can act as skirmishers on the hillsides. Captain, I'll position you and your men on either flank of my cavalry. You can be our sheepdogs should the Romans try to take to the hills."

Baldor found voice. "A suggestion, if I may General?"

"Speak freely, Captain."

"If we could get behind them as well sir, perhaps at the end of the valley, we could cut off any retreat."

"Ideally Captain, yes. That way we would have them all, well and truly trapped. However, as you will know, trapped men are likely to fight like cornered rats and thus it would be prudent to have some infantry support alongside your horse. Also, the time it would take you to get into position I think would prove too long?"

"If you could spare me some of Captain Tercero's spearmen sir? They and my troop could try if you wish? My horsemen are predominately Spaniards and Gauls and used to the hill and forest, we can move quickly."

Maharbal looked thoughtful and summoned a scout forward. "What do you think of the Captain's suggestion, is there time?"

"It would be tight sir and the riding taxing; the route the Captain needs to take is across the hillsides parallel to the track we are on, hard going. The infantry I surmise, would slow the Captain further."

"General, if I may." The stout, black-bearded, infantry Captain stepped forward. Maharbal nodded ascent and gestured for the man to speak.

"We are mountain men General; I vouch my lads can move as fast as the horses across these hills. If you can spare some of us, we could support Captain Targa with closing the trap."

The quiet but charged atmosphere of the briefing heightened as men considered the suggestions. Harbro spoke up.

"If we have sufficient men General, I am also willing to accompany Captain Targa's men; my lads are of similar mix, Spaniards and Gauls. If we arrive late it would be no matter, some may escape, however if we are on time it may be decisive if the Romans see they are completely trapped."

Maharbal cupped his chin. "We have the numbers to spare but the two columns heading for the defiles also have hard riding. They need to swing wide from here then climb the rearward hills and drop down into the defiles, it's going to be hard on men and horses; all will be tired before we even close with the Romans. We'll need to finish the fight quickly and four thousand men is a large force to overcome."

"Better if we can block their retreat and hold them for you then sir, giving a chance for the trap to close. Would you venture some of Captain Tercero's spearmen and Captain Harbro's troop and mine try?"

Maharbal raised his head and looked into the trees, his brow furrowed in thought before he nodded decisively.

"Aye, Captain Targa! Why not? Let's chance it; I think we have all eventualities covered. Captain Tercero, leave me a hundred of your lads to act as sheepdogs; that should suffice for my needs. You and the other four hundred go with Captains' Targa and Harbro." He looked around the circle. "Gentlemen, any other questions, objections or suggestions?" Grim smiles and silence were the only response. "Let's to it then. Captains' Targa, Harbro, Tercero, I'll send a detachment of Numidians with you as well, they will be faster again and can act as pathfinders for you."

The calls to mount up rippled through the forest. Like a disturbed ants nest the force split into three large columns and Baldor's small force of Harbro's cavalry and Tercero's infantry, these being joined by a detachment of Numidians. Baldor reined alongside Harbro as they trotted through the trees and offered his hand.

"I feel better now you are with me."

Harbro smiled, winked and shook his hand. "I heard this voice in my head saying. 'Keep an eye on the lad' I'm not sure if it was Balaam or Gestix!"

Baldor smiled warmly. "Blessing upon them both and on you."

"And on you Baldor." They rode on in silence for a while before Harbro spoke again. "I'm glad we're away from the other columns."

When Baldor gave a quizzical look, Harbro expounded. "That bastard, Bodeshmun. He was at the briefing; did you not see him?"

"No, no I didn't."

"Well, at least you won't have to watch your back this time but take care Baldor; I've seen his like before, damned Lordling! He won't let the argument go, no matter what the General says."

"Yes, I'll mind it." He replied quietly. "I know how Sakarbaal and his family are."

"Good man! Keep your wits about you and your eyes open."

The troops pushed on throughout the afternoon moving as fast as the terrain would allow. Tercero's Spaniards loping along seemingly effortlessly beside the horses. The heat remained oppressive, punishing both horses and warriors, the going hard. Riding across the slope of the hill, the men tried to follow the well-worn goat and sheep tracks where they could, avoiding the irregular clumpy and broken ground. The Numidians on their sure-footed desert ponies seemed to eat the ground up effortlessly and managed to keep ahead of the other troops so to direct them on the best paths.

General Hanno's column, initially riding alongside Baldor's and Harbro's, had turned back northwards into the hills and toward the valley some time ago. Baldor now quietly fretted as he watched the sun slowly sinking. He pushed his mount alongside Harbro.

"Do you think we'll be in place and there'll be a fight before darkness falls?"

"I'm not sure, Baldor. Malo has gone ahead with the Numidians; he'll be able to gauge time if he can see ahead at all, though it's difficult in these hills."

The troop had to slow again as they encountered a hillside covered in yellow flowering, gorse. Forced to follow a single, narrow sheep track through it, they stretched out in long single file. Exiting onto clear hillside again Baldor, still agonizing over the slow progress wiped the sweat from his eyes as he stared into the heat haze.

"Harbro! Look." He pointed to a plume of brown dust on the hillside in front of them and saw Malo and two Numidians forcing their mounts for more speed.

"They've seen something; else the valley end is close?"

The three men reined in, in front of Baldor, their mounts white with spume, the stink of horse sweat strong on the breeze.

"Captains, battle is joined ..."

"Damn it! We're late." Baldor thumped his thigh. "How far to the valley end, Malo?"

"Another five stades or so Captain, not too far. However, there is a small but deep river to cross."

"Fordable for men and horses though?"

Malo's expression was grim. "No sign of a ford sir, we'll have to swim it."

Harbro cursed loudly and looked at Baldor. "That'll slow us up and what about the infantry, getting them over will be difficult. Do we leave them and push on?"

Malo interjected. "The Romans are not giving any ground yet, General Maharbal is holding them and the other two columns haven't come up yet."

"That still gives us some time Harbro, the Romans are unlikely to panic until the other columns appear on their flanks. I don't want to abandon the infantry either; they will be useful if we are trying to block a retreat." Baldor said as he turned, looking around at the men and horses scattered across the hillside.

"Captain! Captain Tercero!" He shouted and waved to the infantry Captain who hurried across to Baldor's mount.

"Aye Captain!"

"We have five stades or so to go and a river to cross. Have your men mount behind Captain Harbro's and mine. It'll save your wind and a swim and we can arrive together." When Tercero looked unsure, Baldor continued quickly. "It helped us at the Trebbia, we mounted the infantry behind us and it saved their breath and energy for the fight." He extended his hand to Tercero. "Come on! Up behind me."

Tercero grabbed Baldor's hand and clambered up behind him while calling for his men to mount up. The cavalrymen seeing what was happening, helping the infantry to mount up behind them. As Baldor urged his mount on the Spaniard lurched and grabbed for support.

"Hold on to me, Captain and grip the horse with your legs."

"I would have rather run."

"What about the swim?"

Tercero didn't answer immediately.

"We're mountain folk, swimming is not natural to us, some of my men may be able to swim but most, likely not, I can't."

"You'll thank me when we get over then!"

With the horses' double loaded, the going was slower and most of the infantry pillions nervous and awkward atop the horses. The land however, became less steep as they approached the river and the straggling column began to bunch up on the river margin waiting to cross. The Numidians were already across with a handful remaining to guide the arriving troops to a point where the bank was less steep and the horses could enter. As the first horses edged down the bank to the water, the infantrymen tightened their grip with their legs and hunched closer to their cavalry comrade. The only exit onto the other bank was further downstream and as the horses angled across the flow, the current carried them swiftly towards it, the deep-water making for a relatively smooth but daunting crossing. As Baldor guided his mount into the river, he heard Tercero mumble his prayers, as the water washed around their waists and the horse began to swim, Baldor felt him push closer and his hands scrabble for purchase.

"Just hold onto my belt Captain, the horse will get us over; clamp your legs if you can and lean forward with me." Baldor reached behind him and took hold of Tercero's belt. "I won't let you go."

The river was soon full of horses making their way from bank to bank. The crossing progressed smoothly; the only noise was the snorting of the horses labouring with their double load and then the splash as the first hooves touched the shallows of the opposite bank. The first ashore exited the water up a dirt bank, their hooves throwing dirt and grass sods as they sought purchase. The bank was steep and becoming wetter and more slippery as more and more animals climbed it, the slips and stumbles occasionally toppling the infantryman off the back of the horse. Thankfully, it was only bruises, the occasional soaking and damaged pride that the infantry suffered as they reluctantly climbed back onto the horses. Baldor extricated himself without incident, though he had to haul Tercero forward by his belt as the man's legs slipped on the horse's wet coat.

"Thank you Captain, thank you! And thank you Nabia, Goddess of rivers and streams for seeing us both safely across."

Baldor was already reining the horse about. "Malo! How far from here to the valley entrance?"

"Three stades or so, sir." He shouted as he pointed and turned his mount up toward the valley entrance.

Baldor nodded and looked to Harbro who was marshalling the men as they continued to emerge from the river.

"Three stades Captain and we are there."

Harbro waved acknowledgement as he bellowed at the last of the men to hurry up. Moments later the soaked and double laden column was on the move at speed towards the valley.

As they came closer, Baldor could hear the first faint sounds of battle but could see nothing. Anxious and wanting to push on, he forced himself to wait for Malo and the Numidian scouts returning again. Harbro pushed alongside.

"Well, we're here, Captain."

"Aye, but ..."

"Malo won't be long." He said as he managed a smile. "It's hard when you can hear battle, the instinct is to either join it or run from it, anything is better than waiting."

"I'd rather wait than ride another horse or swim another river."

Tercero interjected.

Harbro chuckled lightly and Tercero managed a smile. Baldor however was grim.

"I hate it. I just want it over. It's worse this time as this venture was my idea, my suggestion. I'm responsible to make a difference if I can and to keep as many of us whole as possible."

"We'll manage lad." Harbro patted his horse's neck as it tossed its head causing him to look up. "We've got this far and I think we're in time." He flicked his head towards the valley to where Malo and a handful of Numidians had appeared. Malo, recognising Harbro had seen him, reined up and was now waving him on towards him.

Baldor and Harbro trotted their mounts forward while bringing the column on; Malo had to shout above the rumble of hooves and rattle of harness. The men talking as they rode.

"The valley is quite long and the Romans are further up where it broadens. They were making camp by the looks of things, just as the General surmised."

"Is there a narrow place, a choke point where we can best use our numbers to hold them if they turn to run?"

"Further up the valley Captain, it narrows before opening out again, that may suffice, sir."

"Have the other two columns joined the fight yet, Malo?"

"The column from the south was just coming over the hills into the valley when I turned back for you; the one from the north had not appeared yet."

Baldor felt his heart lift a little and smiled grimly at Harbro. "We may be just in time."

Harbro nodded and urged his mount on.

In the valley proper, the Romans had rallied surprisingly quickly to Maharbal's surprise attack. Roman trumpets had summoned a dozen turmaes of Equites, not yet encamped who rode out screening the camp, giving the others time to arm, remount and form up. The initial clash, at speed, accounted for many casualties on both sides, now the battle slowed into a wheeling, pushing match of horseflesh. Men abandoned spears and fought with swords, hacking and thrusting as the two forces crushed together. Men died but couldn't fall, the press of horses being so tight. The weight of Maharbal's numbers however, was steadily pushing the Romans back towards their camp. When

Hanno's men appeared over the hill from the south, in strength, amidst the lilting blare of war horns and made a ragged but heavy attack into the Roman flank, the fight began to shift across the valley floor to the north. In the camp, the Romans were still mounting and forming turmaes and cantering forward to join the fight.

The valley floor resonated with the cries of men, screams of horses and the clash of weapons, the battle looking like a colourful, moving sea as it flowed and eddied across the ground. The Romans, despite the constant stream of reinforcements from their camp were being slowly forced to the foot of the northern hills. As Hanno's men gained ground on the valley floor, he directed newly arriving detachments to attack the camp. In the camp, some Equites were still strapping on their armour when the Carthaginians hit them. Many were killed before reaching their horses as the mounted warriors swept through, slaughtering men, firing tents and cutting horse lines. The loose horses adding to the mayhem as they reared and bolted trying to flee the flames and the stink of blood.

When the crest of the northern hills darkened with Himilco's men and horses, and the brassy tones of trumpets had them spilling down the hillside to attack the Romans in the flank, panic ensued. Boxed in now on three sides and with the enemy seemingly innumerable, the Equites looked to the only avenue of escape, a retreat back down the valley. Those still unengaged in combat were the first to peel away. The fleeing Romans thundered through the remains of their camp, fighting Hanno's troops who tried to block their path and riding their own men down as they sought help else got in the way.

"There sir!" Malo shouted to Baldor as he pointed just ahead to a narrowing of the valley.

Baldor glanced around quickly. The narrowing was flanked on either side by steep sided hills, no risk of the position being easily outflanked and he reckoned he had enough troops to hold the gap. They would be the cork in the bottle. The Romans were trapped.

"Here! We stand here!" He bellowed.

Tercero had already jumped off the horse and was running to the centre of the gap.

"Infantry here! Form up on me!" He pointed across the gap with his spear.

The infantry jumped down from the horses and rushed to form a shield wall across the gap. Tercero knew his business and soon there were two lines of shields and spears filling the gap. Baldor and Harbro marshalled their men close behind the infantry line. Baldor trotted his mount across to Andulas and Armaco.

"This is it. I hope I haven't led you astray in this venture. My blessings and may your Gods keep you both." He bowed his head and placed his fist over his heart.

The big Gaul smiled and dipped his head. "And you Baldor. May Epona grant you life."

"It's a good position Baldor, you're learning!" Armaco sniggered and shook Baldor's hand hard. "Baal keep you, my friend."

The sounds of battle were much louder now and as men waited, they fidgeted, flexing shield arms and setting their stance. Some talked loudly or guffawed in exaggerated laughter, others were at prayer, some just silent. Baldor stared ahead and strained his ears listening for the inevitable rumble of hooves he knew would be coming their way. Harbro saw the tension on Baldor's face and he eased his mount close, speaking quietly.

"Won't be long now, Captain. We're in position and ready, you've done well to get us all here."

"No, we've done well, Harbro. You, Tercero, the men and the horses." He gave a brief smile, secretly glad to talk and spare his nerves. "Now for the hard part."

"We'll manage Baldor." Harbro smiled and offered his hand. "In case I don't see you till it's over; Baal protect and keep you, lad." He saluted then kneed his mount across the line to his troop.

"And you Harbro. Thank you for the support." He touched his fist to his heart and bowed his head.

Left alone again to his thoughts, he ruminated. He was halfway through his mission, he was in position, a good position and in time but now, he had to hold the ground, now he had to fight. The men had quietened now and he saw nearly all had taken to prayer. He wondered once more at his lack of piety, his self-enforced refusal to accept the Gods, blaming them still for his dead wife, comrades and his misfortune. Briefly considering his own mortality, a tinge of fear swept over him, making him shiver despite the heat. Sneering at his trepidation, he stiffened his resolve and raising his face to the sky, he mumbled his own reverences.

"Father, Gestix, help me lead well, help me to be brave and worthy of my name."

His heart still thumped in his chest, his stomach heavy with the same oily feeling it always had before combat, then the rumble of hooves coming close snapped him from his thoughts. The infantry line shuffled, wood clattered as men overlapped shields and sought the closeness of their comrades. Hands tightened on spear shafts and twisted in shield straps, horses tossed their heads and some whickered as they picked up the scent of the incoming Roman horses. Malo drew three arrows from the quiver on his mount's trappings, holding two and laying the other on his bowstring. Baldor slipped a falcata from the scabbard on his back and hefted his shield across his chest.

The first Romans arrived at the gallop in panic and loose order. Surprised at the unexpected appearance of the Carthaginians, they had to adjust quickly as their mounts shied from the close ranked warriors and protruding spears. Malo loosed his arrows in rapid succession across the heads of the infantry into the oncoming Romans, bringing down three horses, others following too close behind tripping over the fallen.

"Javelins, loose!" Tercero shouted and the infantrymen with javelins hurled them into the turbulent mass of men and horses. Horses screamed, whickered and went down. Such was the incoming speed that a few slid along the ground, legs flailing, screeching in agony from their wounds and crushing their riders.

Deadly chaos ensued as Equites and horses succumbed to the javelin shower. The Romans, confused and shocked, failed to respond as javelins and arrows continued to knock more men from their mounts; others killing the horses and catapulting their riders through the air as the animals collapsed beneath them. Desperate to be away from the wood and flesh barricade, the Romans tried to rein up and about-turn, just as a second salvo of javelins tore into them adding more bodies to the carnage.

Some infantrymen made to step forward and slaughter the Romans struggling to their feet or already limping away.

"Hold the line there! ... Shields up, there'll be more coming!" Tercero prowled the line pushing men back into position as he bellowed commands.

The next wave of Romans, having warning of the Carthaginians by survivors of the first group, were better prepared and came on in line with raised spears. Tercero's infantry stood their ground, throwing any remaining javelins into the tight ranks and decimating them. The Romans still came on, closing the gaps in the line where their comrades or mounts had fallen until the horses reached and shied in front of the raised shields. As the horses reared and milled, the Romans thrust their spears down over the shield rims, the Carthaginians thrusting back at both horses and men. The battle noise was deafening; spear shafts clattered and rattled like branches in the wind, swords and spearheads banged on shields and rang on helmets like bell clappers. Horses stomped and whickered, wild-eyed in fear as their riders forced them into the fight. Men shouted, cursed in hate and grunted in effort, else screamed and howled as metal found flesh. Hot, wet blood misted and sprayed, covering men and horses. The weight and pressure on the shield wall was becoming intense as more Romans arrived, Baldor seeing it shouted to his men.

"Harbro! Those men with javelins, loose … loose!"

Javelins arced over the heads of Tercero's men into the Romans, killing and maiming men and horses and the attack faltered. When gaps appeared, the horses turned into them desperate to be away from the noise, huge bright painted shields, stabbing spears and the stink of blood. With no breaches appearing in the shield wall, the Romans finally turned away raising cheers and whoops from the infantry.

With the respite, Tercero had his dead and injured removed and the shield wall shrunk, the men that remained whole or still capable of fighting taking the chance for a drink. Baldor, seeing Tercero pulling men from the second rank to extend the first, beckoned Harbro to him.

"I'll dismount half my men and join the infantry, if we can hold this line the Romans will never get past. I'm hoping those that have fled back into the valley may induce the others to surrender. Hold your men ready to follow us if we take heavy casualties."

Harbro nodded grimly while Baldor split his troop, leaving the mounted half with Andulas and Armaco. Calling for horse-holders and for his men to dismount and help fill the gaps in the second rank of the shield wall, he sheathed his falcata and picked up a fallen spear. With horrific memories of a shield wall and a battle long ago, he tried to hide his fear by encouraging his men.

"Come on lads, we just need to hold them a while longer, be strong!"

As always, cavalrymen made reluctant and poor infantrymen but with encouragement from Baldor and coercion from Tercero, the second rank formed. No sooner had the Carthaginians settled than the rumble of hooves came again, this time louder than before. Men's mumbled prayers became faster and louder, the tension rose higher as men braced themselves for what was coming. Suddenly the Romans burst into view, the horses at full stretch, men riding knee to knee, the line tight, spears raised, someone was instilling order. The horses thundered towards the shield wall. With no javelins left, the Carthaginians could only wait behind their shields. Malo loosed his last two arrows and two horses stumbled and slammed into the ground, once again tripping others coming closely behind. The dead horses and men in front of the shield wall broke the Roman line, horses swerving or jumping over the carcasses. A moment later, they were in front of the shields.

Tercero's infantry, seasoned and trained against cavalry attacks never moved other than to raise their shields higher and shout their hate. Desperate to be free of the slaughter coming behind them, the Romans battered the shield wall, the first rank bellying and flexing under the pressure. Baldor urged his second rank tight against the first, thereby adding morale and physical support with closeness, weight and additional spears. Harbro pushed his horsemen in tight behind Baldor's line. The shield wall was a terrifying experience for the cavalrymen, used to fast, open warfare and space; they were now hemmed in tight to their comrades as close as lovers. The stench was nauseating, spilled guts and opened bowels mixed with stale sweat and the iron smell of blood. The howls of men and screams of horses resonated in the warrior's ears as they stood shoulder to shoulder in the claustrophobia of the wall. The Roman horses, terrified by the thrusting shields, spears and the stink of blood and offal gave ground as the Carthaginians pushed back. Baldor thrust his spear hard over the man in front of him, hitting and scraping down a Roman shield, the man knocked sideways with the force.

"Keep tight! … Stay with the front line!" He screamed as the front rank pushed the Romans back a pace.

"Kill the horses!" Tercero yelled.

The Romans, desperate to be past the Carthaginians and out of the valley, fought like demons but despite their numbers and pressure, the shield wall refused to give. The horses could finally take no more and despite the bullying of the riders, the attack faltered. The slaughter in front of the wall was horrendous; bodies of men and horses littered the grass, twisted and broken in death, the carnage however, adding to the shield wall's defence.

More horsemen arrived from the valley and joined those standing off from the thin wall, raising groans and curses from Baldor's troops. There was brief, agitated exchange between the new arrivals and their battered comrades followed by gesturing back down the valley and at the shield wall. Then the Carthaginian standard came into view amidst wide, solid lines of horsemen. The Romans began throwing down their weapons and shields. Baldor's men raised spears and shields and broke into ragged cheers; General Maharbal was here.

Chapter Nineteen

The cart rumbled over the cobbles and stopped with a jolt outside the Scipio villa. Cornelius, stiff from sitting eased himself gingerly off it, wincing and gasping as his broken ribs objected to the movement. The two gate guards, recognising him, called for the Steward and then came quickly down the steps to help. Declining any assistance, he straightened his back and tried to tidy his appearance with his good arm. He turned to Gaius, who was still laid in the cart.

"Will you not stay with me, Gaius? We both need a physician …"

"Thank you Cornelius, but no, I have a house slave who will see to my needs. Anyway, it wouldn't do for the likes of me to be lounging in your home, what would the nobilis or senators think?"

"I don't give a damn what they think." He growled. "Until they have gotten off their fat arses and fought like we have fought, they can keep their opinions to themselves."

"Shush lad, keep it down!" He hissed. "Thank you for the offer but I will be fine."

Cornelius smiled sadly and offered his good hand. "Thank you, thank you for …"

"Thank you, lad! We look after each other, eh?"

The pair shook hands warmly as the Steward appeared at the gate.

"Sir, sir, you're here! We had news of your imminent arrival from Decurion Herminius. Jupiter be praised, you're safe!" He shouted as he came down the steps apace. "You! You can go!" He waved a dismissive hand at the carter.

"No, he can't! I promised this man recompense for his trouble and damage to his stock." When the Steward frowned and looked down his nose at the man waiting by the cart, Cornelius snapped. "Pay him!"

When the Steward dallied, fishing in his purse, Cornelius took it from him and walked back to the carter. Emptying the contents into the man's hands, he asked. "Is it enough sir, for your trouble and your stock?"

The man gawped at the silver. "Yes, yes sir, more than …"

"Thank you." He closed his hand over the carters and flicked his head towards Gaius. "See my friend to his home and Jupiter's blessings upon you my friend, I'm sorry we took you out of your way."

Leaving the man still staring at the silver, he made his way up the steps into the villa. The Steward stepped alongside, jabbering and fussing, Cornelius put a hand on the man's shoulder.

"Aureus, enough." He said, not unkindly. Weary and aching, he ran a hand over his face and brow, before easing the pressure from the makeshift sling. "You can help me by sending for a physician, organising a bath and finding me some clean clothes. I will see my mother if she is home? Is there any news of my father and uncle and the war in Spain?"

"Yes, yes sir. Your mother, the Lady Pomponia is home and the news from Spain is encouraging."

"It is?"

"Yes sir! Word is your father and uncle are waging a successful campaign against this Hasdrubal Barca, Hannibal's younger brother; we have regained some provinces previously lost."

"They are both hale?"

"When last we heard, sir."

Cornelius was about to enquire further when the house doors opened and his mother stepped out.

"Cornelius!" She gasped, her hands coming up quickly to cover her mouth and stifle a cry. Despite trying to maintain her decorum, her eyes went wide, her face a mixture of relief and fear as she stepped quickly towards him. Shaking her head in disbelief, she paused to look at him

He, unshaven and filthy, his tunic in tatters, patches of dark dried blood still discolouring his mail, cuts and scabs showing on his bare skin and his arm in a sling, smiled and bowed his head.

"Mother."

Scampering the last few paces, she flung her arms around him, he groaning slightly from the tight embrace.

"Son! Son! We feared the worst when we didn't hear. We … we

thought you …"

"The Gods are good mother; see I am whole, battered but whole." He smiled again trying to make light of his injuries. Feeling her warm tears on his skin, he turned to the Steward. "Thank you, Aureus. Will you call the physician then see to my bath and clean attire."

Aureus bowed and left.

"Your arm, it's broken?" She asked, easing him back so to see him, her features tight with concern.

"Yes, and some of my ribs." She was about to ask further when he continued. "I'm lucky mother, very lucky. I'll heal and I'm home."

"Yes! Yes! My prayers have been answered." She wiped at her tears, trying to regain her composure. "If I could have your father home too, I would ask no more of the Gods."

He smiled and hugged her again gently. "From what Aureus says, he and uncle Gnaeus are being more successful than us."

"You should have gone with him, son …"

"I couldn't mother. I have to go where my legion is sent."

"Well now you don't have to go anywhere, your duty is well served, more than. You have served two consecutive campaigns; let someone else take their turn."

Cornelius chewed his lip and sighed. "No, I'm sorry mother, I can't just stand by, I have a duty …"

"No! No! Your duty is here, to the family." Her eyes flashed in anger and her voice rose sharply. "I will not lose all my men folk!"

"Lucius is here mother, he will …"

Her anger dissipated as quickly as it had risen, changing to sad acceptance. "Your brother went to Capitol Hill last week for the choosing, he was accepted and enlisted."

"What?"

"He's of age; he said and would not stay home when his father and brother were fighting." She broke down again and hugged him. "All my men, all of you …"

"Shush now, shush." He said softly as he pulled her close.

"You could have taken a higher rank, served under your father as a Tribune, why did you have to start at the bottom." She managed between gasps.

"I did not want to see my father accused of favouritism; these senators don't need another reason to attack good men. Also, for myself, I wanted to see men as they are, to understand them, share their lives and dangers and earn their respect, if I can. You raised us to be men, mother, to do our duty. We are doing that."

She sniffed and eased slightly away, again wiping at her eyes, trying to be calm. Composing herself, she took back the mantle of the woman of the house.

"Yes, yes son, you're right. We have raised men, good men. Men to be proud of." She stroked her hand down his face. "Oh, I'm sorry! I've placed being a mother before duty and Rome, it's just … just I'm fearful."

"Be strong mother, just like you taught us to be. You didn't raise us to shirk our duties and responsibilities." He smiled and kissed her forehead. "Things will be well, I promise you." He said, purposely neglecting to make mention of Baldor or the bandits in the forest.

She smiled at last. "You are your father's son Cornelius, seeking to give comfort and allay fears, you're a good man."

Cornelius hugged her gently. "I'm a hungry man, mother, I …"

"I'm so sorry son. Forgive a mother who prattles. Aureus!" She shouted, then clapped her hands loudly and within moments the Steward appeared.

"My Lady?"

"Food for my son and wine, quickly!"

"Already prepared, my Lady. Where will you take it, sir?"

"In the bath, Aureus. My stomach thinks my throat's been cut." He smirked at the grim humour as he turned to follow Aureus and didn't see his mother cringe.

Much later, fed, bathed and with his ribs bound and his arm in a cloth sling and enjoying a proper dinner with his mother, he asked. "Does Aemilia know I'm home?"

"We only heard of your coming yesterday evening son and I wanted to see you and let you rest for a night before I sent a message. I will send word for her to come tomorrow."

****

As more and more Romans threw down their weapons and dismounted, the shield wall broke into ragged cheers. Baldor however, could only look at the destruction wrought on his men. Staring at the dead pushed out in front of the lines and the wounded, battered and bleeding who sagged against their comrades, else sat to hold their hurt, trying not to show their pain. The ranks had shrunk, and then despite the infill of his cavalrymen shrunk again. He looked at the first rank and saw Tercero, the man was bloody but whether it was his or Roman blood, he couldn't tell. He pushed his way through the line and offered his hand and his thanks; the Spaniard smiled grimly and dipped his head.

"We did it sir, you said we could and we have."

"Yes, but at what cost Tercero, look what I've done to your men."

"We can't fight without cost; Captain and I swear there's many more of those bastards dead than us and it would seem the rest have surrendered. Yes, I grieve for my men but I don't blame you for it, we came willingly."

Baldor nodded and managed a sad smile. "That was well fought by your men; they never flinched in the face of those Equites, brave men all!"

"It helped when you reinforced our line, sir. We couldn't have held otherwise methinks."

Baldor grimaced. "It's a grim place the shield wall, Tercero. I hope I never need venture there again, twice is twice too many."

Tercero grinned. "That's how I feel about horses and swimming rivers! Each to his own Captain."

Baldor smiled and clapped Tercero on the shoulder then turned away back to the horse lines seeking Harbro, Armaco and Andulas. Casting his eyes quickly along the rank, he saw all three were still mounted and though bloodied and battered were without serious wounds. Approaching each, he offered his hand and thanks.

"Messengers coming through." Someone shouted from the front rank as two horsemen, one bearing the standard of Carthage weaved through the infantry towards Baldor.

"Captain Targa, sir. General Maharbal sends his compliments and gratitude for the stout defence; you prevented any escape."

Baldor dipped his head. "The General is well?"

"He is Captain and also well pleased, we have their whole force contained and our losses appear very light." The man's horse tossed its head and whickered, not comfortable in the close confines of the infantry ranks, he patting its withers to settle it. Clearing his throat and trying not to sound nervous, he pointed to a low hill. "While the General takes custody of the prisoners here, he asks that you accompany me up that hill yonder to see if you can talk those last few

Romans into surrendering?"

Baldor looked to where the man pointed towards a small hill, now crowned with a contingent of Romans.

"The Romans will only deal with those they deem worthy, the General thinks you've earned that accolade, hence the request."

Baldor flushed at the praise. "And if they won't surrender?"

"We withdraw and he will send General Himilico's men up to slaughter them without quarter, his men being the freshest."

Giving a sigh of relief that it wouldn't be his men doing any more fighting, Baldor called for his horse.

"My compliments to the General, I'll see what I can do." He said to the other messenger as he mounted. The man saluted and turned his mount back to the main force. "Andulas, Armaco, Harbro, Tercero see to the men and give me the butcher's bill." He turned to the Standard-bearer. "Let's go ..." He gestured for the man's name.

"Bardaan, sir."

"We've no white spear for truce, Bardaan and they've been ambushed once today so we go slowly. Stop, if I say and don't make any fast moves."

"You've done this before sir? That's comforting."

"Only once and that was because they killed the first man I sent."

"Baal protect us." Bardaan hissed and eased his shield around from his back to cover his chest.

"You would have been better leaving that shield on your back, if we have to turn and run for it ..."

"Baal almighty, I didn't think of that! You, you haven't even brought your shield!"

"I can ride away faster!" Baldor managed a forced laugh making Bardaan chuckle and curse at the same time. "Just keep the slow pace, they may tell us to stop, if not, I'll stop us when we can talk without shouting."

"Must we go that close?"

"Yes. While I talk you count heads, just don't make it obvious."

The pair edged their mounts towards the slope at a walk. Their advance was noted and those Romans who'd dismounted to rest their horses mounted again, all along the line, weapons and shields were readied. The pair continued their progress letting their horses pick their way steadily upwards. Baldor noticed the uneven and broken ground dotted with rabbit holes and small rocks that littered the hill, an attack upwards would be hard enough but over this terrain, difficult and slow. At fifty paces from the Roman ranks, Baldor's skin seemed to itch; his senses heighten. He felt his chest muscles tighten and his hands clamping the reins become damp with sweat, he could hear Bardaan mumbling his prayers. At thirty paces, a voice bellowed from the Roman line.

"Stop there or we'll skewer you! Who are you and what do you want?"

As he reined up and took his time settling his horse, Baldor swallowed hard and tried to moisten his lips from a very dry mouth.

"I'm Captain Targa of Carthage … and you are?"

There was some brief discussion amongst the Roman ranks before a dappled horse pushed out of the line. Its rider slouched slightly on its back as the horse stepped smartly towards the two men. The man wore no helmet, his face pale and gaunt; his mouth and chin stained with blood. A bandage stuffed beneath his mail shirt at his right shoulder and armpit was red and sodden, his forearm covered in rivulets of fresh blood. He walked the horse right up to Baldor, pulled himself up proudly, wiped blood from his lips and cleared his throat.

"I'm Gaius Marcus Centenius, Propraetor or Proconsul of Rome. I command these men." He gasped for breath and stifled a cough. "What can I do for you Captain?"

Expecting arrogance, Baldor was taken aback by the politeness and equanimity of the reply. Immediately changing his thoughts and response, he inclined his head slightly in respect.

"Sir, I come seeking your surrender." Growls and curses came from some in the line that could hear; Gaius raised his hand for silence.

"I think you have your answer, Captain."

Baldor looked at the lines of angry, defiant faces, guessing their numbers at two, maybe three hundred at most, and then thought of the rough ground. The outcome was inevitable but the cost would be high.

"Sir, you and your men have fought bravely, their honour proven. We have you trapped in this valley, if my General comes up here, he will slaughter you all."

"You've heard the answer, Captain. I thank you for the courtesy and bid you good day." Droplets of blood sprayed from his mouth as he finished speaking and pulled on the reins to turn his mount.

"Sir, you will all die here, there's no need."

"I'm already dying, Captain."

"Your men then, will you not save your men?"

"We would rather die with honour than face slavery, Captain. Let your General come, we will extract a high price and you know it, you saw the ground." He gasped and sagged a little, unsteady in his seat.

"Hear me out, sir." Baldor said quickly.

Gaius turned again, the wound causing him to flinch. "Go on …"

"Lay down your weapons, armour and anything of value, dismount and we will escort you back to our camp. From there, you may go with one garment apiece on the road to Rome or wherever you will."

Gaius coughed into his hand and gasped for breath. "You would release us? All of us?"

"I can't speak for the men in the valley; they've already surrendered on no terms. I offer you and your men here my terms."

"And on whose authority, whose word, would these terms be kept?"

"I'm sent here on the authority of General Maharbal to speak for him and you have my word sir, as a Captain."

Gaius looked thoughtful. "A moment Captain, if you will?"

Baldor nodded as Gaius turned back to his men. He and Bardaan waited quietly, deigning not to speak keeping their eyes straight ahead. The sun was still hot and Baldor felt the sweat trickling from beneath his helmet wetting his cheeks and neck, his tunic beneath his mail shirt soaked through and sticking to his skin. Ignoring the heat and discomforts, he nonchalantly patted his horse's neck. When Gaius walked his horse back to him, he straightened his back, trying to read the man's face. Gaius seemed paler than before; he gave a sad smile then slowly lifted his baldric carrying his gladius off his shoulder.

"You strike me as an honourable man, Captain. My sword, and we accept your terms."

"Thank you, sir." Baldor dipped his head respectfully as he took the sword, imagining that under different circumstances he would have liked this man. "Sir, have your men leave their weapons, dismount and walk their mounts down the hill, you ride with me and let us see to some care for you at least."

Gaius seemed to wilt further, unsteady in his seat. "You do your General much credit, Captain. There should be honour amongst enemies should there not? I've failed my men and my city so I will walk with them. I'll bid you good day once more and may your Gods keep and bless you." He dipped his head, saluted and turned back to his men.

Behind Gaius, the Romans began to dismount and throw down their weapons and then a slow, steady stream of men and horses began making their way downhill. Sending Bardaan ahead to relay the outcome to the General, Baldor motioned his horse to one side and watched as the Romans walked past. His initial assessment of numbers was dwarfed as more and more men appeared from the blind side of the hillcrest. If it had come to a fight, the losses for both sides would have been considerable. Following the last of the Romans down, he felt a glow of satisfaction for what he imagined was the saving of his comrade's lives, his concern now, would the General like his terms?

At the foot of the hill, he was met by General Maharbal himself. The man smiling and walking his horse across to offer his hand.

"Well done, Captain. A good finish to a good day and with no more lives lost. That's almost eight hundred men you've talked into surrender; it would have been a hard fight otherwise."

"You are happy with the terms I offered sir? I was generous but I don't think they'd have come down otherwise."

"A great victory cheaply bought is what it is, Captain. I've seen the ground and the numbers and I think you've done well, very well. Losing good men to win a few slaves makes no sense to me either; I knew I'd sent the right man for the job. Come, we are camping here tonight so dine with me, it's only soldier's fare but I have wine."

"Thank you sir, willingly. Just one thing if I may?"

"You may."

"The Roman Propraetor, their commander, he needs care, he seemed a decent man."

"He's dead, Captain. His men carried him into camp; a spear had ruptured his lung they think. A decent man you say? That's a rare find amongst these sons of the wolf."

****

As the sun slipped behind the western hills, Lasairiona lit the oil lamps then took her place at the small table as Sulis set the evening meal down for them.

"Do you think we'll be moving on as soon as the men return?" Sulis asked between mouthfuls.

"I'd imagine so; the army has stripped the country hereabout of everything useful. From what I've heard the General will move on to keep supplied while destroying what can't be carried and driving the populace before him, trying to bring the Romans to battle again."

"Do you not worry that the General may be defeated and where that would leave us?"

"No, I think the Romans have met their match this time. I do worry that Baldor may not come back. Soldiering is a risky business."

Mischief spread across Sulis's face as she smiled. "Baldor now, not Captain, eh! It's love then?"

"No!" Lasairiona snapped, though the corners of her mouth teased into a tight smile before becoming serious again. "Then I would worry what would become of us?"

"Yes, he's a good man." Sulis left her seat and went to tie the tent door flap shut as Lasairiona cleared the plates. "I wonder where we are headed from …" She stepped back quickly, startled by a man suddenly stepping into the doorway. "Who are …?"

"We're looking for Captain Targa, mistress; we've a message from the General." He replied amiably and stepped further in; another two men followed him.

"The Captain isn't here, he's …"

"That's alright mistress, we'll wait."

The other two men were already moving deeper into the tent.

"You can't come in here … who are you?"

"See to the door." He flicked his head at his comrade then glanced around the tent.

"Get out! … Out! Now! Ere I call The Watch."

"Quiet you old bitch!" The man pushed Sulis backwards forcing her deeper into the tent. Stepping after her, he thumped her hard in the stomach taking the wind out of her. As she collapsed to her knees gasping for breath, he turned towards Lasairiona.

Lasairiona, recovering quickly from the surprise hurled the plates at him, stalling his advance while snatching a small knife from the table. The second man laughed and stepped forward quickly, his hand snatching and rolling in her dress dragging her towards him, his other hand raised to take the knife.

"Give me that, you stupid bitch."

Lasairiona spat in his face. As he instinctively raised a hand to his eyes, she stabbed the blade into his neck. Shocked at the attack, he backed away but too slow as Lasairiona stepped after him and slashed the knife across his throat. His hands clasped his throat as he staggered, knocking the table over. A fountain of blood sprayed the tent walls as he collapsed to his knees, his cries drowned in gagging, gurgling noises. The third man growled and pushed forward dodging Lasairiona's knife thrust and knocking it from her hand. Twisting his body around, his other elbow came up quickly hitting her in the jaw. She staggered under the blow. Grabbing her by the hair, he dragged her close then slapped her hard across the head, knocking her on her back. Stepping after her, he hit her twice more in the side of the head; she didn't get up from the ground.

"Steady there you fool!" The first man snarled. "She's worth good coin but not if you damage her."

"The bitch has done for, Bannus!"

"Too bad! If she's out cold, gag her and start searching the tent, start with the Captain's quarters through there."

They ignored their comrade who thrashed on the ground still holding his throat, his mouth opening and closing like a landed fish, blood pouring through his fingers. The first man pulled Sulis to her feet, slapped her hard then grabbed her throat stifling her cries.

"Now, old wife!" He hissed; forcing her hard against the tent pole and pushing his face close. "Where's the money, the valuables? A Captain will have a trove somewhere." Sulis struggled in the vice-like grip, her lips opening and closing, only tortured sounds coming out. The man eased the pressure slightly. "Tell me and I might let you live." Sulis pulled her purse from her belt offering it. "Very good but where's the Captain's money, his trove?" He eased the pressure again as he slipped the purse into his tunic.

"There is nothing, no trove!" She managed in low, hoarse tones.

The pressure came back on her throat closing off her air. "I'll ask you for the last time. Where's the trove?"

Sulis's eyes had begun to bulge, terrified, her face bright red. The pressure eased again.

"Well?"

"Please ... there is no, no trove ..."

"No reason to let you live then."

The grip tightened again. The man dropped his other hand to his dagger and then rammed it hard under Sulis's ribs, pulled it out and stuck it in her chest, bursting her heart. Sulis sagged in his grip, her eyes flickering. As she wilted, he let go, she dropped to the ground beside the now dead man.

"Anything?" He growled to the other man who was busy quietly ransacking Baldor's quarters.

"No coin! Some armour and helmets, a nice looking falcata though and some expensive looking wine jugs and goblets."

"Put them in the sack, they'll sell." He turned to Lasairiona. "Now, you red headed Harpie, apart from your body what have you got that's worth having." Rolling her limp form over with his foot, he ran his hands over her body, checking her neck for jewellery then pushing his hands into her dress and groping her breasts. "Very nice but they're part of your sale price." He grumbled to himself as he frisked the rest of her body, snatching the purse from her belt. Running his hands down her legs to her feet and lifting her dress over her boots, he saw the hilt of a small knife sticking out the top. "You're a vixen all right, eh!" He grinned as he took the knife. "How are you doing back there?"

"All done, not the best pickings, I'd have expected better from a Captain."

"Just as well we were paid for the work then and now there's only us two to split it." He reached down to the dead man and snatched the purse from his belt, then motioned to the other. "Come on, out you go." He ran a knife down the back wall of the tent before ushering his comrade through then passed an unconscious Lasairiona out. "Give her another thump in the head to make sure she doesn't wake up early then take that gag off her. Put your arm around her like she's your woman and she's drunk. I'll bring the sack; I'll just cover our tracks first."

Pushing the table and chairs against the rear wall of the tent, he covered them in cloaks, blankets and rugs then tipped oil from the lamps over them. Scrabbling through the food items and finding an amphora full of oil, he spread the contents liberally about the tent and over the bodies. Taking a lit lamp and ducking out through the slit, he hurled it back onto the table. Hearing the crackle and small roar as the oil caught alight, he grinned, hefted the sack and slunk off into the darkness.

Chapter Twenty

"Cornelius!" Aemilia gasped as she ran across the floor towards him.

He turned side on to her embrace. "My ribs!" He groaned as she wrapped her arms tightly about him.

"I'm sorry, sorry!" She mumbled between sobs while showering his cheeks and lips in kisses. "We thought you were lost, dead!"

"I'm all right … I'm fine, a little battered is all."

She stepped back looking at his splinted and slung arm and the bindings around his ribs just visible beneath his robes. He looked older, more severe, the scabs and scars on his arms adding to his grim seeming persona.

"Oh Cornelius, Cornelius!" He felt her wilt into him as she cried softly into his shoulder, her tears hot on his neck. "I prayed to Juno to keep you safe; I begged …"

"Hush! … Hush, Come on, it's all right now. I'm home and in one piece." His good hand lifted her head up and he kissed her on the brow. "Come, let's sit in the garden, it's a beautiful day." He escorted her out onto the stone patio seating her on a bench in the shade of a pink-blossomed mimosa tree and poured wine for them both.

"Is the pain bad?" She asked as she took his good hand.

"No, not now. The strapping has helped my ribs and Gaius made such a good job of splinting and slinging my arm that the physician didn't need to reset it."

"I'm so glad you are home." She managed between sobs and dabbing her eyes. "When there was no word or sign of you after news came about the battle, we feared the worst."

Cornelius chewed his lip, seeking the right words, when they evaded him, he settled for. "It was difficult."

"What was? Was it this Baldor Targa again? Did you kill him? … Tell me, so I can understand."

Cornelius dropped his head and felt his gut twist as he remembered the fight on the beach. "I'd rather not talk about it, Aemilia. It's over." His words and manner curt. When she looked startled at his manner, he softened his tone. "I'm alive and I'm home, the Gods are good."

She didn't say anything for a while, just snuggled closer. He rested his head on hers, enjoying the closeness and the scent of her hair and perfume, his hand on the smooth skin of her arm.

"I'm frightened Cornelius." She blurted.

"There's no need, Aemilia. We lost a battle, that doesn't mean we'll lose the war."

"But another battle and so many men are gone, only a few have returned."

"Men were scattered over a great distance and Rome is a long way from Lake Trasimene. It takes time to regroup, for men to get home, look how long it's taken me … On the positive side; Consul Geminus's legions remain intact."

"His cavalry don't!"

"What? How do you know that? What's happened?"

"I overheard a messenger relaying the news to my father. Consul Geminus dispatched his complete cavalry arm towards you at Trasimene …"

"Yes, yes, I heard that? What's happened?" He interrupted sharply. Taken aback by his terse manner she didn't answer. "Well, Aemilia … what happened?"

"They were ambushed by the Carthaginians in the hills near Spoletium." She said quietly. "Why are you so sharp and angry with me?"

"Spoletium!" Ignoring her question, he sat up sharply; his ribs flexing with the sudden movement making him wince and gasp. "That's well south of Trasimene, Gods above, Hannibal is moving fast!"

"And no doubt closer to Rome!" Aemilia added, her body giving a small shudder.

Realising Aemilia was becoming more frightened; he hugged her gently and lowered his voice. "How many of Geminus's men have come in?"

"Only a handful. How many would he have sent?"

He swallowed hard, stopping himself before he mentioned numbers. "You shouldn't eavesdrop, Aemilia!" He scolded gently then kissed her.

"I'm treated like a child, no one tells me anything."

"Your father is protective of you that's all; any good father would be the same."

"I'm a woman grown am I not? The same age as you!"

"Yes, yes you are." His voice warm, he hugged her close.

"So how many?" She badgered.

He sighed deeply. "Three, maybe four thousand I'm told."

She shuddered again. "Promise me you won't go back." When he didn't reply, she pushed. "Promise me!"

"I can't, Aemilia, I have a duty."

She sat up, pushing him away, her face clouding with anger. "No!" She shouted. "Not anymore!"

"Aemilia, hush! Not this again."

"I will not be hushed and stop talking down to me; I'm not a slave to be chastised!"

Cornelius lowered his voice though his tone remained firm. "Listen to me, Aemilia …"

"I don't want …"

"Listen!" He snapped forcefully when she tried to interrupt again. "As soon as I've recovered, I'm returning to my legion. More than ever the city needs men, I will not stand back while others go … We have an invader in our country and vengeance to take for our fallen."

"But our marriage … Does that not mean …"

"When this is over and the country is our own once more, and if you will still have me, I'll gladly marry you."

Aemilia got up from the bench and stared at him. Her eyes misting again and her skin flushing as her temper rose. "You've changed, Cornelius!" She spat. "Your duty is well served yet you return again and again. Am I not worth staying home for?"

"Jupiter Almighty, Aemilia!" He growled as he threw his head back, exasperated. His robe opened to the middle of his chest, some bruising showing above the swathe of white bandages. She peered at his neck, a frown spreading across her brow.

"You don't even wear my gift around your neck! Do you care so little?"

Cornelius sighed and reached to his neck. "That's a long story."

"Another that you don't wish to relate?"

"It's not that …"

"Well, what then?"

"I gave it to a woman in …"

"You did what?" She hissed, her face clouding, eyes narrowing and her lips curling into a snarl.

Cornelius stood quickly. "No, that's not! … Listen to me, let me explain …"

"I don't want to listen to you anymore …" She stepped away from him. "I … I don't believe …"

"Listen, Aemilia." He growled reaching for her arm.

She twisted from his grasp. "Get away from me! Get away! … You bastard, Cornelius! How could you?" Tears spilled down her cheeks as she continued stepping away. "How could you? … How could you?" She shook her head, her words fading and lip trembling.

"For the love of the Gods let me explain!" Coming after her and trying to take hold of her hand, she snatched hers away and slapped him hard on the cheek.

"Get away! I hope I never see you again. Go back to your whores and your precious legion, I …"

Shocked and stung by the blow, he persevered. "Aemilia, you need to listen! The jewel was payment for …"

Aemilia had already turned away, walking briskly back towards the house ignoring his protests.

Cursing quietly, he slumped back hard on the bench then groaned as his ribs objected.

The following morning, having breakfasted with his mother and suffered her condoning of Aemilia's thoughts on his return to the legion, he excused himself. Upset, angry and restless he donned his straw sunhat and walked off into the city seeking Gaius.

The streets were busy but lacking the bustle and everyday banter of people and shopkeepers, being replaced by an atmosphere of apprehension. People still went about their business but with a quiet urgency, as though there was no time for talk or pleasantries.

It was approaching midday when he rapped on Gaius's door, after a wait and a second rap a woman eased the door ajar.

"Yes! What do you want?" Her manner abrupt.

"Cornelius Scipio to see Master Laelius." His reply just as curt, his temper already worn thin.

"He's sleeping and not to be disturbed." She snapped and made to close the door.

Cornelius stepped over the threshold and jammed his foot against it. "He'll see me, wake him!"

"Go away else I summon the Watch!" The woman forced the door onto the arch of his foot.

Grunting as the door raked over his foot he shouted through the gap. "Gaius! Gaius! It's Cornelius!"

"Go away!" The woman shrieked as the pair pushed on either side of the door.

"For the love of Venus! What's all the shouting?" The voice resonated from down the corridor, there was a tapping of a stick on stone tiles, and then Gaius came to the door. "Cornelius! Come away in man."

"I would but this Harpie has my foot jammed under the damn door."

"Sir, you were sleeping. I did not want you disturbed, this … this oaf here was forcing his way in."

Gaius grinned and then chuckled. "It's alright Vita; this oaf is my friend, Cornelius."

Vita scowled and reluctantly opened the door causing Cornelius to gasp as it scraped off his foot taking a lump of skin with it.

"Come through, lad. This is a pleasant surprise; I thought you would be busy entwined with Aemilia." He turned down the passage, Cornelius limping behind him. "Vita, wine for us both please, in the garden."

Gaius led Cornelius through the house into a small but beautiful garden surrounded by high stonewalls and covered in a profusion of white jasmine, a veritable suntrap. Stretching out carefully on a cushioned pallet set amongst gardenia bushes, he bade Cornelius, sit.

"So, how are you? Mending well? You certainly look better, except for your foot!" He pointed to the bloodied skin. "I think that's called putting your foot in it!" He chuckled and Cornelius gurned his face. "I'm sorry, bad joke; Vita is a little protective that's all."

"Protective! A bitch as fierce as that should enlist!" He grumbled as he bent to smooth the remaining rumpled skin back over the gash.

Gaius stifled a chuckle in a smirk. "Come on, it's not so bad. How are you?"

"I'm improving thank you, you made a good job of my arm, and the physician was impressed. Yourself?"

"My shoulder is good but it will need exercise. The hip is better for resting and keeping the weight off it. It seems I may be lucky; they think it's only badly bruised or the plate cracked."

"It will heal all right?"

"Time will tell. If it's a bruise it will repair quickly, if the bone is cracked it will take longer as it needs time to knit together, the more I stay off it and rest, the quicker the recovery."

"If it's broken?"

"The physician thinks not, I would be in much more pain and deep trouble."

"Thank Jupiter for Decurion Herminius and the cart then; that must have helped."

Vita appeared with two cups of wine, offering one into Gaius's hand and clattering Cornelius's down on the table, scowling at him as she did so. She smiled at Gaius then disappeared back into the house.

"Looks like your usual boyish charm isn't working today, Cornelius. Good health!" He smirked as he raised his cup.

Cornelius just stared at his wine.

"Drink up lad; it's the Falernian, the good stuff. I think we've earned it. I'm done keeping things for special occasions, let's enjoy."

"I'll wager she's spat in mine, feisty bitch!"

Gaius broke into laughter. "Well, if she has, it won't kill you, here take mine." He passed his cup.

"You obviously think she has spat in it then!"

Gaius's face crumpled as he laughed hard. "Don't be daft, lad. She wouldn't do that; I just enjoy baiting you."

"Huh! It seems to be a national pastime at present." He muttered as he took a large mouthful.

Gaius stopped laughing. "Why, what's to do? Who's rattling your cage?"

"It doesn't matter; I didn't come here to give you my woes."

"It does matter! I'm your friend. What's happened?"

Cornelius looked down and chewed his lip.

"My mother's not happy that I'm not with my father and that I want to go back to the legion. Then … then, Aemilia and I had a huge falling out, she's not happy about me going back either but worse than that, she thinks I swapped the jewel she gave me for a night's pleasure with a whore."

"What? How in Jupiter's name did she come to that conclusion?"

"Oh, I don't know, things just escalated, became heated, she wouldn't listen and then she stormed off. I think the betrothal is over and the wedding off."

"No...! She wouldn't really believe that. I'll explain about the jewel if you like, you gave that to pay for my care. She'll see sense."

"To be honest, I'm past caring. Maybe it's for the best. As soon as I'm well, I'm heading back to the legion. Anyway, what have you heard about the state of affairs? Did you hear about Geminus's cavalry?"

"I heard yesterday. What a bloody mess!"

"What happens now then? We've no Consuls and the army is broken."

Gaius took a drink. "Well, we have Geminus's legions still, that's a start and the senate is already putting out the call for more men."

"What do you know of this Dictatorship, how does that work?"

"Well, he will have absolute power ..."

"That sounds like a King; I thought we were totally against Kings?"

"I don't know lad, but that's what we have, he only has the position for six months, perhaps that's how they keep reins on him? Anyway, he is head of operations from here. Interestingly though, they've not let him choose his own 'Master of horse' but have appointed a political opponent of his, a Marcus Minucius Rufus, maybe he's there to keep an eye on him."

"Gods above, is there to be no unity amongst us? We're a nation in crisis and that's the best we can do."

"What do you expect from fat-arsed senators? As you rightly named them." He smiled. "They look to themselves and their own interests and control every time ... bastards!" He grimaced and swilled his wine.

"Agreed! So why do we fight, Gaius? What makes us carry on, what makes us put our lives on the line for the likes of them?"

Gaius drew a big breath. "I'll tell you what it is Cornelius. Good men, ordinary men, like you and me fight for our people, for our way of life and for our freedom. When savages like the Carthaginians invade, burn, murder, rape and destroy our land, all it needs is for good men to do nothing and they will prevail. That's why we fight."

"Aye, I think you have the rights of it. I love my city and my people but can we recover from here though?"

"Vita! More wine, here. Yes Cornelius, we can and will recover from this. We have the manpower …"

"We just need better leaders."

"Excluding your father, yes, that would help."

"Why did they send him to Spain, Gaius?"

"Opening another front to distract the enemy actually makes good military sense, lad. If it is successful, and I hear your father is being successful against Hannibal's brother, this Hasdrubal, then all the better. As you can see, it's preventing any joining of the Carthaginian forces from Spain with Hannibal.

The way I see it, this war is going to be a marathon, not a sprint and as I said we have the men and the supplies, Hannibal is starved of both. He has many problems to face; despite his victories only a few Gallic tribes have gone across to him, he's in hostile country and if we hold out during the rest of summer, he has winter to face."

Cornelius managed a smile at last. "It's good to talk, Gaius."

Gaius winked. "We're down lad but far from out. Vita! Vita! What are you doing girl? Where's the bloody wine? Cornelius says you should be whipped for your laziness!"

Cornelius cringed. "Now she really is going to spit in my cup!"

Chapter Twenty one

The sunlight glinted and flashed from the standard of Carthage and helmets and spearheads of Maharbal's men as the column came into camp. Folk left the bread ovens and everyday tasks or emptied from tents to watch and raise loud cheers and applause. The huddled groups of Roman prisoners, all roped together and following behind, being jeered, spat on and pelted with food scraps. In the middle of the column, Baldor his men and the prisoners from the hill were followed by the remainder of Tercero's infantrymen.

A messenger trotting back down the column saw Baldor and reined in.

"Captain Targa?"

"Yes, soldier."

"Sir, General Maharbal requests you accompany him to place his report to General Hannibal."

"When soldier? I need to see to my men."

"Er, now sir."

"You'd best go Captain. Armaco and I will see to the men and the prisoners." Andulas said.

Baldor nodded to Andulas and urged his mount out of the column following the messenger. As he rode, he thought of his last meeting with Hannibal and his anger and disappointment at him for his actions towards Bodeshmun. At least this time there should be no issues, Maharbal was grateful of his actions at the battle, perhaps Hannibal and he could revert to their earlier camaraderie and friendship. Coming up on the General and his command group his spirits rose as Maharbal smiled and waved him close.

"Come Captain, you were most instrumental in our victory; I think you're entitled to help me relay our report and good news to General Hannibal."

"Thank you sir, you do me a great honour."

"No Captain, you and your men earned that."

As they rode, Maharbal began dismissing his commanders to see to their men and the distribution of spoils. Before he and Baldor had time to talk further, Hannibal's tent was in sight, with Hannibal waiting outside. Shading his eyes from the sun, he smiled as the men approached. As the pair reined up in front of his tent, he took the bridle of Maharbal's mount and reached for Baldor's.

"General Maharbal, greetings! You sir, are a wonder! The scouts tell me of a great victory and from what I see, little cost. Captain Targa, it's good to see you again and hale!"

The pair offered their greetings and salute then dismounted. Hannibal beamed at both men.

"Come, come, I have wine and food prepared; we'll dine while you tell me of your victory."

Baldor felt his heart lighten as Hannibal showed no trace of his previous anger towards him. Hannibal threw his arms over the pairs shoulders and ushered them through the tent door. Settling each in a seat, he poured wine for them all then settled himself across the table from them while calling for the servants to serve the food.

"In truth, I was becoming a little concerned with you being gone almost four days."

"The Romans were further away than we thought sir, just north of Spoletium."

"Spoletium eh! They can't have been moving fast then. A token gesture from Geminus to cover his lethargy, do you think? Anyway, too little, too late!" He chuckled. "So, tell me! Tell me all and please eat, you must both be hungry." He smiled, snatched up a chicken leg and raised his cup in salute.

"Our scouts had done their work well sir and found us a valley to trap them in. The challenge was to get the timing right."

"As always."

"We were close to the valley by late afternoon of the second day. We had to really push on as we wanted to bring them to battle before sundown, it helped that they'd decided to make camp in the valley."

"Their scouts?" Hannibal laughed and raised a hand. "Sorry, I keep interrupting."

"Taken care of General and replaced with ours. We hoped to hit their main body before they'd have expected the scouts to report in."

Hannibal chuckled, swilled his wine and pushed both to take a refill while gesturing Maharbal should continue.

"Having the men and the element of surprise we opted for a tactic of double envelopment. I led the main body directly into the valley, while General Himilco and his division headed north; General Hanno turned south, both to act as the pincers. The good Captain here, offered to take the hard road and close the door in the Roman rear." Hannibal smiled and raised his cup to Baldor. "As you would understand sir, the timing was the concern, we didn't manage total accuracy but the Romans had nowhere to go except back the way they came."

"And thus, on a collision course with the Captain here."

"Yes sir. As you can imagine, he had the furthest to go and with the smallest force."

"Hard riding followed by hard fighting, Captain?"

Baldor cleared his throat. "Yes sir."

Maharbal began again. "I was amazed he managed to move his men and Captain Tercero's infantry into position, sir. It was a late decision to try and close the door."

Hannibal raised his eyebrows at Baldor. "Short of time and trailing infantry, how did you manage that, Captain?"

"Captain Tercero's Spaniards kept up well sir but when we came to a river and with time pressing, I copied General Mago's tactics that he used at the Trebbia and we mounted the infantry behind us."

Hannibal chuckled into his cup. "They wouldn't like that!"

"Er, no sir." Baldor smiled. "Not at all."

"They'd be invaluable though once you reached your position."

"Yes, sir. Without them, we could not have held. You know the value of a shield wall against cavalry."

"Your losses, gentlemen?"

Baldor cut in quickly as if needing to be rid of the numbers.

"I lost one hundred and eighty-seven of Captain Tercero's infantry, dead. In addition, twenty-eight badly wounded, not likely to recover and another thirty-three lightly wounded. Mine and Captain Harbro's cavalry losses were, eighty-two dead and twelve wounded that will recover."

Hannibal nodded. "I think that's acceptable Captain, for your men will have borne the brunt of desperate men seeking escape, and yourself General?"

"Sixty-four dead sir, mainly from the initial clash and twenty-seven wounded all of which will recover. We caught the Romans unawares, some not even armed or mounted, we were over them before they knew it. As you said sir, Captain Targa's men bore the brunt."

Hannibal took a moment. "So, gentlemen, by my reckoning, including the fatally wounded we have lost; two hundred and fifteen infantry and one hundred and forty-six cavalry plus some seventy two wounded that will recover?"

"Aye sir, that'll be about right."

"And Roman losses?"

"We slaughtered over two thousand Roman Equites and captured around three thousand horses."

"And prisoners?"

"Around fifteen hundred prisoners, sir."

Hannibal beamed and refilled the cups again. "Well gentlemen, I'm pleased, no delighted! Considering the numbers involved, the heavy Roman losses and the minimal losses for us, I judge that a great victory. Most importantly, this is another blow to Roman prestige, to their elite troops. I am well satisfied with that."

Both men mumbled their thanks between sips of wine and mouthfuls of food.

"I tell you." He smirked. "With the prisoners from Trasimene and now these fifteen hundred, the slave market will flood and the price will fall."

Baldor cleared his throat. "Sir, not all the prisoners can be sold."

"Not sold, how so? There wouldn't be any non-Romans amongst their cavalry, they reserve that arm for their nobles and those of influence and money. Are they short of men enough that they are recruiting outsiders into their cavalry?"

"No, sir no." Maharbal replied. "All are as you say, Roman citizens."

Hannibal frowned, looking bemused. Baldor found his voice.

"Sir ... sir. After we stalled their attempts to escape and General Maharbal closed in on their rear, some eight hundred took to a hilltop, looking to defend it, I ..."

Maharbal interjected. "I sent the Captain up to seek their surrender, General. I saw the hill was steep and the ground broken, far from ideal for a cavalry assault and Captain Tercero's infantry were no longer numerous enough or in good enough shape to help.

We could have left them up there and waited as there was no water on the hill and I surmise they would have had to come down within a day or two. However, as we'd already been gone from camp longer than planned I did not want to add time to it."

"Seems wise, General Maharbal but why can we not sell all the prisoners?"

Baldor flushed and cleared his throat again. "Sir, I gave their commander my word that if they laid down their arms, armour and horses they could go free with one garment apiece, once we returned to camp."

Hannibal's face clouded. "We've never offered terms before, why now?"

Maharbal cut in quickly again. "General, I commended the Captain's decision. If we'd had to go up and drive them off that hill, it would have been a bloodbath. No doubt we'd have triumphed, but at what cost in men and time?"

"And if we release them, there will be eight hundred men we'll need to fight again."

"I'm sorry General; I thought it was the right decision, a chance to save our men's lives. A victory cheaply won." Baldor said quietly.

"Yes, it is but the prisoners will be sold, I'm not interested in having to fight these men again."

"You can't sir! I gave my word."

"Gave your word! To who?"

"Their commander, Gaius Marcus Centenius, a Propraetor or Proconsul of Rome."

"A Proconsul?" Hannibal's face lightened. "So we have a Proconsul as prisoner."

"No sir, he died of his wounds."

"Damn it! That would have been a fine catch. Anyway, if he's dead there's no need to worry about your word then, the prisoners can be sold."

Baldor chewed his lip. "His men will know, sir. I know …"

"The Romans are without any honour Captain, so it matters not."

"But I gave my word."

"Then ungive it, Captain!" He snapped.

"Sir … sir, I cannot."

Hannibal stood quickly and rounded on Baldor, his eyes narrowing and a snarl twisting his lips. "You, Captain will do as I say! It's an order."

"Sir, I …"

"Damn you, man! I am your General, your commanding officer; you will obey my orders else suffer for it!"

"Very well General." Maharbal interjected quickly while getting to his feet and placing a heavy, cautionary hand on Baldor's shoulder, stifling any retort. "I admit I agreed with the Captain's actions." He raised a placating hand before Hannibal could speak. "However, it will be as you command sir, we'll see to it. Will that be all sir?"

"No! That is not all." He barked.

Both men stared at their now glowering commander. Hannibal took a moment, making a physical effort to control his anger.

"General Maharbal, support of a junior officer is normally commendable but not in this case. Captain! Though I know of and commend your bravery, both now and in the past, I grow weary of your insolence and temper, I've warned you of both in the past … Have I not?"

"Yes sir."

"I'll suffer no more! Do you hear?"

"Yes sir."

"Then mark me on it!" Hannibal gripped his cup and swilled the last of his wine. "Now! The matter is closed; you may go. General, thank you for your report."

Hannibal turned away and went to his desk, slamming his cup down hard on it. Maharbal and Baldor saluted and left the tent.

It was still hot outside and the warm breeze did nothing to cool Baldor's red face or his temper. He looked at the ground as they walked.

"I'm sorry sir; I didn't mean to involve you."

Maharbal waved the comment away. "I thought your decision was good Captain, but you need to give it up when the General pushes. His hatred of the Romans runs deep."

"Yes sir … my mouth outstrips my head sometimes but it was my word, I gave my word. I care not a fig for those Romans but my word and pride are all I have left." His words were bitter and growing quieter as if he talked to himself.

"Listen lad, if I can give you some advice. War is what it is, a dirty and bloody business. Men will do all kinds of things, occasionally terrible things in order to win, and sometimes honour is too high a price to pay.

Get some rest; I thank you for your support and your bravery, you saved many of our men's lives, that's a good feeling to fall asleep to."

"Yes sir, thank you."

Maharbal smiled and clapped Baldor's shoulder. "If I can give you one more piece of fatherly advice." He chuckled making Baldor smile. "Learn to pick your battles, lad! I can see you have the courage to try and change things which are wrong. However, what you cannot change you must learn to ignore or endure, while having the wisdom to know the difference."

"Thank you, sir." Baldor offered his hand.

Maharbal gripped it hard and shook.

"The General will get over it, I've known him most of his life and he's not one to hold a grudge. Just don't make a habit of upsetting him."

"I won't sir."

"Good man! I'll bid you good evening, Captain."

"And you, General."

Making his way across camp to his tent, Baldor punished himself as he walked. What had been a great victory and thus cause for celebration had turned sour, all because he didn't know when to be quiet. Gods above! Would he never learn! How much trouble had he brought on himself this time with his temper and lack of forbearance? When would he learn that enough was enough? Cursing himself as he went, he wandered to the nearby stream and sat on the bank to think, trying to clear his head and change his frame of mind before returning to his tent. Knowing that if he ventured there too early, he would drink himself to sleep – yet another promise to himself broken.

With the sun slowly sinking, the fierce heat had subsided and he enjoyed the pleasant evening warmth on his body. Breathing deeply, he relished the sweet scent of the grass and meadow while listening to the birds evening chorus and the soft gurgling of the water over the stones. He found his heart slowing and his body relaxing; his eyes flickered as exhaustion crept in. Tempted to lie back on the bank, he made a supreme effort to rise to his feet, groaning slightly as his body objected to the movement. Picking up his helmet, he walked back into the camp towards his tent.

Within half a stade of his tent, he saw Armaco, still mounted and kicking his horse towards him at speed. Baldor wondered at the urgency. Armaco reined the horse in hard as he came alongside.

"Baldor! Baldor, where have you been? We've been back to the General's tent looking for you."

"I went for a walk. Why? What's to do?"

"Your tent! It's burned … burned down!"

"What? … How? When?"

"We don't know; we're told it happened almost two days ago."

Baldor set off at the run, Armaco trotting his mount alongside. Andulas was waiting by the remains of the tent.

"I'm sorry Baldor."

Baldor looked past Andulas at the black, charred wreckage and the scorched grass, the stink of burning still strong. Virtually nothing remained except some charred wood from the tent poles and his armour stand.

"Where's Lasairiona and …" His voice dried in his throat.

"We don't know sir."

"Are they alive?"

Andulas lowered his voice, his face morose. "No one knows, Baldor. The little we've learned is; there were two bodies in the tent."

"Both of them then, Lasairiona and Sulis." He swallowed hard.

"No sir, they think one body was a woman but the other a man."

"A man? Who?"

Andulas hesitated. "It was impossible to say, both bodies were too badly burned. All we know is, going by the size of the bones; one was male and the other female."

"There was a big difference in height and size between the women." Armaco added somewhat untactfully.

"There was a difference in the shape of the hips that much they could tell, so one is male and the other female." Andulas added.

"So where and who is missing?" Baldor almost shouted.

"I'm sorry sir, we don't know."

Baldor's hands knotted into fists, his face screwing into anger, as he looked skywards, his voice rising to a shouted rant.

"Baal Almighty! Is there no end to your spleen? No end to the misery you visit upon me? I curse you! Curse you …"

"Baldor! That's enough!" Armaco growled when he saw Baldor's outburst was drawing attention. Baldor however was not listening.

"I curse you Baal and all the Gods, you vicious …"

Andulas stepped close and grabbed him, pulling him into his chest and stifling his shouts. "Baldor! … Sir! Sir, you're drawing attention." He said quietly.

"Get off me! Get away!" Baldor yelled as he struggled against the embrace. Andulas, being much stronger held him fast while talking calmly to him. Eventually Baldor quietened and his body lost some of the tenseness. His body shook but whether it was from anger or sorrow, Andulas wasn't sure. He relaxed his grip a little and spoke softly into Baldor's ear.

"We'll find out what happened Baldor, I promise … Come on, you're staying with me. Its late and we all need some rest."

"Yes …yes." Baldor's words were no more than a whisper.

Andulas tentatively released him but placed a hand on his shoulder. "Come on, things generally look better in the morning." He turned Baldor away from the blackened mess, throwing his arm over his shoulder he pulled him close, steering him away and towards his own tent.

When Baldor awoke the following morning, it was to an instant feeling of dread. Andulas heard him moving about and shouted through.

"Breakfast's up."

Andulas, a Gallic Lord in his own right, had a large tent, a cook and servants, he gestured to them that breakfast could be served, while waving Baldor to the table.

"Did you get some sleep?"

"Yes … thank you." He said quietly. "I was exhausted."

"We all were. A hard few days methinks. The General will be pleased though."

Baldor just stared at his bowl as porridge was ladled into it. "He was, until I opened my big mouth."

"What, but …"

Baldor just shook his head. "My temper … no wonder the Gods hate me. Now I'm doing my best to make mortal men hate me."

Andulas thought better than to ask further and bit a chunk of cheese then tore a piece of bread off a warm loaf, seeking a subject away from Hannibal and the burned tent.

Armaco arrived, dismounting and throwing his reins at a servant before limping awkwardly into the tent.

"Good morning, did you sleep well?"

"Yes, no rocking required." Andulas smiled as he gestured Armaco to sit and clicked his fingers at a servant to serve the new arrival.

Armaco tore at the bread, dipping it in the olive oil and then with his mouth full turned to Baldor. "I meant to ask you last night; how did it go with the General?"

Andulas immediately shot him a sharp glance and shook his head slightly. Armaco, untactful and blunt as always just carried on.

"What? ... I'm just asking if the General was happy. Baal knows; he should be."

When Andulas discreetly tried to shut him up again, Baldor spoke up.

"He was happy, Armaco. Very happy, until I opened my big mouth about giving my word to release the prisoners."

"I did tell you! ... To Hades with the damned Romans, the ..."

"Armaco!" Andulas growled, and then softened his voice. "Let's not go there, eh?"

Armaco slumped back heavily into the chair and shrugged.

"Fair enough then. Once we've had breakfast let's see what we can find out about the tent and the women."

Andulas just sighed, shaking his head at Armaco.

"I'll remind the General never to send you on a diplomatic mission."

"Armaco's right, Andulas. I need to know what happened." He went to get up from the table.

"Fair enough but breakfast first." When both men continued getting up, he growled. "I said, breakfast first!" His tone sharp and commanding. Baldor and Armaco slipped back into their chairs.

"Yes, my Lord." Armaco smirked and bowed his head.

Andulas stared at him then burst into laughter, even Baldor had to laugh at his friend's irreverent flippancy.

Later that morning after the three men had questioned the occupants of nearby tents they began rummaging through the burnt remains.

"Anything?" Armaco asked.

"Nothing. I didn't have much but everything is gone, my Roman helmet and cuirass, Captain Balaam's sword, my leather armour and the ornate wine jug and cups."

"So, it's a robbery that turned to murder and they burned the evidence to hide their tracks." Armaco ventured. "What do you think Andulas?"

"The Gaul sighed and chewed his lip. "It's looking that way. That would account for the man's body."

"But who's missing? Is the woman's body Sulis or Lasairiona's?"

Andulas cleared his throat and spoke quietly. "I asked the man that buried the bodies, if he could say if the female was tall …"

Baldor looked up waiting for him to finish. "Go on."

"He couldn't say. When bodies are burned in a fierce heat they shrink."

Baldor just nodded then stood and wiped the charcoal from his hands.

"So, nobody saw anything untoward; no strangers, no survivors, just the tent on fire."

"No, nothing." Andulas looked as if he was about to speak further.

Baldor seeing the hesitation, pushed. "But? …"

"Nobody saw anything but they did hear a commotion, crockery broken and a loud crash."

"And no one thought to investigate?"

"No, and in truth why would they? This is an armed camp, if it's men fighting among themselves and you don't know them or even a domestic altercation and thus none of your business, you let the Watch sort it out."

Baldor nodded slowly. "Aye, it makes sense. But after the fire, when they realised one body was a man and they are used to seeing two women, would they not wonder what happened and be suspicious?"

Andulas shrugged. "I asked that too. They told me that having heard raised voices both male and female, along with the noise of breaking crockery and furniture that they surmised a domestic fight had turned ugly. Then, after the tent burned down and there were only two bodies, one being male, that the other woman had ran off, for slaves and servants are known to do that when a situation turns bad and blame will be laid. Moreover, until you returned yesterday, they thought that the man's body was you. I'm sure they meant no insult by all that." He added quickly.

Armaco stopped examining the wreckage and looked up. "Well, we know it wasn't a domestic issue or anything else but a robbery and it strikes me as coincidental that you have two men wanting you dead. So where were those bastards, Bodeshmun and Samilcar?"

"Keep your voice down Armaco!" Andulas chided.

"Bodeshmun was with the column, same as us. He wasn't here." Baldor mumbled as he stared at the debris.

"That matters not; the likes of him would send someone else to do his dirty work, no fear of him dirtying his hands."

"He hates me alright … but this?"

"Oh, come on Baldor! Remember that Samilcar bitch, she was prepared to pay for your murder. Anyway, what about her brother? That young Lordling arse, Sakarbaal. Where was he?"

"I don't know …"

"Hah! There you go then!"

"Steady on Armaco." Andulas said calmly. "We can't accuse anybody without proof, especially not those in high places."

"Why not? They fart, shit and spit the same as us, they're no different. Ahrr! They're all bastards anyway!"

Baldor sniggered then sighed softly. When the others looked at him quizzically, he said.

"It's worrying that so many of my own people want me dead. Ironic don't you think, since we have thousands of Romans ready to do it for them."

Chapter Twenty two

Having had the dirt and sweat scrubbed from his skin by two very attentive slave girls, Bomilcar laid back in the wooden tub and relaxed. More servants appeared with steaming buckets, topping up the bath with more hot water and adding drops of sandalwood oil.

Inhaling the scented steam, he let the heat ease the tension and soreness from his hard worked muscles. The ride through the hills had been long and the fight in the valley had left him bruised and battered when his horse had been killed under him, thankfully, he was without serious injury.

Feeling exhaustion creeping up on him, he dismissed the girls and called his personal servant to him.

"Find me Hephaestus; tell him I want to see him now."

"Yes, my lord." The man dipped his head and left the tent.

Just as Bomilcar was nodding to sleep, the Greek appeared.

"You're seeking me, my Lord?"

"Yes! Where have you been man? I summoned you some time ago."

"Apologies my Lord."

"Here, refill my wine cup and pour one for yourself." He scowled and nodded towards the jug then turned his head to the servants waiting with the towels and his robe. "That will be all, you may go."

Taking a sip of the wine and waiting until the other servants had gone and they had the area left to themselves, he flicked his head and spoke quietly.

"Ensure we're alone."

Hephaestus checked around the tent.

"All good, my Lord."

"Well! Is it done?"

Hephaestus still looked around before lowering his voice to a whisper and answering.

"Yes, sir."

"And?"

"The older woman is dead and the younger taken and no doubt sold."

"A long way from here I presume."

"Yes, sir. I was very clear about that and I warned again of the consequences should anything go wrong."

"They were thorough?"

"Very sir, they burned the tent as they left."

Bomilcar laughed softly into his cup and raised his eyebrows. "Burned eh! I like it."

"The young woman slew one of the men, so they burned everything."

"Baal Almighty! What kind of scum did you find that are unable to rob a tent and two women without getting killed?"

"They looked like they were up to the task sir."

"Apparently not! Sweet Tanith! How hard can it be?"

"They said the woman fought like a tigress; sir …"

"Of course they'd say that, no one admits to being bested by a wench."

"She's a Gaul sir; their women can be formidable, apparently she took a knife to one of the men's throats."

Bomilcar growled into his cup.

"Beg your pardon, sir?"

"Nothing, no matter! All tracks are covered, trails lead nowhere?"

"Yes sir, definitely. At present the fire is been thought an accident or a servant's squabble turned nasty, the woman's disappearance seen as that of a runaway slave perhaps? … However, since Targa and his men returned questions are being asked."

Bomilcar stood quickly, slopping water from the tub. He glared at Hephaestus while clicking his fingers and pointing to a towel draped over the couch.

"That's to be expected sir but they won't find anything, the fire has removed all traces."

"You had better pray that is so, Hephaestus. For our sakes and your family's."

"I'm confident of it, sir."

Bomilcar towelled off and pulled a clean tunic over his head then took another drink of his wine.

"And what of our young Lord Sakarbaal Samilcar, Hephaestus. How did he take his eviction?" He smirked as he looked across the tent at Hephaestus. "Or should I say, how did you take it? You liked him did you not?"

"I do sir. I was sorry that it came to what it did between you both. Lord Samilcar had some fine qualities." Seeing Bomilcar's face darken and about to speak he carried on quickly. "However, my loyalties lie with you first and always. I have served you faithfully these last nine years and you have rewarded me well for it."

Bomilcar raised his head slightly in acknowledgement then rummaged in a small wooden chest. Pulling out a small drawstring pouch he threw it to Hephaestus, the pouch chinked as he caught it.

"And I will continue to reward you well, as long as you continue to serve me well."

"Thank you, my Lord."

Sakarbaal sat in the shadows of the modest tent mulling over his experiences since arriving in Hannibal's camp. Sipping the cheap and sour wine, he reasoned things had not gone well and far from what he thought would be. The fight with Targa, the savage battles and the resulting argument with Bodeshmun. He grimaced into the cup. Perhaps his sister was right; this soldiering was not for him.

Having travelled with Bodeshmun's entourage and given a place as his second in command, he'd only brought as much coin as he deemed he would need. Now, since his dismissal and eviction, both that and his share of spoils from the previous battles had been gobbled up buying some simple furniture and a tent to put a roof over his head, the chronic shortage of such having pushed the prices to exorbitant levels.

At least now, he was attached to General Hanno's command and away from Bodeshmun, though impoverished until he received his share of the spoils from the recent cavalry action outside Spoletium. Too proud to ask for a loan, he'd been forced to let his servants go, paying them what he owed or could with what he had and giving a promissory note to those he still owed. Armistaar, his one loyal friend and one very faithful servant remained with him, both citing he could pay them when he could.

Now it seemed, he was stuck between a rock and a hard place. He couldn't just up and go, having signed to serve, under pain of death should he try to leave before his term of service was up. Though his pride wouldn't allow him to consider travelling home anyway as in his mind's eye, he could hear his sister, Serfina's spiteful words, 'I told you so.'

Seeking permission to send a message home alongside Hannibal's official dispatches to the senate, he'd reluctantly requested money from his estate. Waiting for it to arrive, if it ever did, he mused, would be months from now. Meantime, he would need to fight again in order to put food in his belly and pay his two retainers. The thought of more combat twisted his guts and sent an involuntary shiver down his spine, the training and swordplay he'd revelled in at home was nothing like the fighting he'd experienced.

Now, without influential friends or warriors of his own as support and with Targa and Bodeshmun as enemies, his future did not look bright. Snarling and swearing at himself and his predicament, he poured another cup of wine, anything to help him sleep and take him out of his misery for a while.

Baldor and Andulas were at their midday meal when Armaco arrived along with Malo. Both men stood quickly from the table offering their hands in welcome.

"It's good to see you Malo! Come, come! You too Armaco, there's plenty food for all." Andulas clicked his fingers at the servants intimating another two places should be set.

The Nubian smiled warmly. "It's good to see you both, though I'm sorry to hear of your troubles Baldor, I've come ..."

"I've brought Malo to have a look, see if he can find anything we've missed." Armaco interrupted, looking pleased with himself.

Over the repast. Baldor relayed what information they had to Malo, he listening intently and nodding slowly.

"I'll see what I can find. Though it may be difficult with so many people having disturbed the area and with the burning maybe two or three days ago, signs of what happened will be disappearing. On the other hand, the ground is still soft and we've had no fresh rain to wash anything away, so we may be lucky."

"We finish eating first!" Andulas said firmly, then smiled.

Malo looked at the burned debris for a long time before cautiously stepping amongst it. Squatting down, he carefully lifted pieces of blackened wood and fabric to examine else turned them over, working his way slowly and methodically over the area. Eventually he stood up and looked at Baldor.

"There's not a lot that I can tell as there's been so much disturbance. It will help me to have a picture of how it looked, so I'll describe to you how I think the tent and the furniture was and you tell me whether I'm right."

Baldor looked bemused but nodded ascent.

"The entrance was where you are now, that's obvious. Your private quarters were to this side of the tent and your bed here, facing like this?" He pointed.

"Yes."

"This is the living or main tent area, here?" He gestured with both hands.

"Yes."

"You had a table and chairs here, near the back wall?"

"No, no they were placed to the side of the door so we caught the sun and the fresh air."

"Well, it's been placed over here along with some blankets and rugs piled on top of it. Look! The woods' all burned but some shapes are still recognisable and see; some of the folded fabric hasn't burned right through." He lifted up a small piece of charred rug that still showed a pattern.

"That was on the floor near my bed!"

Malo moved over a pace and squatted again. Sifting through the mess, he pulled gently at something the men couldn't see, he had to stop and move more of the debris before pulling again. Some charred leather began to appear and then patches of burned fur.

"Your bearskin cloak methinks?" He said, while examining the remaining fur and pulling again, trying to retrieve the whole garment.

Baldor frowned. "That was or should have been on my bed, why would it be out here?"

"Were the women cleaning perhaps? Had they piled all the blankets and rugs on the table while they tidied?"

Baldor supported his chin in his hand, deep in thought. Armaco went to speak but Andulas squeezed his arm and shook his head, his other hand holding his finger over his lips.

Baldor shook his head. "This doesn't make sense, we've only been at this site a few days and the women would have cleaned everything before they laid it down, it wouldn't need cleaning again yet."

Malo looked about then stepped back out of the debris. The grass was scorched in the close proximity to the tent but green and lush further away. He paused and squatted again, his hand tracing in the grass. He stood and moved a pace or two forward then crouched again pressing his fingers into the grass.

"Any of you lads wearing Roman boots?" He asked, without looking up. A chorus of no's came back for the three watching men. "Well, someone wearing Roman hobnail boots has been around the back of the tent here."

"That could be anybody in camp, the boots are worth taking and Baal knows there has been plenty to get of late." Armaco said.

"True, but look where the tent is situated, right on the edge of the camp, why would you need to cut behind it, the other tents and latrines are that way." He pointed. "There's no need for a shortcut is what I'm saying. And look here, there are two sets of prints very close together, one is a lot deeper than the other. Come, see." He gestured for the men to walk around the blackened mess and come up behind him.

The three men peered over his shoulder at the grass.

Baldor stared intently. "Where, Malo? I can't see anything."

"Come down here, it's very faint but look." As Baldor squatted alongside, Malo traced his finger over the shapes in the grass.

"I can't see anything!" Armaco grumbled.

"Yes, there … there! I can see it now but only just." Baldor pointed.

"Now look here, just to the side of that print, the other one is a different size and much deeper. It's either a huge man or someone carrying a load? … Just stay there." Malo motioned for the men to stay where they were as he crawled through the grass pointing to the direction of the prints. When they tuned back into the main thoroughfare, he stood and shrugged. "Gone! Whoever it was, there was two of them and they came from behind the tent before joining the usual pathway here."

"The tracks only lead away from the tent, then? No sign of them coming and going?" Andulas asked.

"No, nothing. The tracks only lead away."

"The bastards have come through the front door!" Armaco and

Baldor said, almost together.

"This is starting to make sense, Malo." Baldor growled, his words bitter and his face twisting in anger. "Whoever it was, they came through the tent. I think there was three of them, hence the man's body. They killed one of the women, took the other, and then robbed the tent. If Lasairiona or Sulis had escaped they would have found me by now."

Armaco nodded. "Aye! Perfect sense all right! And I'll wager my last shekel, Bodeshmun or Samilcar are behind it! He'd know we were away, all he had to do was pay some low life to do his dirty work."

Baldor growled like an animal backed into a corner then set off apace.

"Baldor! … Baldor!" Andulas called.

"It ends now, I've had enough!" He snarled. "I'm going to have it out with this bastard!"

The men took off after him, Armaco limping behind them.

"Baldor! … Baldor, wait on!" Andulas shouted. "You can't just march up and accuse …"

"Why not? This wants sorting." Armaco barked as he caught up.

"Armaco, peace! Keep your tongue between your teeth, you're not helping!" Andulas growled. "Baldor! Use your head, not your heart!" The big Gaul grabbed hold of Baldor, twisting his hand in his shirt and stopping him, when Baldor tried to shake him loose, the grip tightened, the power of the hold sobering. "For Epona's sake man, use your wits! The sword is not always the answer."

"Aye, Baldor! Do it properly and take it to the General."

Andulas glared at Armaco. "And say what?" He snapped. "What proof have we, before we accuse? We know what we think but what do we really know? Eh?"

Armaco shrugged.

"Exactly! Now use your bloody heads. If this Bodeshmun or Samilcar are behind this we need proof."

Baldor dropped his head and nodded slightly. "You're right Andulas." He said quietly.

Andulas slowly let go of him, his voice lowering. "I swear Baldor, there's more Gaul in you than Carthaginian!" He smiled, trying to diffuse the situation. "Now listen. Malo has confirmed what we thought, robbery and murder but it's up to us to find the proof. The stolen gear will turn up somewhere in the camp all we need do is look."

"Baal Almighty! There's nigh on forty thousand men here! How are we going to do that?" Armaco groaned.

"By shutting our mouths and opening our eyes."

"And the missing woman?" Baldor asked quietly.

"More difficult, I grant you. I imagine if they've taken her, she would be sold well away from here." Armaco went to interrupt again but Andulas silenced him with a look. "If we find the gear, then ask the right questions, the trail will eventually lead to the woman."

"Which one though?" Armaco asked, unhelpfully.

Andulas glared at him. "I swear Armaco, though I love you like a brother, some days I just want to thump you … It doesn't matter which one but from my reasoning, it will be Lasairiona we find. She is young, beautiful and worth money to those who took her, Sulis I fear, is the one who is dead."

Andulas's sound reasoning and almost regal command of the situation brought peace. Having gained silence, he put his arms out wide shepherding the men onwards, back towards his tent. They walked a few paces before Baldor stopped, the others looking around quickly. He looked at all of them and spoke quietly.

"I swear to you all here, I will kill Bodeshmun and Sakarbaal too, if he's involved. Mark me!"

"I expect you will." Andulas replied in the same quiet tone. "But we do this properly and my way."

For once, Armaco held his peace.

Historical Note

Hannibal did suffer from an eye infection, possibly conjunctivitis, which he most likely contracted when crossing the marshlands of the River Arno. Treated or not, it eventually caused the loss of sight in his right eye. After which, he is thought to have worn an eyepatch or a cloth over it, though none of the later statues or images of him show this.

He was ever mindful of the amount of Gauls his armies had slaughtered, both warriors and civilians and therefore the possibility of individuals seeking revenge on him. The assassination of his brother-in-law, Hasdrubal the Fair at the hands of a lone Gaul, a grim reminder that these people lived by the feud, whether it was a slight to their honour or retribution for a relative. Thus, he had numerous wigs made and adopted disguises to protect himself while in camp from would be assassins.

A Carthaginian fleet, possibly laden with monies, men and supplies did linger off Pisae (Pisa) and the ancient port of Cosa (near modern day Ansedonia) in the late spring of 217 BC. Hannibal however, could either not make contact with it (The ports were possibly blockaded) or in the case of Pisae, he chose to ignore it, having perhaps, already marched past on his way south.

He would not receive any support, either men or monies from Carthage until 215 BC. Thus, the arrival of reinforcements at this point in time, as described in this book, is my own invention.

Hannibal's destruction of Flaminius's legions at Lake Trasimene remains one of the largest successful ambushes in military history. His manipulation of Flaminius's character, the use of the natural terrain and a seasonal phenomenon like the mist cloud, giving further proof of his in-depth knowledge of his enemy, his good reconnaissance and his tactical genius. Even today, over two thousand years later, his tactics are still taught at military schools earning him the mantra as one of the greatest military commanders/tacticians of all time, alongside, Alexander of Macedon and Julius Caesar.

The battle or massacre at Lake Trasimene raged for over three hours and the reported casualty numbers vary. However, the ancient writers, Livy and Polybius both cite between fifteen hundred and two thousand five hundred, Carthaginian casualties and fifteen thousand Roman dead with many thousands taken as prisoners.

Many Romans drowned in the lake while trying to swim for their lives, others were slaughtered in the shallows by the Numidian cavalry as described in this book. An ancient tradition says that one of the small tributaries that fed into the lake ran red for three days afterwards and was renamed *'Sanguineto'* or *'Blood River.'* One can only imagine the ferocity of the fighting that rendered so many casualties in such a short period of time and when the killing method was sword and spear.

Consul Flaminius died fighting, killed by a Gallic nobleman named Ducarius of the Insubres tribe; Ducarius took Flaminius's head as a trophy. Whether this was a chance encounter on the field of battle or Ducarius had sought Flaminius out from some long-held blood feud such as I have suggested is unknown. There is no record of Ducarius or Flaminius's head after the battle.

Livy (59BC - 17AD) writing approximately some one hundred and eighty years after the event, tells us that *'at the moment of the battle'* a great earthquake affected central Italy and a great deal of damage was done to some cities and parts of the landscape. The shaking it is said, did not halt the battle, the effect to the lake while Cornelius and Baldor were fighting on the shore however, is my own invention.

The surviving Romans were hunted down over the following days while Hannibal dispatched General Maharbal and a large cavalry force to the east. Their aim, to intercept an advancing Roman cavalry contingent of some four thousand men sent by Consul Gnaeus Servilius Geminus.

At that time, Geminus was unlikely to have heard of Flaminius's demise. He reasoning perhaps, that sending the cavalry, under the command of the Proconsul or Propraetor Gaius Marcus Centenius, could menace Hannibal's eastern flank, hoping to offer belated support to Flaminius. Hannibal must have been confident of his dominance and his current position after the battle at Trasimene to allow his cavalry arm to leave his main body unsupported.

The Carthaginian cavalry, under General Maharbal, slaughtered half of Centenius's men in a large-scale cavalry battle in the hills somewhere north of Spoletium (modern day Spoleto) a good distance from Lake Trasimene. It is believed that Centenius was killed in battle or died of his wounds. A surviving Roman contingent of some hundreds retreated to the top of a nearby hill but surrendered the next day to Maharbal. He granted them their freedom on condition they surrendered their weapons, armour and horses and after return to the Carthaginian camp, went on their way with only *'a garment apiece.'*
However, upon return to camp, Hannibal overruled Maharbal's decision and had all the prisoners sold into slavery.

When news of the slaughter at Trasimene reached Rome, it caused panic and the senate declared a crisis. Consul Geminus and his legions were recalled and a Dictator, Quintus Fabius Maximus was appointed 'Head of State' with supreme powers for a period of six months.

Quintus's character and tactical approach to Hannibal will be very different to the commanders before him, frustrating the young Carthaginian General and changing the face of the war while Rome recovers from her defeats and raises new legions.

So, Hannibal has his victories in the field but no submission of the senate or the Roman people, thus he must campaign on and Baldor and his comrades must march again. Cornelius and Gaius too must re-enter the fray in a bid to drive the invaders out of Italy.

Also by Garrett Pearson

The Lions and the Wolf series

The Orphan Cub (I)
In Hannibal's Shadow (II)

Other Books

Stamford and The Unknown Warrior